NO
NUMBER NINE

NO
NUMBER
NINE

F J
CAMPBELL

Matador
9 Priory Business Park,
Wistow Road, Kibworth Beauchamp,
Leicestershire. LE8 0RX
Tel: 0116 279 2299
Email: books@troubador.co.uk
Web: www.troubador.co.uk/matador
Twitter: @matadorbooks

ISBN 978 1789013 344

British Library Cataloguing in Publication Data.
A catalogue record for this book is available from the British Library.

Printed and bound in Great Britain by 4edge Limited
Typeset in 11pt Minion Pro by Troubador Publishing Ltd, Leicester, UK

Matador is an imprint of Troubador Publishing Ltd

To S.R., M.B. and N.K.

This book is set mostly in Munich, with a mix of characters from Germany and all over the world. Most of them speak, to some degree or other, German and English.

For the purposes of not annoying the crap out of the reader, it's assumed that, unless otherwise indicated, everyone involved in every conversation understands the language being spoken, whether that's German or English.

Munich, September 1999 $\quad$ 1

Philippa Mitchell was eighteen years old when she left England. She left behind her bedroom, that cocoon of misery in which she'd imprisoned herself; her parents, with their forced, hollow cheerfulness; and the pieces of her heart, smashed to smithereens two years ago with a phone call that came in the middle of the night.

Without a backwards glance, Pip was gone. She'd spent most of the last two years in her bedroom, venturing out only to go to school. Now she was escaping from her bedroom, her house, her town, her country.

As she sat in the train speeding south from Munich airport towards the suburbs, she reread her instructions from Mr von Feldstein. She'd spoken to him on the phone and he'd written this letter, detailing her childcare duties and apologising for not being able to collect her from the airport. The letter was polite and businesslike. In it he'd written, *Mrs von Feldstein is currently living elsewhere.*

In other words, she'd left him.

There might be a million fascinating reasons why Mrs von Feldstein was Elsewhere, but Pip didn't much care about any of them. What she cared about was this job, which she needed, and which she would lose if Mrs von Feldstein took it upon herself to return from Elsewhere.

At Solln station, Pip stepped off the train, slinging her rucksack onto her shoulders. It wasn't heavy – she didn't own many clothes and she'd ditched everything else. Letters, books, photos, CDs. Too many reminders.

She walked along the quiet, tree-lined road away from the station, and within a few minutes found Number Three, Emil-von-Feldstein-Weg. It hadn't clicked before, but it now it did: the family she'd come to work for was ever-so-slightly loaded. Number Three wasn't a house, it was a mansion. And the street was named after someone in their family. Who has a whole street named after them?

She stood opposite the house, gawping at it. It was set back off the road, with high hedges surrounding it. Through the gates she saw a gravel driveway which swept around to stone steps leading up to an arched front doorway. She craned her head around the bars of the gate, up past two storeys to the roof, which was covered with four dormer windows of different shapes and sizes. The garden went on for miles. And was that a swimming pool? Bloody hell.

'Hello, are you Philippa?'

A voice behind her made her jump. She turned to see a middle-aged lady with grey-streaked hair smiling at her. Pip gulped. Surely this couldn't be…?

She stammered, 'I prefer Pip. Are you… Mrs von Feldstein?'

The woman nodded and held out her hand. Pip shook it despondently. *So she's come back, has she? Oh, great.* Pip would have to go home again. 'I wasn't expecting… I thought you…'

Mrs von Feldstein waited, not understanding.

Pip searched for the phrase from the letter. 'I thought you were… currently living elsewhere.'

'Me? No. Oh… I'm not *that* Mrs von Feldstein. I'm Rosa. I'm the sister.' She peered in a kind way at Pip, who hadn't quite caught up yet. 'You're thinking of Dominic's wife, Elisabeth. I live—'

'Next door. Of course, yes, Mr von Feldstein mentioned you in his letter.' *My wife's sister Rosa lives next door with her family.* She thought, *Thank Christ for that,* and said, 'Sorry.'

'Nothing to be sorry about.' Rosa pushed open the gate. 'Come on in. So you know about the family situation, from Dominic's letter? He told you about everyone? The boys, too?'

Pip nodded as they crunched along the drive. The boys. *We have two sons at home, Maximilian (10) and Ferdinand (8). They go to the International School, a fifteen-minute walk away, where you'll take them and pick them up every day except Friday – on Fridays I like to do it myself.* 'I know all about them.'

Rosa said over her shoulder, 'You won't know what's hit you. Come next door to my house if you ever need a break from the testosterone.' She pointed to a wooden gate tucked into the hedge. 'We have two girls, Isabella and Anna. You're always welcome. I hope you know what you're letting yourself in for.'

Pip reckoned she could handle two little boys, whatever Rosa might think.

'So, Dominic will be back tomorrow evening with Max and Ferdi. They're away at the lake house tonight. Until then you can settle yourself in.'

She unlocked the front door and they stepped into a large hallway. Pip took it all in: a grand staircase of dark, highly polished wood ahead of them, and doors leading off the hallway to the left, right and either side of the stairs. Rosa opened them in turn and motioned for Pip to follow.

'Living room, dining room, kitchen on this floor. That door,' she pointed to the left of the staircase, 'goes down into the cellar, where your room is. Leave your bag there – good gracious, is that all you have? I'll show you upstairs first.'

At the top of the stairs, Rosa pushed open the two doors to the left, which were covered with stickers and postcards. 'Max here, Ferdi there, or maybe the other way round, I can never remember. You'll need to get these boys in hand – I've never seen such chaos.'

It was true – in both boys' rooms, it was impossible to see the colour of the carpets. There were Lego models and train tracks, comics and bean bags, clothes, towels and shoes strewn over every surface. Pip liked the chaos; it made her smile to think that these two small worlds of disorder had been created. She thought – she hoped – that Max and Ferdi were going to be fun to look after.

Rosa sighed and closed the doors again, as if by doing so it would make the mess go away all by itself. 'Bathroom's there.' She pointed to the doors on the other side. 'You don't need to worry about those two.' And then she did the strangest thing. She winked at Pip.

Wrong-footed, Pip guessed the doors must lead to Mr and Mrs von Feldstein's room and maybe a guest room. Rosa was looking at her like she expected a reply, so she tried to smile. 'They're not fans of Lego?' It seemed like she'd said the right thing – Rosa chuckled and turned to go downstairs.

Pip, remembering the dormer windows, pointed to another door they hadn't been through. 'Where does that go? To the attic?'

'Yes, that's Dom and… well, Dom's room. Also his bathroom and office. You won't ever need to go up there; he likes to have his own private space. I can show you, if you like?'

'No, not if it's private.' Pip followed Rosa downstairs, where Rosa scooped up her rucksack and opened the door to the cellar.

'Essentially, this is all yours. Although as you'll see, there are other storage and laundry rooms down here. Martina – that's the cleaner – comes twice a week. She cleans the house and does the laundry. Your bathroom is here.' Rosa moved along the dark corridor, flicking on light switches. 'Door to the garden.' She ran her hand along a row of four closed cupboards. 'In here are winter clothes, spare bedding et cetera. The boys store their spare sports stuff here sometimes. It gets a bit smelly, as you can imagine.'

Pip couldn't imagine. What stuff? How smelly could two small boys be?

Rosa continued, 'Of course, they have lockers at the club, but they have so much kit, some of it inevitably ends up here.'

Kit? Club? What was Rosa going on about? Pip couldn't remember reading about clubs in the letter. Must be tennis or golf, something posh. She pictured a country club with gym-toned socialites wafting around in pristine tennis whites and jewellery, drinking G&Ts. Elisabeth would no doubt be captain of the ladies' tennis team, highly competitive on the court and prone to cheat on line calls if she ever found herself at thirty-forty down. Pip, not wanting Rosa to think she was obtuse or inattentive, didn't ask – she wanted to read the letter again, make sure she hadn't missed something obvious. Her German was good, or so she'd thought, but there was obviously something she hadn't understood properly.

Rosa pushed open a door at the end of the corridor and switched on the light. 'This is you.'

The room was large, with a double bed low to the floor, a squishy-looking sofa covered in bright cushions, a widescreen TV, a DVD player, a desk with a laptop on it, and a huge wooden wardrobe. She stood rooted to the spot in shock. This house, this room – it was insane. She thought of the tiny house she lived in with her parents. You could fit the whole of the ground floor into this one room.

'This is all for me?'

'You like it? I can't tell.'

'I love it,' breathed Pip.

'Wonderful. For a moment it looked like you couldn't quite believe what sort of a place you'd landed in.' She gave Pip two keys. 'One for the front door, one for the back – that's your own private entrance, should you need it.' She looked at her watch. 'Oh hell, I said I'd be back at the shop at two. Can I leave you? Take a look around, settle in, unpack… enjoy the peace and quiet before the multitudes descend tomorrow.' She hurried to the door.

'Wait! All this is mine? The TV, the laptop? Or is someone coming to pick it up?'

Rosa waved her hand around the room dismissively. 'All yours to use while you're here.'

Pip blinked and started to say thank you, but Rosa had already disappeared. The sound of her footsteps faded up the stairs and across the hallway, the door slammed, and Pip was alone in the silent house.

She roamed around the house, exploring each room again. Everywhere except for the attic, Mr von Feldstein's private domain – she didn't dare. The two mystery rooms on the first floor were definitely guest rooms. On the wall of each hung one painting, different perspectives of the same castle; the beds were neatly made with crisp white linen; and the wardrobes were bare except for a pair of spare pyjamas and a couple of shirts, probably Mr von Feldstein's. In the boys' rooms, she hung up damp towels and folded crumpled clothes. She took some cups and bowls downstairs and stacked them in the dishwasher. May as well make a good first impression.

The kitchen was – apart from her own – her favourite room. Like something out of a magazine. It had an island unit in the middle, and along one wall there stood an enormous wooden table with six seats on one side and a bench on the other. Above that, the wall was a blackboard covered with chalked messages.

She'd come back to those later. French windows, through which streamed late-afternoon sunshine, led out to a patio. Beyond the patio was indeed a swimming pool, a long, thin one for doing lengths in. Shame she didn't own a swimming costume. She'd grown out of her old one and never replaced it.

The house was light and modern inside, all floor-to-ceiling windows and stripped wooden floorboards. Everything looked understated but expensive. In the living room, there were shelves and shelves full of books and DVDs, which she felt like hugging, so she did. The walls were white and bare except for one single painting of the same castle as upstairs, with a lake in the foreground and a field of lavender in the background. Pip caught a faint whiff of fresh paint – maybe they'd redecorated recently. There was something missing. What was it? She couldn't decide, and it bothered her.

Outside, she'd expected the lawn to be pristine, but it was dotted with patches of bare, scuffed earth, reminding her of the makeshift football goals in the park near her parents' house. She found the back door, her own private entrance into the cellar, next to it an old stone bench covered in moss.

In her cellar corridor, where Rosa had said the spare 'kit' was, she opened a cupboard door to find winter coats and trousers, ski boots, skis and poles in different sizes. In the second cupboard, there were tennis racquets, golf clubs – aha – Frisbees, footballs and some oars. There was a bit of a sweaty odour to it, but nothing she couldn't handle. When she opened the third cupboard, though, it nearly knocked her out – there were about twenty pairs of trainers and Rosa hadn't been kidding about the pong. It was like something had died in there. It was sour and rancid, like decaying vegetables and rotten eggs. Pip recoiled, slammed the door and didn't dare look in the fourth cupboard.

In the kitchen, joy of joys, there was a fancy-pants coffee machine. It looked like something you'd see in an Italian café – stainless steel, nozzles, buttons with pictures on, the works. Pip loved coffee. Was there anything better in the world than the smell of coffee? She peered at it, trying to locate the On button. Terrified of breaking the machine, her fingers hovered over a few buttons but her nerve failed her and she gave up.

The blackboard was a mess of scribbles and smudges. There were messages written by the children: *Dun my homwork* and *Wear are my lukky sox*. There were dates and places: *Konstanz, Padua, Berlin, Amstelveen. 15 September – 1 October*, circled many times over. Why did those dates mean something to Pip? A section of the board was covered with random names: *Pim, Shiver, JJ, Henry, Obermann, Rollo* – some crossed out, others underlined. And there, in the corner, was her name. Someone had drawn a smiley face next to it. One of the boys, maybe, looking forward to her arrival? It startled her to see her name amongst these cryptic messages from strangers' lives.

That night, Pip lay exhausted in bed, her senses bombarded by the newness of her life. The expectation of tomorrow hung over her like a thrilling promise. She fell asleep around eleven.

Next thing she knew, a banging sound woke her. *Shit. What was that? The front door?* Pip checked her watch – 2am. Who was coming into the house at this time? Rosa had said the family was arriving tomorrow evening. Were they back early? Pip didn't know what to do. Should she go up and say hello, or pretend to sleep? *What would a normal person do?* The door had slammed pretty loudly, so they must have known it would wake her. She dragged herself up out of bed and found a baggy old sweatshirt to pull over her pyjamas.

Halfway up the cellar stairs, she heard another sound. A giggle. Murmuring and another giggle, louder this time. She frowned. Was that the kids? It didn't sound like children. It sounded like a woman. She paused. Better go back to bed. It couldn't be burglars, could it? Not laughing like that? She waited, listening to feet moving upstairs. Oh crap, if it was burglars, what was she supposed to do? Had her parents ever told her what to do in a situation like this? If they had, she hadn't been listening properly.

She crept back to the second cupboard and opened it quietly. By feel only, she found a golf club and eased it out without dislodging anything else. Those giggling burglars were going to get it, if they tried any funny business with her.

Slowly, slowly, Pip pushed open the door to the hallway. It was dark and empty and absolutely silent; the kind of silence where no one is there. She heard noises from upstairs, a thump and a laugh, a man's this time. She waited at the foot of the stairs, gripping the golf club, listening.

Before she knew what was happening she was at the top of the stairs, her heart thudding in her chest, edging swiftly and quietly towards the room.

A strip of light under and around the slightly-opened door. One foot in front of the other, closer and closer towards the room. Rustlings, a whisper and then nothing. With the tip of her finger, Pip nudged the door open, minuscule prods, just enough to see into the room. And when she saw it, she felt a great crashing in her ears, blood racing to her head as she gripped the door frame to stop herself from keeling over.

Lying naked on the bed, long blonde hair streaming over the pillow, was an unbelievably beautiful girl. Her eyes were closed, her hands pushed against the wall above her head, her hips slightly raised. Between her legs, a man's head with short muddy-blond hair; clasping her breast, one of his hands. From the girl's mouth issued a series of low moans, becoming ever louder, as she began to buck her hips and slam her head on the pillow.

Pip's eyes burnt as she reversed on iron-heavy legs out of the room. They hadn't seen her. They couldn't have. Please please please let them not have seen her. All she had to do was make it downstairs without them hearing her. She tiptoed down each step in time with the moans, to cover any creaking noises she made.

At the bottom of the stairs, she heard a sound that she'd never heard before. It was like the girl was dying. A long, coarse shriek that made Pip think of endless pain. Was he killing her? Was that what sex sounded like? It wasn't supposed to hurt, was it? She slipped through the cellar door, raced back along the underground corridor and dropped into her still-warm bed.

Oh God. What had she done? Who was that girl? Who was the man between her legs? She couldn't expel the image of them together. The girl's skin, her hair, her doll-like perfection, her eyes scrunched shut in absolute ecstasy. Was she real? Had Pip really seen it? It was outrageous, she felt sick, but why couldn't she stop thinking about it? The sound of it more than anything – that girl had howled like an animal. Jesus. And who the hell was the man? Surely it couldn't be Mr von Feldstein? For obvious reasons, she hadn't managed to see his face. But surely… what was he doing? That girl was Pip's age – no way was she the missing Mrs von Feldstein. He had a lover! Or was she a prostitute? Christ almighty, what kind of a place had she landed in here?

For hours, Pip lay trembling in bed, trying to calm down, forget about it and go to sleep. But racing through her head were the questions, the pictures, the utter mortification and panic if they'd seen her. She was dreading tomorrow – how could she meet Mr von Feldstein, how could she look him in the eye and take care of his children after what she'd seen?

When she woke up in the morning, her first thought was of the couple. What to do? Not hide in her room all day, that's for sure. She'd promised herself that part of her life was over; she had to get up and face… whatever it was she had to face. She showered and dressed, took some deep breaths and walked upstairs.

There was no one in the hallway. She looked in the kitchen. Empty. The house was quiet. Outside she heard the faint whoosh of a car passing by on the road and some birds tweeting.

'Hello?' she tried. 'Hello? Anyone there?' Her German sounded like a made-up language – gobbledygook that a child might speak. It left her mouth and dissipated into the corners of the hallway.

No one answered. She looked out of the front door – no car in the driveway.

'Hello?' she said again, this time louder.

There was no reply from upstairs. No voices or strange, ethereal sex sounds. Nothing. *Right*, thought Pip, *that's it. I have to go and look.* She stomped up the stairs, loudly and slowly, to give them time to get dressed or whatever.

'It's me, Pip. The new au pair. Is anyone there?' Her heart was thumping as loudly as it had last night, but this morning she felt, more than anything else, angry that she had to act like this. Bloody sexers. Couldn't a person come to a new job without having to see a live sex show within hours of arriving? What was the world coming to?

The spare-room door was wide open and when she looked in, there was no one. Last night – had she imagined it? Was it one of those dreams? A wet dream? But didn't only boys have them? Wait – she hadn't left the door open yesterday afternoon, when she'd been exploring. Or had she?

OK. Maybe she *had* imagined it. Weird. She'd never had a dream like that before.

Hang on. No – the room didn't look the same. She walked in and examined the bed: it was made, but not expertly. Yesterday, the white covers had been stretched over it and tucked in neatly. Today they were pulled in a more haphazard way over the bed. And there – aha! A blonde hair on the pillow. Bright, shiny, long – definitely the girl's.

Pip's mind was racing. Two people had been here, in Mr von Feldstein's house, having noisy sex. They'd entered and exited secretly, thinking no one had noticed. It couldn't have been Mr von Feldstein – why would he bring a girl back here and not use his extremely private bedroom in the attic? It must have been burglars. Sex burglars. Was that a thing? It was now.

Pip searched the house, examining every window catch, checking every lock. Outside, there were no ladders or footprints in the flower beds.

She couldn't wrap her head around it, so she had some breakfast. Making no more headway with the coffee machine than yesterday, she had to be satisfied with a couple of deep sniffs. Then she decided a walk might be just the thing.

The sun was out, bathing everything in a mellow glow. Emil-von-Feldstein-Weg was a street of large houses, Rosa's next door a match with Number Three, minus the attic windows. Pip wandered past the station, a bookshop, a bakery and – wonder of wonders – a small cinema. She peered in the window. It was one of those cool art house cinemas that showed interesting foreign films. There were posters in the window for films called *Lola Rennt* and *Todo Sobre Mi Madre*, which was being shown with German subtitles.

After half an hour, she found the river. Sitting on a bench, she watched the water rush by. Despite the sunny day and the pretty view of the tree-lined River Isar, the contented dog-walkers and the chattering families cycling by, she couldn't shift the feeling that this whole au pair idea was a colossal mistake. What was she doing here? This family, this house – even without what'd happened last night, she didn't belong with them. But where did she belong? Would she ever be happy again? She'd forgotten what it felt like to be happy.

FADE IN

EXT. A BENCH, BY A RIVER – DAY

PIP MITCHELL, medium height, plain face, straight up-and-down body, mousy-brown hair – sits watching the river, fat tears rolling down her face.

                          PIP
                      (mumbling)
I wish you were still here, Holly. I miss
talking to you. I don't have anyone to talk to.

HOLLY MITCHELL, 25 years old, beautiful, short dark
hair, fit and tanned – sits next to her and puts her arm
around her.

                          HOLLY
I'm here, kiddo. What d'you want to talk
about?

                          PIP
I don't know what I'm doing here. I'm
lonely. I'm sad. I'm a pathetic loser. And I
don't know what those people were doing
last night.

                          HOLLY
                      (laughing)
He was going down on her, kiddo. You
should try it sometime. It'll make your
brain explode. But seriously, don't give up
on Munich yet. This is a good place to be.
You're not pathetic – you're brave.

                          PIP
I can't do this without you. It's too hard. I
want to see you again.

                          HOLLY
Not going to happen, sis. Even I can't
manage to come back from the dead.

                    PIP
        You can. You have to. You're my hero. You're
        my big sister. I need you.

Pip sniffs and wipes the back of her hand under her
nose. Holly hands her a tissue. She blows noisily into
it.

                    PIP
        Thanks.

                    HOLLY
        Whatever you need me for, I'll be here.
        Tissues, careers advice, Sex Ed, anything.
        Stick at this job, you'll see, it's going to be
        just what you need. No more moping about
        me, OK? Promise me?

                    PIP
        'K. Promise.

                    HOLLY
        And remember what I always say: if it
        doesn't scare you shitless—

                    PIP
        It's probably not worth doing. Yeah.
        Thanks.

                    HOLLY
        That's what big sisters are for, kiddo.
        That and buying you booze when you're
        underage.

Holly stands and walks towards the river, turns and waves at Pip. She walks into the water until it reaches the top of her head. She disappears.

Pip sat a while longer, hating the scooped-out feeling she always had after she'd been crying. Then her stomach rumbled. She walked away from the river, following the path back up towards the house. Along the way she passed a beer garden, full of people eating at wooden tables in the sunshine. Her mouth watered. She wished she had enough money to eat there, but she had to save every last penny this year. Every last Pfennig. There was bread and cheese at the house and that would have to do. She wasn't allowed to eat out; she had to be careful or she'd never afford the flights to Australia for next year.

All afternoon, Pip jumped at the sound of cars on the road, scampering to the front door to check if it was the family arriving. She steeled herself to meet Mr von Feldstein. If he had the same hair as the man in the bed last night, she would have to put a brave face on. She couldn't go back to England. She'd never find a job as well paid as this one, with free accommodation and food, so however strange the family was, she had to stick it out. Plus, she'd promised the fabricated ghost of her dead sister that she'd make a go of it.

At five o'clock, she was lying on the sofa with a book when she heard a car on the driveway, doors slamming and children's voices. *Brace yourself, Pip. Smile. Think of the money.*

She was in the hallway when the front door burst open, two boys careering into the house, shouting and jostling each other. They were alike, with dark curly hair and brown eyes.

'Dad! She's here! Hello. Dad! Are you Pip? Why are you called that? How tall are you? Do you know Harry Potter? Why are you a girl? Where are you most ticklish?'

'Umm. Yes. I don't know. About five foot seven. Who's Harry Potter? Because I am. None of your beeswax.'

'Dad, she doesn't know Harry Potter. Da-ad. Can we send her back?'

Pip heard footsteps clomping up the stairs outside the front door and held her breath. *Here we go.*

Mr von Feldstein's hair was curly, dark and greying. Definitely not him. *Thank Christ for that.*

He put down the suitcases and held out his hand to Pip.

'Welcome and sorry about these two monsters. (No, we can't send her back.) How was your journey? (Take your stuff upstairs and stop badgering her.) Did Rosa show you your room? (I don't know whether she likes *Star Wars*.)' He smiled wearily as the boys trooped upstairs. 'I'm dying for a coffee. Would you like one?'

2

Pip found out what Rosa had meant about the multitudes descending. The house filled with noise and mess. Dominic was at work, so she, Max and Ferdi hung out together, playing games in the garden that involved a lot of sweat or mud or both. When it rained, they built towers and rockets and monsters out of Lego, or watched *Star Wars*, which Pip had never seen. She had no time to herself which, along with the coffee machine, was one of the things she loved most about her new job.

After the weekend, school started and Pip was free during the days. Dominic gave her a travel card, so she took a train to explore a different part of Munich each day. She took a packed lunch and a bottle of water to save money. She'd worked out that if she was careful, she'd be able to afford her plane ticket early next year. She popped into the bookshop Rosa owned, the one Pip had passed on her walk, to talk about books. One advantage of staying in her room for the last two years was that she'd done a lot of reading.

'You can have as many free books as you like,' said Rosa. 'And if you ever get tired of au pairing, come and work for me in the shop.'

They were on their way to school to pick up Max, Ferdi and Rosa's daughters. Pip was still curious about the elusive Elisabeth, and about this club and the lake house Rosa had mentioned. Neither Rosa nor Dominic had been forthcoming about her sister, or his wife, and so Pip thought it might be best to hold off for now with the third degree. She didn't want them to think she was nosy. As she and Rosa walked together through the woods, Pip blushed at the thought of that other burning question and how she might frame it: *Oh, by the way, ha ha, do you know what I saw last Wednesday night? You'll never guess. Burglars performing oral sex!*

They reached the school as the bell rang. The lower-school children ran out first, and while Rosa waited for her oldest daughter, Ferdi, Max and Anna ran around the grown-ups, hitting each other with their rucksacks.

'Stop it, for heaven's sake.'

'Can we go to the club?'

'No, we have to wait for Isa.'

'Can we go on ahead alone?'

'You're not allowed, you know that.'

Dominic had explained that Pip should never let the children go to and from school alone. It was a von Feldstein rule, apparently. Years ago there had been an attempted kidnapping, of a cousin of Elisabeth and Rosa's, and since then, they were very strict about it. He had given her a mobile phone, the latest Nokia, with his number, Rosa and her husband Stefan's numbers, and the direct line to the Munich district police chief already programmed in.

'Can we go ahead with Pip?'

'She doesn't know the way.'

'But we do. Ple-ase Aunty Rosa.'

Rosa agreed and Ferdi and Max each grabbed a hand and dragged Pip away from the school, in the opposite direction from home. They entered the woods, the sounds of the school fading behind them. The boys ran between the trees, pelting each other with conkers and pine cones.

'Are we still going in the right direction?' said Pip. The path led onto a paved road with houses on the right-hand side and a high hedge on the left.

'Yeah, yeah, don't get your knickers in a twist,' said Ferdi.

'Just through here, dumb-brain,' said Max.

'Takes one to know one,' said Pip.

Laughing, the boys sprinted ahead, through a gate in the hedge. Further on, Pip could see a car park and beyond that, the main road and a bus stop. She followed the boys through the gate they'd left swinging on its hinges and then stopped dead in her tracks, her eyes misting over, her whole body pinching together with a pain she hadn't felt for a long, long time.

In front of her and down steps set into a grassy slope was a clubhouse, an old building with ivy-covered walls. Around the first floor ran a balcony, on which people sat at tables, drinking and eating in their sports clothes. She took a few rasping breaths, panicking, because she knew what kind of a club this was, she knew which sport it was and it was the one thing she couldn't bear, the one thing that reminded her so deeply and sharply of Holly that she thought she might scream. On the right of the clubhouse, enclosed behind wire fences, lay two green AstroTurf pitches. More people, including Max and Ferdi, were running around on it with sticks and balls.

Oh. Oh no. Not this. Anything but this. Pip felt tears spring into her eyes. Her throat was thick and her head was thumping. She couldn't move. She couldn't go in.

'Pip? Darling? What's wrong? You're as pale as a ghost.' She heard Rosa's voice behind her, but she was trying to concentrate on breathing so she couldn't reply.

'Has something happened? Are Max and Ferdi OK?' Rosa followed her gaze and saw them by the far goal, playing with the other children. 'Sweetheart, what is it?'

'This is a... hockey club?' Pip whispered.

'Of course. What's wrong? You're scaring me. Come, sit down. I'll fetch you some water.'

Rosa held Pip's arm and led her through the gate, down the steps to a wooden picnic table on the grass by the clubhouse. Pip's legs felt flimsy. She wanted to go backwards, out of here, anywhere but here, but she thought if Rosa let go of her, she'd collapse. She sat on the bench, facing away from the table, and put her head between her legs.

Pip had spent most of her life until she was sixteen in hockey clubs, and not just the one she and Holly had played for. When Holly, eight years older than her, had started playing in the national league, she and her parents had travelled up and down the country to clubs in every corner of England. London, Manchester, Bristol, Leicester, Birmingham. Then, when Holly was called up for England, they watched her – if they could afford it – in the European cities. Brussels, Amsterdam, Berlin, Madrid, Dublin. And twice, when Holly had played for Great Britain, they'd scrimped and saved and gone to watch her in two Olympics. Barcelona in 1992 and Atlanta in 1996. All those clubs, all those pitches, all those clubhouses, all those stadia: Pip knew them. And since Holly's death she'd refused to have anything to do with hockey; refused even to step foot in the club where her parents still coached. She couldn't face the looks of pity, everyone wanting to talk about Holly, the photographs of her still hanging proudly on the wall above the bar.

Rosa materialised with two glasses and a worried look on her face. She said, 'Take your time. There, there. Don't speak for a bit. You look like you're in shock.' She stroked her hand up and down Pip's back as if she were a child. A sob rose up in Pip's body. 'Here, never mind water, have this.' Rosa handed her a glass with brown liquid in it and Pip tipped it into her mouth. It burned her tongue but she swallowed it.

'What was that?'

'Brandy. Listen, are you all right? What happened?'

Pip said, 'I… just… felt faint. I… don't know what it was. I'm better now. I'm OK.' She saw Rosa check her watch. 'Do you have to go?'

'I have a committee meeting. I'll send someone out to you. Wait right there. Don't move.'

Pip started to object, but Rosa was already halfway to the main door of the clubhouse. She reappeared at the balcony upstairs, waved through the open window at Pip and pointed towards a small girl next to her, possibly one of her daughter's friends. Pip groaned inwardly. She wanted to be alone. No such luck. A minute later, the girl crashed down next to Pip on the bench.

'Hey. You all right? Rosa sent me to take care of you. I'm Tina. But everyone calls me Tiny.' She was a redhead, with pale skin and blue eyes. About twelve years old, wearing a pair of red tracksuit bottoms and a clashing pink T-shirt, her left arm in a cast.

'Pip,' she mumbled.

Tiny took the brandy glass from Pip's hand, sniffed it and said, 'Want another one of these?'

Pip shrugged. The first one was doing its job – she felt less faint and nicely blurred around the edges. It couldn't hurt to have another one. She followed Tiny up the stairs to the bar, where a man with a large black moustache was serving drinks. They sat on stools at the bar, Tiny struggling to reach hers.

Before Pip could order from the barman, because she was certain that Tiny was too young to drink, she heard her say, 'Günther, two brandies please. And two beers.'

'Don't you have to play this evening?' he said with a concerned frown.

Tiny held up her cast and waved it at him. 'Off games,' she said. She turned to Pip as he poured the drinks. 'Günther is the worst barman in the world – he's always trying to persuade us to drink less.'

'Wait – how old are you?' said Pip.

'I'm eighteen.' Tiny sighed. 'I know, I know, I look young. You don't have to tell me. I get it all the time. You should see me in make-up and heels, though. I look much older. Fourteen at least.'

Pip smiled.

'That's better. Here, get this down you. On the tab please, Günther.'

'Which tab would that be?'

Tiny pointed towards Pip. 'Hers.'

What? This lot was going to cost a bomb.

Tiny said, 'She's the new von Feldstein au pair.'

Günther did a little bow to Pip and she smiled uncertainly at him. Seeing her confusion, he said, 'Mr von Feldstein called this morning, he said he'd forgotten to tell you – put everything you want on his tab. Drinks, food, anything the boys want. Not sure he had in mind that you and Tiny should be on the hard stuff.' But he winked at her and turned away to serve someone else.

Pip clinked glasses with Tiny and they swallowed their brandies.

'So, are you at school then?' asked Pip. She knew that in Germany, the school leaving age was nineteen.

'Nope. Went to the International School. Like most people round here.' She waved her hand towards the pitch. 'I'm at uni, here in Munich. Studying law.'

A girl about their age passed by and said hi to Tiny.

'That's Tara. She's an au pair too. Been here a couple of years. I'll introduce you later. Do you have a boyfriend?'

The question took Pip by surprise. She hadn't thought about what her answer should be. At home, it was a definite no –

nobody was allowed to know about him. Here, though… maybe it would be OK. If she didn't mention his name. 'Umm. Yes. Sort of.'

'Ah, I see. Actually, no I don't. What does "sort of" mean? Did you split up?'

'No. Well yes. It's complicated.'

'What's complicated?' said a voice behind Pip. 'Yo, Tiny.'

'Pip, meet Caro. She's a medical student. Or a drug dealer. I forget which.'

Caro smiled at Pip. 'Don't listen to her. Unless you want something? No, only joking. Or am I?' She caught sight of the beers. 'I see you've started already. Got to help with the juniors for an hour; after that I'll catch up with you.' She grabbed Tiny's beer and took a large gulp. 'Then you can tell me what's complicated. Bye.'

'She's ever so nosy, that one,' said Tiny. 'So, what's the story?'

'It's nothing. Not very interesting. He moved away.' *To Australia.*

'Tough luck. Well, you can come out with us tonight. You might meet someone who can take your mind off him.'

'Oh, thanks, but I can't.'

'Yes you can. Don't tell me you have to work; I know Dominic always does the school run on Fridays. And they're away most weekends. You are – as of now – at a loose end until Sunday night. Correct?'

'How do you know that?'

Tiny shrugged. 'Everyone knows that. The von Feldstein au pairs bring the kids to training on Thursdays, then they're off the clock till Sunday night.'

Pip thought of Rosa being on the committee and Dominic's tab, and now Tiny knowing her work schedule. 'What is it with the von Feldsteins and this club? Do they own it or something?'

'Yup.'

Pip assumed she was kidding. 'Have there been lots of au pairs? Were the other ones nice?'

'Not as nice as you. They do seem to get through a lot of au pairs, now you mention it. It's a great job, but Lady Muck's not easy to work for. You're lucky – Elisabeth's AWOL at the moment, isn't she?'

Pip nodded and checked that Rosa wasn't in hearing distance. 'Where is she, actually? Nobody's told me.'

Tiny made a fake yawning motion. 'Who knows? She's always buggering off. She does whatever she wants, swanning in and out. Once she had an affair. Once she had some work done on her face. This time – no idea.'

'And Dominic's OK with that?'

'He doesn't have much choice. It's her house and her money. He works for her parents' company. He even took her family name when they married – everyone has to, it's a von Feldstein tradition. The first time she left, it was a major crisis for him, apparently. The next time, not so bad. Now, I think she's done it so many times, he's like the rest of us – he doesn't even notice she's gone.'

Pip and Tiny finished their beers and ordered again. They moved from the bar to a low table next to comfy sofas as three more girls arrived. Pip sat wedged between Tiny and Mandisa, a South African girl; opposite her sat Caro, still sweaty in her tracksuit.

'Just seen Roxy in the gym. That girl is beyond annoying.'

'There's a gym downstairs. You can use it whenever you like,' explained Tiny to Pip.

'But I'm not a member here.'

'I told you – the von Feldsteins own this club. What's Roxy up to now?'

'Oh, just swishing her stupid hair about and hogging the step machine.'

Ferdi and Max bounded in on their way from training to the restaurant. 'Are you coming for some dinner, Pip? Rosa says you don't have to if you're having a nice time here, but you'll probably want to sit with us won't you, instead of with these *girls*?' Max wrinkled up his nose, saying 'girls' like it was something unsavoury.

'Speaking as a girl myself, I think I'll stay here. Say thanks to Rosa.' They stuck their tongues out at her and moved away. She turned back to the girls. 'They have a lot of respect for me, as you can see.'

Everyone laughed and Pip relaxed as she listened to the gossip. Sensing her chance, she asked them questions about the von Feldsteins: what Dominic was like (friendly); what the family business was (a media conglomerate, whatever that might be); and what the girls all did (mostly students, some still at school). She asked them lots of questions so they wouldn't try and find out more about her. When they did, she told them her parents were boring (true); she had no brothers or sisters (true, but not easy to say); and she didn't play hockey (also technically true, or true-ish). She repeated that she'd had one boyfriend but they'd sort of split up when he moved away.

The sofa she was sitting on faced away from the bar and towards the windows that opened out onto the balconies. If she twisted to the left a little she couldn't see the AstroTurf pitches, and if she concentrated hard, she couldn't hear the shouts and whistles from outside. She could almost forget where she was. More and more people arrived, mostly girls about Pip's age, and they greeted each other by kissing twice, once on each cheek. Some shook Pip's hand when they met her, some said hello and some did the double-kiss-thing. Everyone who arrived bought a new round of drinks. Pip did too, Günther never asking her for money. She still wasn't sure whether Tiny was joking about the von Feldsteins owning the club and hoped this mounting bar tab would be OK.

The light was bleeding out of the day, and suddenly the floodlights came on. She blinked at the sight of the shining AstroTurf, an island of green in the darkness, and fought a tidal wave of misery. Outside, next to the pitch, men were gathering, chatting to each other in small groups. She felt a tap on her shoulder.

'Hey, poo-head.'

'Hey, Ferdi.'

'We're going home now with Rosa. You coming?'

'No, she's not. It's her night off and she's staying with us,' said Tiny, shooing him away.

Pip nodded blearily. She couldn't do anything about it. She saw Rosa wave and give her a thumbs-up as she left with the four children.

A few minutes later, Günther put a plate of *Bratkartoffeln* in front of her. 'Rosa says have a great time, see you Sunday and eat these. All of them.'

'Oooh those look good,' said someone, and before Pip could prong a potato with her fork, many hands reached out to the plate, polishing off the food so that Günther had to order some more from the kitchen.

'Pip, how come your German's so good? You've only been here a week.'

'I did it for A Level. How come everyone here speaks such good English?'

'Some of us went to the International School. Some of us have been to school in England. Also, we had an Australian coach working here until last year and he didn't speak any German. So even the little kids are wandering around saying, "G'day" and "Rack off you dag" to each other.'

'Tell us something interesting about you, Pip. Come on. Tell us your absolute best story.'

Pip smiled lopsidedly, her cheeks glowing. 'There's nothing interesting about me. Promise.' This was not a lie. Since Holly had died, she'd gone to school every day, returned home and sat in her room. Studied for her A Levels. Read books and watched films. Not much else. There was nothing else to tell. She desperately wanted these girls to like her. She wished she could tell them something about her life that would make them laugh or want to be friends with her. But she couldn't think of anything.

Friends had been thin on the ground for a while. Anything more than the bare minimum of participation in normal life had been beyond her. She'd had a friend – Nadine Fox, her best friend – but Nadine had moved away with her mum after her parents' divorce in the summer after GCSEs. Nadine would've loved to have been here tonight. She would've been able to regale them with plenty of amusing stories.

She needed the loo, so asked Mandisa where it was and was hauling herself up off the sofa, feeling distinctly dizzy, when she saw another girl come up the stairs into the bar. She was wearing a short, tight dress and knee-high boots. She was tanned and her long blonde hair was loose over her shoulders. She had a lot of make-up on, but she didn't need it: she was gorgeous. And, with a jolt, Pip knew she'd seen this girl before. Lying on the bed in the guest room of Number Three Emil-Von-Feldstein-Weg. Her head about to explode.

The girl sauntered over to the sofa. She didn't smile.

'Hi, Roxy,' said Tiny.

'Hi.' Roxy sounded bored.

'Good summer?'

'The best.' She checked her nails.

'Is it true you're seeing Leo?'

Aha. So the muddy-blond hair between Roxy's legs must've belonged to a man called Leo. But why were they in Dominic's house? Pip steadied herself on the sofa.

'Yes. Yes I am. Is he here?'

What? Both of the Sex Burglars, here? What's going on? Pip saw Roxy's gaze sweep unseeingly over her and the rest of the girls to where the men were standing outside. She ran her fingers through her mane of hair. This Leo bloke mustn't have been there, because she looked back at the sofa and that was when she saw Pip staring at her.

Roxy flicked her eyes down at Pip's clothes and back up again. Her pouty mouth changed into a sneer. 'Who are you?'

Pip blushed, afraid Roxy had seen her last Wednesday night. This was going to be awkward. *No. Actually, no. Who the hell does this Roxy chick think she is, breaking into a stranger's house and being pleasured right in front of my very nose? What a cheek. Bloody blondified short-skirted breaker-and-enterer.*

Pip straightened up, letting go of the sofa. She took a few steps towards Roxy and said, with as much confidence as she could muster, 'I'm Pip.' Copying the other girls, she leant her head towards Roxy's to do the double-cheek kiss. As she closed in, Roxy, who had her hand out in front of her, moved her head and Pip's lips landed on hers.

'Ew. What are you doing? I'm not a lezzer.' Roxy made a big deal of wiping her mouth. She spluttered and grimaced, like she'd kissed a turd.

'Sorry, I meant... I didn't... I was trying to... you know.'

'No, I don't know. Euch. Keep your hands to yourself. Dyke.'

Pip was mortified. She stumbled away, with Roxy's continuing outraged squeals in her ears, everlastingly grateful to Tiny, who was telling Roxy that Pip had a boyfriend and to stop making such a fuss.

Downstairs, she turned left and punched open the door to the ladies'. Inside it was cool and quiet. She sat for a while in one of the stalls, waiting for the heat to leave her cheeks. *Well done, Pip. Really great work there. The first time you have a chance to make some friends, you try and snog one of them – the one who you've already secretly spied on while she's having sex with her boyfriend. Could this get any worse?*

She splashed water on her face and looked in the mirror. Ugh. Her cheeks were still flushed red; her neck too. Her hair, which was at the best of times unruly, now had a fluffy life of its own. She had a spot of ketchup on her T-shirt. Her eyes looked strange and black. She stared at herself, as she'd so often done before in the mirror in her bedroom. Before Holly had died, Pip had always wanted to look like her. Beautiful Holly Mitchell; everyone adored her. But afterwards, Pip had been relieved not to see Holly in her reflection. She shook her head to clear it. She was mega drunk. What was she supposed to do now? What would Holly do? And an idea came to her.

Her mind racing, she walked upstairs to the group on the sofas. She scanned their faces: no Roxy. Where was she? Pip glanced outside and saw her in the middle of the group of men, who were still milling around, warming up and waiting for the training session before theirs to end.

'Right. I've just thought of a good story. It's a bit rude, but it's true. Every word. And it's about Roxy.'

'What? You know Roxy?'

'Not exactly. But I've... met her once before.'

'Sounds juicy. Here, budge up. Sit, Pip, and tell us your best story.'

INT. CELLAR BEDROOM IN VON FELDSTEIN RESIDENCE – LAST WEDNESDAY NIGHT.

Pip Mitchell, the new au pair, is asleep in her bed. A door bangs upstairs – she wakes suddenly, her eyes wide with fear, her fingers gripping the duvet. She calms her breathing, wondering what to do. Her mouth set in a grim line, she rises from her bed and creeps noiselessly along the dark underground corridor. She grabs a weapon from the cupboard in case it's burglars.

'What kind of a weapon?'

'A golf club.'

'Carry on.'

Pip grinned.

Standing at the bottom of the stairs with her weapon ready for action, Pip hears voices. Two voices. Two burglars. She ascends the stairs, gripping the golf club. She is stealth personified. She tiptoes along the upper hallway, listening intently. Strange noises. Giggles. Rustling. A thump.

'Is this true?'

'Yes. Shhh.'

Pip paused for effect, looking around her at the rapt girls. Behind her, she felt rather than saw a couple of people drift over from the bar to listen. They were watching her, waiting for her to continue.

She approaches the door, which is ever-so-slightly ajar. A light is on within. She ea...s...es open the door, slowly, slowly, to retain the crucial element of surprise. Through the open door she sees not two burglars, but... ROXY, lying stark naked on her back on the bed, moaning with pleasure, smacking her head against the pillow, AN UNKNOWN MAN with blond hair... going down on her.

Pip burst out laughing. 'I was so embarrassed.'

There was a nervous silence.

Someone said, 'Roxy was in your house? When was this? Wednesday night? Are you sure?'

'Yes. It was my first night there. No one else was in the house. Dominic was with the boys in Lindau.' Pip felt uneasy. No one was laughing.

Another silence.

All hell broke loose. A man who'd been standing behind her moved so quickly towards the stairs that she only caught a glimpse of his dark hair and furious face as he vaulted the top of the stairs and disappeared. She heard him roar, 'Billy,' and everyone, until then frozen in their seats, scrambled up and rushed over to the window. Pip, not understanding, followed in a daze. What had she said? What had she done?

The dark-haired man reached the group by the pitch and she heard him shout, 'Billy you fucking cunt,' as he swung his arm into the stomach of another man, who crumpled and fell to the ground.

Someone near Pip screamed, but not in horror. A swell of chatter erupted in the room.

'Did you see that?'

'Impressive swing. Ooof.'

'Billy's in for it now.'

'Roxy's such a slag.'

Tiny was laughing so hard, she fell off the chair she was standing on.

'What's going on?' whispered Pip. Nobody heard. Down by the pitch, the man called Billy was still on the ground. Some of the others were holding back the dark-haired man. Roxy's head was swivelling frantically from one to the other.

Pip took a deep breath and shouted, 'Will somebody please tell me what the fuck is going on here?'

Tiny was lying on the floor, howling with laughter, tears streaming down her face. She hiccupped and sat up. 'You legend. You absolute bloody legend. That was the best story I've ever heard.' She pulled herself up onto the sofa.

Pip stared at her. Tiny must be mad. 'What just happened?'

'You...' Tiny hiccupped again. 'You told Roxy's boyfriend that she shagged his brother.'

'What? No I didn't. Why... who was that man? Who punched Billy? Who *is* Billy?'

It was Tiny's turn to stare at Pip as if she was mad.

'Billy? You don't know Billy? Aka Wilhelm von Feldstein? Second son of Dominic and Elisabeth von Feldstein? Seriously?'

'No, I don't know what you're talking about. No one told me Dominic... wait... *second* son? Who... oh no... so what you're saying is... that man who punched Billy...'

'Is Leo, aka Leopold von Feldstein. Aka Roxy's boyfriend. Or ex-boyfriend, thanks to you.'

Pip groaned. 'No no no no.' She remembered Rosa's wink when she'd pointed out the rooms that first afternoon. Those weren't guest rooms – they were Billy and Leo's rooms. She hadn't understood about the 'multitudes' and the 'testosterone'. Why hadn't she asked Rosa? Rosa had talked about 'the boys'. Not two boys. Not just Ferdi and Max. Four boys. Two older brothers.

Pip put her head in her hands. 'This can't be happening.'

'Oh yes, my friend. Oh yes it can.'

3

'Uh-oh, Pip. Look out. Roxy's on her way up and she's not a happy bunny.'

Tiny patted her hand. 'You've done nothing wrong. She was nasty to you, and you were only telling the truth.'

Pip felt a lump in her throat as the girls who'd been at the window gathered around her, smiling sympathetically and murmuring words of encouragement. Her bodyguard. Pip glowed.

'You!' Roxy screamed as she rounded the top of the stairs. 'You fucking freak.'

Deep breath. Stand up. Face her. Here goes nothing. 'Sweet of you to say so.'

'You were *watching* us? I knew you were a pervy lezzer.'

'I wasn't watching you. I saw you. For maybe two seconds. Three, tops. Then I left you to it.'

'You've ruined everything between me and Leo.'

Pip tilted her head to one side and pretended to consider that. 'Actually, I think *you* ruined it between you and Leo. Plus, you didn't sound like you were complaining at the time.'

She heard quiet chuckles around her and saw more and more people emerge from the stairs. The men appeared to have abandoned their training session. That one must be Billy, leaning on a wall near the stairs. She recognised the muddy-blond hair, although he didn't look as pissed off as Pip thought he might've been. In fact, she thought he might be grinning.

Roxy snarled, 'Why the fuck did you blab that stupid story?'

'You deserved it. You were a total cow to me, even though I'm new and I only tried to say hello. Also... also... you were homophobic.'

'What?'

'You called me a lezzer and a dyke. If I *had* been gay, that would have been highly offensive. I have lots of gay friends...' (this wasn't altogether true, since she didn't have any friends at all, but many of Holly's friends were gay, and Pip didn't think the distinction was important; they'd been lovely to Pip when she was growing up), 'and frankly, I found your tone insulting to them. Just my opinion.'

'Hear, hear,' someone said.

'You don't get to have an opinion. You're just a stupid au pair. You should say sorry and then fuck off home.'

'Nice. Homophobic and xenophobic. Oh, am I using too many long words for you? As for saying sorry, I think it should be you apologising to me for the... emotional distress you put me through last Wednesday night.'

Roxy said nothing, her face apoplectic.

But from the wall near the stairs came a man's voice. '*I'm* sorry.'

Pip looked over. It was Billy. He was definitely grinning, along with everyone else in the room except Roxy. Pip felt a smile play on her lips as he winked at her.

Roxy turned away from Pip and flounced over to him. 'Take me home. Immediately.'

'Darling, I'm in no fit state to drive. Plus I have training now. My brother and captain's waiting on the pitch and if I'm not down there in twenty seconds he'll have another excuse to damage further parts of my anatomy. Ones you might not like to be damaged.'

Roxy shot one last dagger-look at Pip, tossed her hair and stomped down the stairs.

Pip flopped onto the sofa. Thank God that was over. The men filed out of the room and down the stairs until only Billy was left. He limped over to Pip and peered at her.

'So you're Pip? The new au pair?' He didn't give her a chance to answer. 'Did you really see me and Rox on Wednesday? Leo wasn't clear – too busy trying to smash my head in.'

Pip blushed. 'Yep. Sorry. For disturbing. I thought you were burglars. Your room – it doesn't look lived in.'

'Well, we have a flat in Schwabing. We use those rooms sometimes at the weekends. Handy for the club. And... ahem... for seeing people I'm not supposed to.' Something caught his eye outside. 'Oops. Gotta go. See you around, Pip.' He hobbled away.

Pip sat back and let out a long breath. She put her hand on her forehead and closed her eyes. But she didn't feel scared any more. She didn't feel overwhelmed, even though when she opened her eyes, everyone was looking at her. She was worried about meeting Leo and seeing Dominic and Rosa – they were bound to hear about this. She knew what hockey clubs were like for gossip. But she had a feeling inside of her that had been missing for ages. Her blood was pumping around her body. She was warm. She felt loose and light. For the first time in years, she felt alive.

One of the girls whose name Pip didn't know, counting on her fingers, said, 'That's the von Feldstein brothers, and last year Roxy shagged Henry and JJ. She's working her way through the first team. What a slut.'

Pip frowned. 'I don't understand it when people use that word. Why isn't Billy the slut? Why is the girl the slut? She's only slept with four men.' She looked around her, suddenly regretting opening her big mouth. Why was she being so bolshie? Probably because she'd been thinking about Nadine, who'd always been loud-mouthed and opinionated enough for the two of them.

'That's just the tip of iceberg.'

'So what? Let me ask you this – how many women has Billy slept with? Look what he did – he shagged his brother's girlfriend. That's the most sluttish thing that's happened in this scenario.'

'Why're you sticking up for Roxy? Thought you didn't like her.'

'I don't, particularly. But the word slut is unfair. Men who sleep around are studs and playboys. When women do it, we're whores and slags and nasty slappers. What's that all about? It's double standards, isn't it?' Nadine would be proud.

'She's right,' said Tara. 'I think we should reclaim the word slut, like the Irish did with Paddy and gays did with Queer. We must all proclaim ourselves Sluts, and be proud of it.'

'Right on,' said Tiny. 'I am a slut and I'll shout it from the rooftops.'

'Then my work here is done,' said Pip, standing up unsteadily. 'This slut needs to go home because she's drunk a teensy bit too much.'

'We're going clubbing at the Ostbahnhof. Come with us.'

'Can't. Shit-faced. Need bed.'

Tiny offered to walk her home, but Pip said she'd be fine alone. They trooped down the stairs together, passing the pitch. Leo gave her a look reserved for something nasty on the bottom of his shoe and turned back to the game.

At the bus stop, she said to Tiny, 'I can't figure out how this happened. Why didn't you tell me about Billy and Leo?'

'Thought you knew about them. Leo was standing right behind you when you started the story – he was listening, he thought it was funny. Until you got to the punchline. Look, don't worry. Billy's not going to hold this against you. Leo – well, he's a miserable bugger anyway. Sure you won't come out tonight?'

'No, best not.'

'I'll come over tomorrow evening.'

'You know where I live?'

Tiny chuckled. 'Yes, Pip. Everyone knows where you live.'

Pip's hangover the following day was merciless. As soon as she woke up, she winced at the memory of what she'd done. How could she have been so tactless? And why the hell had she drunk so much? Waves of nausea and regret rolled through her body.

Good thing it was her day off. Her head was so thick and murky, she couldn't possibly have kept up with Max and Ferdi. She lay as still as she could. Movement would be fatal at this point. Later she'd make herself a bucket of coffee. For now, rest.

She struggled through the day, trying to avoid Martina the Cleaner who gave her grumpy looks whenever she saw her. Her head cleared and after another doze and a much-needed shower, she felt more human.

In the evening, Pip was in her room, considering snuggling up in bed to watch a DVD, when the doorbell rang. Must be Tiny. She ran upstairs and yanked open the door.

'I've got shitloads of questions for you,' she said.

'Have you indeed? Well I'd better come in then.' It was Billy. 'Tiny couldn't make it. These are for you. For your... umm... how did you put it? Emotional distress.' He held out a large bunch of flowers and smiled.

She didn't smile back. 'Don't you have your own key?'

'I thought it would be more polite to ring the doorbell. You know, after what happened last time I let myself in.'

'Very considerate of you.'

37

'Considerate is my middle name.'

Pip took the flowers, stepped aside and let him in. On the driveway stood a Porsche 911 convertible. Swish. She closed the door and followed Billy into the kitchen.

He said, 'Dad's not here, is he?'

'No, they left this morning for the lake. How's your stomach?'

'Why? Do you feel responsible?'

'I mostly feel embarrassed. And hung-over. Don't laugh at me.' She sighed. 'I could lose my job.'

He laughed even more, his eyes crinkling up. 'Don't worry about that. Leo won't tell Dad. Neither will I. Your secret's safe with us.'

Pip was absolutely certain that Dominic would hear about the fight and her part in it sooner or later. If he hadn't already. There must have been twenty people in the bar listening to her story, and down by the pitch there were another twenty at least. All those mouths and ears, working like crazy to spread the word that the new von Feldstein au pair was a vapid halfwit.

Billy was bullshitting. But he thought she'd never stepped foot inside a hockey club before. Pip made a mental note not to trust him.

Billy's head was in the fridge. He emerged with a bottle of wine. 'Hair of the dog?'

Pip shuddered. 'No thanks. Look, is everything going to be OK with you and Leo? I've never seen anyone so angry. Won't it be awkward playing in the same team as him, if you two aren't speaking?'

Billy poured a glass of wine for himself and one for her. 'If you change your mind. Don't worry about me and Leo. This sort of thing – it happens all the time with us. Of course, it's never quite happened like last night. But then again, *you've* never been involved before. Tell me the story you told Leo. I heard it was hilarious.'

'No. No way. Anyway, I didn't tell it to him. I didn't even know he was there. I didn't know who he was – or you. Nobody told me Max and Ferdi had two older brothers. I feel so terrible. But... it'll really be OK with you and Leo?'

'Why don't you ask him yourself?' said Billy, tipping his head towards the door.

Pip almost jumped out of her seat when she turned and saw Leo in the kitchen doorway.

He said without smiling, 'Your concern is touching. But a little belated.' He turned to Billy. 'I thought you said they'd all gone to Lindau?'

'Oops. My mistake,' said Billy, winking at Pip. 'Still, as we're here, may as well get to know each other a bit better.'

Pip was mortified. 'I'll... just go downstairs. Sorry. I'm sorry about... Roxy. I really didn't mean to... sorry,' she mumbled to Leo, standing up.

'Sit down, don't be such a chump,' said Billy. 'Don't be sorry about Roxy, she doesn't deserve it. Neither do I. Now you've apologised to Leo, we can forget about it. Sit. Tell us about you.'

'There's nothing to tell,' said Pip quietly. She watched Leo out of the corner of her eye. He fetched pans and knives from various cupboards and drawers, and started chopping onions and garlic. He filled a pan with water and put it on to boil. He looked like he knew what he was doing. But the whole time, he had a serious look on his face, not angry exactly, but he clearly wasn't thrilled that she was there. Had he loved Roxy very much? Was he heartbroken, because of her?

EXT. MOONLIT GARDEN – NIGHT

LEOPOLD VON FELDSTEIN – a dark-haired, grief-stricken man in his mid-twenties – is on his knees in front of a woman.

LEO

Don't leave me, *Liebling*.

ROXY – a curvy, blonde-haired beauty with cruel eyes.

ROXY

I must go. For I love your brother, Wilhelm. At least, I love it when he makes me orgasm. Loudly.

LEO

But *Schatzi*, I can't live without you. You are my first love. I will never smile again.

ROXY

You will forget me, in time. That au pair girl – who was in retrospect completely within her rights to expose and humiliate me in front of all my friends – will replace me in your fickle heart.

Huh? What? No way should I be thinking along those lines. Leo isn't even that good-looking.

'Hello? Earth to Pip?' Billy was waving a hand in front of her face.

'What? I mean, pardon?'

'I was asking you where you went to school.'

'Why?'

Leo said, 'Billy always does this. He's such a snob. He thinks everyone went to private school in England, and that he'll know someone from your school. It's one of his many irritating habits.'

'But... does that mean... are you saying that *you* went to a private school in England?' After all the other bombshells, she didn't know why this surprised her. She was starting to feel apprehensive.

The world of hockey was a small one. Billy was a hockey player who'd been to school in England; who was only a few years younger than Holly; who'd been coached last year by an Australian. There were too many links. She had to be careful what she said.

'Millfield. Leo too. We boarded there.'

She'd heard of Millfield. Everyone in England had: it was the best sports school in the country. 'So that's why you speak such good English. Will Max and Ferdi go there too?' Pip felt glum. They might go next year, in which case she'd be out of a job.

'Maybe. Dad hasn't decided yet. Mum wanted… wants them to. But she's not here.'

'Will she come back? Where is she?'

Billy hesitated, but Leo cut in. 'Of course she'll come back. She's away working at the moment.'

'Oh. I thought… nothing.'

Leo gave her a look. He really was quite frightening.

Pip desperately tried to think of something to say in the ensuing silence. She looked at the blackboard behind Billy's head. 'What's all this? What are these dates and cities?'

'Internationals.'

Pip looked blankly at him.

'Hockey. International tournaments.'

'You're going to watch?'

He chuckled. 'Hopefully to play.'

She froze. 'You play… for Germany?'

'It has been known to happen.'

Leo growled, 'If he doesn't cock around too much and get chucked off the team in the middle of a European Championships.'

'What?' said Pip, her voice catching in her throat.

Billy looked sheepish. He tapped the board. 'Padua. Last week. We had a day off. I may have had a few beers to celebrate my hat-trick against Belgium. Coach wasn't best pleased. Neither was big bro.'

41

Leo said, 'See, that pisses me right off – it's not *your* win, *your* goal, *your* hat-trick. When are you going to sort yourself out, shit-for-brains, and get it into your thick head that you play a team game?'

'Oh, give it a rest, Leo.'

'Make me.'

'What? *You both play for Germany?*' Pip was aware that her voice had risen to a squeak. Her whole body was rigid. Her heart was thumping loudly. This couldn't be true. It wasn't possible.

Leo stopped stirring the sauce in the pan. 'Are you OK? You look like shit.'

'I... don't understand. You play for Germany – both of you?'

Billy nodded.

'And you were playing in the European Championships last week?'

He nodded again.

'And...' She looked at the dates on the board. 'These dates... that's the Olympics, isn't it? Next year. In Sydney.' She felt a dull ache in her heart. How could this be happening?

'Yes. Seriously, though, are you OK? Tiny said you had some sort of a fainting fit yesterday. You look like you're about to keel over again.'

'I'm fine,' Pip mumbled. *Crap, crap, crap, this whole situation is ludicrous.*

It had just hit her, what had been bothering her all this week about the blank walls of the house: there were no photos. Not one single shot that would have given her a clue about the abundance of hockey players in this family. Where were the photos? And, come to think of it, where were the cups and medals that Leo and Billy would have won over the past ten years or so? She and Holly had thousands of the things, displayed on every surface. They cluttered up the already cramped house, gathering dust, but Pip's parents refused to throw any away or store them out of sight. Why wasn't it the same here? Why was everything so minimalist?

'Here, have something to eat,' said Leo, and put a bowl of pasta with a creamy sauce in front of her. It smelled delicious.

She stared at it, her head down. She could feel tears pricking in her eyes, but she refused, absolutely, to cry in front of these two men.

Pip had done everything to avoid Holly's world since her death. Given up hockey. Refused to go back to her club at home. Ignored calls from any of Holly's old teammates. She'd left home to come here, to make a new start. It was bad enough yesterday, with Max and Ferdi at the club. But now these two. This was an utter, utter disaster. Leo and Billy would be going to Sydney next year. Any other time, she would have found the coincidence funny. But all she felt was irritation – no, anger. This was *her* trip, *her* dream holiday, *her* secret mission to be reunited with the man she loved. How could she go to Sydney without them finding out about it? And then they would find out about *him*, and it would ruin everything.

With the last of her willpower not to cry ebbing away, she pushed back her chair and bolted out of the kitchen.

4

Holly Mitchell met Troy Costa in 1992 at the Barcelona Olympics. They passed in the hallways of the Olympic Village and smiled at each other, even though she was in her GB tracksuit and he in his Australian. At the hockey ground in Terrassa, they watched each other play and train. Holly's GB team won the bronze medal that year; Troy's Aussies the silver. At the closing ceremony in the Montjuïc stadium, they found each other amongst the other nine thousand athletes and, ignoring their teammates, danced and chatted all evening. At the end of the night, fireworks exploding in the dark sky, in front of sixty-seven thousand ecstatic spectators who seemed to be cheering only them, they kissed passionately.

At their wedding two years later, Troy hired a live band to play INXS' *Never Tear Us Apart* for their first dance. In his speech, he said he'd tried to hire Michael Hutchence, on whom Holly had a huge crush, to come to the wedding but he hadn't been available – either as the singer or the bridegroom. Holly and Troy were the golden couple of hockey, young up-and-coming stars for their countries.

After the Atlanta Olympics in 1996, they went to play and coach at a club in Sydney. In June 1997, right after her GCSEs, Pip and her parents flew to Berlin to watch Holly, who'd come back to Europe for the Champions Trophy. That was the last time Pip saw her sister.

On the night of the 9th of September 1997, the phone rang at the Mitchells' house in Canterbury. Troy was on the line, crying, not making sense. Holly had been hit on the head with a ball. She'd died of a brain haemorrhage on the way to hospital.

Pip didn't remember much about that time. Holly's body was cremated and there was a memorial service in Sydney. Troy brought the ashes back to England in October, after the men's Champions Trophy in Adelaide. There was another memorial service, attended by Holly's family and friends, her hockey teammates and coaches, and Olympic athletes from other sports. Piles of flowers, famous faces, David Bowie's *Heroes* playing as her hockey friends raised their sticks to make an archway for Pip, Troy and Pip's parents to walk under. INXS and David Bowie had been the soundtrack to Holly's life. After her death, Pip couldn't bear to hear any of their songs.

Troy remained in Canterbury; he and Holly had been hired as player-coaches at the hockey club for two years. They'd planned to live with the Mitchells in Holly's old bedroom to save money, and then Troy would return to Australia the year before the next Olympics, the big one: Sydney 2000. But he came alone and Pip's parents welcomed him with open arms.

Not one of them knew what to do.

Pip's mum and dad tried to carry on as usual. They went to the club every week to coach the junior teams. At weekends they umpired and spent hours there, talking about Holly, struggling on quietly and stoically.

Troy didn't hide it so well. He was one of the world's best players, but a terrible coach. On the pitch, he'd shout such extreme swear words and rage at the umpires, he'd be sent off. At training sessions, he was always close to boiling point, physically threatening anyone who failed to live up to his unreasonable standards. Afterwards, in the bar, many beers later, he would mellow and apologise, ending the night in tears, someone bundling him into a taxi.

Late at night, Pip would hear the phone ring, shivering in her bed. She hated the sound of the phone in the night. When it rang, it woke her up over and over again with the worst news of her life. But it would be someone from the hockey club, calling Pip's mum and dad to tell them he was on his way home.

And Pip just stayed in her room.

One weekend in November, her parents went away with friends to Wales. She sat watching *Ghost* alone on the sofa, tears welling up in her eyes because Demi Moore reminded her of Holly. Whenever memories of Holly filled her head, she felt a physical pain which seemed endless to her.

Troy came in the door. He was carrying a bottle of whisky and a glass. His jaw was covered in stubble, his blond hair unwashed and greasy.

'Hey, kiddo,' he said, stumbling as he sat down next to her.

Pip brushed away her tears. 'You look how I feel.'

Troy grunted, nodding.

Pip said, 'Can I have some of that?'

'Sure. Why not. You're eighteen, right?'

'Yep,' she lied. She was seventeen. Next week. When Holly was alive, Troy had never taken much notice of Pip and she'd always been in awe of him. She didn't think they'd ever said more than a few words to each other. Now she saw what a wreck he was, but she still didn't know what to say to him. She took a mouthful of the drink. It tasted foul.

'It's an acquired taste.'

And you're doing a lot of acquiring, thought Pip. But she didn't say anything, just stared ahead of her. She heard a sniff and turned to Troy.

His cheeks were wet. 'I just heard – Michael Hutchence died.'

Pip thought, *Who?* It took her brain a while to process what Troy was saying. Michael Hutchence had committed suicide. They'd found his body in a hotel room. She listened to Troy and couldn't feel a thing about the INXS singer's death. How could she? All she cared about, all she thought about, was Holly. She couldn't care less about anyone or anything else. Holly would have been as devastated as Troy apparently was. But Holly wasn't here to mourn him.

There was silence. Pip listened to him crying. He was so huge and had such an enormous physical presence, she felt tiny compared to him. It had been the same with Holly – there had been an energy, a glow of health and power about her. How could she have died? How was it possible that someone so fit and strong could have been extinguished? She put her arm around Troy and he pulled her towards him. They stayed like that, neither moving, for a long time. He didn't smell good, but he was warm and the hug felt comforting. One of his big hands stroked her arm. Neither of them spoke.

Troy shifted on the sofa and Pip edged her face away from his shoulder, which was damp with her tears. 'Oh. Sorry,' she said, trying to wipe them off. He caught her hand and held it to his face. His stubble felt rough on her palm. His eyes were bloodshot. She could feel her lips tremble; she thought she might cry again.

He moved his face quickly towards her and put his lips on hers. Her first thought was to move away from him. But the shock of it, his hard face touching hers, held her there. She panicked but didn't move. Troy made a noise in his throat and she felt his tongue in her mouth, pressing against her teeth, trying to find a way in. She opened her mouth for him. One of his hands was on her back, pulling her to him. She let him.

It was difficult to breathe. He tasted stale. His skin scraped against hers. He was making low grunting noises, his breathing thick as he pushed her back onto the sofa cushions and lay on top of her.

She didn't know what to do. Her thoughts weren't keeping up with what was happening. He was heavy, his knee was between her legs, she moved so that his weight wasn't on her so much and felt his knee move upwards, the force of it parting her legs. She couldn't think straight. What was she supposed to do? Troy was fumbling with his jeans buttons, his big fingers slipping, scrabbling drunkenly. He stopped and looked at her. A shadow passed over his face and he lurched away from her, squashing himself right up against the other end of the sofa.

'Oh God. I'm sorry. I didn't… I'm sorry.' He put his hand on his face, rubbing his eyes. 'Oh God.'

'It's OK.' Pip heard herself say the soothing words. 'It's OK. It's OK.' She crawled to him and kissed him again. This time it was all her. She pressed herself against him, wanting him to respond, her hand on the back of his neck, her tongue flicking into his unmoving mouth. She sat on his lap, her legs straddling him.

It happened so quickly. He pushed her back onto the sofa, pulling down her jeans and tugging off her knickers. His jeans were off; he was inside her, it hurt, a shooting pain, jabbing against her, his face twisted in agony and fear. He kept going, thrusting and grunting as she tried to keep herself in the right position, to make it easy for him. She didn't know whether this was the right way to do it. No one had ever told her how. Her back was against the arm of the sofa, she could feel the corner of it digging into her, and the pain of that felt right. He shouted, shuddering against her, convulsing and hurting her inside so that she had to stop a scream coming out of her mouth.

Pip put her hand onto his hair and stroked it, as he pulled out of her and lay on her chest, sobbing. She held him tightly and listened as he quietened and his movements slowed. She kept whispering, 'It's OK' and stroking him until she felt his body relax, his breaths slowing. He was asleep.

Pip stayed there, half under him, as her eyes strayed around the room, this room they'd grown up in, she and Holly. Everything was the same as it always was. Except Holly wasn't here. And she was. And so was Troy. What they'd done – what *she'd* done – it didn't make her feel any happier, but while she'd been thinking about Troy, she hadn't thought about her sister. The new pain had wiped away the old. She fell asleep to the sound of the end of the film.

In the morning, Troy had been unable to look her in the eye. He tried to pull on his jeans, but she stopped him with her hand. And left it there.

He shook his head. 'I can't. Please. Don't you see how fucked up this is?'

'We both loved Holly. We both miss her so much. Why can't we help each other?'

Troy rubbed his eyes and shook his head again. 'I dunno. I don't know anything any more. I think I should leave. Go back to Oz.'

'No. Please don't leave me here. Please stay – just for a bit longer.' Pip grabbed his shoulders and clung on to him, until he agreed to stay. They went up to her bedroom and had sex again, this time more slowly, Troy kissing her gently and trying not to hurt her. When he came, he cried again.

That night, when Pip's mum and dad returned, Pip was falling asleep in her bed when she saw the door handle dip. Through a crack in the door, the outline of Troy's head. He came in, closed the door carefully and crept into bed beside her. In the dark, Pip kissed him and whispered to him that it was OK. Quietly, they did it again, Troy diving under the pillow to muffle the sounds. She wiped away his tears and he slipped out to return to his room.

The next time, he cried less, and the time after that, not at all. But he never smiled at her, he never said her name, he didn't acknowledge her around the house. There were times when he was away, playing in different parts of the country or in Australia, but when he was there, they did it every night. They were never careless. They never made a noise. Pip went on the Pill and went to school and did her homework and waited for him.

Then the hockey club fired Troy: he'd punched one of the players on his own team and fractured his jaw. He'd been drunk. Time to go back to Australia. He promised Pip he'd write emails to her and call her. He said he had to straighten himself out, he'd been slipping with his training and they were threatening to drop him from the Australian squad. He had to focus on the Sydney Olympics.

'Can I come with you?' asked Pip, but she knew she couldn't. They'd kept their relationship a secret in England because of how her parents and Holly's friends would react. It would be no different in Sydney.

'I can't have any distractions. No booze, no partying. No you. Look, maybe after the Olympics. Maybe then we could give it a go.' He looked doubtful, but Pip's heart leapt. She did the calculations. She had her A Levels next summer, then a year until the Olympics to get a job and earn the money for her flight to watch him play. And stay.

'I love you,' she said.

He smiled at her. 'No you don't, kiddo. But I'll see you in Sydney.'

5

Munich, September 1999

Pip spent the weekend alone, desperately thinking. She hated the thought of staying with the von Feldsteins, but worse would be to go back home to her parents. She didn't have the money for a plane ticket yet, and anyway Troy didn't want to see her until next year. Why on earth had she chosen this job? Why hadn't she asked more questions about Ferdi and Max's hobbies, about other family members, about anything that would have given her a warning? What an imbecile she was.

She stood in front of the fourth cupboard in the cellar corridor, holding her nose before she opened it. There they were – hockey sticks, small ones for boys and larger ones for men. AstroTurf shoes, hockey balls, shin pads, protective gloves, Germany tracksuits. Why the bloody hell hadn't she opened this cupboard on the first day she'd been here? She had no one to blame but herself for the shit she'd landed in.

On Monday, she pulled on her trainers and a pair of old shorts and, after she'd dropped off the boys at school, carried on running through the woods. She was gasping for air within minutes. Got to get fit again, like she used to be, hating her feeble, pale body. Once she'd been the best runner in her school. Like Holly before her, both their names on the school cross-country trophy, *Holly Mitchell, Philippa Mitchell*. Once, a magazine had published an article titled *Holly Costa: The Fittest Female Athlete in Britain?* They'd laughed because the accompanying picture was of her in a sports bra and skin-tight athletics shorts, and more than a few boys at Pip's school told her they had that picture up on their bedroom wall and everyone knows what that means.

On Tuesday, she ran again, through the woods, past the hockey club, feeling the burn of her tired muscles. One foot in front of the other, a memory of speed and strength. She looped around to the river, pushing herself further, her body starting to loosen. On the way past the bookshop, Rosa waved at her and gave her a new book, *The Perks of Being a Wallflower*, which she grasped in her sweaty hand and started reading after she'd showered, sitting in a sunny spot on the kitchen floor with the radio playing. Later, when she took the boys to the hockey club, she sat in a corner of the bar and finished the book, tears stinging her eyes at the end. Now she needed something else to keep her mind off hockey. She could hear, through the open windows, the thwack of the ball, the shouts of the children, the whistle and the coach's instructions. She felt like covering her ears with her hands.

She left the bar and turned away from the pitches, following the wall of the clubhouse around to the left. She wasn't allowed to leave Max and Ferdi; she had to be at the club the whole time. But it was torture. She couldn't stand it. She sat on a bench and tried to steady her breathing. Her blurry vision gradually focused on what was in front of her: three hard tennis courts and a tennis wall. Someone had left a few balls and a racquet lying on the court next to the wall. She hadn't played for years, but thought, *Why not? Better than sitting here feeling sorry for myself.*

An hour later, she heard a voice behind her. 'What's that ball ever done to you?'

She stopped, her arm aching, dripping with sweat. Billy. She shrugged, trying to even out her breathing.

He smiled at her. 'You're pretty good. We should have a game sometime.'

Pip shook her head and blew a strand of sweaty hair off her face. 'It's just to… you know.' She was still panting. 'Get rid of some of the…' She didn't know what to say – anger? Frustration? Grief? Instead, she looked at her shoes. 'You know.'

'Not really. You OK?' He glanced over his shoulder towards the hockey pitch and back to her. 'On Friday – when you legged it out of the kitchen – did we say something?' He stepped closer to her. 'I was gonna come and check on you but Leo said leave it. He thought you might be homesick.'

Pip nodded and looked up at him. 'Yeah. A bit. But I'm OK. Thanks.' She was getting better at lying. She puffed out her T-shirt at the front to stop it sticking to her so much.

Billy ran his hand through his hair and smiled at her. He wasn't much taller than her, but he was solid, his tanned legs and arms taut with muscles. Pip didn't know a lot about guys, but she knew that he was ridiculously good-looking, the sort everyone lusts after. But he didn't make her go wobbly at the knees. She wondered why. Because he was so far out of her league? She knew what she looked like, even without a mirror to confirm the horror. At this moment, her hair would be a mess, her face blotched with heat and sweat. Her T-shirt, jeans and trainers were old and shabby. No make-up. Billy's type of girl, no doubt, was someone like Roxy, who dressed to impress.

He said, 'Good. We thought for a moment you were going to do a runner. Max and Ferdi would kill me. Dad too.'

'Why?'

'Because they adore you. Think you're the bees' knees.'

Pip blushed.

There was a shout from the Astro, just visible around the corner of the clubhouse. 'Billy, stop chatting up the au pair, you slag.'

He winked at her and turned away, jogging towards the other men. In her humble opinion, he really did have a fine bum. She wondered what it looked like under his shorts. But no. No. Altogether not a good idea.

On Wednesday, she played a game Holly had taught her – in a new city, you take a train map, close your eyes and put your finger down. Wherever it lands, you go there and walk around, see where it takes you. She chose a station in the north of the city, but was waylaid by the crowds heading for the Oktoberfest, so followed them instead and spent the morning walking between the beer tents and the fairground rides.

On Thursday afternoon, she took a change of clothes, and a racquet from the cellar cupboard to the tennis wall during junior training, smacking the ball as hard as she could, swapping from her right hand to her left when it hurt too much. She felt the warmth flood through muscles she hadn't used for years, loved the feeling of moving them, working them, flexing them. Her body sang, it shouted for joy, it felt like she was flying.

Two hours passed and it felt like two minutes. She showered in the changing room, her shoulders aching, and had dinner with the four children and Dominic, Rosa and Stefan when they arrived.

'Günther tells me you were worried about the bar tab last week,' Dominic said. 'Go ahead, put whatever you want on it, I don't mind. We're really happy you're here. Max and Ferdi are having a blast. Rosa's a big fan of yours, and I'd like you to feel at home. Become one of the family.'

'Thanks. So much. I do feel at home here.' Embarrassed, she looked down at her plate.

There was a silence and then he said, 'You know you can also use the computer in your room? It's an old one of mine. I can show you how to dial in for the internet – if you want to send emails. Or... if you want to write anything. I've heard you tell a good story.'

She raised her head slowly and saw that they were smiling at her, even Max and Ferdi. *Oh shit. They all know?* She blushed. 'I'm so sorry about that.'

Dominic, laughing, said, 'No, no apology necessary. Billy thought it was hilarious. Of course, you're not in Leo's good books, but he'll get over it.'

'I didn't know, about Leo and Billy. I just thought you had two sons.'

Rosa said, 'It's the silliest thing – I thought Dom had mentioned it in his letter to you. He thought I'd told you when you arrived. We're the ones who should apologise.'

'We hope you don't feel that you've got off on the wrong foot here, Pip.'

'No, it was just a shock.' Something occurred to her. She'd applied for the job when she'd seen it advertised in a magazine called *The Lady*. The librarian had lent a copy of it to her when she'd mentioned she wanted to work abroad for a bit after she left school. She'd given the librarian's and her German teacher's names as character references. Neither of them knew about Holly, or at least that's what she'd thought at the time. 'Mrs May and Mr Schumer – they didn't... say anything about me, did they? I mean, they didn't say that I play hockey... did they?'

Dominic looked at her, confused. 'No.'

Ferdi said eagerly, 'Do you?'

'No... sorry... not... I'm not a hockey player. I didn't want there to be a misunderstanding. Another one, I mean.'

Dominic said, 'They didn't say anything about your sporting proclivities. He said your German was good and she said you were a responsible, intelligent girl. Funnily enough, apart from reading, they didn't seem to think you had any hobbies. Don't you like sport at all?'

'She likes tennis,' piped up Max. 'And cursing. We heard her when she was smashing the cover off that ball the other day. She was doing some really bad swears.'

Pip gave him a warning look and said quickly, 'Yes, tennis is OK. I played a bit at school. But I… don't… well, I mean…' She had to try and make it convincing, so they wouldn't ask her again. 'I suppose, no offence or anything, but I've never understood the appeal of team sports like hockey. Cross-country running, tennis – I liked them when I was younger. But Mr Schumer only came to our school in my A Level year, and I worked really hard that year, hardly did anything else except revision and coursework.'

Dominic said, 'Yes, he said that. Seemed to think you might want to apply for university at some stage.'

'Oh, I don't know. I don't think so.'

'Well, you might change your mind.'

Pip thought about Millfield. 'If you only want me to stay for a year—'

'No, not at all. I'm not trying to get rid of you. I just thought that you wouldn't want to be an au pair all your life.'

'Course she does, Dad. She loves it here. She has to stay forever.'

Dominic smiled in a that's-that-sorted-then way, and they ate.

She stayed at the club after they'd gone home, with Tiny and the other girls. She was quiet, thinking about Max and Ferdi. She liked how they had accepted her straight away. They were so simple. As long as she played with them and read their precious *Harry Potter* to them (they'd finished all three *Harry Potter* books together already) and took them to the club and fed them, they were happy and easy. They weren't cuddlers – 'We're a bit past that, Pipsqueak,' they'd said when she tried to cuddle them – but they always came to her, rather than Dominic or Rosa, when they needed something, help with Lego or homework or a snack. And they had the natural egotism of young children, so were never curious about Pip, her family or her life before she came to them.

On Friday, after the family had left for the lake house in Lindau, on the shores of Lake Constance, she thought, *Maybe I could stay here*. It wasn't so bad. She didn't have to play hockey – she hadn't even stepped close to the AstroTurf. The von Feldsteins were lovely people, they looked out for her – even Billy had worried she was unhappy. They didn't know about Holly, and if she was careful they never would. And it was probably only going to be for a year, anyway. Next year, either Max and Ferdi would be at boarding school, or maybe, if everything worked out with Troy, she'd be living in Australia with him.

That must be why Billy wasn't doing it for her. Because she was still madly in love with Troy.

Within a few weeks she'd found a rhythm to her days that soothed her. She would run and read and walk around town. She played with the boys and, at the club, she'd go to the tennis wall or the gym in the basement if it was raining. In the evenings they sometimes ate at Rosa's, or Dominic cooked. Pip couldn't cook and so they always made her help them prepare the food. Chopping veg, stirring the sauce, measuring ingredients. Slowly she learned how to cook a few dishes and found, to her surprise, that she enjoyed cooking. It was something that Holly had never excelled at, so nothing about it reminded Pip of her.

During the week, she hardly saw Leo and Billy, who had a flat in the student area of Munich, which was by all accounts the place where everyone from the hockey club went for parties. It was on the sixth floor of a new apartment block and they shared with two other flatmates. Pip found this out by listening when Tiny and her friends gossiped. Leo was a medical student. Billy worked, but not often, for his family's company. Leo had been playing for Germany for years, but Billy had only recently broken into the squad.

On Thursday evenings at the club they were there, Billy friendly and flirty, Leo cold and hostile, and at the weekends they often pitched up at the house. She never knew when they were coming. She heard noises from her room and began to identify which of them it was: Leo splashing into the swimming pool and doing fifty lengths before she was even up for breakfast; Billy rummaging around in the storage cupboards, shouting out, 'Where are my lucky socks?', swearing and leaving everything in a mess.

Sometimes she heard noises in the night. She thought it best to stay in her room, so she never knew if it was Leo or Billy, with Roxy or another steady girlfriend, or lots of different girls.

On Friday or Saturday evenings, Leo cooked for the three of them but he never let her help. He said it was because it was her day off, but Pip thought he didn't trust her to do it right. With Leo it was hard to tell what he was thinking. He always made something healthy – boring, Billy said – and glared at Billy if he drank too much. She was still wary of Leo, who for the most part acted as if she wasn't in the room, although at least it meant he didn't ask her too many questions, unlike Billy.

'Where do you come from?'

'We moved around a lot.'

'Like where?'

'All over. It's not very interesting. Have you always lived in Munich?'

'Yes. Why did you move around a lot? Army parents?'

'No. No special reason.'

A new song came on the radio and Billy started humming along to it. 'D'you like this song, Pip?'

'I don't know it.'

'Really? You don't know this song?'

'Well, why, is it famous?'

'It's the theme tune to *Friends*.'

'Oh, yeah, right.' Pip cursed inwardly. Of course she'd heard of *Friends*, but she'd never watched it. There was a lot of music, TV shows, the normal teenage stuff that she'd missed when she hid in her room.

Billy said, 'So, what kind of music do you like?'

Right. Make an effort to seem normal. 'Umm. All sorts.'

'Like what? Pop? Dance? Hip-hop, rock, soul?

What are all those things? She was going to have to start listening to music and see what she liked. 'Yeah, all of those.'

Billy opened his mouth, probably to ask her another question about her non-existent music taste, but Leo said, 'Leave her alone, Bill.'

She smiled at Leo, but he was concentrating on stirring.

'So, tell us about this boyfriend character of yours then.'

Her heart sank. She was going to have to become way, way better at lying.

'Umm. Well, we sort of split up, he moved abroad.' She'd told Tiny this much already. 'We went out for about eight months.' *Seven months, two weeks and two days.* 'I don't really know whether we're still officially together. I suppose not.' She couldn't think of anything else to say about Troy that wasn't a blatant lie, so she used her best acting skills to look dejected and said, 'Can we talk about something else, please?'

Pip was in her room late one Friday evening. She'd already put on her pyjamas and was in bed about to start watching a film. There was a knock at her door and Billy poked his head in.

He wiggled his eyebrows, fake-sexily. 'So you were expecting me.'

She made a face at him, trying to stop the heat rising. As long as he didn't—

'God, you look cute in those pyjamas.'

...Do that. She blushed.

He grinned and saw the remote control in her hand. 'What are you watching?'

'*Good Will Hunting.*'

'Well, that sounds like my kind of film. May I join you? But you have to promise to keep your hands to yourself. I know your sort.'

She rolled her eyes at him and put her hands under her legs. 'I'll try my best.'

Billy jumped onto the bed next to her and made himself comfortable.

She said, 'Where's Leo tonight? Hot date?'

'Ha ha. No idea. Probably studying.' He made a yawning motion with his hand. 'That boy does not know how to have fun.'

'Says he who's watching a DVD with his little brothers' au pair on a Friday night. Why don't *you* have a hot date?'

'Because we're playing in Rüsselsheim tomorrow, early start – and I want to make a good impression. Beck's going to be there.'

'Where's Rüsselsheim? Who's Beck?'

'Near Frankfurt. Beck's the German national coach. He doesn't like me.'

'Not surprised, the way you behave.'

She saw a flicker of annoyance cross his face, then disappear. Had she gone too far? Billy made a joke of everything, but when it came to hockey, some of the lectures Leo was giving him had sunk in: he was taking the Olympics seriously. Pip sighed.

'Hey, what's up? Are you OK? You look like you did the other night in the kitchen when you ran out on us.'

''S'nothing.' She swallowed to stop herself from crying.

'It obviously is. Come on, tell Uncle Billy. Homesick?'

Pip shook her head.

'Missing your boyfriend?'

Pip sighed again and nodded, not looking at him.

He touched her chin and gently turned her face to his. 'I can help you out with that, you know.' He edged closer.

'Billy! What happened to keeping hands to ourselves?'

He held up his hands and laughed. 'Sorry, sorry. Worth a try, yeah?'

'No. C'mon, let's watch the film.'

She couldn't concentrate for the first part of the film and kept stealing glimpses of Billy out of the corner of her eye. He was seriously good-looking – like the male lead in a movie – and he was funny and she knew, even though it wouldn't last long, it would be good and he'd be kind to her. Show her the ropes. And whenever Pip thought about Roxy, the way she'd moaned and screamed… Pip blinked and looked at the TV.

But he was a reprobate; there was no way she should start something with him. He'd been through every girl at the club, according to Tiny. Pip knew she wasn't even close to being pretty enough for him to stay interested in her for long. And he was her boss' son. And her heart still ached when she thought about Troy.

At the club the following week, Leo asked to speak to her alone.

'Billy told me he was with you last Friday. In your bedroom.' His face was pale and unsmiling.

'Nothing happened.'

He raised one eyebrow. 'I never said it did.'

'Well, good, then.'

There was a pause before Leo said, 'He did, though.'

'What? What did he say?'

'He said you let him help you get over your boyfriend.'

'Fucking hell. Excuse me, sorry but your brother is a dickhead. Sometimes.'

'You don't have to tell me that. So, not true, then?'

'Not true. Absolutely. We watched a film. We talked. That's it.'

Leo looked at her, studying her eyes, making her feel like he was deeply interested in hearing what she had to say. It was unnerving, given the amount of stuff she didn't want to say to him.

'Well, whatever you did or didn't do, he was on fire on Saturday. Played the game of his life.'

Pip nodded and said nothing. There was no such thing as a conversation with either Leo or Billy, or any of the von Feldsteins for that matter, that didn't come around to hockey in the end.

'... he scored the equaliser and got Man of the Match. You listening, Pip?'

'Umm. Yep. Equaliser. Man of Match. Got it.'

He frowned at her. 'Do you really hate hockey so much?'

'No. Just... it's a bit... boring.' *Sorry, Holly. Sorry sorry sorry.*

'Right. Well. Would you do me a favour?'

Pip tried to keep her face neutral. What on earth could Leo possibly need from her? He hardly even knew she existed.

'Would you ask Billy around to... watch films with you a bit more? There's a list of matches on the board at home – the night before every game or tournament would be ideal. Next Sunday are the league quarter-finals; the following weekend, hopefully the finals. At the end of October we're in Australia.'

Her shoulders tensed. 'Where?'

'You know, that big island you guys used to send your criminals to.'

'No, I mean where in Australia?'

'We're touring. We play the national team five times, in different towns.'

So Billy and Leo will see Troy. Play against him. The thought of it made her heart thump.

'You OK?'

'Yes. Sorry. Miles away. Your great plan to keep Billy on the straight and narrow – what makes you think he'll go for it?'

'He likes you. He told me he thinks you're funny. Listen, I'll be there sometimes too. To keep an eye on him. But if I can't, and Dad's not there, can you?'

'Funny ha-ha or funny peculiar?'

'A bit of both.'

'I don't know that I'm the right person...'

'I know it's a lot to ask. It would really help. Billy's in with an excellent chance of a place on the team. But if he wants to hit form, he has to stop drinking and take it seriously. Don't you want to help him go to the Olympics?'

Nope. I don't want any of you to go to the Olympics. She crushed that thought and said, 'OK. I'll try. But I can't promise anything.'

'Here's my number. Call me if you need any help.' Leo coughed. 'Any time.' He took her phone and tapped in his number. 'Here's twenty Marks to start you off. I'll give you twenty more every time he comes to a game well rested and not hung-over.'

'Why are you paying me?'

'Well, it's like an extra babysitting job, isn't it?'

'I guess so.' Pip took the note he was holding out. *Think of the money.* He handed her phone back and she looked in the address book. 'Why Leo Stein? Why not your full name?'

'It's the name I use for everything now.'

'For hockey too? On the back of your shirt?'

'Yes.'

She bit her lip: she'd been about to blurt out that it was probably the reason why she hadn't recognised his name from international hockey and connected it to the family before she came to Munich. *Be careful.* 'Why?'

'It's easier. The whole von Feldstein family thing... it's not me. I feel more myself with just Stein.' He shrugged, and Pip looked down at her phone. He'd saved a draft message – *HILFE* (help) – with his number, so she could click it once and he'd receive it straight away.

'Leo. One question. What if he…'

'What?'

'You know. Tries anything on.'

He looked alarmed. 'I didn't mean… God… I didn't mean for you to do anything like that. No.'

'Only joking.' Pip saw Leo's face flood with relief. 'I can handle myself anyway.'

That Saturday, having already raided the DVD shelf, she forced Billy to replace the wine in the fridge and dragged him downstairs to watch *The Usual Suspects*.

'Excellent film,' said Billy, after it had finished. They were sat on her bed, and Pip was sure that the gap she'd left between them at the start of the film had grown smaller. 'The bit about the trick of the Devil convincing the world he doesn't exist – reminds me of you.'

'What? Don't talk crap, Billy.'

'It's true – you never talk about yourself. Leo reckons you're hiding something.'

'Leo said that?'

'Well, I think his exact words were, "Leave her the fuck alone, you're obviously bugging her with your constant nosiness", but basically it's the same thing.'

'If you say so.' Pip had been contemplating what to do about Billy's persistent questions. 'Look, we can carry on like this the whole time, you believing I've got some mysterious past, skeletons in closets, et cetera, et cetera, or you can just accept it – my life is totally anodyne. There are people – on the planet I come from, at least – who have dull parents and they don't have glamorous or exciting lives. By not answering your questions, I'm trying to save you from being bored to death.'

'OK, I will never again ask you a question about your life. If you tell me what anodyne means.'

'It means mind-numbingly boring. Thank you, Mr Billy Considerate von Feldstein.'

'My pleasure, Ms Pip I've-swallowed-a-dictionary Mitchell.' He stretched out on the bed and yawned. 'Can I stay the night? Can't be arsed to go home.'

'No, you bloody can't. You've got a bed upstairs.'

'But I've made this one warm. Please – no funny business, promise.'

'Nope. No way.' She kicked him. 'Get out. You're so lazy, you can't even be bothered to walk upstairs – how do you think you're going to represent your country in the Olympics?'

'Oh, all right then. Can't blame me for trying.'

He hauled himself up from the bed and stretched again. As he did so, his T-shirt lifted and Pip glimpsed his stomach above his belt. It was smooth and tanned. She looked down at the bed, at her hands, anywhere but at the sight that was making her feel... how was he making her feel? Alive? Afraid? Like she'd woken up after a sleep that had lasted two years? Like she wanted to grab him and eat him up, starting with that line of skin she'd seen?

'Night, beautiful,' he whispered, and winked at her as he walked out of the door.

The next morning, she woke early to the sound of a splash in the pool. She dozed for a while, listening for other sounds in the house. Apart from the odd swish of water, there was nothing.

Desperate for a coffee, she pulled on an old hoodie, trackie bottoms that had gone at the knees, and a pair of thick socks. She plaited her hair as she walked upstairs and hoped it wasn't too greasy. Still half asleep, she turned on the radio and pressed the buttons on the coffee machine, watching contentedly as the thick brown liquid spilled out from the nozzle. Mmmm. Add the frothy milk. She took a spoon from the drawer and dipped it in, her taste buds coming alive at the smell. With her hands wrapped around the hot mug, she turned and looked out of the window as Leo climbed out of the pool. Water dripping off him, he rubbed himself with a towel, first his hair and head, then his body. Pip stood at the counter, a newspaper in front of her, risking glances when she thought he wasn't looking. When he'd finished, he wrapped the towel around his waist and pulled a sweatshirt over his head.

They didn't look alike at all, Leo and Billy. Leo was taller than his brother, with wide shoulders and long arms. He was darker, too, and hairier. He was nowhere near as well put together as Billy, and his face wasn't as pretty – he had the telltale bump of a previously broken nose, a small scar on his forehead and another, nastier-looking one on his hand – but there was something about him. She couldn't quite think of how to describe it. Something about the way he held himself, his face so controlled, his body language so neutral and hard to read. You probably had to get to know him before you could truly find him attractive. Which wasn't going to happen, since most of the time he gave the impression he could barely tolerate her.

He opened one of the patio doors and said, 'Morning.' His face was expressionless.

'Would you like one?' Pip said, pointing at the coffee machine.

'Yes please. No milk.'

'I babysat Billy last night. Should be ready and raring to go for the match today.'

'Good work.'

She handed him his coffee and they sat at the table. There was silence. She read the messages and scribblings on the blackboard and wondered what to say. She bit her fingernail and looked at him. He was staring at his coffee cup. She looked away in case he saw her and fiddled with the spoon in her cup.

Why couldn't he say something? He was older than her, cleverer than her, a proper grown-up. Why couldn't he just talk – about anything, about the weather?

Pip heard signs of life from upstairs and Billy's feet plodding down into the hallway. Thank God. Billy would fill the silence. Her eyes flicked to the door and back to Leo, who was frowning at her. She sipped her coffee and tried to stop blushing.

'Morning, you two chatterboxes.' Billy was wearing his club tracksuit bottoms, red with a white stripe on the side, and a denim jacket over the red tracksuit top. He ran his hands through his hair, messing it up deliberately. 'I feel fantastic today. It's amazing what a good night's sleep can do to a man.'

Leo rolled his eyes and Pip smiled at both of them.

'Beck coming today?' asked Billy. 'D'you want toast?'

'Nope, he's in Hamburg, I spoke to him on the phone last night. He says he'll take you to Australia on trial, but you have to be on your best behaviour. You're dropped if you put even a toe over the line.'

'Jesus, how boring,' said Billy, but he had a big grin on his face.

The two of them started talking about the match: Leo was under the impression it was unwinnable, but they were going to scrap for every last goal chance. Pip switched off and ate her toast, said good luck and walked to the door.

'Wait – you're not coming to watch?' said Billy.

'Umm. No. I've… I'm busy.'

'Come and watch. Whatever you're doing, cancel it. It's the league quarters. Come on.'

'I don't… I can't.'

'Why not?' Billy stood up and stepped towards her. 'I want you to come and watch. I'll play better if you're there. I'll dedicate my goal to you.'

Pip knew he was only teasing. Probably said that to all the girls. She shook her head and glanced around Billy to see

Leo staring at her. She looked down at the floor. 'Sorry,' she mumbled.

Billy said, 'But—'

'Leave her alone, Bill, she doesn't want to,' interrupted Leo.

Billy shrugged and let her go. She smiled a quick, grateful smile at Leo and thought she saw him nod his head at her. As she fled back to her room, she thought about Leo and that look he'd given her, and how he wouldn't talk to her, and how disapproving and cold he was. But he understood her better than Billy. He'd said so in that nod: *I'll get him off your back; I see that you're uncomfortable; I know you don't want to do this thing he's trying to make you do; I see you; I know you.*

6

October 1999

Having made her decision to stay in Munich, Pip couldn't shake the feeling that it was all a huge mistake. She was busy – helping out with Rosa and Stefan's daughters too, while Rosa was at the Frankfurt Book Fair – and that was good for her. But Billy and Leo left for Australia until the end of the month, and she found to her surprise that she missed them.

Also, she was winding herself up about them playing against Troy. What would happen if he overheard Billy or Leo talking about her? Maybe she should send him an email, warning him and asking him to keep quiet. It felt disloyal to him that she hadn't done that already. But it would be disloyal to Billy and Leo if she did it. She hadn't contacted Troy at all since she'd been in Munich – what could she say to him? Nothing about Germany or the von Feldsteins.

No, she was going to have to hope that Leo and Billy would forget her existence while they were in Australia. What on earth would they be doing talking about her anyway? What a ridiculous idea – they had more important things to think about than her.

She was exhausted with the extra work, and still pushed herself on long runs and marathon tennis-ball-whacking sessions whenever Max and Ferdi were at the club. Most of their lives were spent there and Pip still hated even the thought of it. But she gritted her teeth and kept putting one foot in front of the other.

'Pip, what're you doing at the weekend?' Tiny, her cast finally off, approached their table one evening when she was eating dinner with Dominic, Stefan and the children. At least, they were eating – she was pushing the food around her plate. 'Oh hello, Dom; hello, Stefan. Can you spare Pip on Saturday? We've only got nine players, we really need her.'

'I thought you said you don't play hockey?' Dominic said to Pip.

'I don't. I can't play, Tiny. I haven't got a clue.'

'Oh, that doesn't matter. We just need you to run around, look like you know what you're doing. Make up the numbers.'

'Tiny, I can't. I really—'

'I've seen how you hit that tennis ball so I know you have great hand-eye coordination. You're fit, you've been spotted running – by my spies. You're not working...' She looked at Dominic and Stefan, who shook their heads. 'Right, so help us out, will you? You never know, you might surprise yourself. I bet you'll love it. We'll convert you.'

'No. I don't have a stick.'

'Hardly a problem in the house where you live.' Tiny crossed her arms in front of her body as if to say, *Whatever your next objection is, bring it on.*

'I...' Pip saw them looking at her, Max and Ferdi included. 'I've...' The room was starting to spin, their faces blurring; she could feel the familiar sting of tears in her eyes. 'It's… just that I… hurt my ankle. I think I twisted it.'

'When? Why didn't you say?' said Dominic, concerned.

She hated lying to him and to Tiny, and in front of the boys, too. She hated what she was doing, she hated herself.

'Sorry, I don't feel… sorry.' She pushed up from the table and walked away with as convincing a limp as possible, as quickly as she could, down the stairs. She saw a couple of the other girls from Tiny's team.

'Hi, Pip, did Tiny ask you about Saturday yet? Are you—'

She wheeled left into the changing rooms to evade them and backed out again to avoid two more players. In the ladies' loos, she pushed open the first cubicle door, locked it and sat on the closed lid, breathing deeply and trying to stop the tears.

Someone came in and there was silence. She lifted her feet from the floor as she heard a person coming her way.

Tiny's voice said, 'Uh-oh. Pip, you should never go in the first cubicle. Don't you know? That's asking for trouble.'

'Why?'

'Can I come in?'

Pip unlocked the door and Tiny squeezed in and stood over her. 'It's lucky you had the lid down. If you sit on that seat, you get pregnant.'

Pip brushed away a tear.

'It's true. Three second-team players last year. The year before that, two from the third team. The year before that, five – I kid you not – five players got pregnant, from sitting on that loo.'

Pip swallowed and said nothing.

"S'up, Pip? I know your ankle's fine. I didn't say anything to Dominic, but I know it's not that. Did I say something to upset you? Did I do something wrong?'

Pip didn't trust herself to speak. She thought the world of Tiny. She wanted to be friends. But she couldn't even say sorry again. She felt a wave of despair and she sat, tears rolling down her face, not speaking.

Was there ever going to be a time when she could bring herself to talk about Holly, and how she missed her with every fibre in her body and loved her so much that she couldn't imagine living her life without her? She felt eviscerated from the pain that never seemed to lessen.

Tiny put her arms around Pip and patted her on the back. 'It's OK. You don't have to tell me. But if you ever do want to talk, you know where I am.'

'It's nothing,' said Pip wearily. There was a dead weight on her shoulders. She felt heavy enough to sink into the ground. 'Honestly, I'm OK, just tired. Thanks.' She stood up and returned Tiny's hug. Her heart was like a stone.

Pip walked away from her, and at the door Tiny said, without even the smallest amount of anger or malice in her voice, 'You don't have to do the limp for me.'

Pip attempted a smile.

'That's better.'

'How come you're so good with children?' asked Tiny in a shop changing room. 'Do you like this top? Does it make me look older?'

'Umm.' Pip decided to ignore the first question. She had surprised herself with how easy it was for her to get along with Max and Ferdi, how much fun she had with them and how they responded to her. At first she'd thought she must be rather immature and silly. But she'd realised that the age gap between her and them was more or less the same as between Holly and her, and she'd slipped, without even meaning to, into some of the old games and ways she'd had with Holly.

She looked Tiny up and down. Last week, Tiny had added blue streaks to her hair. She was trying on a glittery turquoise top with a sheer panel across her stomach. 'It's fab. It definitely adds years to you. You look positively ancient.'

'Thanks. Aren't you going to buy anything?'

Pip blanched. She was not allowed to spend money. She had to be firm – she needed to save and save until she had the money for Australia. 'No. Wasn't going to. Why?'

'For the party.'

'What party?'

'Pip, what planet do you live on? Martin Obermann's birthday party – tonight. You must know this. Everyone knows this.'

'I don't think I'm invited.'

'Of course you are. Everyone's invited.'

'But I don't even know Martin.'

'That's irrelevant. Look, this is how it works when you play hockey—'

'Which I don't.'

'But you are in the employ of the hockey-playing von Feldsteins, which amounts to the same thing.'

'If you say so.'

'I do. So, when you play hockey – shush – and you have a party, you just issue a general invitation and everyone in the club turns up. Otherwise it's no fun.'

Pip pretended that this was news to her. Tiny was always explaining things about hockey and the club that Pip already knew, and she always listened politely and nodded and said got it.

'All right. So I'm invited. But I don't think I'll go. I won't know anyone there. I don't have a present for Martin. I don't even know where he lives…' She tailed off.

'I'll pick you up. I'll buy a bottle of bubbly on the way and we can give it to Martin together, not that he'll notice. Try this on.' She handed Pip a strappy red top. 'Wear it with that denim jacket of yours. I'll bring a scarf that'll look perfect with it.'

'I—'

'Martin lives in Schwabing. He shares a flat – everyone at the club calls it the Sixth Floor – with Leo and Billy. They came back from Australia this morning.'

Pip bought the top and said she'd see Tiny later.

Tiny rang the doorbell and mouthed, 'Ready?' at Pip, who nodded. It occurred to her that she had never been to an actual party, a party for adults, before. She was, to put it mildly, shitting herself. She thought about the things she didn't know how to do – flirting, drinking, mingling, small talk – and wanted to run away. Behind the door, they could hear the thump of the music, and a man opened the door as the swell of voices crashed over them. The place was heaving.

'Hey! Hi! My favourite girls,' said the man, whom Tiny introduced to Pip as Theo, the fourth flatmate. He was wearing a T-shirt that said, *No sex please, I'm British*, and was swaying. He kissed them on the cheeks and ushered them in, as the door to the lift they'd travelled up in opened and the next guests spilled out of it. 'Hi! Hey! My favourite girls,' he shouted at the newcomers.

Tiny pulled Pip by the arm into the flat. She followed her along a corridor to an open-plan living room and kitchen, crammed with bodies. There were already people dancing and the balcony doors were open, more guests sitting at long wooden beer tables and benches outside.

Pip searched the room and found Billy, who was wearing a yellow Australian lifeguard's vest and shorts, mixing drinks behind the bar. He was deeply tanned and his hair was proper blond. She looked about for Leo but couldn't see him. Ah, there he was, on the sofa talking to Roxy. Were they back together again? That was a good thing, right? For the two of them and for Billy, who had presumably been forgiven. For herself, too – maybe Leo would mellow and they might be friends.

Tiny fetched two bottles of beer from a tub packed with ice on the balcony. They clinked them together. Pip recognised some faces from the hockey club. There was a mix of ages, from about her age up to late twenties, early thirties. As she and Tiny moved through the crowd, she heard English voices, Dutch, German and Spanish. They sat with the girls from Tiny's team, then danced to a couple of German songs Pip didn't know. Tiny pointed out two other guys who played for a different club in Munich and had been with Leo and Billy in Australia, playing for Germany. The four of them stood out with their tans against everyone else's pallor.

Mandisa asked Tiny, 'Are Leo and Roxy back together?'

'Why do you ask, Mandi? Interested?'

'No, shut up. But are they?'

Tiny shrugged. 'Doubt it. Not after...' She pointed at Pip, who cringed. 'It was an unlikely relationship anyway – they don't go together at all, except for the fact that he's rich and Roxy's a social climber. And he's too old for her.'

'How old is he?' asked Pip.

'Twenty-five. And she's nineteen.'

Pip bit her lip. Troy was ten years older than her. But that was OK, no matter what Tiny thought. Age didn't matter.

'And there's his rule as well – didn't I hear he had a rule about not dating girls who're younger than him?' said Tara.

'The rule isn't about whether they're younger or not, it's about whether he knew them when they were younger.'

'Huh? Not following,' said Tara.

'He grew up in the club, he knows all the girls from way back when. So, for example, when he was eighteen, I was eleven. He finds it strange, you know, pervy. So he would never go out with me.'

'Yeah, Tiny, that's why Leo would never go out with you.'

Tiny made a face at Caro. 'The point is, he disapproves of it. Says it's creepy. So he doesn't do it. Ever.'

Pip took a sip of her beer to cool her throat. When Troy and Holly had first met, Troy had been twenty-two and Pip had been twelve. So what did that make Troy? Was he a paedo? No, it wasn't like that with them. It was different.

'So why did he go out with Roxy then? If she's six years younger than him, that puts her in the no-go area.'

'Because she only moved here last year.'

'Ah.'

Pip drank her beer and another one, and then a cocktail, and stayed quiet. *Forget it*, she thought. *Leo's wrong. He doesn't know. Tiny's talking crap. None of them have a clue.*

She said, 'Is it true that Billy and Leo fight over girls all the time? Billy told me that after I… you know, after I outed him and Roxy.'

'Yeah. Roxy wasn't the first. There's a rumour that they both went out with Franzi van Almsick. Billy definitely did; Leo won't talk about it.'

'Who's Franzi van Almsick?' said Pip. The name rang a bell.

'Swimmer. World record holder, two hundred freestyle. Drop-dead gorgeous.'

'Oh.'

'They're so different, Leo and Billy,' said Caro. She lowered her voice and they leant towards her. 'Some people say that Billy's not even Dominic's son.'

'Blimey – is that true?'

Caro shrugged and smiled enigmatically. Pip knew to take it with a bucket of salt – a rumour like that could easily have started because Billy had blond hair and Leo dark. Why let the truth get in the way of a good story, after all?

Tiny said, 'Anyway, to answer your original question, Mandi, no, I don't think Leo will ever get back together with Roxy. She's committed what for him is the ultimate crime.'

'Cheating on him with his brother?'

'No, cheating on him with a teammate. There's nothing more important for Leo than his team. Anyone who messes

76

with it, sabotages it, disrupts it – their life is no longer worth living.'

The music changed – *Word Up* started playing, and Billy vaulted over the bar, grabbed Pip and Tiny's arms and dragged them to the dance floor. 'Yo, pretty ladies,' he shout-sang, 'do your thing.' He was bouncing up and down, trying to dance with both of them, bumping into them and flinging his arms around. Like most hockey players, thought Pip more cheerfully, Billy couldn't dance at all, but what he lacked in style, he made up for in enthusiasm. She felt it rub off on her and she joined in, copying what he did, grinding against him when he yelled that he wanted to be a Pip-Tiny sandwich filling. She relaxed, and was having such a laugh, she didn't notice that the song ended and the next one too. There was a slower song and Tiny disappeared. Traitor. Billy put his arms on Pip's waist. He pulled her in closer and she smiled. He was fun. He was messing about and so was she, not wanting anything, not expecting anything either. She shuffled around with him and he chattered in her ear the whole time, about hockey and Australia. She was only half-listening.

Out of the corner of her eye, she saw Leo and Roxy stand up to dance. Roxy was wearing a minuscule dress, an asymmetrical thing off one shoulder, which showed her curves and a lot of flesh. She had her hair down; it reached the middle of her back. She gave it a little toss every now and again, in case anyone hadn't noticed how shiny and thick it was. She had her face close to Leo's, tilted up, a blissful smile on her face. Pip hardly dared look at Leo. Once she did, quickly, but his face gave nothing away – it was as blank as ever. His hands were resting on Roxy's waist.

As opposed to Billy's, which were creeping downwards, slowly but surely. Pip broke apart from him.

'I'm thirsty, shall we find a beer?'

'Not allowed.' Billy scowled in Leo's direction. 'He'll kill me.'

They went outside to the balcony. Billy found her a bottle of beer and opened it, passing it to her with a look of longing in his eyes.

'Did you behave in Australia?'

'Yes, and I nearly died of boredom.'

'Bet you didn't.' She grinned at him and took a swig as they sat down. 'How does it feel to be the new star of the team? Dominic told me you were ace.'

'Well I was, but Beck still hasn't got a good word to say about me. I worked my arse off – early nights, early mornings, did everything he and Leo told me. He's never going to pick me for Sydney.'

'He will. He's probably just being extra strict with you to make sure you stay on the straight and narrow.'

Billy raised his eyebrows and chuckled. 'No flies on you, are there? Since when did you care about my hockey career?'

'I don't. Let's talk about something else.'

Leo crashed down beside them on the bench, followed by Martin and some of the other guys from the club.

'Where's foxy Roxy?' said Billy.

Pip didn't know how he dared call her that, or even speak about her to Leo, after what he'd done. But probably because this happened often between them, they were used to it. Leo certainly didn't look like he was going to knock Billy's block off, so that was reassuring. He shrugged.

Billy said, 'I've been telling Mary Poppins what a good boy I was in Oz.'

Leo said to Pip, 'He was. Never seen him play better.' He turned to Billy. 'I wasn't supposed to say anything, but Beck told me you're in if you carry on like that.'

'See?' Pip said to Billy. 'Does anyone want another drink?' She stood up and counted the hands, leaving the table to fetch them.

As she did so, she heard Leo say, 'There was one game, he was up against this fucking gorilla – mean bastard, he takes someone out in every game I've ever played against him – and Bill ran circles around him. Some people think this guy's the best centre half in the world, but you made him look ordinary. It was such a joy to see.'

'Who's that?' someone asked.

'Troy Costa.'

Pip's insides went cold.

'Is that the guy who smashed Fischer's jaw last year?'

'The very same. He's a fucking psycho. He's pretty much on a red card every game nowadays.'

'Isn't that the one…'

Pip knew what was coming. This had happened to her a thousand times before, at hockey matches she'd watched with her parents, when people in the crowd had started talking about her sister, not knowing that her family was sitting right there and could hear every word they said. 'Check out that number nine – she's well fit', or 'Holly Costa's playing like a donkey today', or 'She can handle my stick any time.' Pip had heard it all. She wanted to leave, to walk through the door, out of the apartment and leave the party but she couldn't move her feet.

'… whose wife died, a few years ago?'

There it is. The pain ripped through her, as sharp as it had ever been. She curled her hands into fists and tried to breathe through it.

'Yes, but he was a psycho before then. She, on the other hand, was amazing. How he got her to marry him I don't know.'

'Who was amazing?' asked Billy.

Here it comes…

'Holly Costa. She was a lovely girl.' Leo's face had a wistful smile on it.

Wait, Leo knew Holly? Pip couldn't take much more of this. She'd go insane. She put her hand on the door frame to steady herself.

'God, yes, I remember her. She was gorgeous,' said Billy. 'A total babe. It was fucking tragic, what happened to her. She was hit on the head with a stick, wasn't she?'

'Ball,' said Leo. 'Costa went completely off the rails. Like I said, he's always been a nasty piece of work, but after that he got meaner. I saw him at the Champions Trophy in Adelaide just after it happened; he shouldn't have been playing, he was a mess. But they never dropped him. I tried to shake his hand, tell him I was sorry about his wife, but he nearly decked me. We'd had a falling-out over her before – he thought I was coming on to her in Atlanta, which I wasn't, but the guy has mental problems.'

Pip was rooted to the spot. She had no strength in her legs – their words and the memories of Holly had hollowed her out, stripped layers off her skin. If she tried to move, she thought she'd fall over. Why was no one sticking up for Troy? He'd lost his wife. It wasn't his fault that he was so angry – why couldn't anyone understand that? Little by little, Pip manoeuvred herself so that she was leaning against the wall. A patch of it felt cool and refreshing against her face. She closed her eyes.

EXT. BALCONY IN SCHWABING – NIGHT

A crowd of party guests is sitting around a table drinking and talking. Among them, LEO VON FELDSTEIN, BILLY VON FELDSTEIN, TINY, ROXY and PIP MITCHELL, a bit drunk, looking quite all right in her new top.

PIP
Poor Troy. Who could blame him, if he was messed up after his lovely wife died?

LEO
That's no excuse. The man is dangerous. He hurts people.

                         PIP
Can't you just have a little bit of humanity?
What makes you the expert on how people
behave? You're so judgemental.

                        BILLY
Why are you so bent out of shape about
this, Pip?

                         PIP
Holly's my sister. And Troy Costa happens
to be a *very* good friend of mine, if you
know what I mean.

                         LEO
                  (judgementally)
You're kidding me. That's indecent.

                        BILLY
                    (excitedly)
Yo, pretty lady. I knew you liked hockey
players.

                         TINY
                     (kindly)
So that's what's been up with you.

                        ROXY
                 (hypocritically)
You are so gross. How could you sleep with
your sister's husband?

Stop, stop. Pip rubbed her forehead and opened her eyes. The
conversation had turned. Plunging her hand into the tub of iced

                          81

water, she retrieved five beers, opened them and handed them out. She slipped away to the now-deserted corridor.

It was after midnight. Along one side were four doors. She tried the first two and backed out sharpish. Couples in both of them, mercifully not yet in compromising positions – she really didn't want to go there again. The third door was open, full of people watching a football match on TV. The fourth door was locked. She turned away and then back, just in case – she reached up to the top of the door frame and swept her fingers along until she felt a key. Aha. Oldest trick in the book. She used it to open the door and stepped inside.

It was quiet and cool in the room. She looked around and saw a double bed, an exercise bike, a shelf stuffed with medical textbooks and a bedside table piled with books about sports psychology. On the windowsill, medals and trophies piled up – so that was where they were. There was a small TV sitting on top of an old video player, and stacked next to it VHS tapes with names of countries on them. *Pakistan vs. England; India vs. New Zealand.* He'd taped matches to watch and learn from. Holly used to do that, too. Another door led to an en-suite bathroom, which was clean and neat. On a chair near the door were a folded set of running shorts, Leo's pale grey sweatshirt and a couple of T-shirts, and underneath the chair a pair of pristine trainers.

She could hear the thump of the bassline, but the party seemed far away. She sat on the bed and picked up the books on his bedside table. *In Pursuit of Excellence. Advances in Sport Psychology. The Mental Edge.* She flicked through a few pages of one of them and settled back onto the pillows, reading sentences and chapters, the words reminding her of Holly and the way she used to talk about sport. There was a notebook with a plain black cover. Inside it were handwritten notes about games – dates, venues, with scores, moves and tactics. Pages and pages of diagrams and instructions. Words and phrases in different languages – Spanish, Dutch, French, other languages she didn't recognise; some spelt out phonetically. She'd never seen anything like it.

Pip lost track of time. She felt drowsy, and put her head on a pillow. It smelled clean, of mint and shampoo. She propped up the book in front of her and the words swam before her eyes. She drifted, eyes heavy, body warm, and the noises of the party melted away...

A soft click. Another click. Footsteps, quiet, stopping, then approaching. She was dreaming. A hand reached out and took the book from her limp fingers. A soft blanket fell over her body. Movement on the bed behind her. A deep sigh. A rustle and gentle, regular breathing. She slept on.

Pip smelled the coffee before she opened her eyes. Oh, bliss. She was warm; there was sunlight streaming in through the gaps in the blinds. One side of the room consisted of only windows. Did it? That didn't seem right, not in her cellar room. She tried to concentrate, had a fuzzy sense of something amiss. But how could it be, when she felt so comfortable? Oh. Wait. She opened her eyes, slowly, carefully, and bam, she was awake, the fuzzy feeling giving way to panic.

She was in Leo's room. More to the point, she was in Leo's bed. She lifted the blanket. Fully dressed. Thank Christ for that. The other side of the bed had been slept in, but there was a pillow down the middle. Leo had put it there. Had he? And the coffee? Was that from him too? Where was he? Her eyes searched the corners of the room: empty. No sounds from the bathroom. The door to the corridor closed. The rest of the flat quiet.

What did I do? Did she have some sort of a crazy wish to humiliate herself in front of Leo? *Why, oh why did I fall asleep in his bed?* Of all the beds in this flat, in the whole of Munich, it was exactly the wrong one to fall asleep in. What must he have thought? Did he think she was throwing herself at him, after he'd danced all night (well, one dance) with Roxy? But he'd put a pillow between them and not woken her up and thrown her out, and made her the coffee – with foam and a spoon, how she liked it.

She sat up and sipped the coffee. It was the right temperature. What should she do now? Drink this, leave without anyone seeing, go home? Leave him a note? To say what? *Thanks for letting me sleep in your bed, smiley face, kiss kiss*? No, no way. Better to pretend this hadn't happened. Always better to do that. And where was her coat? Tiny had taken it yesterday and hung it on a hook near the door, hadn't she? Oh, what was she going to say to Tiny, who was probably out of her mind with worry?

Pip swallowed the rest of the coffee and crept into the bathroom, smearing toothpaste around her teeth with her finger. She looked longingly at the shower – she smelled pretty rank – but no. Leo might be in the kitchen. He might walk back in at any time. She hastily splashed water on her face, redid her ponytail and straightened her top. She couldn't bear to look at her reflection for too long.

She pressed her ear against Leo's door but heard no signs of life in the corridor. His running gear was gone from the chair. So that's where he was. She looked at her watch – 8.30. Bit on the late side for him. He was probably still jet-lagged. *OK, time for the Walk of Shame. Now or never. Take a deep breath, edge open the door, peer into the empty corridor.* Left was the living room, right the front door. About ten steps away. She listened again, terrified of Billy, Theo or Martin coming out of their rooms.

One, two, three, four steps. She froze as music blasted from one of the bedrooms. Five – quick – six, seven. Made it to the hook. Grabbed her coat and heard a *thump-thump*, someone shouted, 'Shut the fuck up,' and the music stopped. Eight, nine, ten, reached the door, pulled down the handle, out of the flat and quietly, swiftly, pushed it shut behind her.

She couldn't wait for the lift, so started walking down six flights of stairs, pulling on her coat. She reached into her pocket and found her phone. Five missed calls and three messages, all from Tiny.

12.43: Where r u? xxT
01.05: Did u go home? xxT
02.54: Saw Leo – said u r home safely. Going home self. xxT

Leo had told Tiny she was safe? When? When he'd gone to bed, found his room unlocked, and Pip asleep like Goldilocks in his bed? Lucky for her he wasn't Daddy Bear. What must he think of her? He already hated her for causing his break-up with Roxy. He might've wanted to get it on with Roxy last night but Pip had been there, wrecking his plans yet again.

She reached the bottom of the stairs, where there was a lobby with postboxes on one side and bikes and recycling bags on the other. She opened the front door and came face-to-face with Leo.

'Oh. Hello.' She looked down at her coat and pulled it closed.

He was covered in sweat, even though it was freezing. His breath formed clouds in front of his mouth. He was steaming.

'Did you sleep well?' he said, his face impassive.

'Yes. Thank you. And thanks… thank you… for not… for… umm. Thanks for the coffee.' She looked at her shoes. 'Sorry.'

'What for?'

'For… well… umm, well, for… sleeping in your bed,' she mumbled. It came out wrong – she still had the Goldilocks image in her head, and emphasised the word 'your' without meaning to.

'Were you looking for someone else's?'

She looked up at him, to see if he was joking. His face was blank. 'What? No.' What did he mean? She blushed and didn't even know why. 'No… I… was tired. It was the only free room.'

'It was locked. Not exactly what I would call "free".' His voice was stiff and cold.

Pip deflated. She had thought, since he'd taken care of her last night, left her to sleep with the pillow between them, sorted out Tiny and made her a coffee, how she liked it, maybe he was going to be friendly to her now. But it was the same as ever.

'Got to go. Thanks. And sorry. Won't happen again,' she muttered and dodged past him, hurrying away. She heard a door slam behind her and looked back. The pavement in front of the door was empty.

When the first snow fell in November, Dominic took one look at her denim jacket and shoes and told her to help herself to proper boots and a down puffer jacket from the cupboards in the cellar. Her shoes had holes in the soles and she'd been wearing two pairs of socks to keep her feet warm and dry, changing her wet socks when she came back to the house. She took the most masculine-looking boots and a coat, which also had a book-sized pocket on the inside, trying to avoid borrowing anything of Elisabeth's, whom no one had mentioned lately. Would the woman ever come back? Didn't she miss her children? And yet, Pip didn't want her to come back.

Max and Ferdi's hockey training had moved to the indoor hall at the International School, so Pip sat in the school reception area and read *Der Vorleser* while they played. She didn't know when the men's training was, and felt foolish asking.

There were no more matches scribbled up on the blackboard in the kitchen, and Billy didn't come over for DVD nights. She went to the cinema along the road instead, alone, watching anything that was showing – English or American films, German films, children's films, documentaries – didn't matter, she loved everything. She supposed, now the outdoor season was finished, Leo might have relaxed his rules about drinking and going out; in the whole of November, he and Billy only came over once for dinner. Pip didn't speak much, staying away from Leo, not looking him in the eye.

She turned nineteen at the end of November, but didn't tell anyone. She hadn't celebrated her birthday since 1996 anyway. Who would wish someone a happy birthday when they are plainly one of the unhappiest people they've ever met? Her parents sent her a card, signed *With love*, nothing else.

Another card arrived from her old friend Nadine, with a letter enclosed. Pip vaguely remembered other cards and letters from Nadine that she'd stored unread in a shoebox under her bed. She'd called a few times, too, Pip was pretty sure. Her mum had relayed messages to her when she'd refused to answer the phone: *Nadine says hi. Nadine sends her love.* But Pip had ignored her, along with everyone else who'd tried to comfort her. She hadn't known the right words. What could she say, anyway? *What are you up to these days, Pip? Oh, you know, nothing much, nothing at all actually, zilch, zip, nada, my life is an empty, meaningless black hole of misery – how about you, Nad?* The only comfort she found was in the pages of books, where she could disappear for a while into other worlds, and in the arms of Troy.

Pip sighed and opened the letter. It was typical Nadine – five messy pages long, full of hilarious, foul-mouthed anecdotes describing her life at Manchester University, the pubs, the hangovers, the boys, the parties. At the end she'd written, *Don't leave me hanging, Pip. I know you're busy working now, but you're still my best friend and I miss you like hell. Besides, I'm never going to leave you alone. I'll never give up, I'll just keep bugging you until you give in and call/email/write.*

Pip smiled. She could do it. She had something to say now: she would write Nadine an email and tell her about Munich – about her first night here, the sex, Billy and Leo, the hockey club, the sluts. She could imagine Nadine cracking up as she read it and the thought cheered her enormously.

Pip had opened a post office account and Dominic paid in her wages every month. She'd been to the local travel agent's shop to ask about the price of a return ticket to Sydney. She'd have enough by February at the latest. *Sydney, here I come. Troy, here I come.*

'What's the plan for Christmas this year, Daddio?' said Billy, a few days into December. He and Leo were sitting in the kitchen and had called Pip in from the garden where she'd finished building a snowman with Max and Ferdi. She was glad – next on the agenda, Max had declared, was a snowball fight. Boys against girl. To the death.

Christmas. Pip hadn't thought about that. She didn't want to go home to Canterbury. Christmas was the absolute worst time of year for the Mitchells since Holly's death. Even they couldn't summon up their usual fake cheerfulness, because Christmas Day was Holly's birthday. She wanted to ask Dominic if she could stay in Munich. She'd work through the holidays for nothing if it meant she could blot out the memories. The happy ones of Holly coming home every year, no matter where she was in the world, because she never wanted to celebrate her birthday and Christmas anywhere else. The terrible ones of that first Christmas after she was gone; the suffocating feeling of being the only child left. The awkward silences. Even Troy hadn't been there – he'd flown home to Australia and she'd missed him, his body, his warmth, the way he made her forget the pain. Her body had ached for him in the night as she'd cried herself to sleep. The second Christmas, also without Troy, last year, when she'd drunk too much and ended up phoning him in the middle of the night. It was so loud where he was, he said he'd call her back the next day. He never did, and Pip didn't want to risk calling him again in case her parents saw the phone bill. *Merry Christmas: don't think so.*

'We can go to Lindau or we can go skiing in Verbier. Up to you,' Dominic was saying.

Billy said, 'Verbier' as Leo said, 'Lindau.'

Leo turned to Billy. 'We can't ski. You know that, don't you?'

'What? Why not?' Billy looked petulant.

'You break your leg, your arm, twist your knee, anything, you've ruined your whole training schedule. If you even manage to get fit again in time, Beck's not going to select you.'

'We could ski slowly. Oh come on,' Billy said as he saw the sceptical look on Leo's face. 'We can take those slopes any day of the week. If I promise to go easy, you won't tell Beck, will you?'

Leo said nothing.

Dominic turned to Pip. 'What are you doing for Christmas, Pip? You're welcome to join us. Or do you want to go home?'

'If it's OK, can I come with you? My parents aren't planning anything special.'

'You've spoken to them already?'

'No, but I will. If it's OK with you.'

'Of course, the more the merrier. Can you ski?'

'No. But I'd like to try.'

'So is that your vote, then?'

'I have a vote?'

'Of course. Max and Ferdi get half a vote each and they'll be for Verbier. Billy too. Leo votes for Lindau. I do, too. Keep Billy away from temptation. What do you say?'

Pip wanted to go skiing. She'd never been before and she reckoned she'd love it. But she was too scared to vote against Leo. Max and Ferdi barged into the kitchen, dripping snow.

'I don't want the deciding vote. It's not up to me.'

'The siding vote for what?' said Ferdi.

Ignoring Leo's glares, Billy said, 'I want to go skiing at Christmas. Boring Dad and even more boring Leo are voting for Lindau.'

'Me too, us too, we want to ski. Yessss!' shouted Max.

'So that's two for Verbier, two for Lindau. Pip needs to vote.'

'Pip, vote for skiing, vote for skiing. Come on, Pipsqueak.'

Billy sat back in his chair, folded his arms in front of him and smiled at the carnage he had caused. Max and Ferdi danced around Pip's chair.

'Do it, Pipsqueak, or we'll put this snowball down your neck.'

'Do it, Pip, or we'll fire you.'

'Vote for skiing, or we'll never let you play with our Lego again.'

Dominic was trying to keep a straight face. Leo was furious, his mouth set in a hard line. Billy was smirking. The noise of the children and the silent, still adults and the steamy heat of the kitchen were getting to her. She sweated in her winter coat and wished that she had said she wanted to go home. No, never. She never wanted to go home. She dug her hands deep into her pockets, panicking, and felt a coin. A coin. Of course. She didn't care whether they went to Lindau or Verbier.

'OK, ratbags, settle down. You're hurting my ears. We'll flip for it: heads is Verbier, tails is Lindau. Everyone all right with that?' Around the table, heads nodded. Billy leaned forward in his seat. There was a hush. She threw the coin high up into the air, it bounced off the ceiling and fell quickly into her hand.

'Nice catch,' said Billy.

'Thank you.' She slapped her hand onto the table and closed her eyes, moving it slowly away from the coin.

'Yippeeee!' shouted Billy, Max and Ferdi. She opened her eyes. The three of them were hugging each other and bouncing up and down. She glanced at Leo, who was looking out of the window.

Dominic said, 'Verbier it is. On one condition.' Everyone fell silent. 'Leo, Billy, you're skiing slowly, right? So that's perfect, then – I'll go with the boys and you two can teach Pip to ski.'

December 1999

7

'I'm not going in your car.' Leo and Billy had turned up in separate cars, Billy in his Porsche, Leo in an old VW Golf, onto which he was fixing a roof rack. 'You drive like a maniac.'

Billy yawned. 'You drive like a granny.'

'You don't even have snow tyres.'

'So?'

'So it's illegal. I'm not going with you. You either let me drive or we go separately. If you crash, it's your own stupid fault.'

Billy humphed and rolled his eyes, loading his bags into the boot of Leo's car. 'What's with the facial hair, Leopold?' he said.

'Makes me look scarier.'

'What, to the opposite sex?'

Without looking at him, Leo thumped Billy on the arm and carried on loading the car.

'Want to go with them or us?' said Dominic out of the corner of his mouth to Pip. Max and Ferdi were already in the back of his car, sitting quietly for once, looking at an *Asterix* book together.

'You, please,' said Pip.

'Sensible girl.'

They drove for six hours, through Switzerland and into the mountains, playing I Spy and listening to CDs of *Charlie and the Chocolate Factory* and *The Jungle Book*.

Pip had expected to be making beds and cleaning and shopping – she'd told Dominic she wanted to help as much as possible – but the chalet was ready, with a fire set in the grate and the fridge full of food. There was even a cake, freshly baked, sitting on the table.

'I'll take my usual room,' said Dom, 'and Pip can have the other bedroom with the en suite.'

'What? No, I'll have this one,' Pip said, pointing to the smallest room at the end of the corridor.

'Nonsense. The boys can share a bathroom. You need your own.'

She squirmed with embarrassment. She had the best bedroom, her own bathroom and was on a free holiday where she didn't have to work. Max and Ferdi were going to ski school tomorrow morning, and she had two personal instructors, with all the equipment supplied. She knew that spending vast amounts of money meant nothing to the von Feldsteins – she supposed they didn't care about it, unlike people who didn't have so much – but she felt the differences between them when they were so generous.

She set her alarm for early the next morning, but didn't need it – at 6.30 she was wide awake. Outside her window she saw the village sloping down the mountain, the strings of Christmas lights and the snow-topped roofs of the wooden chalets glowing white in the still-dark dawn. It was like a postcard and she shivered with excitement – she was here, in the postcard. And wasn't her whole life with the von Feldsteins like a postcard from a holiday? The easy job, the relaxed family, the free time she had, her walks through Munich. She sighed with happiness.

In the kitchen she searched through cupboards and the fridge and got going. First, coffee. She smiled to see a machine, the exact match of the one in Munich. She made porridge, bacon and eggs, and toast, and squeezed fresh orange juice. No need to wake anyone up when it was ready – the smell must have drifted up to their rooms. All five men, big and small, wandered into the kitchen in pyjamas or ski underwear, eyes half open, sniffing the air.

Dominic and the boys left first for ski school. Billy and Leo took Pip down into the basement and dug out their skis, poles and boots, finding everything she needed.

'Pip, sweetheart, how much do you weigh?' called Billy from an adjoining storeroom. He appeared, clutching two pairs of boots and skis. 'We have to fix the boots into the skis and I need to know your height – what are you, about one metre seventy? So these skis should do you fine for now. And your weight?'

'I don't know.'

'Rough guess?' He lined up the boots in front of her.

'Umm. Sorry, no idea.'

He looked at her in surprise. 'You are a strange kind of girl. You don't know how much you weigh? I thought all girls weighed themselves endlessly.'

Pip shrugged.

'Leo, how much would you say the lovely Pip weighs?' He looked her up and down with a wicked grin on his face. She cringed. 'Let's see if we can work it out.' He wandered around the back of Pip, who looked at Leo for help. But Leo ignored them both. One of Billy's hands knocked the back of her knees so she stumbled into his arms as he lifted her up. 'Mmm. I'd say about fifty-five kilos. What d'you reckon, Leo? Want to try?'

Leo didn't look up from fitting boots into skis and adjusting the bindings with a screwdriver. Pip kicked, and Billy put her down.

He knelt in front of her. 'Give me a foot.' He touched his hand on the back of her right leg. *Is it hot in here?* 'Come on, I won't bite. Much,' he said, but she was having trouble keeping her balance, especially since his head was level with her crotch. *Flashback to my first night in Munich. Oh God.* He shifted her leg over one of the boots and gripped it harder, pushing it into the stiff boot. 'I think we're in. Wiggle it around a bit. Feel good?'

'What?'

'The boot, darling. Concentrate, will you?'

Leo clattered a pair of skis down near the door and disappeared into the other room.

Billy looked up at her. 'Alone, at last.'

Pip frowned down at him. 'Stop it, please.'

He laughed. 'But it's so much fun, babe. You're so easy to embarrass. You should see your face.' He reached out to touch it and pretended it was on fire, making a sizzling noise and shaking his fingers.

Pip slammed her left foot into the other boot. There. Done. Without his help.

Still kneeling in front of her, Billy reached out his hand and said, 'Help me up, will you?' She grabbed it and hauled him up, losing her balance in the heavy boots. His arm shot behind her back and he steadied her, their faces a few centimetres apart. *Don't blush, don't, just don't.* Billy was looking into her eyes, his smile soft and contrite.

'Knock it off will you, Bill,' said Leo, who'd come into the room without Pip noticing. His voice was flat and hostile and, although he was talking to Billy, the hostility was largely directed at her. 'Come on, we don't have time for your arsing around.' Billy winked at her and let her go.

They took her to the baby slopes and helped her onto the button lift, following behind her. As she was dragged up the side of the slope, she watched the toddlers as they whipped down it with no fear, their skis pointed straight down the mountain.

At the top, Billy checked her skis were clipped on and Leo showed her how to turn and stop. They set off, Leo in front demonstrating, Pip in the middle, Billy calling out instructions from behind. She fell, it hurt, she stood up, she skied faster, she fell again. Over and over again until they reached the bottom.

'Good. You're getting the hang of it.' Billy checked his watch. 'I am?'

'Yup. Listen, you'll be OK doing these slopes if we leave you here?'

Pip looked at the button lift, with two slopes coming off it either side. 'Umm. OK.' She started sliding off towards the bottom of the lift.

'Whoa there. Wait, Billy, what do you think you're doing?'

'Come off it, this is so boring. No offence, Pip. We can't stay here all day. You said we had to ski slowly, but this is like standing still. It's torture. Look at that fresh snow, man. Just think what the powder will be like on the Backside of Mont Fort.'

'Are you fucking kidding me? You're not going anywhere near the Backside. Do you hear me?'

But Billy, if he had heard Leo, was showing no signs of it. He was already halfway to the cable car.

Leo turned to Pip, a grim look on his face.

She said, 'You can go too, if you like. I'll stay here and do these slopes today. I'll be fine, honestly. I'll see you back at the chalet this afternoon.'

'No, I'm not leaving you alone on your first day of skiing. He's just being a dick as usual.'

'What's the Backside of Mont Fort?' said Pip as they made their way to the lift.

'It's the end of Billy's Olympics.'

Leo was a patient teacher, which surprised Pip, who'd expected him to become bored. He showed her over and over again what she was supposed to do and his face showed a flicker of pride when she managed it. She graduated from the baby slopes to the steeper blue pistes, which were reached by T-bar lifts. She had to share with Leo, sitting close to each other to balance it, with their hands gripping the middle bar. She could see couples chatting and laughing in front of her; once, a man and woman started kissing on the T-bar in front of them. Pip pretended not to see it, and looked at the view instead.

By mid-afternoon, Pip was exhausted, the muscles in her thighs and calves burning. Her arms felt like pieces of string. But there was no way she was going to give up. She wanted to show Leo she could keep on going, keep on improving. After she'd fallen over for the seven-millionth time, he led her to a restaurant and made her take off her skis.

'Sit. Rest.'

'Yes, sir.'

He bought them both a hot chocolate and they sat on two deckchairs on the terrace that faced the slopes. They sat and sipped their drinks silently until a shout came from the chair lift.

'Leo, you hound – stop chatting up the au pair girl.' It was Billy, grinning and waving at them.

Leo shook his head. His face was glowing, with two red patches on his cheeks above his dark beard. 'He's such a kid. I don't know what goes through his head sometimes. Lunatic.'

Pip curled her toes in her ski boots and took a sip from her cup. She shivered with the cold.

'You OK? Shall we go inside?'

A cloud passed and the shadows fell away from them. Pip felt the sun on her skin, smiled and closed her eyes. She wasn't looking at him, so felt brave enough to say, 'Ah, Mr von Feldstein, you absolute wonder – you made the sun come out for me.'

He was silent. She opened one eye a tiny amount and saw that he was looking at her with a strange expression. What was he thinking? Perhaps he was offended by her pathetic attempt at flirting with him. It was disconcerting not to know him at all. He lay back on his deckchair and closed his eyes too.

'Tell me a story about the lunatic, something from when you were growing up.'

She heard him exhaling. She waited.

'I used to have this sort of tradition – it started the first time I went to a junior hockey trial, when I was about twelve or thirteen. I needed a haircut and my mum did it for me, the night before I left. At the trials, I played well and so after that, I always asked her to cut my hair the night before a big tournament.'

His voice was soft and steady, warmer than she'd ever heard it.

'The first time I played seniors for Germany, I was twenty-one – it was at the Europeans in Dublin. I was freaking out, because Mum wasn't there. By that time, we didn't get on so well, but still – I was taking this massive step forward and I couldn't have the haircut.

'So, the afternoon before I leave, Billy gives me this envelope with an address in it. "Go there," he says. "I can't arrange Mum for you, but this is the next best thing." So I'm really pleased because Billy's not usually so clued-up about other people's feelings, and off I go, thinking he's given me the address of a barber's. I arrive at a flat in town, go up to the door and the hairdresser lets me in. It's in her private flat, but there's a chair and a mirror and scissors all set up. I sit down and she starts cutting my hair. She's kind, she says complimentary things about my hair and does a great job. But the whole time I'm more and more uncomfortable because she's giving me a head massage, and when she's finished the cut, she starts massaging my shoulders and telling me she likes me, and then I'm about to stand up and leave when she just… starts undoing my jeans.'

'What?' Pip sat up and sploshed hot chocolate on her ski trousers. 'She did what?'

Leo shook his head and grimaced. 'Turns out she was a hooker. Billy had bought me a haircut *and* the haircutter, for the night.'

'Oh Jesus, no, what did you do?'

'What do you think I did?' He was looking at her, half-smiling.

Put me on the spot, Leo, why don't you? Panic. Argh. 'You... what... I think... You left?'

'Of course I left. Billy's unhinged if he thinks I'm going through with that. It's not only that I prefer to sleep with women without having to pay them to do it; it's also that he completely misunderstood what the haircut was about. I mean, it was supposed to be...'

'Your mother doing it?'

'Yes.'

'So he shat all over that sweet little tradition, then?'

'That's putting it mildly. After that, I had to go to a normal barber's every time.'

'And how did you play – in Dublin?'

'Not badly. We won. I played in a few games – good enough to go to the '96 Olympics.'

Atlanta. Pip had been there. Holly's last Olympics, though none of them had known that. Holly and Troy were married by then. Pip and her parents had stayed in a rented apartment in a complex with a dirty swimming pool and a spider infestation. There had been no furniture – they'd had to buy camping mattresses and sleeping bags. They'd tried to laugh about it, but they were bitten so badly, and the bites were so swollen and painful that they had to go to the doctor. They'd moved out and booked into a campsite instead.

That must have been where Leo had met Holly. Leo at his first Olympics; Holly at her last. Pip couldn't remember whether the German men's team had won a medal. Holly's team had just missed out on the bronze. Pip was fifteen and had been allowed to go out afterwards with the GB girls, who bought her drinks and looked after her. She felt a lump in her throat. She missed those girls – they were like big sisters to her, all of them. Why did everything, even an anecdote about a prostitute, remind her of Holly? How long did she have to carry this grief, stooping under the weight of it, being ambushed at every turn?

Leo was saying something about Billy, but he stopped. 'What's wrong?'

'Nothing.' Pip blinked back the tears in her eyes.

'You always look… when I talk about the Olympics… like you're in pain.'

'No I don't.' It came out angrier than she meant it to.

'Pip. What is it?'

Could she confide in him? About Holly? About Troy? He would understand, wouldn't he? Because of his mum, he knew what it felt like to miss someone you love. But no. He was so proper, so upright. He would judge her, especially about Troy, whom he hated, and their relationship, which he would think was creepy because of the age thing.

'Shall we go?' She swallowed the last of her hot chocolate and stood up. 'Race you to the bottom.'

Leo's face, which had been worried and confused, snapped back to normal. Shutters down, brisk and formal. She couldn't blame him – he'd been kind and she'd shut him out.

They clipped on their skis and Pip pushed off first, trying to stay steady, transferring her weight like he'd taught her. On her turns she couldn't see him, he was way behind her, she was going faster and faster, she was beating him, it felt great, she straightened her skis and pointed them down the mountain with a rush of adrenalin, the cold air streaming past her face, the scrape of ice beneath her skis. She whooped with joy as she came to a halt at the bottom of the cable car. She looked up the slope, into the sun, gasping for air, her cheeks burning, to see how far behind he was. Someone tapped her on the shoulder. She turned.

'Not bad,' said Leo. He already had his skis off.

'Wh… how…? I thought…'

'You thought you beat me?' He laughed. 'I like your positive attitude. It'll get you far.'

'But… you're not supposed to go fast. I thought…'

'Pip, come on. I've been skiing since I could walk. You think you're going to beat me after two days? Even with a broken leg I could ski faster than you.'

'I might bloody well test that sometime,' Pip muttered. She really thought she'd beaten him.

Leo looked at her, still laughing. 'Who knew you were so competitive?'

He stayed with her every day, and she worked hard to win his approval. He didn't give it easily. When she fell, he hauled her up. When she was tired, he made her practise more turns. When she skied well, her reward was a 'Not bad' or a 'Better than yesterday.'

On the fifth day, Pip was concentrating on her turns when she felt a loud whoosh of air and someone barrelled past her, missing her by centimetres. She screamed, lost her balance and fell over.

'Are you hurt? Are you OK?' Leo was at her side.

She nodded, scanning the mountain for the snowboarder, and caught sight of him near the lift. Leo gave her his gloved hand; she took it, heaved herself up and carried on. Leo overtook her and stopped next to the snowboarder, who had sparked up a cigarette. Pip could see Leo shouting at the man, and as she skied up to them she heard him swearing in German, but the snowboarder shrugged. Leo switched to English.

'You were too close. Learn how to board properly or you'll kill someone.'

The snowboarder shrugged again.

Leo pointed at her, but looked at him. 'Apologise, you fuckwit.'

The snowboarder took a drag from his cigarette, looked Pip up and down and smiled at her, still not saying anything, not understanding, or pretending not to. He gestured towards Leo, as if to say, *What's this loser going on about?*

Pip said to him, '*Il dit que tu devrais t'excuser a moi de skier comme une merde.*'

The snowboarder said, '*Et moi, j'te dis que tu devrais te taper ton mec plus souvant, pour qu'il soit moins merdeux.*' He stubbed out his cigarette and pushed off down the slope.

'How come you speak French? What did he say?'

'A Level. Nothing,' she said, wondering if she should tell him that the Frenchman had recommended she should be having sex with Leo more often.

In the evenings, they ate together and Pip helped Dominic put the boys to bed. After dinner, Billy went out. He'd met some old school friends who'd come out from England on the first day. Leo joined him the first night, but when Billy invited her, she said she needed to have a bath and sleep. She'd seen the prices in the mountain restaurants and knew she couldn't afford her round. On the second night, Leo stayed home too, and read one of his sports psychology books by the fireside. He was deeply immersed in it, underlining bits.

Every night before she went to bed, Pip ran her hands over her legs, which were aching and sore but becoming firmer. She loved her new muscles. She'd paid for them with pain and sweat and nearly tears, if she hadn't been too proud to cry in front of Leo. 'My thighs of steel,' she whispered to herself as she drifted to sleep.

On the morning of Christmas Day, they skied together, Max and Ferdi racing with Billy, Pip hanging back with Dominic and Leo. Billy taught the boys the lyrics to The Pogues' Christmas song, so she could hear the three of them sing-shouting down the mountain, something about a bum and a punk – *did they just say 'slut'?* – then scumbags and maggots, and *oh no, not faggot, surely not; Billy, please stop*, which just made them sing louder. Happy Christmas the von Feldstein way. They stopped at eleven and returned to the chalet for a huge Christmas lunch, cooked by a Swiss couple Dominic had hired from a restaurant in the village.

'Do you want to phone your parents?' Dominic asked, and Pip started. It had just hit her – it was Holly's birthday. She'd forgotten. How on earth could she have forgotten the birthday of the most important person in her whole life?

She spent five minutes on the phone with her mum and dad, who sounded far away and distracted. She hadn't spoken to them for weeks, and it occurred to her that when she'd told them she wasn't coming home for Christmas, they'd not asked where she was going or what she was doing. It had ceased to bother her years ago, even before Holly's death.

After the call, they gathered around the fire to open their presents. Dominic gave Pip a beautiful scarf, Billy gave her some expensive perfume and Leo gave her a pale blue cashmere jumper, lovely gifts that Pip suspected Rosa had chosen.

'I didn't buy you anything,' she said, once the wrapping paper had been ripped off every present. Max and Ferdi groaned whilst Dominic, Billy and Leo shook their heads, insisting it wasn't necessary and she shouldn't worry. 'But… I did sort of make something for you.' She took an envelope out from behind a cushion and put it on her lap. 'It's a bit silly. I thought it might be fun for this afternoon.'

To quizzical looks, she pulled out the pieces of paper from the envelope, printed pages stapled together, six copies in all.

'It's a story – well, a play really. I wrote it.' She handed out the pages. She had listed their characters on the first page and highlighted each of their parts. Dominic read quickly, a bemused smile on his face. Billy was chuckling, Leo impassive, Max reading bits out loud, Ferdi shushing him, his chubby finger following the words as he read silently, his lips moving.

It was a short play, only five scenes, and they spent the afternoon reading their parts aloud and performing in costumes Billy found in the cellar. Leo relaxed the no-drinking rule for this one day, so Billy kept filling up their glasses with wine and champagne and became more raucous and merrier as the afternoon turned to evening.

On the last day, although Pip told Leo that he should ski with Billy, if only to keep an eye on him, he wouldn't leave her.

'It's fine, really, I'm OK alone,' she said.

'Are you trying to get rid of me?'

Was Pip imagining it, or was that a smile on his lips?

They skied, Pip trying her hardest to keep up with him, Leo infuriatingly good.

'What's that you keep saying to yourself?' he asked her, when they took a break by the side of the slope. 'When we're skiing. I hear you saying or singing something. What is it?'

'Umm. It's stupid really. Well, not stupid, just... you know. Someone used to say it to me, and when I'm skiing it sort of helps. She said, "If it doesn't scare you shitless, it's probably not worth doing."'

'Huh,' said Leo, thinking. 'It's not stupid at all. I like it. Your mantra.'

Later that afternoon, as they opened the door to the chalet, they were greeted by a strange hush. Max and Ferdi were sitting quietly on the sofa. Dominic was standing by the door, a concerned look on his face.

'What? Where's Billy?' said Leo, barging past his father. 'What's happened?'

Pip followed him. Billy was sitting on the chair by the fire, his leg raised on a stool in front of him. He was staring at the flames, his face set in pain. Oh no. Leo knelt by his side, asking him what had happened, where did it hurt, had he seen the doctor? Pip thought he'd be angry, but his voice was soft and full of worry. She walked slowly to the sofa and sat next to Ferdi, put her arm round him and he buried his head in her shoulder. Hang on. What? Ferdi, who wouldn't allow her to touch him? She looked at Max. His mouth was twitching and he covered his face with his hand. Was he crying? But Max never cried. Something was... Pip looked at Billy, who turned his head from the fire and, while Leo was examining his knee, gave Max a quick wink. The traitors. She disentangled herself from Ferdi and jumped up off the sofa.

'How could you? You lot are the pits.' She turned to Leo. 'Stop. You don't need to do that.'

Leo stared at her like she was mad.

'They're having you on. Look at them.' Ferdi was sniggering behind his hand. Max gave a muffled snort from behind a cushion. She glared at Dominic, who looked a little shamefaced. 'You, too?'

'Calm down, Pip. It's only a joke,' said Billy, laughing his head off.

'You're horrible and a disgrace. All of you. But mostly you.' She walked over to Billy and jabbed her finger at him. 'You know how much this means to Leo. All he wants is for you to be there, playing with him at the Olympics. It's his dream and you're shitting all over it. Excuse my language. You should be ashamed of yourself.' She gave them one last glare and stamped out of the room. She didn't know where to go. Upstairs to her bedroom? No, because they might follow her and she didn't want to see any of them. She grabbed her coat and hurriedly pushed her feet into her snow boots, rushing out into the snow, to go anywhere, anywhere she could get away from them. She ran down the street towards town, passing groups of families and friends. She had just reached the corner when she heard footsteps behind her.

'Pip, stop, I'm sorry, OK?'

She turned and realised that she *had* wanted to be followed, but not by Billy, who looked truly apologetic; not by Billy, who kneeled down and started grovelling, begging her forgiveness, until she smiled and shook her head at him and told him to stand up and stop acting like a three-year-old. Not by Billy.

8

'But why aren't you changed? I said we had to leave for the club at 7.30,' wailed Tiny. She was standing in Pip's bedroom doorway, wearing a long coat over a black dress. She had dyed her hair dark brown and had on a lot of make-up. 'You're not bailing on me again, are you?'

'Yes. I'm not coming. I don't have anything to wear.' She knew she sounded like a wet blanket.

'You always say that.'

'But this time it's true. It's ridiculous, anyway – who has a Bond Girl dress hanging in their wardrobe? And it's unfair – the men wear their DJs and look suave and dashing, and we agonise about what to wear, spend far too much money and look ridiculous.'

'Welcome to the world, Pip.'

'What are you wearing? Show me.'

Tiny took off her coat and showed Pip the black evening

dress Teri Hatcher wears in *Tomorrow Never Dies*, with the fluffy, feathery sleeves.

'Paris Carver. You look amazing.'

'Yeah? Does it work? How old do I look?'

'At least forty. And totally sluttish.'

Tiny grinned. 'Thank you.' Then her face fell. 'But I won't go unless you do. Can't you just put on one of Elisabeth's dresses?'

'No way. I'm not going and that's final.'

'What's final? Is everyone decent?' A head appeared round the door. 'Ah, shame.'

'Hello, Billy. Please help me persuade, or force, Pip to come to the party. It's New Year's Eve. It's the millennium. When your children and your grandchildren ask you what you did on the millennium New Year's Eve, are you really going to tell them that you stayed at home watching telly? Are you that sad?'

'Yes. That is how sad I am. It's not that I don't want to come, but I don't have a dress.'

'Well then, it's lucky I'm here,' said Billy with a grin. He moved into the room, wearing a DJ and looking suave and dashing, with a dress bag over his arm. He put it on the bed and unzipped it. 'Would you prefer to be Elektra King from *The World Is Not Enough* or Anya Amasova from *The Spy Who Loved Me*? It's all they had left in your size in the dress-hire shop. Apart from the Honey Ryder bikini and I thought you might be a little chilly in that.'

Tiny jumped up and down, squealing with excitement. 'Yes, yes, yes, Billy, you hero.' She picked up the dresses and held them to Pip's body. The first was a red-and-black lacy number with spaghetti straps; the second a long black dress, low-cut with a glittery trim.

Pip touched the dresses and realised Billy wasn't joking. He had actually gone to a dress-hire shop and found not one but two Bond Girl dresses for her.

'Well? Aren't you going to try them on?' he said.

'Yes. But you have to leave the room. Not you, Tiny, I need your help with the zips.'

'I can do zips.'

Tiny pushed Billy out of the door. 'These ones need to go up, not down. Shoo.'

Pip stripped off and tried on the dresses. They both fit her more or less, and Tiny said that with some safety pins she could make them perfect. The Anya Amasova dress was much more glam, and Pip loved that character from the film, but it was so low-cut that Pip didn't think she would stop blushing all night; so she chose the Elektra King one. It was beautiful. She smoothed it down, running her fingers over the fabric and adjusting the straps.

Tiny shouted, 'Billy, you can come in now. Pip, let down your hair. Perfect. You have about three minutes to do your make-up.'

'I don't have any make-up,' said Pip, wet-blanketing again.

'You can borrow some of mine,' said a girl's voice at the door. That wasn't Tiny's voice. Pip whipped up her head and goggled. Nadine was standing at the door.

'What...? But... How...?'

'The look on your face,' said Nadine, rushing to Pip and hugging her. 'It's priceless.'

'What are you doing here? Why didn't you tell me you were coming?'

'Surprise. But there's no time to explain now.' She pulled off her clothes. 'I have to get dressed – I'm so glad you chose that one; I had my eye on the black one but Billy said you had to have first choice.'

'What? Billy said what?'

Billy knocked and came in the door. Nadine was in her underwear. She didn't miss a beat, just smiled, turned her back on him, unhooked her bra and slipped on the dress. 'Did I hear you say you were good with zips, Billy?' She lifted up her hair at the back and waited.

Billy, for once, was speechless. He stepped forward and pulled up the zip, then stepped back again, all the time staring at Nadine. Pip caught Tiny's eye and grinned.

'C'mon, do your make-up, let's go or we'll be late,' said Tiny, all business. 'Billy, you will drive us there, won't you? Do you have any shoes, Pip? Nothing with a heel? Oh, they'll have to do I suppose.'

Nadine parted her straight black hair in the middle and expertly smoothed lip gloss onto her lips. 'Let me do your eyes, Pip. I'll make you look smokin' hot.' She came towards Pip, brandishing numerous sticks and brushes. When she'd finished, she stuffed the make-up into her handbag, along with a travel toothbrush, a condom, her passport and a spare pair of knickers. She saw Tiny and Pip staring at her and said, 'What?'

'Your passport, Nad?'

Nadine shrugged. 'I will spend this evening asking myself, *What would Anya Amasova do?* And she would definitely never be without her passport.'

Leo, clean-shaven and extremely handsome in his DJ, was waiting upstairs and Pip couldn't look him in the eye. She kept fiddling with her straps until Nadine gently knocked away her hand. 'You look gorgeous. Relax.'

Max, Ferdi and Dominic rushed downstairs, Dominic in a DJ, the boys in their normal clothes – they were allowed to go to the party until midnight, when Dominic was going to bring them home, but had refused to dress up.

'Pipsqueak, you look horrible.'

'Why thank you,' she said. 'I'll take that as a compliment.'

Billy held open the front door and they walked to Leo's car. Billy offered the front seat to the girls, but Pip piled into the back with Nadine, too shy to sit next to Leo and desperate to hear what the hell Nadine was doing in Munich with Billy of all people. Tiny squished in beside them.

'I called a few weeks ago for you,' Nadine giggled. 'I thought I was speaking to Mr von Feldstein and told him I was your friend, but then this guy was asking me in a ludicrous fake-dad voice what I look like, and I knew it was Billy. So we got chatting and I said I was thinking of coming to visit you, and we made the arrangements and here I am. I arrived earlier today, he picked me up from the airport and we went into town to collect the dresses.' Nadine mouthed, 'You're right – he *is* lush', and Tiny cracked up.

'I heard that,' said Billy.

'I didn't mean you, I meant Leo,' said Nadine, quick as a flash.

'Hear that, Leopold? You have an admirer,' Billy said, but his eyes didn't leave Nadine's.

Leo said nothing. Pip could only see the back of him. Was he smiling, or did he think they were all beyond silly? They pulled into the car park, the lights in the clubhouse shining out and the air filled with loud music. Billy took Nadine's elbow and Tiny tottered along beside them in the highest heels Pip had ever seen. Pip shivered.

'Are you OK? Are you cold?'

She risked a glance at Leo and her stomach flipped. She was so nervous, she couldn't talk. She shook her head and looked towards the clubhouse. She didn't know what to do.

'Your dress is nice.'

'So's yours. I mean… you know what I mean.'

Leo coughed. 'You look nice.'

'Yes. Thank you.' There was a pause.

'Nadine seems…'

'Nice?' said Pip. She looked up at Leo and he was smiling at her. She felt like her insides were melting. But… shit. Nadine – she had to tell Nadine to keep her mouth shut about Holly. 'I have to… sorry… see you later,' she said as she ran away from him.

She caught up with Nadine as they reached the door. They said to each other at the same time, 'I have to speak to you.'

'Oh. OK. You first,' said Nadine. Billy and Tiny went inside and up the stairs. Pip pulled Nadine into the women's changing room. She checked it was empty.

'No one knows about Holly here. Please please tell me you didn't talk to Billy about her.'

'What do you mean, they don't know about Holly?'

'Did you tell him?' Pip squawked.

'Why? No, I didn't,' Nadine said quickly. 'Calm down, OK? We didn't... we talked about other things. But why?'

'Oh my God, thank you. Sorry, I didn't mean to give you a fright. I haven't told them. I didn't want them to know. I didn't want to have to talk about her. Have people feel sorry for me or whatever. And that was even before I knew they're hockey players. I haven't told them I played hockey, nothing. They've all heard of Holly. And Leo... he met her once.'

Nadine bit her top lip. 'It's still bad, isn't it? For you, I mean – it's not got any easier?'

Pip shook her head. 'It hurts. Every day. Everything reminds me of her. Even... just being alive when she's not... it... I can't bear it sometimes.'

Nadine hugged her. 'It's OK. I didn't say a thing. I totally understand why you're not telling them.' She stroked the top of Pip's arm. 'Are you OK? You seem really well and happy. Apart from that moment of drama just then. It's good here, right?'

'Yes. It's good here. Mostly. I mean, always, I think.' She smiled. 'Let's try and forget about it for tonight, shall we?'

'Yes, you're right.' Nadine looked down at her dress, or more accurately at her cleavage. 'Let's hit the bar, shall we?'

'What did you want to talk to me about?'

'What?'

'You said you wanted to talk to me.'

'Oh yes. Umm... do you know if Billy has a girlfriend? Stop laughing. I've got a huge crush on him.'

'Really? I hadn't noticed.'

'Do you think he likes me?'

'Do you mean before or after you took your clothes off in front of him?'

Nadine giggled. 'I've never done anything like that before. I think it's millennium fever.'

'Should I even ask what that is?'

'Seriously, though – girlfriend?'

'Not as far as I know.'

'And how about you?'

'No. Nope, I don't have a girlfriend.'

'Ha ha. But I mean – do you like him? You don't, do you?' Nadine put her finger in her mouth and started biting her nail. 'From your emails, it seemed like you did. The way you wrote about him – how hilarious he is, and good-looking. And all that stuff with that girl, Rosie.'

'Roxy.'

'Whatever. Phew.' Nadine flapped her hand in front of her face. 'I'm getting more of that millennium fever just thinking about it. I won't lie to you, it's my ambition tonight to have some of that.'

'Nadine!'

'It's what Anya would do. Look, if the world is going to end, I know where I want to be at midnight. And what I want to be doing. And who I want to be doing it with. If you know what I mean.'

'Yes, Nadine, I know what you mean.'

'But you haven't answered my question: do you or do you not fancy Wilhelm von Feldstein?' She held her fist in a microphone in front of Pip's mouth.

'I do not,' Pip said. Nadine squealed with delight, smacked her on the bum and pushed her out of the changing room.

The bar was packed, it was already eight o'clock and they'd missed everyone arriving. As predicted, the men were in DJs, but the women had made a monumental effort. Pip saw a Pussy Galore, an Octopussy and a May Day. A whole team of the younger girls had come in *Moonraker* yellow jumpsuits, and some of the older women were playing it safe, sticking to the Miss Moneypenny side of things. There was a buzz, a swell of chatter and laughter as everyone tried to guess the films people's costumes were based on. She saw Billy and Nadine chatting by the bar, laughing loudly. Pip tried not to, she tried her hardest, but her eyes kept roaming around, searching for Leo. He was sitting at the bar, talking to an older couple. She took a sip of her drink and tried to look away, but kept sneaking glances at him. What was she doing? Why was she being so ridiculous about Leo, of all people? She knew she had absolutely no chance with him – he was way out of her league and she wasn't even sure he liked her at all.

When Nadine had asked her about Billy, she'd felt a momentary pang. *Do I?* she'd thought. Perhaps she had a bit at first. He had always been so sweet – the little things he did to look after her. The big things too – like the dresses for her and Nadine tonight. But the warm wave that flooded through Pip when Nadine asked her the question wasn't because she had feelings for Billy – it was because Nadine had asked her. Nadine, who used to be her best friend but had moved away, still liked her enough to come and visit, spend NYE Y2K with her, and be considerate enough of her feelings to give Pip first dibs on a boy she was clearly lusting after herself.

Pip danced a lot that evening. Mostly to stop herself gawking at Leo all night. She danced with Tiny and Mandi. She danced with Caro. She danced with loads of boys – some from the club, some she'd never met before. She was relieved she'd worn flat shoes (Tiny was now barefoot), and that she'd chosen the red dress (Nadine was having trouble dancing; she kept popping out of her dress, Billy kindly helping her put them back in again). Billy and Nadine were both hammered, but they wouldn't let Pip go off by herself. They kept grabbing her and pulling her onto the dance floor whenever she tried to leave them alone. Pip saw Max and Ferdi a few times, racing about in their socks, skidding and sliding on the dance floor with a few of the other children, including Anna and Isa, Rosa's daughters.

Leo didn't dance. Not even when Roxy, who was looking stunning in the Honey Ryder bikini – only she could have pulled it off – shimmied over to him. Pip watched from where she was slow-dancing with Theo. She couldn't hear what they were saying, but Leo shook his head and Roxy sat down on the bar stool next to him, accepting a drink he bought her. His face was calm and neutral as he chatted to her, but when she stood up, he shook his head again and she walked away.

'Go and ask the Party Animal to dance,' shouted Billy over the loud music to Caro later.

'Leo? No way. He's just blown out Roxy, she's blubbing in the ladies'. Bloody drama queen. If he won't dance with her…'

'What do you mean?'

'He's still mad about her,' said Caro.

'No he's not,' said Billy.

'It's so obvious. He can't stop staring at her. He's totally smitten.'

'If so, why won't he dance with her?'

Caro shrugged. 'You tell me.'

'OK, I will. He's staring at her because she's practically naked and she's fit as fuck. He's not interested in her because she's high-maintenance and basically a nightmare girlfriend to have in an Olympic year. He's not dancing with her because he's stone-cold sober and hates dancing.'

'In that case, I'm not asking him to dance either.'

'Fair enough,' said Billy. 'Why don't you ask him, Pip?'

Pip gave him a look. 'Ditto what Caro said.'

'I'll do it,' said Nadine, and she strode away from them. They watched her, Pip's heartbeat speeding up. Nadine approached Leo and whispered something in his ear. His eyes flickered over to where they stood. He gave a quick nod of his head and stood up, following Nadine, who had a triumphant look on her face, to the dance floor. *How on earth did she manage that?* thought Pip.

It was another slow dance – *No Scrubs* by TLC. Pip danced with Billy, but kept looking around him at Nadine and Leo.

Billy said in her ear, 'I like your friend.'

'She likes you too.'

'Where's she from? I mean, is she English?'

'Her mum's half Indian and she's got another grandparent who's black – her paternal grandfather, I think. That's where the dark hair and eyes are from.'

'She doesn't have a boyfriend, does she?'

'Would you really care if she did?'

Billy laughed. 'Are you taking the little men back home tonight? After the fireworks?'

'No, Dominic said he'd do it. And there are other guests staying in your room and Leo's, so don't go barging in later with Nad.'

Billy did a little salute to thank her for the tip.

Leo's hand was on Nadine's bare lower back. Billy saw where Pip was looking.

'Amazing girl. Can't believe she got old Leo to dance.'

'Must be the millennium fever.'

Before Billy could ask what that was, Pip heard Nadine say, 'Switch', and Billy stepped away from her, taking Nadine in his arms. The song faded and Pip stood opposite Leo, praying for the year to end and the computers to crash and the lights to go out and the planes to fall out of the sky, or for something to happen that would mean she wouldn't be rejected by him. What would the next song be – a fast one, so that he had an excuse to sit it out, or a slow one, so that he would put his hands on her back, the thought of which made her knees shake?

The strings from the next song began and a thrill ran through her. *I Try.* It was her favourite song from this year. Every time she listened to it on the radio, she loved the lyrics and Macy Gray's raspy voice and the beautiful, haunting music that made her feel so sorrowful and joyful at the same time. She thought about millennium fever, took a deep breath and stepped towards Leo, taking his hands and placing them on her waist, putting her own hands on his shoulders, and looked somewhere in the direction of his chin. Trying to stay calm and to keep a friendly, neutral smile on her face, she swayed clumsily and felt his hands hold her more firmly.

They moved together without speaking and Pip's mind was racing all over the place. He was dancing with her out of politeness. He probably wanted to dance with Nadine again and would do the switch thing as soon as he could. Compared to Roxy, she looked boring; she *was* boring, she didn't have anything to say to him and there was nothing she could talk about, not hockey because she hated it, not her family because of Holly, not Troy. Definitely not Troy. Nothing was ever going to happen between her and Leo – if he thought Roxy was high-maintenance, what would he think of her, with her overwhelming grief for her dead sister and her screwed-up relationship with her sister's husband? *A nightmare girlfriend in an Olympic year.* Billy didn't know the half of it.

'What are you thinking about?' said Leo quietly.

'Nothing.' Well, what was she supposed to say? She looked at his eyes and away again. She could have screamed with frustration. Why couldn't she chatter away, like she did with Billy or Tiny? It had been fine in Verbier, but the camaraderie she'd felt with Leo then had disappeared, especially after she'd told off the others for the trick they'd played on him. They'd taken her out that night to a pizza restaurant to say sorry, even though Pip said it was Leo they needed to apologise to. Leo had sat next to her and told everyone how much she'd improved at skiing and what a natural she was, and how she had a real knack for it. But that was then. And now he felt like a stranger again.

'Want to go outside?' he said.

INT. DANCE FLOOR AT A PARTY – NIGHT

PIP and LEO dance. The words he has just spoken hang in the air between them. Everyone around them melts away and disappears. They are alone. The music winds around them, spiralling along their bodies like wisps of silver smoke.

LEO
Want to go outside? For the fireworks. It's only five minutes until midnight.

Pip blinked and looked around her. The other couples were drifting to the windows and the doors that led out onto the balconies. Oh.

Where were Nadine and Billy? She couldn't see them anywhere. If they were where she thought they were, doing what she thought they were doing, she hoped no one walked in on them. She certainly wasn't going anywhere near the physio room in the basement until they reappeared.

'You OK? You look pissed off about something.'

'I'm fine,' Pip lied. 'Just tired. I think I'll go home after the fireworks too.' Everything was starting to weigh down on her. Nadine being here, and Nadine with Billy, and the way she felt about Leo, and how he clearly had no interest in her, and even if he did, he'd run a mile if he knew anything about her. And as always on occasions like New Years and anniversaries, she felt engulfed by misery that Holly wasn't here with her, or at least somewhere in the world, enjoying it too. She would've been twenty-eight years old. She and Troy would have been standing together in Sydney Harbour, waiting for the biggest year of their lives to start. What was Troy doing now, without Holly? Thinking about her, or trying to forget about her? Or was he thinking about Pip?

Pip was ambushed by a thought – that in trying to get over Holly's death by being with Troy, she'd only made it worse. Because now she had the guilt about the sex to add to the grief itself. Not to mention the fear that someone might find out about Troy, and her uncertainty about their reaction to it.

'Five... four... three... two... one.' The fireworks began and Pip felt tears running down her face. She swallowed the sob that rose up inside her. She brushed away tears and saw Leo watching her, frowning. Someone slapped him on the back and hugged him. A woman kissed him on both cheeks. Everyone was shouting, 'Happy New Year', shaking hands, kissing and hugging each other. She stepped back, slipping into the clubhouse and scurrying towards the stairs.

Out of the door, she saw Max and Ferdi with Dominic and the older couple Leo had been talking to earlier, stepping into a taxi. She asked if she could catch a lift home, replying to Dominic's concerned questions with assurances that she was tired but yes, she'd had a good time and yes, the fireworks were brilliant, and to Max that no, she didn't think that zombies were about to take over the world, and to Ferdi that no, the moon probably wasn't going to explode.

Back in her room, she stepped out of her dress and hung it in its bag, stroking the material and wondering if she'd ever wear anything so pretty again. She washed the make-up off her face, scrubbing at her smudged eyeliner and mascara and feeling like crying again.

What a mess. How could she have allowed things to go so far: to lie to these lovely people about Holly and take advantage of them, take their money, live in their home? She was a fraud. And her best friend had arrived and whisked Billy off his feet and they were probably on their way back to his flat for a night of passion. She felt an aching loneliness. Would she ever be able to put herself out there like Nadine had with Billy, just take a leap and hope she didn't fall flat on her face? Also, she was confused about Troy and what he meant to her. What was she going to do when she saw him in September? Would she have to lie to him about the von Feldsteins, like she was lying to the von Feldsteins about him? How difficult she'd made her life. And did she even care enough about him to lie to him?

Because when she closed her eyes and that Macy Gray song drifted back into her head, it wasn't Troy's face that she saw. It wasn't the lack of him that caused her to ache. She was hopeless, pathetic, ridiculous to have fallen for someone so far out of her reach, he might as well have been living on the moon.

9

January 2000

After New Year, everything went flat. Nadine left, having spent the weekend with Pip during the days and Billy during the nights. A few days later, Billy and Leo left for Barcelona where they were playing in a tournament. School started again and within a week, Pip had the feeling that the skiing holiday and New Year's Eve were so long ago, they literally felt like a different century.

She missed Nadine. They'd talked a lot about how Pip was doing; how there seemed to be some days when she didn't feel so low about Holly's death; how lovely the von Feldsteins were. Pip told Nadine about Billy's jokes and kindnesses, and asked her not to go into too much bedroom detail.

'"Bedroom detail"? You crack me up. But you're sure we're all right about this?' Nadine had fretted.

'Bit late for worrying about that, isn't it?' Pip took Nadine's hand. 'I absolutely, sincerely, truthfully am all right with this. It's just, when it comes to Billy's sexual abilities, I've seen and heard enough to last a lifetime.'

Nadine sighed, a glazed, dreamy look in her eyes.

'Oh please, stop. I'm going to be sick,' Pip groaned.

And now that Nadine was gone, and Billy and Leo too, Pip's life felt empty. Even Tiny had less time for her – she had an important paper to write for her course and said she'd be back in action in February. There was a huge snowfall, so Pip struggled to run around the uncleared paths in the woods. The sun barely had time to rise above the houses before it started to sink again. She woke up often during the night, hearing floorboards creaking and windows whistling in their frames, the house echoing her loneliness. The food she ate tasted dry and bland. The day Leo was due back from Barcelona, her heartbeat quickened whenever the front door opened, only to crash back down to reality when it wasn't him.

'Pip, can you do me a favour today? Can you collect a folder from the travel agent's, the one on Sollner Street? They called to say it's ready to pick up,' Dominic said as she was walking out of the door to take the boys to school.

'Sure.'

While she was in the travel agent's, she checked the prices for flights to Sydney but didn't buy them there. She had made up her mind that she was still going and that she'd decide about Troy when she saw him. But she didn't want to buy the tickets in Solln, in case the people who worked there said anything to Dominic. There were plenty of other, more anonymous travel agents in the centre of Munich.

Back at the house, she checked Dominic had gone to work, made herself a coffee and sat down to open the folder because she thought she knew what was in it. Travel documents for Sydney. She wrote down the times and dates of their flights, the event tickets they had and the hotel they were staying in.

He'd booked a two-room suite in a hotel on Macquarie Street, with views of Sydney Harbour Bridge. Sounded swish. There were four reservations for everything – Dominic, Elisabeth, Maximilian and Ferdinand von Feldstein. And they had tickets to the opening and closing ceremonies, as well as athletics, tennis and beach volleyball. They wouldn't need hockey tickets – Holly had always been allocated tickets for her family, and it was probably the same for the German team's families.

Pip already had the schedule for the men's and women's hockey written down – she'd found it on the internet and copied it out. It was going to be tricky, but she had to try and avoid being anywhere near the hockey stadium when Germany were playing, in case one of the von Feldsteins saw her. She wanted to watch as many of Troy's games as she could – he would give her tickets for them – but she didn't know if Germany and Australia were going to be in the same group. They were both strong teams – they might also be in the semis or the finals, playing against each other. She also didn't know if she wanted to watch any of the women's matches – Holly's old team – if that would be something she could cope with. If, if, if.

When Dominic arrived home from work, late that evening, Pip had already put Max and Ferdi to bed and was sitting on the sofa in the living room, reading. She heard him stomp the snow off his boots and walk through to the kitchen. He appeared in the doorway with the Sydney folder, a bottle of wine and two glasses.

'Hi, Pip. Thanks for picking this up. Glass of wine?'

'Yes, please.'

He poured the wine and sat, opening the folder. 'It's our tickets for Sydney.'

'Oh?' said Pip.

'We'll be away for just over two weeks. I'll write the dates on the board. If you want, you can take a holiday, go back home and see your family. Or you can stay here. I don't mind.'

'I think I would like to go home. Thanks.' That would cover her tracks, if they thought she was going in the opposite direction.

'I hope Billy makes it into the squad. Then we'll all be there, the whole family.'

Pip thought it might just about be OK to ask. 'Is Mrs von Feld... I mean, Elisabeth. Is she... sorry, I don't mean to be nosy. It's only... you said the whole family. Will she be there, too?'

'Yes, hopefully.' Dominic took off his glasses and rubbed his eyes. He looked at Pip. 'If you want to ask about her, you can, you know.'

'Oh. OK. Well, no, it's OK. Thanks. I don't want to pry if it's a family thing.'

Dominic gave a short, low laugh that wasn't really a laugh. 'Actually, it would be a relief to talk about it. She's not been very well. Max and Ferdi don't know the details. We've kept the worst of it from them. She's had problems with depression and alcohol dependency. She's in a facility near Lindau.'

'Facility?'

'Psychiatric.'

'Like rehab?'

'Yes. Near her parents. I go and see her when I'm down there, but she won't see Max and Ferdi so they don't know.'

'And Billy and Leo? Will she see them? Do they visit?'

'Billy does. Leo hasn't been for a while. They aren't close. Also, Leo likes things simple, you know. He's so focused – as you've probably noticed – and steers clear of distractions and complications. The last time they saw each other, it didn't go well. They were both upset afterwards. Leo won't want to see her until after Sydney.'

'But she's going to be there, watching. Won't that distract him?'

'He said it's OK. He'll be busy with the team – they don't see their families much during the tournaments. We'll be in our hotel and he'll be in the Olympic Village. Even when they have days off, he believes quite strongly that his place is with the team. Elisabeth and I can do our own thing with the boys. If she's well enough to travel.'

Pip nodded. She hadn't seen much of Holly either, when she'd been at the two Olympics with her parents.

'I do have a question, actually. You might think I'm being nosy. But when I came here, and we had that whole mix-up about Leo and Billy, I wondered – why are there no photos of them on the walls?'

'Ha. Yes. Good question.' Dominic eased himself out of his chair. 'Come with me. I'll show you where the photos are.'

Pip followed him up the stairs, through the door to the attic. There was another narrow staircase which opened up into a bedroom, a small office and a bathroom. Covering the walls were framed photos of Leo and Billy when they were little, with a beautiful blonde-haired woman who must be Elisabeth. Of all four boys playing hockey. Elisabeth alone, with a baby on her lap. Dominic and Elisabeth on their wedding day. Leo and Billy in school sports uniforms. An adorable picture of Leo in a cowboy costume. Leo collecting medals on podiums. The whole family, including Rosa and the grandparents, at the lake house, which was basically a castle – the one in the paintings downstairs. Elisabeth with Rosa. Elisabeth wearing an evening dress. A tennis dress. Elisabeth with Leo, smiling. The family on the beach. Leo and Billy pushing Max and Ferdi on swings.

Dominic stood silently while Pip walked around the rooms, taking it all in. Occasionally she asked which baby was which. Billy was easy to pick out – he was the only one with blond hair. When he'd been little, it had been bright, almost white. But Leo, Max and Ferdi's hair was dark. She could see where those rumours came from about Billy having a different father. Not that she believed a word of it.

'I prefer to keep them up here. We've had some happy times. But shortly before you arrived, she had a breakdown and left and it was difficult for me and the boys. I moved everything up here. It seemed easier for us to keep everything plain and simple downstairs. Then we could move on with our lives. No reminders.'

'I understand.'

'Do you?' He looked at her. 'You seem very old for your age sometimes.'

'I feel very old for my age sometimes.'

They went downstairs and sat in the kitchen with their wine, Dominic eating leftovers for his supper. He offered her some but she wasn't hungry.

Pip said, 'Why doesn't Leo get on well with Mrs von Feldstein? Sorry, I'm being nosy again.'

'It's OK.' He thought for a few seconds and said, 'You know what, I don't blame you for asking, but I think that's something that Leo would prefer to keep to himself. He'll get around to telling you sometime in the future, when he's ready.' Dominic finished his wine and poured himself another glass. 'With Billy, it's always been different. She... I guess she always preferred Billy, even as a baby. That happens sometimes. It shouldn't, but it does.'

Pip nodded. She knew what it was like to be the least-loved child. She wondered if it was the same for Leo as it was for her: she never remembered it upsetting her; she simply accepted it and it had made her love her parents less, perhaps out of necessity. The grief of losing Holly should have united her family, but afterwards she'd felt more than ever like she was the second-favourite daughter. That was a competition she was never going to win. So she'd given up.

'But Leo is highly driven, absolutely single-minded, always has been, and especially so this year. He's good at shutting out things that will make him lose focus. It's quite impressive.'

Pip was silent, sipping her wine, thinking about Leo. Those psychology books he had. The way he shut down his face. His icy composure.

'What's he like when he plays?'

'You haven't watched him? No, of course, I forget. You don't like hockey. He's staggeringly good,' Dominic said proudly. 'He's so assured and so precise, he can take the ball off anyone before they even know he's there. When he moves, it looks effortless, almost lazy.'

'Like he's a different speed from everyone else?'

Dominic smiled at her. 'Yes. That's exactly right. But of course there's nothing lazy about Leo. He's worked so hard with his hockey. Harder than anyone. He fully admits he's lucky – he has the money to do it full-time. He doesn't need to work and he's taken a year off university. Not everyone has that luxury.'

'The other German players work?'

'Actually, this year, they're a young squad – all students. But that just shows you what a huge commitment it is, playing an amateur sport like hockey to this level. When you're past student age, you have to make a decision. Do you carry on playing, and then what do you do for money, or do you give up and find a proper job?'

'Leo wants to be a doctor, doesn't he?'

'Yes, and he'll be a very good one. It's going to take him longer than most to graduate – he may take another year off before the next Olympics. But he'll get there in the end.'

Pip was aware she was asking too much about Leo. 'And Billy? What does he want to do when he grows up?'

Dominic grinned. 'Touché. He has a couple more Olympics in him, if he wants to. Then he can work for the family firm. On paper, he's employed by Feldstein AG. But we never see him. And that's fine, for now.'

Dominic stood up and rubbed a few old scribblings off the board. He wrote up the dates they'd be in Sydney. He also wrote, *1–6 Feb Egypt* and *16–25 Feb Kuala Lumpur*.

More tournaments, thought Pip, and sighed quietly.

Jan? Dubai.

'When are they going to Dubai?'

'They're there already. I think they're going straight to Egypt from there. That was the vague plan, anyway. Depending on how it goes, they might also stay there between Egypt and Kuala Lumpur.'

Pip's heart sank. So Leo would be away until the end of February. She wouldn't see him for six long, grey weeks. She tried to keep her face calm as Dominic told her they were training with some amazing fitness instructor, who would get the two of them in the shape of their lives. She thought that if this was a movie of Billy and Leo's road to Sydney, there'd be a montage now, with them working out to an inspirational piece of music, something like *Eye of the Tiger*, ending with them standing on top of the Burj Al Arab, arms raised triumphantly in the air. Six weeks, though. Six.

Pip took her wages out of her post office account and went into town to buy her tickets to Sydney. It had always been the plan to stay on in Australia with Troy. But the man in the travel agent's explained that she couldn't buy a one-way ticket unless she had a student or work visa. She was relieved – the decision had been made for her.

She had saved so much that she had some money left over, so she splurged on a new swimming costume (a boring Speedo), a bikini (as small as she dared), new jeans (the most expensive ones she'd ever owned), and underwear (necessary as all of hers was falling apart). She was now completely skint and couldn't even go to the cinema with Tiny during February. But she had the tickets. She was going to Sydney. She emailed Troy for the first time since she'd arrived in Munich, with her flight dates and to ask if it was still OK to stay in his house. She told him she was working as an au pair for a family in Germany. She wrote a quick email to her parents and a longer one to Nadine, to whom she'd got into the habit of sending a long email every week, describing her daily life, a bit like a diary. As she was about to turn off the computer, she saw Troy's reply in her inbox.

From: troytheboy@hotmail.com
To: pipmitchell80@hotmail.com

Kiddo,

I was starting to think you'd disappeared off the face of the earth. Kraut-land? Is that where you've been hiding? I didn't know how to find you. I didn't want to ask your Olds in case they suspected and I haven't really been in touch with them anyway. Was meaning to give them a call on Christmas Day but I didn't get round to it in the end.

All good here, hockey's going great, last year we ruled at Oceania and Champions Trophy. I've got a new stick sponsor – they're bringing out a new range, personalised, I helped design it – the Troy Costa stick. Get me. Sydney, here we come.

And yes, of course you can crash here. As long as you like. I'll be in the Village from the 15th onwards, so you can stay in my room. Maybe I can sneak out and see you sometimes… The guys I share with, Glen and Dean, they're OK – kind of derros but hey, what do you expect? You only have to sleep there. You'll like my room. I've still got some of Hol's old stuff, I like having it, hope it's not gonna be too sad for you.

Afterwards, I've got some time. Do you want to head up the coast together, get away from Sydney? We could have a holiday. I'll book something. Just the two of us.

I've been thinking a lot about what to do and I don't know how you feel about this plan, but what if we told everyone we got to know each other after the Games and go from there? I can't get my head around whether people will think it's sweet or just plain sicko. Do you know what I mean? And after Sydney I have to think about what I'm going to do next – no sponsor or TV station or club's gonna come near me if I fuck it up now.

Bet you never knew I could think this much about anything, eh? Well, kiddo, what can I say, you're on my mind a lot. I've been a dick for most of my life but somehow the Mitchell girls are there to sort me out.

What do you reckon?

I think this is the longest email I've ever written.

Love Troy xxx

Pip sat in front of the screen and read the email again with a lump in her throat. She was on his mind? It sounded like he'd been waiting for her all this time. He was worried about the future? About them being together and what people would say? It sounded so serious. He was way ahead of her. But he was thirty. This might be his last Olympics. What had she been expecting?

She tried replying, but couldn't phrase anything with the right amount of enthusiasm. She gave up after deleting four different versions of the same email and decided to try another day, when she'd had time to think.

And she did think about him, constantly, endlessly, over the next few weeks. She had to reply soon or he'd think something was wrong. But something was wrong, wasn't it? She had booked her tickets to Sydney, but return tickets, leaving on the last day of the Games. She didn't want to go somewhere with Troy, just the two of them. She didn't want to sleep with him again. It made her cringe to think about the sex they'd had. At best it had been sad, and at worst, utterly and disgustingly wrong.

The weeks slid by, everything the same, Pip becoming desperate about what to say to Troy. She couldn't even ask Nadine, because of course she hadn't told her about Troy. Nadine knew him from way back when and had never been exactly effusive about him. She also steered clear of writing about her feelings for Leo, which were growing stronger all the time, but which she wasn't ready to share with Nadine yet. They were too new at the moment, too fragile and easy to shatter if Nadine cracked a joke about it.

Troy had sent another two short emails, asking if she was OK and asking for her phone number. She couldn't ignore him any more, so wrote that she was looking forward to seeing him play and that they would have to talk about everything after the Games. She gave him her mobile number, hoping that the expense of calling it would put him off. She'd have to be careful not to leave it lying around, in case someone else answered it by mistake. Her email was too formal, too unfriendly, but she hoped Troy wouldn't notice or read too much into it.

When she thought about Sydney and its complications and potential dangers, she wondered if it was worth going. She could bump into the von Feldsteins. She could be spotted by one of the players, German men or British women, from the pitch. She could find she wasn't in love with Troy any more and – if he did sneak away to see her – she'd either have to tell him so and risk upsetting him in the middle of the Games, or sleep with him to avoid that. She tried to harden herself to the possibility – after all, wasn't that what had happened when she'd slept with him the first time? If she could do it when she was sixteen, losing her virginity with him, she could surely manage it once more. She cringed at the thought of her sixteen-year-old self, climbing onto his lap and forcing herself on him. How had that happened? It was as if she was a different girl.

But if she didn't turn up in Sydney, wouldn't that also upset Troy? She could make up some excuse nearer the time, say she'd been in an accident, broken her leg or something. Lies piled on top of lies. A downward spiral leading to who knows where. No, she had to go there, face up to what she'd done with him and end it.

And what about Leo? She couldn't ignore the fact that she was – what – in love with him? Was *that* what she felt?

By going to Sydney, she'd be in the same city as him, even if she couldn't talk to him or see him play. That was something. And afterwards, when they were back in Munich, she'd confess everything and ask the von Feldsteins to forgive her for lying. They would understand. She and Leo might become friends. That was something, too. She hoped they wouldn't fire her, and that she could keep the mess that she had created under wraps until after the Games.

At last, it was the end of February. Pip thought she might go mad if she thought about Troy any more, and about Leo and what she was going to say to him and how she should behave around him. She had to try and calm down. She hadn't been sleeping well. She lay in bed every night, letting everything rotate in her head. Tiny invited her out to celebrate her birthday, but she had no money until the 1st of March so she was going to have to stay in.

'Why are you broke? Don't they pay you?' whined Tiny on the phone.

'Sorry, I blew my wages already.'

'Ask Dominic for an advance.'

'I can't. Sorry, it'd be awkward. He's too good to me already. I'll make it up to you – let's go out next weekend, my treat.'

'This sucks big time, Pip. I want you to come tonight. You always say no to me. You always have some excuse.'

'OK, well how about this? To demonstrate my undying love for you, I'll come out with you next Saturday night. And... and I have to say yes to you all night. I have to do everything you tell me to do.'

Tiny perked up. 'Every single thing? I can tell you to do anything and you'll do it?'

'Absolutely anything.'

'Oooh. That sounds like fun. Yes, it's a deal. I hope you realise that I have a whole week to think up stuff to make you do.'

'Yes. Yes, I'm just realising what a huge mistake this was.'

'Too late to take it back.'

'OK, well then, have fun tonight. Who's going anyway?'

'The usual. Everyone from the club. Mandi, Caro, Tara.' She rattled off a few more names, including Theo and Martin. 'Oh, and Billy. And Leo and Roxy.'

'Roxy? You invited Roxy?'

'Well, I had to. What with her and Leo being back together.'

Pip tried to control the wobble in her voice as she gripped the phone hard. Thank God she wasn't face-to-face with Tiny. 'Oh? Really? Wow. How... how do you... how did that happen?'

'Apparently, she went out to Dubai on holiday, just by chance – yeah right, Roxy, whatever – and pitched up at their hotel. She's such a stalker. But somehow she managed to wangle herself back in there with Leo. Seems like Caro was right at New Year: he is still mad about her. She went to watch them play in Kuala Lumpur and flew back with them. They're inseparable. Joined at the hip. According to my sources.'

Pip put down the phone and lay back on her bed, thinking what an utterly silly, pathetic fool she was. She'd always known Leo didn't like her, let alone anything else. She knew it and she'd still let herself hope, even though there was a substantial list of reasons why she had no right to hope: one, despite what Roxy had done with Billy last year, Leo had forgiven her, that's how much he loved her; two, it was Pip's fault that he even knew about Roxy and Billy; three, she'd seen them dancing happily together at Martin's party; and four, Pip wasn't in Leo's league – talk about punching above your weight.

Pip spent the night of Tiny's birthday alone in her room in her pyjamas watching *Rushmore*, which she loved for its quirkiness. She was about to start watching the extras when she heard noises upstairs. It couldn't be Dominic and the boys; they were in Bayreuth all weekend at a junior hockey tournament. Shit. It must be him. Quickly, she turned off the TV and DVD player and switched off the light. Whatever she heard, whatever was going on upstairs, even if they came down to say hello to her, which was unlikely, she would pretend to be asleep. In the dark, she lay and listened for minutes that seemed to stretch into hours. Low voices in the kitchen. The radio playing a song she couldn't quite hear. Drawers opening and closing. Steps in the hallway. The door to the cellar opening. Footsteps in the cellar corridor. She closed her eyes and slowed down her breathing as much as she could.

A soft knock. The door handle turned. The door opened.

'Pip?' Leo's voice. *Leo*.

She lay still, keeping her breathing even. The click of the door closing. She thought he'd left, but she heard soft footsteps on the carpet. No other noise. What was he doing? Should she pretend to wake up? Were her acting skills good enough? Her heart was pounding so loudly in her chest, she was certain he could hear it. Where was he now? Close to her, but she couldn't hear his breathing. This was getting a little weird. And as usual, she'd put herself into a situation where she could only lie or make a total dick of herself to get out of it. Did other people do this, or was she the biggest idiot on the planet?

'Hey, Pip.' It was the quietest of whispers. He didn't want to wake her up. She felt like he was casting a spell over her. She had to concentrate so she didn't screw up her eyes too tightly. 'Missed you.'

Did he just say that? There was silence for such a long time, and she felt so blissful that he'd come to see her, that she drifted, drifted, down, down into the best sleep she'd had for weeks.

10

March 2000

When she woke she was, for a moment, confused as to whether it was still night-time. But through her narrow window streamed daylight. And there was no sign of Leo. She went to her bathroom to shower and make herself look presentable, but changed her mind and instead pulled on her hoodie over her pyjamas. Otherwise it would be too obvious she'd made an effort for him. On absolutely no account could she allow him to know how she felt about him, especially since he was with Roxy again.

Upstairs, the radio was playing and there was a tempting smell of coffee. Oh well, she had to face him sometime. She pushed open the kitchen door, her heart slamming in her chest, and plastered on a smile that she hoped didn't look too fake.

'Pip! You're a sight for sore eyes.' Billy bounded forward and gave her a bear hug, ruffling her hair. 'How're you doing? You look thin. What's up, Mary Poppins? Why are you smiling so strangely? Did you miss me?'

'Yes,' she lied, relaxing her mouth. She flashed a look at Leo over Billy's shoulder. He was sitting at the table reading a newspaper. He looked up and then down again. *That's it? That's all? Not even a quick smile?* They were both tanned and had short haircuts, their faces leaner than when she'd seen them at New Year. Billy was wearing a T-shirt cut off at the arms and a pair of hockey shorts. She looked down at his legs and saw the sharp definition of his calf and thigh muscles. His arms were sculpted and smooth.

He saw her looking and flexed his arms. 'Check me out. Guess who's been working hard?'

She should try to act normally, at least with him. 'May I?' She put her hand on his raised arm and squeezed the muscle. 'Buff.' She moved to the coffee machine, turning her back to Billy and Leo and pressing the button, at the same time trying to stop her whole body trembling. Because if Billy had worked hard and felt like that, then Leo would have worked twice as hard, and his arms and legs would be solid muscle, not an inch of fat on him, and his stomach would be taut and brown and... *You have to stop this, right now. Get a grip on yourself.*

She took a couple of deep breaths and concentrated on the wondrous smell of the coffee as it gushed into her cup. 'I thought you were out with Tiny last night? How come you're here?'

'We flaked out after a couple of hours. Jet lag, and also my New Year's resolution.'

'Which is what?'

'No fun until Sydney.'

Pip managed a weak laugh as she turned and walked to the table. 'That sounds more like Leo's idea of a resolution.'

Leo didn't look up from his newspaper. *Please look at me, smile at me, say something. Missed you too. I haven't seen you for weeks. I know you're in love with someone else but please just say hello.*

'Heard a rumour about you last night,' said Billy, serving up three bowls of porridge. He placed them in front of Leo and Pip.

135

'Daddy Bear. Mummy Bear – you need feeding up. Baby Bear.'
Billy sat down and started attacking his porridge like he hadn't
eaten for a week.

'Whatever it was, I didn't do it,' she said.

'Not yet, anyway.'

Pip frowned. 'What're you talking about?'

Billy's mouth was full, so Leo said, 'Tiny told us that you've
promised, as her birthday present, to go out with her next
Saturday and do everything she says. She was collecting ideas
last night.'

'But… that was supposed to be a girls' night out. Not
everyone… who? What ideas?'

'I gave her some,' said Billy, winking at her.

'You can't join in. That's not how it was supposed to work.'

'You're not allowed to say no. It's the Night of Saying Yes.'
He rubbed his hands together. 'You're in such a lot of trouble,
my friend.'

'You keep out of this, Billy.'

'I'm sorry to say that I'm the least of your problems.'

'And what's that supposed to mean?'

Billy was laughing so much he was crying. 'Mourant.
Bredenkamp. Wolters.'

'Which Wolters?' Pim Wolters was a Dutch guy who played
in the first team. His younger brother Hendrik, who was in his
last year at the International School, played for the seconds. 'I
don't even know who Bredenkamp is.'

'Both Wolters wanted in on the action. Jamie Bredenkamp
– brick shithouse, third-teamer? And money was changing
hands.'

'What action? What money? Billy, for fuck's sake, what are
you talking about?'

Billy couldn't talk, he was laughing so much.

Pip turned to Leo, panicking. 'Leo, you're the sensible one.
Please tell me what he's going on about.'

Leo took a sip of his coffee and fixed his eyes on hers over the rim of his cup. 'They were trying to give Tiny money so that she would tell you to do stuff with them.'

'Stuff?' she said quietly.

'Use your vivid imagination.' Leo gave an impatient motion with his head.

'Shit.'

'Yes, indeed. Shit.' His voice was deadpan.

She couldn't tell if he was annoyed or amused. He was probably just bored. Pip started to worry. Tiny wouldn't humiliate her like that, would she? It would only be silly dares – tequila shots, flirting with a waiter. That sort of thing. 'She didn't take the money, though… I mean, please tell me she didn't take the money. That was a joke, right?'

Billy stopped laughing and scraped his bowl clean. 'All I can say is, whatever happens, you're going to have quite an audience next Saturday night.'

Leo finished eating too. That song – the Macy Gray one – started playing on the radio. He stood up and left the room.

While Billy and Leo went to the gym at the hockey club, Pip ran through the woods, slushy and slippery with melted snow. Afterwards, she tried calling Tiny, but there was no answer.

09.33: Need to talk to you, xx Pip
11.05: Why won't you answer? x Pip
13.55: What are you planning next Sat? xP
16.41: Call me, P

Finally, that evening, Tiny replied and Pip's blood ran cold.

20.23: This is going 2b the best birthday present EVER!!!!
20.24: Bring condom, passport, toothbrush and spare pr knickers

That week the temperature rose to above ten degrees and training moved outside onto the AstroTurf, which meant that, although Tiny still wasn't answering her calls, Pip would see her on Thursday evening when she took Max and Ferdi to the club after school. She needed to gauge how far Tiny was going to take this and try to talk her out of it, or prepare herself for mayhem. Or just run away.

Was she being paranoid, or were people at the club looking at her strangely? After she'd hit the tennis ball with several months' worth of pent-up energy, she showered and afterwards settled into her usual sofa with a book, glancing up every now and again when she thought she was being watched. As well as fretting about the Tiny thing, she was also on the lookout for Roxy. And Leo. And Roxy and Leo.

The women started to arrive for their training. Tara waved at her. Caro shouted hello from where they were warming up.

'Where's Tiny?' Pip shouted back, but they were too far away to hear, or were ignoring her on purpose. 'Mandi, hi, have you seen Tiny?'

Mandisa shrugged and joined the others on the far side of the pitch. They started their practice, but there was still no sign of Tiny. Roxy arrived wearing the shortest of shorts, and even from the balcony of the clubhouse, Pip could see that she was glowing with a deep tan and the fulfilment of all her sexual needs. *Curses*, thought Pip. *So it's true, then: she has been to Dubai.*

18.23: Are you coming to training tonight? xx Pip
18.25: Busy with a BIG list. CU Saturday. Meet @7 nr Münchner
Freiheit station. Wear sth sxy. xxT

Pip groaned and called Tiny, but she didn't answer. She left a message saying she wouldn't come unless Tiny swore to be nice to her. Two minutes later, her phone beeped again.

18.31: U promised. Undying love, remember? xxT
18.32: Do you have any whipped cream?

Max and Ferdi finished training and they had dinner together. Behind her, she could hear the men arriving. She heard Billy's laugh and turned to see him with Pim and Hendrik Wolters, who walked away when they saw her looking over, and another man, a hulking giant who stared dopily at her with his mouth slightly open and who she supposed, with a sinking heart, must be Jamie Bredenkamp. Billy waved at her and pointed his finger at the giant behind his back.

'Are you OK, Pipsqueak? You look like you're about to puke,' said Max.

'Fine,' she mumbled. 'Don't say puke at the table.'

'You did.'

She was silent.

'You're no fun today. Can we go outside and play?'

'Sure. Just don't go beyond the gate.'

She sat alone, slumped in her chair. She felt a tap on her right shoulder and turned automatically to the left. For years, this had been a joke between Holly and Pip – they had tapped each other on one shoulder and appeared behind the other. Billy grinned at her.

'All ready for Saturday night?'

'Don't start.'

He tickled her. 'Oh come on, Pipster. Don't lose your sense of humour now.'

'I just want it to be over. Whatever "it" is.'

'That's the spirit.' He slapped her on the thigh. 'Right, duty calls.' He stood up and stretched his arms above his head. 'Fitness session today, worse luck.'

'Should be a breeze for you after Dubai.'

'Yeah. You're right. As usual.'

Pip frowned. 'What do you mean, "as usual"?'

He sat down again. 'You remember what you said in Verbier, about Leo's dream, about Sydney? Well, that made me think—'

'You can think?'

'It has been known to happen. Not too often, because it really hurts. But I'm going to do this. I'm going to work my arse off and I'm going with him to Sydney. No matter what it takes.'

'OK. Good. Now get out on that pitch and run until you puke.'

'Sir, yes, sir.' He bounced up and jogged away.

On Friday, Pip ran for an hour along the river, which was swollen from the rapidly melting snow. She thought about when she'd walked down here on her second day in Munich, and how miserable and lonely she'd felt. The shocks of that first week – seeing Roxy and Billy together; finding out about the club and Billy and Leo – it hadn't been a great start to her career as an au pair. She could laugh about it now. Ish.

She felt the sun on her face, warming her after the months of snow and freezing temperatures. She took off her sweatshirt, tied it around her waist and ran in shorts and T-shirt, earning curious looks from passers-by: mums with babies wrapped up in blankets in their prams; old people in knitwear doddering along; a group of kindergarteners dressed in woolly hats and gloves and thick coats. But she needed some sunshine on her skin, and it felt exhilarating to stretch herself out. She flew alongside the raging river, the rhythm of her strides and the beating of her trainers on the path chasing out the gloomy thoughts that had become a part of her whole being, ingrained like dirt in the creases of her skin.

Now that the outdoor hockey season had begun, and Billy and Leo were back from Dubai, she might see them more regularly. Billy had said that they were going to be at the club every day, using the gym in the basement and practising set pieces on the AstroTurf. Once Tiny's birthday debacle was out of the way, Pip could look forward to her weekly routine at the club, seeing Tiny and the other girls, messing around with Max and Ferdi, playing tennis against herself. She still wrote weekly emails to Nadine, trying to amuse her, now that she knew some of the characters in Pip's story. Nadine's short but enthusiastic replies always made her laugh and encouraged her to write more. Even the thought of the AstroTurf itself, which had tormented her last year, wasn't filling her with that panicky, sweaty feeling any more. Maybe she could even bring herself to watch sometimes.

The boys were upstairs packing some toys for their half-term holiday in Lindau while Dominic packed the car.

'Will you see her?' asked Pip quietly.

'Yes. She's doing well. If she carries on like this, she's going to come home at Easter.'

'Here?' Pip tried not to show her shock.

'No, sorry, I meant home as in Lindau. We'll see about here – maybe later in the spring or early summer.' He put the last of the bags in the trunk. 'So, I hear you have a big night tonight.'

It didn't surprise Pip that Dominic had heard about it. 'Yes,' she said through gritted teeth. 'If I'm not here when you get back next Sunday, I'll be chained to a lamp post or something.'

'Good luck. I'm sure you're up to whatever Tiny has in mind.'

The afternoon dragged. She swam some lengths in the pool, took a long shower and washed her hair. She chose an outfit from her limited wardrobe, and then wandered around the house, drinking too much coffee and trying not to imagine what was in store for her that evening. At six, she walked to the S-Bahn station and wondered if it would be possible to catch a train going the other way, towards the mountains, to hide out in a cave forever.

INT. A DESERTED TRAIN CARRIAGE - DAY

PIP MITCHELL sits staring out of the window, brooding.
HOLLY COSTA takes the empty seat beside her.

                    PIP

Hello, sis. So you know too, do you?

                    HOLLY

Everyone knows. How're you holding up?

                    PIP
                 (shrugs)

Well I've been better. But then again, I've
also been worse.

                    HOLLY
                 (laughs)

Yeah. I'm sure there's something worse
than being humiliated in front of everyone
you know. I just can't think of what that
might be right now. You seem to have quite
a talent for getting yourself into sticky
situations, kiddo. But seriously, it'll be fine.
Tiny - she's your friend, right?

                    PIP

I'm about to find out.

                    HOLLY

Course she is. And she's a hockey player.
We look after each other. All for one and
one for all. Like I have to tell you that. Get
yourself into that bar, neck a couple of

drinks and do whatever she says. It'll be a
laugh. Remember my hen night?

PIP

I'll never forget it. They made you dress up
as a cheerleader all night. And call Troy on
speakerphone and tell him you had cold
feet.

HOLLY

Yup. He freaked out and got so angry with
me when he found out it was a joke. He
nearly called the whole thing off. The girls
sent him cards to apologise. So chill out,
kiddo. At least it won't be as bad as that.

PIP

Guess not. Yeah, you're right. I'm going to
do it. Whatever she says. She's my friend
and it's the least I can do after I missed her
birthday. You wait, Holly – you'll see, I'm
going to astonish and astound them all. I
just wish you were going to be there too.

HOLLY

I'll be there, kiddo.

Holly puts her arms around Pip for the rest of the journey.

At Münchner Freiheit station, Pip followed Tiny's directions to a
side street near the Englischer Garten. She looked at her watch.
Seven. Right on time. She pushed open the door to the bar and
came to face-to-face with the usual crowd from the hockey club.
It looked like most of them had been drinking for a while.

'Hurrah! She's here,' screamed Tiny, grinning her head off.

'Happy belated birthday.' Pip smiled. 'I see you've started without me.'

'Bit of last-minute planning,' said Tiny. Tara and Caro balanced a tray of beers and some evil-looking liquids in shot glasses.

'Right, I'd better catch up then,' said Pip. She took a shot glass and necked it, grabbing one of the beers to take the taste away. She grimaced and sat down next to Tiny. 'How was your night out last week? Where did you go? Tell me all about it. Every last detail. Don't miss anything out. I don't care if it takes hours, I want to hear it all.'

'Very good, Mitchell. Don't try and put me off.'

'The thought never entered my mind.'

Pip's eyes scanned the bar. At the far end of one of the long tables sat Billy, Theo and Martin. No Leo, though. He must be with Roxy. Maybe they were coming later. Billy had a soft drink in his hand; he was moving glasses around in front of him, explaining a hockey tactic to the others.

She tried to be nonchalant. 'Roxy and Leo not here?'

'Oh no, God, that's so funny. I forgot to tell you. I got that story totally wrong,' said Tiny.

Pip felt a fluttering in her stomach. 'So she wasn't in Dubai?'

'Yes, she was there and she made a terrific play at him. And he turned her down.'

'But I thought you said she followed them to Kuala Lumpur and watched them play and they were inseparable? Where did you hear that? Was it a different girl?'

'No. A different guy.'

Billy. Pip felt sorry for Nadine. If Roxy and Billy had slept together, how was she going to feel about it? Nadine was crazy about him; they'd swapped phone numbers and email addresses and Billy had told her he'd fly over to Manchester soon to see her. 'Who – Billy?'

'No, Billy has more sense than that. Never thought I'd say that

144

sentence. After Leo sent her packing, she found some Italian guy – an older man, apparently – to get her hooks into. She didn't go to Kuala Lumpur at all – she just happened to be on the same connecting flight to Munich as the German hockey team. So you can rest easy, your boys are safe and sound, unmolested by Roxy.'

'I don't care either way.' But she did care, she did, and she couldn't help the smile that was creeping over her lips.

'Riiiight.' Tiny, Tara and Caro were looking at her.

Caro said, 'The question is, which one of the von Feldsteins are *you* interested in molesting?'

'None. Neither. Don't know what you're talking about. What's your first dare, birthday girl? Come on, let's get this over with.'

'Love the change of subject. Ready for a dance yet?'

'Are you askin'?' Tiny was supposed to say, 'I'm askin'' and Pip would say, 'I'm dancin'', but instead Tiny shook her head and smiled. A Robbie Williams song was playing.

'Follow me, please. I would like you to dance with...' She stopped halfway along the table. 'Hendrik.'

Hendrik reacted by turning beetroot red. He couldn't even look Pip in the eye.

She felt sorry for him. 'Your wish is my command. Hendrik, will you do me the honour of this dance?'

He stood up too quickly, knocking over his glass. 'Sorry,' he stammered. 'I'm a bit clumsy.'

'That bodes well for the dance, then.' But she said it kindly. It was a slow song – one that Pip didn't recognise, surprise, surprise. She'd been trying to learn the names of some of the songs on the radio, but she had two years to catch up on. She faced Hendrik, and falteringly he put his hands on her waist. She smiled at him. They danced for a while in silence.

'So, Pip, where do you come from?'

Pip thought it was some cheesy chat-up line. When he didn't say the punchline, she prompted him. 'How d'you mean?'

He shrugged. 'Just – you know – where do you live?'

'We moved around a lot.'

'OK, then where did you live, which town, in the time before you came to Munich?'

'Why do you want to know?'

He mumbled, 'Tiny said you'd do this.' He seemed to strengthen his resolve. 'I'd like to know more about you. It's a simple question. I come from Rotterdam. Where do you come from?'

Pip glanced over to where Tiny was sitting.

Hendrik said, 'Are you going to answer or do I have to go and get her?'

'What?' Pip stopped dancing. 'What are you talking about?'

'For her birthday, Tiny would like you to dance with me and answer my question.'

'Why?'

Hendrik turned away from Pip, put his finger and thumb in his mouth and whistled loudly. Tiny stood up and came over.

'What seems to be the problem?' she said.

'Pip's not playing nicely,' said Hendrik.

'What? What's going on?' said Pip. By now, some of the others had come over to the dance floor. 'Tiny, what I am supposed to do?'

'It's easy – dance with Hendrik and answer his question.'

'But I don't want to. It's private.'

'What did you ask her, Hendrik? What her bra size is? What her favourite sexual position is?'

'I asked her where she comes from.'

Tiny crossed her arms in front of her and raised her eyebrow at Pip. 'He's really stepped over the line there, Pip. How dare he?'

Pip was starting to feel uncomfortable. Everyone was looking at her. 'I... still don't understand.'

Tara stepped forward. 'Pip, it's quite simple. We want to know more about you.'

Caro said, 'We've known you for six months now and we

really like you. But we don't know anything about you.'

Tiny chipped in. 'We were sitting around last Saturday night trying to think of stupid dares to give you, to embarrass you. But we realised that none of us has a clue about you. You never talk about yourself. Your family. School. Friends.'

'It's private,' muttered Pip again.

'We're your friends, you massive idiot. You can't expect us to like you and spend time with you if we don't know anything about you. So that's my birthday wish – every single person in this room has a question for you and you have to answer.'

Pip shook her head.

'You promised. You said you were up for it. It was your idea.'

'Come on, Pip, how bad could it be?'

'We love you, Pip, don't be a stranger.' Everyone laughed at Theo.

Pip couldn't help herself – she laughed a bit too. She looked at Tiny, who was smiling at her hopefully. OK, she could do this. No panic. It was simply a matter of telling them everything – up to, but not including Holly and Troy. She could be eighty per cent honest. That would have to be enough. She nodded.

'Yay. Group hug,' said Tiny, and everyone surged forward and enveloped Pip in many arms. When they had all disentangled themselves, Pip took a deep breath and said to Hendrik, 'I come from Canterbury. It's a city in Kent.'

Hendrik said, 'I know Canterbury. We played there once.'

Of course he did.

The song ended and the next one started. Pim said, 'My turn', and the others drifted away.

'So, what do you want to know?' said Pip.

'Don't be grumpy.'

'Ha. Easy for you to say. You're not the one being interrogated. Come on then, what's your question?'

'Favourite holiday ever.'

'Is this going to be reported back to Tiny?'

Pim shrugged, meaning, *Yes, but what're you going to do about it?*

She couldn't say Barcelona or Atlanta, but they weren't her favourite holidays anyway. 'When I was fourteen, my family spent the summer holidays in Ireland. We went to Dublin, then we travelled to the south-west coast. We learnt sailing and surfing and kayaking. It was really beautiful. And fun.' She, Holly and their parents had spent four weeks together after watching Holly play in the World Cup in Dublin. It was just before Holly and Troy's wedding. She'd loved that holiday.

'There, that wasn't so bad, was it? Cool. Sounds great.' He laughed and shook his head. 'I've found out more about you in twenty seconds than I have done in six months.'

They danced until the song ended and Pim stepped aside. 'Thanks, Pip. See you around.'

He made way for Theo, who asked what her parents did for a living.

'Typical English question. Nothing special: they're retired coppers.'

'Both of them? Your dad and mum?'

'Yup.'

'How come they're retired?'

Pip bristled. 'Don't you get only one question?'

'Humour me.'

She sighed. 'They had me when they were quite old. They're over sixty now. They retired a couple of years ago.'

Martin asked her what she wanted to do for a career.

'I honestly don't know, and that's not me trying to dodge the question. I want to be an au pair at the moment. Then I don't know. It's a bit pathetic really, when everyone else seems to be so sure.'

'I'm not.'

'But I thought you were studying law?'

'Yeah, but I don't know if it's for me. It seemed like a good idea, but I'm playing for time really.'

Pip thought, *This is OK, quite normal. Not so bad.*

Henry asked her what her favourite movie of all time was.

'Good question. Difficult question. Probably *The Graduate*. Or *Shawshank*. Or *L.A. Confidential*. I don't know. I need to think about that one. What's yours?'

'*The Godfather*.'

'Which part?'

'All of them.' They laughed. 'It says a lot about a person, what their favourite movie is. Like now I know that you're rebellious and have a romantic streak.'

'And wouldn't like to be incarcerated for a crime I didn't commit?'

'Yes, that too.'

When Pip had danced with the boys, it was the girls' turn. She sat next to Tiny and said, 'Seriously – are you writing this down?'

'Seriously – are you still whingeing?'

'Who, me? No – I'm actually having a laugh.'

'Good. Here's mine. Why do you never have any money?'

Tricky. Ah well, here goes. 'I'm saving up for a holiday. With my ex. We're meeting up in September. We've had it planned for ages, to see if we're going to be friends or boyfriend-girlfriend.'

'Which do you think?'

'I don't know yet. I thought I'd wait until I see him.'

'Where are you going?'

'Don't know. We haven't booked it yet. Somewhere sunny. Just the two of us.'

'What's he like? What does he look like?'

'Tall. Blond. Fit.' *Heartbroken. Drinks too much. Ten years older than me.*

'Sounds yummy. Where's he from?'

'He's lived all over the world. But he's originally from Australia.'

'No wonder you want to split up with him, then,' said Billy, sitting down opposite her. Pip had been checking the whole time: there was no sign of Leo. If he wasn't here with his friends and he wasn't with Roxy, where was he? Probably not interested. Oh well – he wasn't with Roxy, and that was enough. Billy said, 'When do I get my dance?'

Pip took a sip of her drink and stood up. They went to the dance floor and Billy put his arms around her.

'So what's your question? Bring it on.'

Billy shook his head. 'Nope. No questions. I promised I would never ask.'

Pip felt a rush of gratitude and relaxed. They danced for a while longer and Billy told her about training on Thursday, when Leo and the coach had cracked the whip so hard that a couple of the players had indeed thrown up by the side of the pitch. Pip thought it might be safe to ask.

'Where is your brother tonight?'

'Coming soon. First he had to go out with Beck for dinner. Beck says he wants to talk to him. Don't know what about.'

'Don't you? Don't you even have a clue?'

Billy shrugged and gave her a puzzled look. 'No. Why would... what do you know? Has he said something?'

'No, but it's obvious, isn't it?'

'What's obvious? You've lost me.'

'Didn't I hear that the German captain – whatshisname – hasn't been on his best form recently, has had lots of injuries? It's Olympic year. After Sydney, he'll probably retire. So Beck needs to start thinking about his replacement. He'll want someone who's injury-free; a solid, reliable captain who inspires people to up their game, who can bring the team together and get them working like one big hockey-playing machine. Because he leads by example; because he himself is a hockey-playing machine. Someone like your brother, in fact.'

'You think?'

'I do.'

Billy thought about it and chuckled. 'You know, Pipette, I think you might be right. How about that, then? My brother, the captain of the German hockey team.' He wrapped his arms around her and lifted her off her feet. 'My God, you are so amazing. What would I ever do without you?' He gazed into her eyes and put his hand on her cheek. A few months ago, Pip would have felt self-conscious and wondered if Billy was going to try and kiss her. But it was different now between them. After he'd got together with Nadine, she knew it was only bluster. There was no lust in his eyes, just friendship and a sort of brotherly love. Billy reminded her, more than anyone, of Holly.

Pip pecked him on the cheek and said, 'Shall we celebrate? Champagne?'

They turned from the dance floor and saw Leo standing at the bar. He was wearing jeans and a dark blue V-necked jumper with a white T-shirt underneath, and Pip felt her heart crashing against her ribs.

Billy asked him about Beck, and Leo said he'd fill him in later. It was impossible to tell if he was pleased or excited; he was his usual composed self. They ordered a bottle of champagne anyway and a couple of apple juices, and sat down, the three of them, at the end of the table.

Billy looked with longing at the champagne and said, 'I haven't had a drink for eight weeks.'

'You must be quite thirsty, then,' said Pip. She'd just read a book Rosa had given her, *The Girls' Guide to Hunting and Fishing*, and it was one of her favourite lines.

The noise in the bar was deafening. The DJ was playing faster songs and everyone else was dancing. Billy went to dance with Tara, and Leo turned to Pip.

'Everything OK? They weren't too hard on you tonight, were they? Tiny told me what they were planning.'

'I hate talking about myself. But I appreciate that I've been a bit evasive since I arrived.'

Leo nodded.

'It was fine in the end. Turns out I have things in common with lots of them.'

'Even Bredenkamp?'

'No. Not him. Actually, he didn't ask me a question. Said he'd only come for the dance. He was very… umm… tactile. Wandering hands.'

'Fucking creep.' Leo glared around the room.

'It was OK – I told you, I can look after myself.'

'You should've sent me a text. You still have the *HILFE* text saved on your phone?'

'Yes. But I wouldn't… I mean, I sort of wanted to save it for a real emergency. So you know, if I send it, that it's serious and not just something silly.'

There was silence as they watched the others dance. Leo's thigh was jogging up and down under the table, she could feel the vibrations.

She said, 'You're not going to ask me a question, are you?' But she wanted him to ask her something, to show he was interested in her.

'No. If I did have a question, I wouldn't force you to answer it. None of my business. Not everyone has a perfect life or a perfect family or wants to talk about it all the time.'

'Right.' Pip had rarely known Leo so chatty, unless he was talking about hockey. She supposed he was on a high about the captaincy. 'Did your dad tell you we spoke a bit about your mum?'

'Yes. He told me what he told you. And what he didn't.'

'I was being nosy. Sorry. I understand about you wanting to focus this year. But maybe after Sydney, if you want to talk about it, I'm a good listener.'

'I could say the same to you.'

'Why don't you, then?'

He half-smiled. 'OK. After Sydney, we'll talk. You can tell me why you're so unhappy and I'll tell you why I am, quite literally, a son of a bitch.'

'I'm not unhappy.'

Leo looked at her hard for a second and then shrugged.

Pip knew that although it might be OK to tell Leo that she'd lied about Holly, she could never tell him about Troy. She would end it with Troy while she was in Sydney, no matter how that might affect his playing, and it would be as if it had never happened. Troy wouldn't tell anyone. He had a lot to lose, more than Pip, because her youth would to some extent mitigate the appalling thing she'd done. And although her parents would never speak to her again, they never spoke to her anyway.

Tiny crashed down on the bench next to Pip, hot from dancing. She proceeded to tell Leo every single piece of information about Pip that had been supplied to her. Pip thought, *He's going to think I'm so dull.* And he did seem completely indifferent to everything. He looked as though he was barely listening. Pip tried to stop her several times but Tiny was not to be deterred.

When she'd finished, she said, 'It wasn't so bad in the end, was it?'

'No. I thought you were going to make me do dares.'

'What makes you think I'm not going to? The night is young.' She reached into a bag under the table and called everyone over. 'Ta-da! Your next challenge, should you choose to accept it, which you will because you promised, is to wear this costume.' She held up a red dress and a blonde wig.

Pip looked at her, confused.

'It's from *There's Something About Mary.* The scene where Cameron Diaz goes out on a date with Ben Stiller. But you have to collect the last piece of the costume yourself.'

'You're fucking with me.'

'Impressive film knowledge, Pip. You know what it needs, though…'

'Hair gel? Please let it be hair gel.'

Tiny shouted around the bar, 'Anyone have any hair gel? No, didn't think so. So, if you'd like to retire to the ladies' loos and change, that should give Bredenkamp time to produce the goods.'

The rest of the evening was a blur, but she said yes to everything. The Night of Saying Yes. She said yes to the spunk-covered wig. She said yes when Tiny told her to sing …*Baby One More Time* in a karaoke bar. She said yes when they made her dance alone for an entire song on the deserted dance floor of a nightclub. And in the same nightclub, when she had to go and ask a man she'd never heard of (but who was apparently a famous Bayern Munich footballer) for his autograph, and if she could sit on his knee while Tiny took a photograph, she also said yes, groaning with embarrassment.

Pip thought, *I've done it. I've had a normal night out with friends who told me they love me.* She lay in her bed that night, Billy and Leo having brought her home safely, the room spinning and her head buzzing from after-effects of the loud music, but with a big grin on her face while Billy tried to make her drink water and said he'd stay with her to make sure she didn't vomit in the night. *Because Leo must think I'm a mental case, but he doesn't hate me because he said he wants to tell me about his family, and he said Bredenkamp was a perv and he's not going out with Roxy and maybe I can hope and… and… and…*

11

Pip woke alone, with a throbbing head and a dry mouth, to the sounds of doors and feet. She dragged herself upstairs to the hallway, where Billy was gathering sticks and bags. He kissed her on the forehead and asked how she was.

'OK. Where are you off to today?'

'The club: training game.'

The kitchen door opened. Leo held a coffee in his hand, which he gave to Pip with a sardonic smile. She took it and thanked him as he disappeared out of the front door.

She whispered to Billy, 'Did they give him the captaincy? Did you ask him?'

'You were right. Mayerhöfer's told Beck that Sydney'll be his last Olympics. Then Leo's up. He has to have a rock-solid Olympics. Like that's not going to happen. But mum's the word. See ya.'

Pip was at a loose end. After she'd drunk her coffee, showered and sent Nadine an email with the details of last night – what she could remember, anyway – she decided to go for a walk. Didn't matter where, but before she knew it, she was in the woods on the way to the club. As she pushed open the gate, she heard the whistle for the start of the game and, instead of heading for her usual spot in the clubhouse, she forced herself to walk towards the AstroTurf.

She made it to a bench about three metres from the fence before she had to stop and sit down. Her heart was beating fast, she felt nauseous, this wasn't going to work. *Breathe, breathe, calm down, don't panic.*

In front of her lay the bright green turf, white lines measuring out halves and quarters and D-shaped goal areas. Twenty-two men, two umpires, plus subs and coaches in the dugout. The sight of it was simultaneously familiar and yet utterly alien to her. She shivered and bunched up her legs on the bench, wrapping her arms around them. Billy flashed past on the wing nearest to her. He was passed the ball, which he controlled as if it was magnetically attracted to his stick. He flicked it up, once, twice, passing it to a teammate in the D, who cracked it into the goal. It was magic. She watched him for a while longer, mesmerised by the speed and energy he showed whenever the ball came near him.

She switched her attention to Leo. Dominic was right – he was in a class of his own. Every attack from the opposition was closed down, every ball repossessed with such ease that Leo looked like he was hardly trying. The goalkeeper behind him, a South African player called Rollo, at one point sat on his back board and started reading a newspaper. Pip chuckled.

When the half-time whistle blew, Pip went into the clubhouse for a coffee. It was deserted apart from Günther. She sat at the bar and chatted to him for a few minutes, Günther complimenting her on how much her German had improved. It started raining, so she took her cup onto the balcony and watched the second half from there.

The teams had switched ends, so Leo had his back to her and Billy was attacking the goal at the far end. The game settled into a series of long passes, neither side able to get near the other's goals. Pip contented herself with watching the ball skim across the wet surface, landing on the ends of sticks and being controlled with a satisfying skill she hadn't seen for years. And she was content: she was thinking about Holly, but it didn't hurt so much any more. Here, on this balcony, at this clubhouse, watching this match, she surprised herself by at last gaining pleasure from the game of hockey without the gnawing grief of losing her sister. She smiled to herself.

She saw Billy break into the D at the other end of the pitch. He smacked the ball towards the goalie, who saved it on his kicker, it sailed up into the air, as if in slow motion, and hit Billy on the head. He slumped to the ground.

Someone screamed. A mist covered Pip's eyes and the air around her thickened, the balcony tilting beneath her feet. A face looked up at her from the pitch. Günther was behind her, are you OK, sit down, put your head between your legs. Günther's shouts. More voices.

'Pip.' A soft voice in her ear. 'Are you OK?' She raised her face slowly to see Leo peering at her, touching her hand. 'Jesus. You're as cold as ice.'

'Billy?'

'He's OK. Look.' Leo pointed to the pitch, where Billy was sitting up, holding his head. Pip watched as he was helped up and walked to the edge of the pitch.

'Ambulance?' Pip gasped.

'He'll be fine. There wasn't so much power in the ball.' He stood up and held out his hand. 'Come on, come with me. See for yourself. Slowly. Steady. You've had a shock.'

They walked down the stairs in silence together, Leo holding the door open for her. He was watching her closely, a concerned look on his face. It was throwing it down, and she blinked as the rain ran down her face. When they reached the gate that led onto the AstroTurf, Pip hesitated. She turned and followed the fence on the outside until she reached the dugout where Billy was sitting with an ice pack on his forehead. As she approached, she stumbled and righted herself. Players standing near the dugout, drinking water, turned towards her. Billy stood up. He was smiling at her like she was crazy, shaking his head.

'What?' she said. *Why is everyone staring at me?* 'Are you OK?'

'I'm fine. How're you doing, sweetheart?'

'What?'

Some of the younger players were openly laughing. The older ones were trying to keep straight faces.

Billy came to the waist-height fence where she was standing. He was close to her, close enough for her to see the red lump on his head and his blue eyes crinkling up with a smile. His hair was plastered to his scalp, dark from the rain. He said in a low voice, 'You screamed so loudly, we all thought someone had died.' Pip gripped the edge of the fence to stop herself falling over. Tears pricked her eyes. 'You kinda stole my thunder.'

She let the tears spill out and mix with the rain on her cheeks. *He's OK. He isn't even concussed. He's joking about it.*

'So that's what I had to do to get your attention.' He kissed her full on the lips while Pip's ears roared with relief and the sounds of wolf whistles.

Someone shouted, 'Put her down, Feldstein.' The umpire's whistle blew shrilly and he broke away from her, winked and ran back onto the pitch.

Pip wasn't remotely embarrassed by the kiss that Billy had plonked on her lips. There had been nothing sexy about it – he'd been showing off in front of the team like a little boy in the playground. She *was*, however, embarrassed about the fact she'd nearly passed out when he'd been hit. She should have known better than to think a deflection off the keeper from that far away, and with that trajectory, would kill someone. She'd panicked, of course she had and she knew why, but no one else could.

She was sure that Dominic would hear about Billy kissing her and she most definitely didn't want Leo to think she had initiated – or enjoyed – it. So when Dominic, Max and Ferdi returned from Lindau, she cooked a meal for them and steered the conversation to Billy's injury. He had a multicoloured bruise on his forehead but the swelling had gone down.

'Tell us again how it happened, Billy,' said Ferdi.

'Why don't you ask Pip? She had the bird's-eye view.' He wiggled his eyebrows at her.

She said, 'It was pretty impressive, from where I was standing. Billy hit the ball hard. It arced back towards him and seemed to smack him right in the middle of his head. I even thought I could hear the sound of it from the clubhouse. He went down like a stone.'

'You're such a girl, Billy,' said Max.

'Unfair to girls,' said Pip. 'This is the bit I don't remember very well. I freaked out. I thought he was really badly hurt and apparently I screamed. I don't even remember.'

'Did she, Leo? Did she scream?'

'She did.'

'Was it blood-curdling?'

'It was.' Leo was scratching the surface of the table with his fingernail.

'So Günther's trying to calm me down and Leo comes up to help and he tells me Billy's fine, so we go to have a look for ourselves. And then, obviously under the mistaken impression that I need comforting, Billy decides to snog me in front of everyone.'

'Oh, gross.' Max and Ferdi made sick noises.

'Yes, it was a bit gross. He was all sweaty and stinky and had this great big egg sticking out of his head. It was like kissing a frog. Except he didn't turn into a prince afterwards.'

159

Billy laughed. 'Well, that's told me, then.'

'Yeah, Billy. Hands off her,' said Ferdi.

Dominic was laughing too. 'Think you might have some competition for Pip's affections, Billy.'

'Don't touch her again, or we'll get you,' said Max.

Billy, closely monitored by Max and Ferdi, was as good as his word. Through March and into April, Pip went to the club and watched one or another of the von Feldsteins play or train. They were there almost every day, and the club was full of friendly faces. After the Night of Saying Yes for Tiny's birthday, she could relax more. She listened as Henry raved about *Gladiator*, which he'd seen the night before, and arranged to go the cinema with him the following night to see it again. She sympathised as Tara complained about her job and how she never had time off on Saturday nights. She met Caro for a drink when she split up with her boyfriend and needed someone's shoulder to cry on. Tiny and Mandi and the others were always there, and they made her feel wanted even though she didn't play.

When Leo and Billy left for another tour of Australia, she wasn't plunged into her usual despair. The Germans were playing South Africa, India and Australia, the third time since she'd arrived in Munich that Leo and Billy would play Troy, and now she barely gave it a thought. If it was going to happen that Troy found out she was working at the von Feldsteins', it would have done so already. No point worrying about something so out of her control.

She thought about Leo, of course she did, but she wanted to try and be cheerful while he was away, not mope or spend hours daydreaming. She wasn't over him, not by a long stretch, but she had to try and survive without him. As a symbolic gesture of her new attitude to life and love, she went to the hairdresser's for a radical haircut.

'You sure?' said the bubblegum-chewing hairdresser.

'Yes, very. Cut it all off to above my shoulders. I'm fed up with being Rapunzel and waiting in my room for a prince to come along and fall in love with me. Snip away, dear lady!'

The hairdresser looked at her like she was mad and started cutting. When she'd finished, Pip felt lighter and younger and she loved it. 'In your face, Rapunzel,' she said to no one in particular.

'Whatever,' said the hairdresser.

Dominic was organising a team for the annual 'Von Feldstein vs. the Rest of the World' tournament.

'How many players do you have?' asked Pip.

'Let's see. Me, Billy, Leo, Rosa, Stefan, Maximilian – my father-in-law. Then we have the cousins, Christa and Felix, from Hamburg. Sofia, Alex and Helene from Berlin. So we need another female player.'

'You could ask Tiny.'

'She's not a von Feldstein, or married to one.'

'What about your family?'

'My parents are no longer with us. I'm an only child of only children.'

'I'm sorry, I didn't know. Why are you looking at me like that?'

'How about it, Pip? You don't have to do much – just make up the numbers.'

'No way. I'm not family either.'

'As good as. It would really help me out.'

'Why can't Max and Ferdi play? Or Anna and Isa? They're girls.'

'They're too young. It can be quite competitive and rough. A few years ago we brought in the rule that players have to be over sixteen, so none of the kids are hurt.'

Pip crossed her arms in front of her. 'But it's OK for me to be hurt?'

'Ha. You play rough. You're ruthless with that tennis ball. And I've seen you winded from a football Max kicked with all his might. You dusted yourself off and carried on. You're as tough as old boots.'

'I'll take that as a compliment. But I can't play hockey.'

'It doesn't matter in the slightest. Tell you what, I'll put you down as a maybe and keep calling around. There might be another cousin somewhere who can make it down for the weekend.'

'I'm not playing. Sorry, Dominic. I can't.'

'Can't or won't?'

'Both.'

Dominic considered for a moment. 'Is this something to do with the head injury?'

Pip froze.

'It is, isn't it? You said you freaked out when Billy was hit.'

Oh, Billy, yes. 'It is sort of to do with that. But also, I just… when I came here, you know, I had no idea you were a hockey-playing family. No one told me.'

'Ah yes, the letter with the missing key facts. Once again, I apologise.'

'I never would have come here, taken the job, if I'd known.' Pip felt anger rise inside her. Anger at herself and the lies she told daily to cover the truth of who she was; anger at Dominic for pushing her about this. 'So you can't make me play and you have to accept that I'm never going to play or even go near that AstroTurf. Watching from the sideline – that's the limit. That's it.'

'Message received and understood,' he said with a bemused smile.

'Good. I'm sorry – I don't mean to be rude. I'll do anything else for this family – for the boys and for you – but not that.'

'And I'm sorry I tried to force you to play when you've made it so clear that you're not interested. Can I put you down for another job? Would you be OK to help Günther behind the bar?'

'Of course.' Pip relaxed. 'How does it work, then, this tournament? Who's in the Rest of the World team?'

He looked at his list. 'So, over sixteen years old. A minimum of five women on the pitch at any time. And the Rest of the World team is only allowed one player per country on the pitch. Rollo's in goal.'

'South Africa.'

'Henry's playing.'

'USA,' said Pip.

'Theo.'

'England.'

'Pim Wolters.'

'Holland. Wow, this is amazing.'

'Natalia.'

'Argentina,' she said.

'Tara.'

'Ireland.'

'Tiny and Caro are substituting for each other.'

'So that's Germany.'

'Annie.'

Annie was the women's coach. 'Where does she come from?'

'Zimbabwe. Roxy's playing for Switzerland – spurious, apparently her grandmother is Swiss, but we'll let that one slide. There are two male players, Dev and Ajaz, coming over from England who used to play here. Dev's Indian and Ajaz is from Pakistan. So that's the lot.'

He showed her the list and Pip was amazed at how international the club was. She doubted there was another club that could have found so many players from so many different countries.

She said, 'You're certainly taking this seriously. Cousins coming down from Berlin; players flying over from England. Is this a life-or-death situation?'

'Something like that,' said Dominic grimly. 'You haven't met my father-in-law yet, have you?'

The game was at three o'clock on Good Friday. Dominic, Pip, Max and Ferdi walked through the woods early, to help Günther set up and prepare the clubhouse for the after-match party. Pip was going to work until seven, then she had to take Max and Ferdi to a friend's house for a sleepover. After that, she was free to join the party. The following day, the von Feldsteins, including the cousins, Rosa, Stefan and the girls, and Billy and Leo, who were back from Australia, were spending the Easter holidays at the lake house in Lindau.

'Would you like to come with us this time, Pip?' said Dominic.

Pip was torn. She imagined that spring would be the perfect time to see the house at Lindau. The lavender fields behind it, the lake shimmering, and everywhere the trees and flowers bursting to life. And to spend more time with Leo was tempting. But Dominic had said that Elisabeth was going to be home, hopefully for good, and she didn't want to intrude on their first time together as a family. She said no, maybe next time and Dominic replied, 'Yes, you're quite right.'

She started serving the first drinks before the game began, Günther showing her how to pull the beer so it frothed up the right amount. There was quite a crowd – two hundred people, Pip reckoned. She and Günther stood on the balcony watching, and at half-time, two-nil to the von Feldsteins, everyone surged up to the bar to order drinks. Shortly after they started playing again, Theo limped upstairs with an ankle injury, and a couple of minutes later, one of the von Feldstein cousins came off the pitch clutching her elbow.

'There'll be blood soon. There's always blood,' muttered Günther.

Pip gulped and hoped that neither Billy nor Leo would be injured. They shouldn't even be playing, five months before the Olympics. But she watched them for the second half and realised they were both mucking about, to the frustration of their grandfather. All of the players on the pitch were quality – the von Feldstein cousins looked like they could play Bundesliga. Some of them, like Rosa and Dominic, were slow, and some, like Tiny and Roxy, were quick but couldn't keep hold of the ball for long before they were borne down upon by some man who was twice their size. Dominic hadn't been kidding that the game was rough. The score was three-two to the Rest of the World. The von Feldsteins were awarded a penalty flick because Rollo sat on the ball and couldn't stop laughing. Maximilian insisted on taking it, but Rollo saved it easily and Pip could see that the von Feldsteins, with five minutes of the match to go, were starting to take it seriously. Leo took charge again in defence and started pushing up with Billy, and the Rest of the World players peeled away as the two of them made short work of anyone who tried to tackle them. Pip's mouth hung open. Four minutes to go. They were passing so quickly to each other it was a blur, and the crowd was screaming and roaring and Pip knew that she'd never see anything so awesome again, such a display of absolute perfection and timing, as if the two brothers knew exactly what the other one was going to do, every move coordinated, beautifully synchronised, like they were one person with four legs and two sticks. She saw it all slowed down, and knew they could do this blindfolded.

Rosa and a Hamburg cousin, who were playing up front, took their markers away from the D and gave Billy the space he needed in front of the goal. Rollo, realising that he had no chance of saving anything that Billy shot at him, ran out of his goal, bellowing like a deranged animal, trying desperately to disturb his concentration. Billy sidestepped him and pushed the ball with aching slowness into the goal, Rollo howling with frustration and diving after it, only to watch it trickle over the line. Three-all. The final whistle blew.

Billy bowed to the crowd; he and Leo high-fived.

Pip rushed back behind the bar. 'No blood today,' she said happily to Günther as they started serving drinks to the players and crowd who had poured into the clubhouse.

'Not yet,' said Günther and gestured towards Maximilian, who was stomping up the stairs, following Billy and Leo.

'You didn't take that seriously, not at all. I'm terribly disappointed in you. I expect to win this game every year, especially this year. That was preposterous, what you two did out there.'

'Is he for real?' whispered Pip to Günther, who nodded. Billy was trying and failing to keep a straight face. Leo looked bored.

'We win, the von Feldsteins, it's what we do. You showed us up today, Wilhelm. Leopold, you too – I expected more from you at least. You need to buck up your ideas.'

Pip didn't hear Leo's reply to his grandfather, but the older man gave him a scathing look and left the room, muttering.

'Two of your finest beers please, serving wench. Love the haircut,' said Billy, and Pip poured them each a lemonade. Neither of them had even broken a sweat, but the other members of both teams were trooping up the stairs, red in the face and exhausted. She was enjoying herself, serving as quickly as she could, when an Indian man ordered a round of drinks and she looked up to see a green Canterbury Hockey Club tracksuit. *Stay calm, Pip, you don't know him. He won't recognise you.* He ordered his drinks, thanked her and moved away.

She served the von Feldstein cousins, who were glamorous and intimidating. She served Tiny and the other girls, who kept asking when she was off duty and admiring her new hair. Günther asked her to go and collect glasses outside, where long wooden beer tables and benches had been set out in the sunshine. The loudspeakers from the clubhouse were pumping out music, and on the grill, sausages were sizzling. She wished she could sit for a while and join in, but the bar was packed and she and Günther were hardly able to keep up. She carried tray after tray of empties upstairs and stacked them in the dishwasher.

As the end of her shift neared, Pip watched Max, Ferdi, Anna and Isa, who were playing on the AstroTurf with some of the other children from the club. Out of the corner of her eye, she saw one of the boys bend over by the side of the pitch. Had he been hit? Pip squinted over to see what he was doing. Dominic had seen too, and was walking to him and started patting him on the back, soothing him. Pip looked more closely and saw that it was Ferdi, and he was throwing up. She went back behind the bar, thinking, *He's eaten too many sausage sandwiches and run around straight afterwards.* She only had twenty minutes, then she'd take him home and he'd be fine.

At seven, Leo and Billy came to take over from Pip and she went to find the children. She took Max and Ferdi through the woods towards home, to collect their overnight bags. Their friend lived a few streets away.

'You OK, little dude?' she asked Ferdi. He looked pale, but he smiled and nodded.

As they approached Number Three, Max grabbed the gate and vomited onto the pavement. It splattered Pip's shoes, which were soaked in beer anyway. She sighed. Both of them had overdone it. Maybe they shouldn't go to their friend's house? She sat them down on the front step, fetched a couple of buckets and told them to stay put while she cleaned up the mess. By the time she'd finished, they'd both thrown up again and Ferdi was lying on the step, his face white and his hair slicked to his head with sweat.

Over the next few hours, she swilled out buckets and stuffed sicked-over sheets and pyjamas into the washing machine when they missed the bucket. There had been a message on the answering machine from the mother of Max and Ferdi's friend, to cancel the playdate – they'd come down with a stomach bug that was going round the class. She'd texted Dominic and Leo, but doubted they'd hear their phones in the loud clubhouse.

By eleven o'clock, the time between upchucks had lengthened and Pip wearily hung up the last wash of sheets and pyjamas, showered quickly herself, gratified that her hair was much shorter, and got ready for bed. She still hadn't heard anything from Dominic, so she pinned a note to the front door to explain what had happened, and that she was going to sleep upstairs in one of the spare rooms so she could hear them if they were sick again. She chose the room she thought was Leo's, rather than the one she'd seen Billy and Roxy in. She fell asleep straight away, and just before she woke up, she dreamt someone was stroking her hair.

'Pip,' said a voice in her ear.

She blinked her eyes open. 'What time is it?'

'Just past midnight.' Leo was sitting on the bed beside her. He was wearing a baseball T-shirt, white with dark green arms. Pip had a wild urge to put her hands on his chest. She crushed it. 'I thought you said you weren't going to sleep in my bed ever again?'

'Oh, I'm not… it's… umm…'

'Relax, I'm only kidding. I saw the note, and I've just seen your message on my phone. Sorry – I didn't hear it beep. Has it been awful?'

'I think the worst is over. They haven't been sick for a while.'

'They're both fast asleep. How are you feeling?'

'Oh, I never get sick,' said Pip. 'Are you staying here tonight? I mean…' She realised it sounded like she was inviting him into bed with her. 'If I go back to my bed, will you… sorry, I'm half asleep. Will you stay here and listen out for them, or are you on your way back to the Sixth Floor?'

His face was closer to hers than it had ever been. In the lamplight, she could see his features clearly. The scar on his forehead, his long, dark eyelashes, his bashed-up nose and wide, straight mouth, turned up slightly at the corners.

He said gently, 'I'll stay. Dad and Billy'll be back soon – I'll wait up for them and tell them what's happened. Go and get some sleep.'

Pip dragged herself out of the warm bed and checked Max and Ferdi one more time. 'Night,' she said sleepily as she went downstairs.

She slept so soundly that she didn't hear Billy and Dominic coming in an hour later, and she didn't hear them leave for Lindau early the next day.

In the morning, she swam lengths in the pool and afterwards sat on her patch of kitchen floor in the sunshine, drinking coffee and reading *White Teeth*. The empty house was silent around her – the air seemed to be suspended in time, like it was waiting too, restless and thick with yearning, for its men to come back to it and fill it with life again.

12

At lunchtime, the phone rang. Pip let it go to the answering machine, putting down her book as she listened to the female caller.

'Philippa – hello, are you there? Please do pick up if you're there.' An exasperated sigh. 'Oh, she's not there. Where on earth is she? No, I don't like those dratted things. You do it.'

Who was that? A moment later, her mobile phone rang. She picked up straight away.

A man's voice said, 'Philippa? Where are you?'

'I'm… at home. I—'

'We're in a bit of a fix here.' The voice, which sounded angry, became muffled. She'd heard that voice before – was it Max and Ferdi's grandfather?

'Excuse me?' said Pip.

A new voice came on the line. 'You're needed here. I'd like you to be on the next train to Lindau; there's one leaving in…

forty-nine minutes from the main station.' This was the female voice from before. It must be the grandparents. Why didn't any of these people introduce themselves properly? 'Get a taxi at this end.'

'What's going on? I mean, why am I needed?' She stumbled over her German, saying the wrong words and trying to correct herself.

The voice continued, in perfect English, 'There's no time to explain now. Just be on that train.' She hung up.

Pip would have to get a wriggle on if she was going to catch the Lindau train. She grabbed her travel card, phone, keys and book and closed up the house, running to Solln station and barely making it to the S-Bahn into town. She found the right platform at the main station and prayed that her travel card was valid for the whole journey. At the Lindau station taxi rank, she realised that no one had told her the address of the house.

'Umm. I need to go to... do you by any chance know where the von Feldstein family live?' she said to the taxi driver.

'Course I do. Hop in,' he said.

From the train station, he drove on a road bridge over the water and took a left on the mainland, along a lakeside road and past a tennis club. A few minutes later, the taxi turned into a private road through a small wooded area, coming to a stop outside the castle that Pip recognised from the paintings at the house in Munich.

The paintings had softened it – flattered it. She was ready to have her breath taken away by its beauty, but the building was boring, ugly even. It was painted yellow with a red roof, and was square and plain. It was the setting that was beautiful. The house was separated from the lake by sloping gardens and surrounded by fields and woods. She was disappointed to see the fields were green, rather than the lavender in the painting in the living room. Talk about artistic licence.

'Hello?' she called, outside what she thought was the front door. She couldn't see a bell or a knocker anywhere. She tried the handle and pushed open the heavy wooden door. 'Hello? Is anyone—'

'Ah, Philippa, at last you're here.' A woman was walking towards her, dressed in a neat tweed skirt, a cream blouse and pearls. Her hair was a dark grey colour, in one of those posh old-lady sets that didn't move at all, even in the strongest wind. She didn't smile at Pip or shake hands or offer her any other greeting. Pip was waiting for her to introduce herself, not that it was necessary. This was clearly Mrs Maria von Feldstein.

'Follow me, please. I'll show you your room, and then if you could help me with the children, that would be wonderful.'

'Umm. Yes. Of course.'

Mrs von Feldstein moved with determined speed up the stairs and turned right into a long corridor with ten doors leading off it, five on each side. It had a thick carpet on the floor and the walls were lined with old portraits.

'But... I mean... please – has something happened? You said... your husband said you were in a fix.'

'Oh, it's been chaos here. Maximilian and Ferdinand are fine now but the others have come down with it, one by one. We've hardly been able to cope. You knew they were ill, didn't you?'

Pip had the feeling she was being blamed for something, but she didn't know what. 'I... yes, I told Dominic.'

'Well, that's by the by. Here's your room.' She opened the first door on the left, into a room with a single bed in it, beneath a window that looked out onto the fields at the back. Opposite Pip's door, she opened another one. Two small blurs rocketed towards Pip and nearly knocked her over.

'Pipster, you're here, we've been waiting for you, it's so boring, everyone's puking their guts up.'

'Maximilian, that is unacceptable language and Philippa is not interested in the sordid details.'

Pip winked at Max and straightened her face. 'Is everyone ill?'

'Yes. First it was Leo, then Isa and Anna, then Billy and Dad and Rosa and Stefan. It's like a tidal wave of—'

'Lovely, well, why don't you tell me about that later?' said Pip. She might be blamed for their language as well as the illness itself. She turned to Mrs von Feldstein. 'What do you need me to do?'

'The boys will show you downstairs. You can help Marlene with the washing.' Pip presumed that Marlene was some kind of servant. A bit like her, then. 'They'll need entertaining – they are the only ones who are healthy, and are rather boisterous.'

'Are you and your husband feeling OK?'

'Yes, we're fine. I'm of the belief that our generation is made of sterner stuff.'

Pip couldn't think of anyone whose stuff was sterner than Leo's, but she kept her mouth shut. Mrs von Feldstein didn't seem like the kind of person who would appreciate being talked back to.

'It's dreadfully inconvenient. We had to cancel our other visitors. My nephews and nieces, who'd come all the way from Hamburg and Berlin, have had to change their plans.' She sighed like there was nothing worse in the world than a cancelled house party, and wandered off downstairs.

Max and Ferdi showed her to the kitchens in the cellar, where Marlene turned out to be one of the least friendly people Pip had ever met. She grunted at Pip and pointed at piles of washing, gabbling all the time in a language that sort of sounded like German but wasn't. Pip was going to need subtitles to understand her.

'Why can't I understand Marlene?' Pip whispered to Max.

'She's Austrian. Just nod and smile. That's what we do.'

She started unloading and loading sheets from the washing machine, spotted a line outside and hung everything out in the sunshine. She followed a mumbling Marlene, who slapped a bottle of disinfectant in Pip's hand and pointed upstairs. There she found Max and Ferdi loading dangerous-looking water pistols in the bathroom, and told them to drop their weapons and come with her on a secret mission.

The room next to Max and Ferdi's was Isa and Anna's. Both sound asleep. Two buckets needed emptying and the room stank of sick. Pip cranked open the window to let in some fresh air.

After she'd emptied and cleaned the buckets in the bathroom next door, and Max had replaced them quietly, she pushed open the fourth door. Rosa and Stefan. 'Anyone need anything? It's Pip. Anything I can do?'

'No thank you, we're fine. Are the girls OK?'

'Fast asleep. Any water? Or soup? Marlene has some ready.'

'Oh, yes please, a little water, if it's no trouble,' whispered Rosa.

'I could manage some soup,' said Stefan. 'Thank you. You're an angel.'

Pip sent the boys to the kitchen. The last door on the right was Dominic's. He was sitting up in bed wearing pyjamas, his face pale, reading.

'Hello, how are you?' said Pip from the door.

'I thought I heard you. What are you doing here? Come in.'

'Mrs von Feldstein phoned and asked me to come and help with the patients. I feel a bit like Florence Nightingale.' She entered the room, leaving the door open.

Dominic shook his head. 'I'm sorry, Pip, that was unnecessary. You shouldn't have to come down here and do this—'

'I'm happy to help. The house in Munich is too quiet without you all, anyway.'

'I don't want you to catch it too.'

'Oh, I won't. I never get sick.'

Dominic smiled. 'Is that right?'

'Could you manage soup? I'm keeping Max and Ferdi busy, being waiters.'

'Good. Yes please.'

As Pip turned to leave the room, she remembered another question. 'Elisabeth? Is she here?'

Dominic motioned to the other side of the corridor. 'She's not ill. She's had to keep her distance, which is terribly frustrating for her. But she's fine. You'll probably bump into her in the garden, or at dinner tonight.'

Pip left the room and crossed over to the other side, missed out Elisabeth's room, knocked on the next door and went in. It was dark and stank of sour body odour and sick. The bucket by the side of Billy's bed was half full. Pip tugged open the curtains and the windows. Billy was tangled up in his duvet, wearing only boxer shorts, his hair greasy and messed up, blond stubble on his chin.

'Mary Poppins? Is that really you?' He smiled weakly at her. 'I feel like death.'

'You look like death too.' She picked up the bucket. 'I'm going to empty this, but you can do it next time. You'll have to look after yourself a bit better. Surely you can make it to the bathroom? And it smells like hell in here. You need a shower.'

Billy stretched and yawned. 'Blimey, you remind me of a cross between Nurse Ratched and Maria von Trapp. It's very, very sexy.'

'Only you could be thinking about sex at a time like this. Get up, come on, and I'll change your sheets. You are the most disgusting, smelly person I've ever met.'

Billy groaned and sat up, scratching his stomach. There was the sound of giggling from the doorway.

'Max, Ferdi, get in here and help your big, fat, lazy brother into the shower. You can pretend he's a prisoner and squirt him with the water.'

'Be gentle, you ratbags,' Billy said, but allowed himself to be led to the bathroom. Pip pulled off the sheets and found some clean ones downstairs. She swilled out the bucket and placed it back by the side of his newly-made bed.

After the bathroom on this side, there were only two rooms left – hers at the end, and what must be Leo's. Heart hammering, she knocked softly on the door, turned the handle and pushed it open.

'It's me, Pip.' No answer, but the sound of gentle snoring from the bed. She crept into the room and closed the door behind her, tiptoeing to the bed. Only his head was visible above the duvet. His short, dark hair against his pale face, his forehead furrowed, his lips slightly parted. Apart from the stubble, he looked like the little boy in one of the photos she'd seen in Dominic's attic room in Munich. She stared at him, losing track of time, the picture of him soaking into her brain.

His room was neat and smelt of him. There was no bucket by his bed – he'd probably been the first to become ill, and therefore the first to recover. On his bedside table sat a pile of books and a glass of water, half drunk. She had a mad desire to drink from it, to have her lips where his had been. She put her hand on the wall and thought, *Through there is where I'll sleep. My head will be next to his, separated only by this wall.*

She moved away from the bed towards the window. The view was the same as from her room. She peered out of the glass at the green fields and the woods behind them. There was the faintest tinge of purple. She whispered, 'Is it my imagination, or are the flowers starting to come out?'

'Could be,' said Leo's voice. 'In a couple of weeks it's going to be beautiful.'

She jumped. 'Hi. How're you doing?'

'Better. You?'

'I told you—'

'You never get sick.' He sat up, rubbing his eyes. 'What time is it?'

'Six.' She added, 'In the evening.'

'I'm not that out of it.' He stood and walked to the window. 'Did you know, my father had all this planted for my mother?' Pip was silent, so he carried on. 'They went on holiday together to Tuscany and she loved the views of the lavender fields. So he asked my grandfather for her hand in marriage – totally old-fashioned – and if the field behind the house, which was fallow, could be planted with lavender seeds. He brought her down here in the summer of 1972 and proposed to her. They married a year later, and a year after that I was born.'

'It's such a romantic start to a marriage.'

'Yeah, and look how it turned out. Goes to show that grand romantic gestures are just that – gestures.'

'But they still love each other, even after everything.' It wasn't a question. She couldn't conceive that a man who'd planted a whole field of flowers would ever not love the woman he'd planted them for, or that she would ever not love him.

'They can't seem to do without each other for long.'

'That's not the same thing.'

'It's a sort of love. They need each other. And they remember what it was like before.'

'Before...?'

'Before I was born.' His voice was doleful.

She wanted to say to him, *How could anyone believe* your *birth could mark the end of love?* 'Sorry, I'm making you unhappy.'

'And what's making *you* unhappy, Pip?' he murmured, but so quietly, she thought he meant it to be to himself.

She swallowed. One more look at the field, then she turned and said, breaking the moment, 'Are you hungry? There's soup, or dinner probably, soon.'

'I'll be expected at dinner. Any of the others up?'

'Only Max and Ferdi. Not sure what I'm supposed to do. Maybe eat in the kitchen with Marlene.'

'No. You'll eat in the dining room with me. Come on. I'll show you the way. If you get lost, we'll never find you again.'

He led her out of the room. 'What do you think of the von Feldstein residence, by the way? Romantic lavender fields notwithstanding?'

'It's not quite as castle-y as I thought. The setting is lovely.'

'You can say it, you know. It's monstrous.'

She smiled. 'All this will be yours, one day.'

'I'll raze it to the ground.'

'And lay an AstroTurf here instead?'

'Not a bad idea. Oh, hello, you two. Anyone hungry?' Max and Ferdi appeared from their room.

Pip said, 'Did you sort out Billy? Is he sleeping again?'

Max and Ferdi opened their bedroom door wider, to show Billy asleep on one of their beds, face down and naked.

Pip jumped back and blushed. 'You horrors.' She couldn't look at Leo. She didn't know where to look. 'I should quickly check on the girls.'

Leo clutched her arm. 'They'll be fine. Dinner. Come on.'

They stomped downstairs and Max and Ferdi ran in front of them, singing, 'Pip saw Billy's bum', making Pip blush again. She would have liked to have cleaned herself up before dinner – she was sure she'd seen a film or something on TV about people who lived in posh houses putting on their finest for dinner around a massive table, with servants in white gloves unveiling plates from under domed silver covers. But no doubt that was a long time ago, and in England. Leo was wearing a hockey shirt and a pair of old tracksuit bottoms with a hole in one knee and creased from where he'd slept in them, and Max and Ferdi were in shorts and T-shirts.

As they entered the dining room, Pip caught a look of disapproval from Mrs von Feldstein. She was seated at the furthest end of the long table from her husband, and next to her sat Elisabeth, who Pip recognised from the photos on Dominic's wall.

'Darlings. Are you hungry?' Her voice was thin, and it matched the rest of her. The beautiful woman in the photos had

178

been replaced by this ravaged person, with a head too large for her body and dry hair that wisped, rather than fell, onto her shoulders. Elisabeth held out her arms to Max and Ferdi, who moved towards their mother and each gave her a quick kiss on the cheek, before sitting in the two places to her left. 'Leopold, you're up. At last. Must you look so scruffy all the time? And would a shave have killed you? No sign of anyone else?'

Leo said, 'Mum, this is Pip Mitchell.' When there was no reaction, he added 'The new au pair.' He pulled out the chair next to his for her to sit in. 'She's been with us since last September. She's great, isn't she?' He addressed this to Max and Ferdi, who nodded.

'She is. She can build the best towers out of Lego. She climbs trees, too, higher than us. And she taught us how to whistle.'

'How useful.' Even Max and Ferdi understood the sarcasm in Elisabeth's voice.

Marlene, who had been standing in the corner, started serving. Pip stood to help her, but sat down again as Marlene glared at her as if to say, *Don't even think about it*. Pip kept her eyes on her plate. Marlene piled it with food: boiled potatoes and a pile of long, ghostly white things, with rounded tips that could only be described as phallic, covered in a yellow sauce. Pip didn't know what they were, or if there was going to be any meat, so she waited. But everyone said, '*Guten Appetit*' and got stuck in, so she did too.

She watched Max and Ferdi. They ate the white things first, meaning they liked them the least, which surprised her because they didn't much like boiled potatoes either. They were making faces as they ate each bite. She risked a glance at Leo, who was picking at his food. He usually ate like a horse. She'd skipped lunch, and so braced herself and put a mouthful of everything together, determined not to show herself up as the plebeian that she knew, and everyone else knew, she was. OK, the white things were definitely vegetables. Not anything she'd eaten before, but with a bit of sauce slapped on them, quite tasty.

'Would you like some wine, Philippa?' said Mrs von Feldstein.

Before she could check herself, Pip glanced at Elisabeth, and quickly away, hoping no one had seen. She could do with a drink right now. But was that the right thing to do in front of a recovering alcoholic? To be on the safe side, she said, 'No thank you' and sipped her water. Elisabeth shot her a scathing look. So she had seen. Crap.

Mr von Feldstein began talking about the hockey match, describing every move in detail, using words like 'debacle' and 'showing off'.

'Honestly, Grandpa, what do you expect? Bill and I shouldn't even have been playing. It's supposed to be fun. Every year you take it too seriously.' Leo pushed a potato round his plate.

'What did you think, Philippa?' said Mrs von Feldstein.

'About what?'

'The hockey match? On Friday.'

'I don't know.' *It was sublime, it was incredible, it was the most fluent, instinctive, mind-blowing five minutes of sport I've ever had the honour to witness.*

'She's a civilian, Grandma,' said Max.

'Excuse me, a what?'

A civilian: someone who doesn't play sport seriously.

'She doesn't know the first thing about hockey.'

Mrs von Feldstein said, 'What do you do, Philippa, when you're not looking after my youngest grandsons?'

'Umm.' *I think about your oldest grandson in a totally inappropriate way.* 'Not much. I like to read.'

'Is that so?' Mrs von Feldstein reacted as if Pip smelled bad. Which, she realised, she did. 'And in England – what do your parents do? Your surname is Mitchell, is it not?'

'Yes. They're retired police.'

'Scotland Yard?' She turned to her husband. 'Wasn't there a Sir Hugh Mitchell, darling, who we met at lunch that day – the commissioner?'

'There was indeed. Are you related to Sir Hugh, Philippa?'

Pip nearly choked on her food. 'I seriously doubt it.' She felt a movement next to her, but didn't dare look at Leo. 'They were constables. In Canterbury.'

'And did you go to King's?'

King's School was the posh school in Canterbury. Pip couldn't help it – she looked at Leo. He was smiling at her, one eyebrow raised. She managed to keep a straight face and said, 'No. I went to Simon Langton.'

'Is that private?'

'Grammar.'

'Oh.'

Pip imagined them talking about her later: *Darlings! Just think – she wasn't privately educated. Her parents are constables. She's not even related to Sir Hugh. Awfully common.* She finished her food and put her knife and fork in the same position as everyone else had done.

Elisabeth said, 'Do you like asparagus and hollandaise?'

'I've never had it.'

Max and Ferdi burst out laughing and Pip wondered what she'd said that was so funny. She felt her face heat up. She could smell the sweat on her, from lugging buckets and bedding around all afternoon, and a faint tang of sick that clung to her clothes and hair. She looked, for want of anywhere else to look, at Leo, who was tapping his knife on the leftover penis-y things on his plate. Of course. She could have kicked herself.

She didn't even know what asparagus was.

'What are we doing tomorrow, Grandma?'

'You've a riding lesson booked at nine. Then in the afternoon, if it's fair, we can take the boat out.'

Pip knew exactly which questions were coming next.

'Philippa, do you ride?'

'No.'

'And do you sail?'

'No, I'm afraid not.'

Simply amazing – the girl does nothing.

'She couldn't ski either, but Leo taught her.'

'Gosh, how dull for you, Leopold,' said Elisabeth.

'Not at all. She's a fast learner. And her French is excellent.' Pip could hear him smiling.

'What's that got to do with anything?' said Elisabeth. 'If you don't ride, that's not a problem. You can take the boys to the stables – it's not far from here, the owner is a family friend – and pick them up again after their lesson.'

'OK.'

'And in the afternoon, you can *read*,' she said the word like she was suggesting Pip should stand on a street corner selling her body for crack cocaine, 'or whatever you want.'

Leo said, 'Pip doesn't actually need to be here this week, does she? I mean, we're on the mend and Marlene can cope, and we can pitch in.' Pip couldn't figure out whether he was trying to be kind or trying to get rid of her. His voice was so neutral all the time, she found it hard to read between the lines.

'Nonsense. We need her here. The boys will drive me mad, they have far too much energy these days. It's very wearing.' Why was Elisabeth talking about Max and Ferdi like they weren't here? 'And you can't do anything with them – you'll need to train this week, won't you?'

'If Friday was anything to go by,' said Mr von Feldstein, 'you really do need to up your game.'

Leo pushed up from the table and calmly walked out. There was silence. And there were looks. Dark ones.

Max said, 'May we get down too? Please?'

'Yes, certainly.'

Pip stood up, thinking perhaps if the children were allowed to leave, she could too. It was a delicious feeling to take the boys out of that room, so full of tension that the slightest wrong move might make it explode. All those barbed remarks and nervy undertones – she couldn't handle people who behaved like that. Leo clearly hated his mother and his grandparents. He hated the castle, even the name von Feldstein. She'd never seen him like this before – he was normally so polite and in control. Here, he seemed to be constantly wound up, snappy and argumentative.

She played and watched TV with the boys in a room at the back of the house that they called the nursery. It was unlike the other rooms in the house – stuffed full of cosy, comfortable chairs, shelves of books and toys, and an old TV with a precarious pile of videos on top. Elisabeth frostily asked Pip to put the boys to bed as she had a headache. Afterwards, Pip sat for a while longer, watching TV and the door, hoping that Leo might make an appearance, but he didn't, so she turned in herself.

It was only when she reached her room that she realised she had nothing with her – no toothbrush, no pyjamas, no clean clothes for tomorrow. She snuck into the bathroom on her side of the corridor and cleaned her teeth as best she could using toothpaste from a tube she found there, smearing it around her teeth with her finger. She would have loved to have soaked for ages in the tub, but there was no lock on the door. And what to do about her clothes? Rosa wasn't her size and she couldn't even contemplate asking Elisabeth or Mrs von Feldstein. She realised that tomorrow was Sunday, and the following day Easter Monday, so all the shops would be shut – how on earth was she supposed to make it through to Tuesday with one set of clothes and no washing things?

She listened to the sounds of everyone going to bed and made a decision. Taking a sheet from her bed, she crept downstairs to the laundry room in the cellar. She took off her clothes and wrapped herself in the sheet while she ran them through a quick wash cycle. In the morning, she'd borrow soap and shampoo from Rosa, and walk to a garage to see if she could buy a toothbrush.

When her clothes were clean, she took them back upstairs, still wrapped in the sheet. She'd hang them up and they'd be dry by the morning. The floorboards on the stairs were creaky, so she had to step lightly and hold on to the banister to keep from making too much noise. She needed a wee, so tiptoed towards the bathroom and was nearly there when she saw Elisabeth at the far end of the corridor.

They stared at each other. Pip knew what this looked like – she was naked under a sheet, clutching her clothes, right outside Leo's room. She panicked. *If I go back to my room and pretend I didn't see her, then it might just be possible that she wasn't there. She could be sleepwalking. She might not remember in the morning.* Pip ducked her head, turned around and dived into her room. She was desperate for the loo but didn't dare go out again. She searched around her room, under the bed, in the cupboard, and found a tatty-looking ceramic jug with a flower pattern on it. With a sigh of relief, she squatted over it and emptied her bladder. After she'd hung up her clothes and tucked the jug in the corner of the room, she put her lips against the wall nearest Leo's room, whispered, 'Goodnight', lay down and fell asleep.

Max and Ferdi woke her in the morning by bouncing on her bed.

'Come on, sleepyhead. Breakfast time. Billy and Dad are up, and Isa and Anna. Then you have to take us riding.'

She shooed them out and put on her clothes, which were still slightly damp but smelt better. As she walked alone down the corridor towards the dining room, she heard raised voices and paused outside the half-open door.

'...and I think you're doing it deliberately to wind up your mother,' Pip heard Mrs von Feldstein say.

Leo said acidly, 'You think I'd study medicine to wind someone up? In what world is that even possible?'

'We simply don't understand it, Leopold. You have such a good brain and it belongs to Feldstein AG, not to some germy hospital or dreary waiting room.'

'My brain doesn't belong to anyone but me. And you don't understand it because you never listen. I don't want to work for the family. I've looked at the company in detail, with Dad, and there's nothing that interests me.'

'It shouldn't be a question of interesting you, rather how you can give back to the family what it has given to you. Look around you. All this – it has to be earned.'

'Billy can earn it, then. I'm not interested – either in the job or in the "all this".'

'We'll see where your so-called hockey career lands when we pull the plug on your allowance.'

There was silence. Pip thought, *How could they be so disdainful of Leo's hockey, when he's about to be captain of the German team? Why aren't they proud of him? What is wrong with these people?*

'Ah, now we have your attention. You like the allowance, don't you, young man, but you're not willing to give anything back for it.'

'I play for Germany. I play for my country, for nothing, and I'm the best in the world at what I do.' Leo's voice was low and dangerous. 'And I want to be a doctor, for Christ's sake. Not a pimp or an arms dealer or a brain-dead corporate robot. You want me to give that up to work in an office for the rest of my life, doing something that will slowly but surely kill me?'

'Don't be so dramatic. You are so grouchy. And really, why haven't you managed to shave yet and change your clothes? There are standards. A shower and a smart shirt and chinos, surely you can manage that.'

'It's not important. I can't think about that sort of stuff at the moment. If the way I look is offensive to you, then I'll leave.'

'This is supposed to be a family week together. For your mother. So that you can all be together again.'

'And yet Pip's doing everything with the boys and Mum makes it clear she doesn't want anything to do with them. Same old story.'

'Would you please stop sticking up for that au pair girl? What is it about her that you all find so wonderful? I can't see it myself.'

'Nothing. There's nothing wonderful about her,' said Leo, and Pip deflated a little. 'She's good at her job. The job that Mum should be doing but can't be bothered.'

'That's a cheap shot. Give your mother another chance.'

'I have done. More than once. And all I get for it is criticism from you about what I'm studying or wearing. For once can't we have a conversation that doesn't involve slagging someone off?'

'Please lower your voice. You're behaving like a spoilt child.'

'There's only one spoilt child in this family.' Pip heard the sound of a chair scraping along the floor. 'I'm leaving after breakfast.'

He was coming out of the door. Pip looked around her – there was nowhere to hide. She heard footsteps in the opposite direction, too; the children coming down the stairs. She turned back to the door as Leo came out, but he didn't seem to see her, just strode past. She waited until the children caught up with her and went in to breakfast.

Billy appeared with Dominic and Elisabeth. Pip didn't look at Elisabeth, but sat quietly, hoping she wouldn't say anything.

'Where's Leo? Thought he was feeling OK again,' said Billy with a yawn.

Mrs von Feldstein said, 'He's leaving, to go back to Munich. Philippa, he seems to be of the opinion that you should leave too. Would you like to go back to Munich with him?'

Faces turned to her. The children were quiet, not understanding. Pip looked at Elisabeth, whose face made it clear that she had seen Pip last night, and that she knew exactly what Pip was up to with regards to her firstborn son and heir.

'No. Not if I can be helpful here,' said Pip, screaming inwardly. She'd be missing out on a couple of hours alone with Leo. But what choice did she have? 'I can take the children to their riding lessons and help Marlene in the kitchen until everyone's back on their feet.'

'Thank you, Pip, that would be very kind,' said Dominic.

After breakfast, she took the children upstairs to change into their riding clothes. She came out of their room and saw Leo, a bag slung over his shoulder, talking to Billy.

'You should come back too. If you're not with me, you won't train properly this week.'

Billy shook his head. 'I'll stay with Mum a bit. I can handle her. You go, I'll come back on Wednesday, OK? Hey, did you know Franzi's in town? You planning to see her, you old dog?' They saw Pip, which was a shame because Pip thought they might be talking about that famous swimmer and she would've loved to have heard the answer. Or maybe not.

Leo said to Pip in a gruff voice, 'Are you coming back with me? They don't need you here, you know. They're being lazy.'

'I said I'd stay and help out.' *Yes yes yes, please can I come with you?*

'I'll bring her back on Wednesday,' said Billy. 'By then everyone will be OK. And I'll do some running and swimming. No booze. All right?'

Leo shrugged and walked past Pip, not saying goodbye.

Billy walked with her and the boys to the riding stables, and afterwards went for a run along the lake. Pip returned to the house, tidied the children's rooms, peeled a mountain of potatoes for Marlene and spent an excruciating ten minutes trying to explain to Mrs von Feldstein why she'd gone to the toilet in an antique jug and then left it in her room. Apparently, Marlene had gone in there to clean and shown it to her employer in disgust. *The girl is a savage.* Wearily, Pip went outside with her book and sat on a chair on the lawn near a pretty boathouse. Rosa and Stefan wobbled out to join her about an hour later.

'We're so sorry you've had to be our nursemaid, Pip,' Rosa said. 'I can't understand how this thing swept through all of us and you remained unscathed. You must have a stomach lined with steel.'

Pip laughed. 'That's what my... mum used to say.'

'How can we ever thank you?'

'Well, actually, it's a bit awkward but I came here in such a rush, I forgot to bring any spare clothes or wash stuff. Can I borrow some shampoo, and can you tell me where I can buy clothes and a toothbrush around here?'

Rosa looked appalled. 'You poor thing. Yes, of course; borrow anything you like from me – my washbag is in my room. And I'll take you into Lindau tomorrow. A friend of ours has a lovely little shop there; she'll open it for you if we ask her.'

'I'll take her,' said Billy, who had run up behind them. 'Shit, that hurt. I'm zapped.' He took off his T-shirt, lay on the grass behind them and started doing sit-ups.

'Take it easy, you've been ill.'

'I'm fine. Fit as a fiddle. I think all that puking has cleaned out my system. What do you need in town, Pippi Longstocking?'

'I forgot to bring any clothes.'

'We'll go first thing tomorrow. Then we can have lunch somewhere. I'll get you drunk and have my wicked way with you.'

'Leave the poor girl alone,' laughed Rosa. 'Actually, don't; make sure you treat her. She's been a lifesaver these last few days.'

Pip stayed out of the way of the grown-ups for the rest of the day. Most of them went sailing and she took the time to explore the grounds, the woods and the gardens by the lake. No matter what Leo said about the house, it was spectacular here. She gazed across the shimmering lake, behind which the snow-capped Alps rose like islands in the sky. When Leo was older, he could bulldoze the house and build something prettier on the land. *What a life*, she thought, *to live in a place like this and ride and sail and play tennis all day.* But maybe Leo found it too boring, too easy. It would probably suit Billy better, to be the playboy landowner.

The following day, Rosa told Pip she'd take over the childcare duties for the day. Billy took her in a little speedboat back towards the island where the train station was, mooring it at a wooden jetty. They walked through the streets of the old town until they came to a shop in a cobbled alleyway. Billy rang the bell.

'You know what would be fun – pretend you don't speak German,' he said. Pip was about to ask why as the door opened.

'Ah, so this is the young lady who needs something to wear,' said a woman who kissed Billy and shook Pip's hand. She spoke in German.

Pip shrugged, pretending to look confused.

Billy said, 'She's English – doesn't understand a word of German.'

Pip stood, feeling awkward, as he rifled through the racks of clothes, pulling out sundresses and tops and skirts with the shop lady. They made a pile of clothes on a chair in the middle of the shop, chatting about the colours and the styles and, excruciatingly, her body.

'She has lovely legs, very athletic,' said the shop lady. 'Such a slim figure, not too busty, which will suit more something like this… or this… oh no, darling, not that. We don't want to make her look too old. She has a lovely innocence to her – don't spoil that.'

It was eye-wateringly embarrassing. Pip was glad to escape to the dressing room. The shop lady bustled in and out with more clothes, pushing Pip out into the shop to show Billy. He bought three strappy summer dresses for her, four T-shirts and two pairs of shorts. He added a pair of calf-length trousers to the pile, and a blue cardigan.

He said, 'Oh, she needs underwear, too.'

'Something like this – to please you? Or more like this?' She held up two pairs of bras and pants – one lacy and sexy; the other plain. Pip reached out her hand towards the latter.

'Shy, is she? Well, I'm sure she'll warm up for you soon, Billy. They all do, in the end. Even a sweet little baby like this one.'

God, this is mortifying.

'This is so much fun, don't you think?' whispered Billy.

'I'm going to kill you.'

Billy paid for everything and walked Pip, face still flaming, to a restaurant by the water. He ordered a bottle of white wine and some water for himself.

'Right. Let's get you good and sloshed.'

'Your English is perfect,' said Pip as the cool liquid slipped down her throat. 'You don't even have the slightest German accent.'

'I love speaking it, better than German most of the time. You Brits have so many excellent swear words. And you have about a thousand ways to say drunk.'

'Like sloshed. And hammered.'

'Bladdered, battered, shit-faced.'

She laughed. 'Rat-arsed, tanked, plastered, blotto.'

'Trashed, trousered, trolleyed and my personal favourite – wankered. I wonder who made them up.'

'Some drunkard, I expect.'

Billy seemed to know everyone at the restaurant. People stopped to say hello, some pulling up chairs and joining them for a drink. He kept Pip's glass full, saying she was drinking for the both of them. When she was away from the castle with its long, chilly corridors and gilt mirrors and suits of armour and antique chairs you weren't allowed to sit on, just with Billy, she could relax and be herself. She was all wrong with the von Feldstein elders. They were stiff and bony and unwelcoming, with their own set of rules she could never hope to learn. No wonder Leo avoided it, given half a chance.

When it was time to go home, Pip stood up and had a head rush. Billy gripped her elbow.

'Oops. Mullered. There's another one. I think I may've had too much to drink.'

'It's not possible to have too much to drink.' He slung his arm around her and walked her back to the boat. She nearly fell into the water when she stepped onto it, wobbling it from side to side, but he steadied her and sat her down.

Back at the house, they sat by the water's edge in the chilly dusk, his arm still around her. She shivered and he nudged in closer.

'You're not going to try and kiss me again, are you?' she said.

He laughed. 'No way. Not after your feedback last time. Unless you want to practise a bit? See if I can do it better this time?'

'Thanks, but no thanks. You're so lovely, though. Like an older brother.'

'That's the saddest rejection I've ever had.' But he was grinning.

She stood up with her bag of new clothes. 'Thanks for these, Billy. I had a lovely day. I guess I should go up to the house now, see if anyone needs me.'

'Righto, little sis. I'm off out again – the night is young and all that. Sleep tight, Pip, and don't let the bedbugs bite.' He jumped into the boat and zoomed off into the darkening night.

Until she left on Wednesday, Pip worked hard with the children and Marlene in the kitchen, determined to give the elder von Feldsteins no reason to criticise her. Dominic, Rosa and Stefan were slowly coming back to life, and on Wednesday morning she said goodbye to them and the boys and climbed into the car with Billy. She'd never been in a Porsche before. Billy drove ridiculously fast. Pip pretended not to notice, hoping that he'd become bored of showing off and drive normally. He didn't.

'What did you think of my grandparents?'

'They frightened the life out of me.'

'Ha – yes, they tend to do that. Leo and I used to hide in that playroom when we were Max and Ferdi's age, trying to avoid them. Of course, I think they preferred that anyway – they're not exactly child friendly.'

'You seem to rub along with them OK nowadays.'

'I do, because I'm a charming bastard. Leo won't play the game, though. He'll probably be cut out of the will one of these days.'

'All the more for you, then.'

He laughed. 'Harsh but fair. I won't keep it to myself, though – what's mine is his.'

'I'm not sure he'll want it, will he?'

He paused. 'You're pretty astute, you know, Pip. For a girl of your tender years. Sweet little baby.'

'Thanks. And may I congratulate you on using the word astute?'

'Did I do it right?'

'Yes, gold star for you. You're not as stupid as you look.'

'As my older brother often tells me, I'm just about clever enough to know how stupid I am.'

Pip chuckled. Holly used to say the exact same thing about herself. Billy was a male version of Holly – insanely talented, ludicrously good-looking, universally loved. She sighed and settled her head back on the seat. 'What's next for you? How long to go now?'

He knew what she was talking about. 'Five months. Next week, first outdoor Bundesliga game. Season lasts for two months. End of May, Champions Trophy in Amstelveen. That's in Holland.'

Pip knew that – she'd watched Holly play there in 1993. The Dutch hockey crowds were something else: a sea of orange, nine thousand screaming fans, players fêted like rock stars. She had loved watching hockey in Holland.

'End of July, three matches against Korea in three different German cities. Start of August, in Hamburg against GB, Holland and Korea. Mid-August, selection. Then, all being well, first week of September, Sydney, here we come.'

She closed her eyes. It was like this every Olympic year. Everything stopped. Nothing else mattered. Every year of her life that she could remember had been marked by a World Cup or a Champions Trophy or European Championships, but most of all, the four-yearly Olympics. For hockey teams, the Olympic gold was the biggest prize of all. Pip's life was measured not by her birthdays or achievements at school, but by her sister's injuries or goals or medals won and lost. That was how it had been with the Mitchells and the Costas. And now with the von Feldsteins.

Troy had told her once that for him, it wasn't in the ambulance when Holly was pronounced dead that he'd fully comprehended what had happened. It was when he was dialling the Mitchells' number to tell them. He'd paused before he pressed the last number, and had to hang up and start again several times.

'I just couldn't do it,' he said. 'I knew that you were asleep on the other side of the world, no idea about Holly, no clue what had happened. Your lives were still intact and normal, and I was about to call and say a few words that would crush them forever.' He cried as he went on, 'I had this picture in my mind of you three in your house, perfectly happy and oblivious. I wanted to leave you be, never tell you. And you'd just carry on, in a different life, everything as it was.'

Pip couldn't help wondering if there was a parallel universe somewhere out there, where Holly was a 'civilian' – a teacher or a banker or a mother – and Pip was a normal person, with a big sister who was alive and had normal problems like mortgages and flat tyres on her bike and whether to go on holiday to France or Italy this summer. That Pip would be happier than this one, she thought. That Pip wouldn't have a clue about base strength and complex carbohydrates and how long it took to recover from a hamstring pull. That Pip would never have met Troy Costa. She'd be working as an au pair for a normal family, where Billy and Leo were students and Max and Ferdi played computer games and she took them to playdates on Thursday afternoons. In that world, there was no need for her lies. In that world, by the time she'd met Leo and fallen in love with him, she would have had a couple of normal boyfriends, with the things under her belt that teenagers had under their belts – a broken heart, a crush on a boy in the year above, a holiday romance.

But Pip was here, in this universe. The one where she loved Leo but didn't know how to tell him, or how to behave with him in the way that a normal nineteen-year-old person would behave. There must be signs, but she had never learnt how to read them. She could ask Nadine, or Tiny, or even Rosa, and they would tell her what they knew about men. But she already had years of watching other people in films fall in and out of love and kiss and have sex and flirt and betray each other and argue and make up and whisper sweet nothings and laugh at each other's jokes and take each other's clothes off and sneak out of bed quietly in the mornings and die in each other's arms and hold hands in the park and eat from each other's forks and throw vases at each other and have affairs and get down on bended knees and play in the snow with each other and frankly not give a damn and sing on the top of a piano and catch a glimpse of someone from a train and sing in the rain and ask if they'd like to seduce you and carry you out of a factory in a white uniform and be king of the world and promise they'll never leave you and always have Paris.

No, Pip didn't need the advice of others. She needed to do it herself.

13

May 2000

As Pip let her in the front gate, Tiny said, 'You look different. Why are you so… why are you glowing?'

'Don't know what you're talking about.'

Tiny gasped. 'Did you sleep with Billy?'

'Billy? What? No. He's in Holland at the Champions Trophy. Has been all week.'

'Why are you whispering? Are Dominic and the boys here?'

'No, they left this morning – Germany's in the final tomorrow against Holland and they wanted to go and watch.'

On their way to the patio, Pip and Tiny passed a row of seedlings, sunflowers that Pip had planted with Max and Ferdi last month.

'Anyway, why Billy? Why would you ask that?'

'Because – oh, you know, some things people say.'

'Which things? Which people?'

Tiny shrugged. 'It's just that you flirt all the time, you and Billy.'

'I do not. Well, not that much.'

'And you dance. And you spend a lot of time with each other.'

'And he slept with my friend at New Year. And I work for his dad.'

'Ah. Oh, yes. I see. Well, don't worry about it, anyway. It's just gossip. Hockey clubs are terrible for gossip.'

I know, thought Pip. *I know about hockey clubs.*

'But you still haven't told me why you're glowing. If it wasn't Billy, who was it?'

'What makes you think it was a someone? I might just be in a good mood.'

Tiny looked at her sceptically.

'OK, OK, I admit it. I went on a date last night.'

'And?'

'And it was nice.'

Tiny pulled a face. 'God, I hope not. Who was it? Anyone from the hockey club? Anyone I know? It wasn't Pim, was it?'

'No. Please stop pairing me off with hockey players. It was a friend of Tara's, a student. Tara's been asking me for a while if she could set me up with her friend Sven who's single and so I said yes.'

'Very daring of you.'

'Well, I was in a daring mood. I asked myself, *What would Anya Amasova do?* and so I said yes.' Pip hadn't been in a daring mood so much as a desperate one. She had, predictably, done nothing about her vow six weeks ago to go out with other men and discover the magic formula for being a normal nineteen-year-old. How was she supposed to meet men anyway? She was wary of the hockey club and its hotbed of rumours that spread like wildfire. And then she remembered Tara's friend. She was fed up with herself – she'd come to Germany to try and leave behind her the years of staying in her room, feeling sorry for herself and waiting for Troy. Now it was a different room and a different man – but it had to stop. Hence the blind date.

What she couldn't tell Tiny was that she'd gone out with Sven for practice. She didn't know the first thing about men. She didn't know how to flirt with them, or how to behave on dates. She didn't know what food or drinks to order. How far was she supposed to go with them? How do people know these things? She didn't even know how to kiss men. With Troy, it occurred to her, there hadn't been much kissing. And before him, she'd kissed the sum total of one boy at a party after GCSEs, which didn't count because he had train-track braces and it had been a little bit revolting and a lot metallic. But how could she tell Tiny she needed practice, when Tiny knew she'd had a boyfriend? And undoubtedly she would want to know for whom Pip wanted to practise, and that wasn't something Pip could share with Tiny, now or ever, probably.

And there was also the small matter of Leo and Billy playing in Amstelveen against the Australians. Troy would be there, and yet again Pip fretted that they would talk about her, but berated herself for her ridiculous self-obsession. Why, in the middle of a tournament, would any of them give her even a second's thought when they were fighting for every ball, concentrating on not getting injured and sussing out the opposition teams for the last time before the Olympics? Leo had rung Dominic – they'd beaten the Aussies on Friday, Billy scored two goals and was shown a yellow card, and they were playing Holland on Sunday, without Billy because he had a hamstring strain; nothing bad but they wanted to rest him. Leo had four spare tickets, which were like gold dust because it was Holland and the final was sold out. Dominic had asked Pip if she wanted to go, but she panicked and said no, so he took the boys and one of their friends from the club.

Pip had agreed to a double date with Sven, Tara and her boyfriend the week before, and last night she'd met Sven alone at a restaurant. It was awkward. Drink-too-much-wine awkward.

They went back to his apartment and had sex: real, proper sex with prolonged kissing and slow undressing, and more kissing and he'd even gone down on her, which was quite an eye-opener.

Tiny insisted on hearing all the bedroom details. She clapped her hands together. 'You are such a wicked slut. Love it. Will you see him again?'

'We swapped numbers. But…'

'But what?'

'I don't know, I'm not sure about him.'

Tiny said, 'Go on, call him now.'

'No way. It only happened last night. And also maybe again this morning.' Pip wiggled her eyebrows and they both laughed. 'Look, it's nothing serious. I like him, but it's not that overwhelming feeling that I must see him again. You know?'

'Are you saying it's casual sex?'

'Might be.'

'Pip Mitchell, what's got into you? Apart from Sven's tongue, that is. Frankly, I'm shocked at the change in you. One night of passion and you become a total floozy.'

'Ha ha. We don't have much in common.' Pip had asked Tara whether Sven played sport, and when Tara replied that she thought he was the least sporty person she knew, Pip said, 'Perfect.'

Had she thought about Leo at the restaurant and wished it had been him sitting opposite her? Yes, she had. And had she thought about him again when she and Sven were at his flat, when he was driving her crazy with whatever he was doing down there, and when she'd had her first ever orgasm? Yes, definitely. It wasn't her finest hour, it wasn't fair to Sven, but yes, she had. It occurred to her afterwards, as she drifted off to sleep in his bed, that most normal people would have been thinking, if they were thinking of anyone else, of Billy when he was with Roxy, but he hadn't been there in her head, not for a second. Oh God, Tiny was right, she was a floozy. And she was in so deep with Leo that not even the best sex she'd ever had would erase how much she loved him.

Later, Pip wrote an email entitled *Bedroom Details* to Nadine about the date and the sex-practice. Nadine's reply came straight away – *Proud of you. Keep up the good work, you big, gorgeous slut.*

The following week, the house was full again. Dominic collected Elisabeth from Lindau and brought her back to Munich. Leo and Billy came over for a swim on Tuesday morning. Billy said he'd stay all week but Leo left straight afterwards, making what sounded like an excuse about seeing his university tutor. Pip realised with a pang that, now Elisabeth was back home, she'd see less of Leo, who would avoid contact with his mother. It was unfair to him, to Dominic and to the boys, but there it was. She had to get used it.

On Wednesday morning, Pip returned to the house after her run to find Billy and Elisabeth on the patio, relaxing on the sunloungers.

'Philippa, did you remember Maximilian's PE kit today?' said Elisabeth.

'Umm, no, he has PE on Mondays.'

'Oh, silly me. Could you go over the house with a duster and perhaps a vacuum today? I do like it spick and span. If you have time,' she said pointedly.

'Of course,' said Pip. She went downstairs to Martina's cupboard, fetched the duster and started with the bookshelves in the living room. Through the open windows drifted Elisabeth's whiny voice.

'I don't know what that girl does all day. Dominic pays her a fortune and she just seems to hang around here. She may as well keep herself busy. I told Martina she could have the rest of the summer off. Now I'm back, I can take care of Maximilian and Ferdinand and *she* can take on the household tasks.'

'Are you sure you're up to that, Mum? Why don't you let Pip carry on with the boys? She's really good with them.'

'Nonsense, Billy. How can you say that? The best thing for children is their own mother. No, Philippa needs something to do. I might suggest she signs up for a language course in town.'

'Her German is perfect. She doesn't need to do a course.'

'Then a cookery course. She can't cook. Everything she cooks is burnt – probably because her head is always stuck in a book. Also, she can't drive. What is the point of her, I wonder?' Elisabeth paused. 'And I think it's time she understands that she needs to stop stargazing.' Her voice was hard.

'Whatever do you mean?'

'I've seen her fluttering her eyelashes at you. You lead her on.'

'Mum—'

'You can't give these people hope. It's cruel.'

These people? What is she going on about?

Billy chuckled. 'You're letting your imagination run wild. Pip isn't like that. She hasn't shown the slightest interest in me or Leo since the moment she got here.'

'Is she one of those... sapphists?'

Billy roared with laughter. 'Because she doesn't fancy me or Leo? Oh, Mum, you should hear yourself. That's a classic. I'm absolutely certain she has no gold-digging or lesbian tendencies. She's good with children. She's quite sensible and awfully good fun. You should give her a chance. You might like this one.'

'Just as long as you don't,' said Elisabeth.

Pip left the room and vacuumed upstairs. By the time she turned off the Hoover, their conversation had, thank goodness, moved on from her. They were talking about how difficult it was to resist alcohol and how tempted they were, all the time, to drink. Billy said they could be dry together.

When she had finished cleaning and showered, Pip decided to escape out of her back door, to go to Rosa's shop or down to the river. But Billy was alone on the patio, lying on his sunlounger in swimming shorts and sunglasses, listening to the radio. He motioned her over.

'Mum's upstairs having a nap,' he whispered. 'You don't have to make yourself scarce.'

'Is it that obvious?'

'Only to me.' He smiled at her. 'It's OK, she's like this with every au pair. Ignore her if she's snarky.' He patted the sunlounger next to him and Pip sat. 'I know she's not easy. You just have to understand where she's coming from. She wants to get better and come back to the family, but when you're here she doesn't feel useful. But Max and Ferdi need you to stick around. Whenever the au pair leaves, it's more disruption and Mum can't cope and we have a terrible time of it, then she goes back to the clinic and Dad has to find a new au pair.'

'Maybe it'll be different this time,' said Pip hopefully.

'Yes, maybe,' said Billy, not so hopefully.

Pip was silent. She felt sorry for them, even Elisabeth. But mostly Max and Ferdi. However rude Elisabeth was to her, Pip wanted to protect the boys from the worst of the disruption. And if Billy and Leo needed her to provide stability so that they didn't have to be involved in the mess she was inevitably going to cause, she would do it because she owed them that.

'I'll stick around. Whatever happens,' she said.

'Good girl.' He patted her hand. 'Now, can you clear up something for me? Did you or did you not try to sneak into my room at the lake house at Easter? Mum says she saw you in the middle of the night, up to no good. But I distinctly remember you saying you had only sisterly feelings for me. Care to explain?'

'I was on my way to the loo.' Pip blushed, but relief flooded through her. Wrong brother.

'Thought so. Ah well. Now, would you mind cleaning all the bathrooms? And I think I saw a speck of dust on the stairs.'

'Shh. She might hear. Then you'll be for it.'

'Oh, not me, I'm the favourite son.' He stretched his arms above his head and reached for his feet, wincing.

'Hamstring?'

'It's OK. I've got physio at the club this afternoon. Nothing to worry about. Bloody annoying to miss the final in Amstelveen, though.'

'Still, if it means you're fit for Sydney…'

'Yup. And I did screw up the Aussies' chances last Friday. Two goals. They didn't know what hit them.'

'Even though you do say so yourself.'

'Wish you'd been there to see it. One of their players – total headcase – it's like he has a personal vendetta against Leo. But he can't get past him. No one can.'

Pip lay back on the lounger and looked up at the sky. She knew who he was talking about and didn't know what to say, so she stayed silent.

Billy continued. 'This guy was raging by the end of it. Refused to shake hands and there was some trouble in the dressing room; of course they didn't tell us exactly what.'

Pip had seen Troy like that before, and had heard how he'd been when he was coaching in Canterbury after Holly's death. She felt desperately sorry for him.

'He's a world-class player. But rumour has it, he's not very popular in the team. Leo thinks that's the be-all and end-all – the team is everything. He reckons this fella will self-destruct soon. Hopefully in Sydney.'

'How do you mean?'

'He can't control himself when things go wrong, and he can't handle the pressure of the big events. And there's nothing bigger than the Olympics; for hockey, it's bigger than any other tournament, even the World Cup. This time it's in his home country, his home town, and it might be his last Olympics. And it's the first one since his wife died.'

Shit. I can't leave that statement unquestioned. He'll expect me to ask about the wife. Pip faked a yawn. 'Sounds like he's got a lot on his plate. You'll have to tell me more about it another time. I need to go into town before I collect your brothers.'

Billy looked at his watch. 'I'll give you a lift in, if you like.'

'It's OK, really—'

'No problem. I'll just shower and then I'll drop you off... where?'

'Marienplatz.'

Pip waited for Billy, and when he came downstairs again, freshly showered, she said, 'Oh, you know what, I don't think I've got time after all. I don't want to miss pickup time.'

Billy shrugged. 'OK. Fair enough. Laters. Oh, I forgot to ask – what are you doing on Saturday night?'

'Nothing.'

'You are now – it's Leo's birthday. Party at the Sixth Floor. Don't tell him or he'll say he doesn't want a party.'

'Why are you having one, then?'

'Because if Leo got his way, we'd never have any parties.' He made the sign of a square in the air in front of him. 'See you, Pipsqueak.'

Pip made herself some lunch and, when she heard Elisabeth moving about upstairs, fled to the basement to eat it there. It was a beautiful day and she had an hour or so before school pickup time. She weighed up whether it was worth the risk of bumping into Elisabeth if she snuck out of the back door and left to find a bench in the woods where she could read undisturbed. How everything had changed since Elisabeth had returned. The house wasn't a place where she could relax any more, except in her bedroom. Even the smell of it had changed – everywhere, she smelt traces of Elisabeth's cloying perfume, which caught in the back of Pip's throat and lingered in rooms long after she'd left them.

Out of the back door, through the garden, worse luck: Elisabeth was on the patio, reading a magazine, flicking over the pages with her perfectly manicured and painted fingernails.

'Oh, there you are. Could you nip over to the organic market and pick up a few things for me? Here's a list.'

Pip looked at her watch. 'Sorry, I'll have to do it later. I have to pick up Max and Ferdi.'

'Oh, no, I'll do the school run from now on. Take the list for me, and do be careful to buy exactly this brand of olives. Oh, and you may as well go to the dry-cleaner's on the way back – I need this dress cleaned. Make sure they do it by Saturday night. Dominic and I have an engagement.'

'Are you going to Leo's party too?' Pip said without thinking.

Elisabeth blinked at her. 'What do you mean, Leopold's party?'

'I...' Pip realised she'd put her foot in it. 'Billy's planning a surprise party.'

'What on earth for?'

'For his birthday.'

Elisabeth stared at Pip, her thin mouth pursed. *Shit*, thought Pip, *she's forgotten her own son's birthday. And I've pointed it out to her. Double shit.*

'My dear girl, the last thing Leopold wants is some wild party.'

'I...' Elisabeth seemed to be blaming *Pip* for the party.

'And are you under the impression that you will be attending this event?'

'No, I... yes, well, Billy asked me.'

'Well, he can un-ask you. We'll need you to be here with Maximilian and Ferdinand. This is your job, isn't it?'

'Yes, that's fine. Sorry, yes, of course.'

'As of now, you're going to have to ask me first if you have any plans. I will need you to be more... present. You have a lot of spare time, don't you?'

'Well, yes, but I'm happy to do more. To help.'

'That goes without saying. Things are going to change around here.' Elisabeth flapped the shopping list and the dress at Pip impatiently. It was a dismissal.

'Umm. I... do you have...?'

'What is it, Philippa? I can't understand when you mumble.'

'It's just that, I'll need some... money. If... for the shopping. Please.'

'Money? Oh, goodness.' She fluttered her hand over her forehead, like Pip was a particularly irksome fly she wanted to swat away. 'Dominic will reimburse you. Make sure you keep the receipt.'

Pip took a deep breath. She didn't have enough money in her room to pay for this shopping. She'd have to walk all the way to the post office.

'Is there a problem?'

'No. I'll... goodbye.' She had to be helpful. She had to try and stay calm when Elisabeth was winding her up. Swallow her pride. She left the garden, walking towards the main road. As she put her phone in her pocket, she noticed a missed call from Dominic. She rang him back and he picked up straight away.

'Pip. Hello, sorry to disturb. I forgot to tell you before I left for work. If Elisabeth says she's going to pick up Max and Ferdi, please make sure you're on standby. It's the sort of thing she forgets, if she has a nap or something else distracts her. It's just a matter, I'm afraid, of keeping an eye on the time and if it looks like she's not going to manage it, to pop round to the school yourself.'

'Oh. Elisabeth's asked me to go to the market and I have to go to the post office first to withdraw some money, and she said she was going to pick up the boys every day. I'm so sorry, I didn't know, otherwise I would have made sure I was there.'

Dominic paused, and Pip could imagine him frowning. 'OK, no problem. I'll call her now and remind her. You go ahead to the market. Wait – why are you going to the market? Is Martina ill this week?' Martina usually shopped for the family groceries.

Pip cringed. 'I... it's just that Elisabeth has asked Martina to... not come. For the rest of the summer. So I can do more around the house and she – Elisabeth, I mean – can take care of the boys.'

Dominic sighed. 'OK. Don't worry, I'll sort this out.'

'I'm not worried. I can do more. Please don't tell her I was complaining or anything; I'd like to be more helpful to her. To you. To everyone.'

'Of course. I understand. I'll tell you what, I'll talk to her this evening. See if we can't find a compromise. And it'll be coming from me, so there's no need for you to worry that she'll think you're not doing a great job here. Which you are.'

'Thanks.'

'Right, goodbye.'

That evening, Pip put the boys to bed because Elisabeth was feeling tired, and afterwards read in her room, sitting on her bed. She was dreading seeing Elisabeth the following day, if Dominic was going to give her the impression that Pip had been trying to shirk off. She had to work hard, to make sure Elisabeth could rely on her and trust her. Also, Pip would have to take care how she behaved with Leo and Billy when Elisabeth was around – clearly Elisabeth thought she was after becoming the next Mrs von Feldstein. She wasn't too far off the mark, thought Pip as a warm glow spread through her. *You have to rein it in. Stop thinking about Leo.*

She set her alarm to wake her early the next morning. She was first in the kitchen and switched on the coffee machine before Leo arrived, waving the day's newspaper at her through the window.

'You're up early,' he said with a smile.

'So are you.' She took the paper. 'Coffee now or afterwards?'

They heard footsteps on the stairs. 'Here's Billy. Afterwards, please.'

Billy, who was already wearing his swimming shorts, waved sleepily at Pip and went straight out to Leo, where they stretched and talked in low voices. She tried not to stare as Leo took off his T-shirt.

Dominic interrupted her ogling with a polite cough. 'Morning, Pip. Before Max and Ferdi come down – I had a word with Elisabeth last night. We'll ask Martina to come back and she'll do what she always does, but if there's any extra bit of shopping or cleaning Elisabeth needs, I said you'd be pleased to help. Does that sound OK?'

'Yes, sounds great. Thank you.'

'She's adamant she wants to walk to school for the afternoon pickup; she won't hear of you doing it. She didn't like my suggestion that you remain on standby if she's too... umm... busy.' He looked worried. 'But she's sometimes unreliable and I don't know what else to suggest.'

'Could Rosa be the standby?'

'Good idea. I'll stop in on the way to work.' Pip stood with Dominic at the window, looking out at the pool where Leo and Billy were doing lengths. He sighed. 'I'm glad you're here, Pip. Not just for Max and Ferdi.'

Pip smiled. 'I'm glad I'm here, too. I'll go and wake them up.'

Elisabeth kept Pip busy with errands that took up a large part of her day. Pip didn't mind the work, but she hated the way Elisabeth talked to her. She shopped, she ironed, she cleaned, she cooked as best she could, she washed and tidied and dusted. Never once did Elisabeth smile or say please or thank you. Pip wondered why everyone thought that posh people had nice manners.

On Saturday, she set her alarm early again and went for a jog in the quiet streets. Through the woods, around the hockey club, past strawberry fields, down to the river and back again. She ran for an hour and felt euphoric from the exertion. The sky was overcast, but as she arrived back at the house, the sun broke through the clouds. There was a lone swimmer in the pool. She wiped the sweat off her face with her T-shirt and tapped him on the shoulder as he neared the end.

'Happy birthday.'

Leo pushed his goggles up onto his head and blinked at her. 'Didn't know you knew.'

She tapped the newspaper she held in her hand. 'Front-page headline in the *Süddeutsche Zeitung*: *Handsome Hockey Hero Turns Twenty-Six*.' She hadn't meant to say 'handsome' – it had slipped out – but he didn't seem to have noticed. Hopefully he had water in his ears. He looked at the paper, startled, as she unrolled it to show the real front page. 'Gullible, aren't you?'

'Very funny. Five more lengths to do.' He pushed off the side and she walked to her room via the back door, picking up the package she'd wrapped last night, returning to the kitchen and pouring herself a coffee.

She was hoping to be alone with Leo to give him her present, but there were thumps and bumps from above her head, which meant that Max and Ferdi were awake. She heard voices on the stairs before the whole family walked into the kitchen one after the other, carrying wrapped presents and cards. Pip slid along the bench so that she was right in the corner, underneath the countdown to Sydney (ninety-five days), and hoped no one would see her and her present. She stirred the frothy milk in her coffee with her spoon and kept her head down.

'Morning, Pip, what you got there?'

'Nothing,' murmured Pip, embarrassed. She wished she'd kept it in her room – or better still, stayed in her room herself. She was sweaty and thirsty from her run and hungry too, but didn't want to draw attention to herself or fetch her own food until everyone else had eaten.

Leo came in, wearing a red T-shirt and a pair of tracksuit bottoms he'd cut off into shorts. They sang and made a fuss of him. Dominic handed him a coffee and he sat down to open the presents: expensive clothes and CDs, sunglasses, a wallet and a Lonely Planet guide to Sydney.

Elisabeth said, 'It's not much, I'm afraid, but I'm sure you'll have a lot more at your party tonight.'

Billy groaned. 'Mum! It was supposed to be a secret.'

Elisabeth turned to Pip angrily. 'You didn't tell me it was a secret. For goodness' sake, Philippa, you've ruined everything.'

Pip was sure she'd told Elisabeth that Billy was organising a surprise party. 'Sorry,' she said.

'I knew anyway.' Pip glanced at Leo and thought she saw him smile quickly at her, but the smile was gone in a flash, as if it had never been there. 'I overheard Theo talking about it on the phone.'

He unwrapped some lacy lingerie with holes in strange and uncomfortable places, to which he remarked, 'Pretty tame for you, Bill.'

'One year he gave Leo a fibrater,' said Ferdi, giggling. 'Ugh, don't,' he squealed as Leo put the bra on Ferdi's head. 'Disgusting.' He picked it off with his fingertips and threw it to Pip. 'Here, you have it.'

Pip blushed and shook her head as Billy rocked with laughter. Max grabbed the knickers and threw them at her too.

'Oh, do take that away, Philippa. It's awfully tacky stuff, Billy, I don't know where you find it.'

'I found it in a sex shop in Schwabing. The vibrator too.'

'Can we go there, Billy?' asked Max.

'Sure. We can find some more stuff for Pip.' He winked at her.

Pip didn't know where to look – Max and Ferdi were shrieking with laughter and she couldn't look at Leo or Billy in case Elisabeth thought she was being flirtatious. She grabbed her present to Leo, which she hoped no one had seen, and the underwear from the table and ran out of the kitchen. As she left, she heard one of the boys ask Billy if there were also women in sex shops who sold kisses to men, which made Billy roar again as he tried to tell them about brothels. She needed to have a serious word with him about the stuff he was telling them, and talk to Max and Ferdi about respecting women before they were indoctrinated with Billy's dodgy ideas.

209

Once she'd thrown the idiotic underwear in the bin, showered and changed and calmed down, she decided to leave the house by the back door. It was her day off, after all, so she would spend it by the river, treating herself to lunch in a beer garden. She packed a rucksack with water, some fruit she kept in her room for just this eventuality, and a book. She was leaving her room and thinking about texting Tara or Tiny to see if they would join her, when she bumped into Leo, who'd been sitting on the old stone bench, but had stood up as soon as the door opened.

'Are you off out?'

'Yes. I… to the river, probably. I have to be back later this afternoon; your mum and dad are going out so I'm looking after the boys tonight.' She was aware she was gabbling, but couldn't stop. 'So I won't be able to come to your surprise party which I did tell your mum about, she must have forgotten—'

'Yes, she does that.'

There was silence between them.

'Did you have a present for me?'

'It's nothing. It's silly.'

'Well, why don't I be the judge of that?'

She dropped her eyes. 'I'll fetch it.' But when she turned back towards the door, she heard him follow her. They went inside her room, Pip's heart beating out of her chest. *He's never been in this room with me alone*, she thought. Except when he came back from Kuala Lumpur. Unless that had been a dream? She walked towards her bed and straightened her duvet, not wanting him to think she was slovenly, when she knew his bedroom was so neat. She hoped it didn't smell too bad in here, but feared it did – her running clothes and trainers were lying in the middle of the floor and they probably stank.

'Oh. You threw these away, did you?'

She whipped her head around. Leo was pointing at the lingerie in the bin.

'I… I thought… Did you want them? Sorry.' *Calm down. Don't be such an utter plank. Just because you're standing in your bedroom with the man of your dreams talking about sexy underwear, it's no reason to act like a moron.*

She didn't know what to do. Should she take them out of the bin for him? She wished he'd say something. He was standing still, looking at the bin. He didn't smile at her, or do or say anything.

Eventually, the silence became too much for her to bear. 'Your present?' she said, but it was barely audible. She cleared her throat. Her stomach was lurching. *Please don't be sick.*

He looked up at last, as if he'd been miles away. 'Pardon?'

'Your present?' She managed to pick it up from her bed and stretched out her arm. She took one step towards him and stretched out again, not wanting to be any closer. She might lose it and topple over at his feet.

His took it and stared at it for a moment. 'Thanks very much. It's lovely.'

'You haven't opened it yet.'

He tore off the paper and turned the book over in his hands. She said, 'It's one of my favourite books ever.'

He read the title: *The Power of One.*

'I mean, I don't even know if you like reading fiction. I'm sure you don't have time. It's silly really, sorry, I just thought, it's quite inspirational, and I thought because it's sort of about sport, and, you know, you're… sorry. I should have got you something better—'

'Thanks,' said Leo stiffly.

Pip felt the air go out of her. He hated it. It was boring. Of course he didn't read novels – he had his hockey and his medical degree, he read those sports psychology books and was busy with three brothers and loads of friends and parties and holidays and family commitments and a sick mother.

'Well, have a good birthday,' she said as she tried to sidle past him.

'Wait. Did you say you were going down to the Isar?'

Pip nodded.

'Want to jog down together? Oh, or are you meeting someone?'

'No… it's just, I already jogged today, for an hour.' *Damn it, why did I do that? Idiot girl.*

'Oh.'

'Won't Billy want to go with you?'

'He's resting until next week.'

Pip desperately tried to think. 'I could cycle beside you? While you run.' She'd done this many times for Holly when she was younger. Lifetimes ago. 'If you need to keep the pace up, that would be even better than me jogging; I'd only slow you down.'

'That would be great. If you don't mind?'

No, I don't mind at all. I can't think of anything better to do in the entire world. 'Don't you want to do something more exciting, on your birthday?'

'Still have to train.'

'And at least there's your party later.'

'Yes, can't wait,' he said sarcastically.

Pip put a second bottle of water and her rucksack into the basket of one of the bikes in the garage. She left the house separately from Leo and they met around the corner. The two of them set off for the river, at first in silence. Pip started pointing out her favourite parts of Solln – a house she liked because it was the only old one left in a street of new-build apartments; a park where she and Max and Ferdi played football; a café that sold delicious coffee. Leo was stopped three times by people wishing him happy birthday.

'Really was on the front page,' Pip teased.

Finally they reached the river and Leo turned left.

'Uh-uh, don't go that way. That's where the FKK is.'

'The what?'

'The FKK – Freikörperkultur. The nudist bathing area. Don't you know what that means? I thought you were German?'

'I know what "FKK" means, but I didn't know that you did. Good to see you've been learning the crucial words of my language.'

'I can swear like a sailor too.'

'Billy?'

'Got it in one. But I figure, if he's teaching me filthy words, maybe he'll hold off teaching Max and Ferdi, at least for a little while longer.'

'Good thinking. So how did you find out it was FKK? There's no sign.'

'The first time I jogged along there. I didn't know where to look for all that flesh. Never run so fast in my life.'

Leo laughed. 'I can imagine it. Must have been an interesting anatomy lesson.'

'Yes, if I'd needed a lesson in the effects of ageing on the human body. Sagging, wrinkling, drooping, et cetera. There was no one under the age of eighty.'

'Ah, I see.'

Pip pointed the other way. 'There's a good flat bit this way, if you want to do shuttles or sprints. I can time you.'

'Lead the way, coach.'

She sat on a log in the sunshine and timed Leo's sprints until he lay at her feet, gasping for breath.

'You going to be sick?'

'No.'

'Then you're not trying.'

'You're a hard taskmaster.'

'You'd better believe it.'

He lay on the ground, his eyes closed, with his head cradled in his hands and smiled. Pip couldn't help staring at him. His T-shirt was soaked with sweat, sticking to his body in all the right places. His arms and legs were so muscly and strong, she caught her breath as she imagined them wrapped around her. She could disappear into this man. She felt her eyelids dip and a stirring between her legs, her stomach rolling and catching, her head buzzing. She closed her eyes too, raising her face to the warm sun, and gripped the log to keep herself from falling off it.

She kept them closed as she heard him shifting on the ground. *Come to me. Kiss me. I'll do anything you want. I'm totally at your mercy.* Her blood pulsed through her body. She wanted to make him touch her by the power of her thoughts alone. She heard him move and tensed herself, ready. But the sounds were steps away from her. She opened her eyes and saw him beside the river, stripping off his T-shirt. He waded in and swam into the middle, turned and waved at her, beckoning her into the water.

She couldn't even stand up, let alone strip off and swim out to him. The river was about twenty metres wide at this section, sloping gently on both sides but with a deep drop in the middle and a strong current. She'd probably drown.

Go get him, tiger, said Tiny's voice in her ear.

Don't be such a chicken, said Nadine.

If it doesn't scare you shitless… said Holly.

'…it's not worth doing. Leave me alone, all of you,' mumbled Pip. She took a deep breath and unbuttoned her shorts, stepping out of them. Before she could change her mind, she raised her T-shirt over her head and walked to the river, which seemed to shimmer at the edges, over the pebbles on the sloping beach, looking down, concentrating on not tripping. The water was cold against her toes but she waded further until there was a drop-off. She dived under the water to cool her face and body, which felt as if they were on fire, and swam towards him. She felt like she was moving towards a firing squad. *Shoot me now.* Her heart pounded so strongly it hurt her.

'Hey,' he said softly, and smiled with one side of his mouth. The air between them changed. There was something forming inside her – a solid, small thing that she thought might be hope. He reached out his hand and she looked at it, paralysed. She couldn't touch him, she just couldn't. Otherwise she was going to dissolve into the water. 'What's wrong?'

She shook her head.

He moved closer to her. 'Don't you want to?' he said quietly. There were drops of water on his eyelashes.

She nodded, not trusting herself to speak.

'But…?'

'There's no but,' she whispered.

'Good, because I hate buts,' he said.

He kissed her. Every part of her body liquefied; she felt only his warm lips on hers and everything else slipped away. His hand was on her back, and she knew that if he let go, she'd sink. His body was warm, still, from the sprints. He put his tongue in her mouth, she couldn't breathe, she was drowning in him. She pushed his shoulders weakly with her hands, but he felt it and pulled away from her.

She felt tears in her eyes as she said, 'Don't.'

He didn't say anything, just looked at her, confused. His hands dropped off her and she had to struggle not to float away.

'I can't. I can't do this,' she said, louder than she meant to. She needed to be away from him. She swam further into the middle of the river and towards the opposite bank. As soon as she could, she put her feet down to steady herself.

'Pip, wait. What's wrong?' He was following her.

Please leave me alone. Please. Don't follow me. But do follow me. Don't leave me alone. Kiss me again.

She felt the stones beneath her feet and dragged herself through the water, up onto the shore, and collapsed on the sunny bank. She could see, over the other side of the river, the log where she'd been sitting and their clothes on the ground near it. She put her head in her hands and scrunched her eyes shut.

Please go away, please don't, I'm all yours, do whatever you like to me.

He sat down next to her, leaving space between them. 'I'm sorry. I didn't mean to scare you. I shouldn't have done that. Only I've been wanting to kiss you for so long and I thought – but I was wrong. I suppose it's Billy, is it?'

She looked up at him. 'Billy?'

'It's him you want.' It wasn't even a question. His voice was so flat and glum, she felt a tug in her heart.

'No.' She was trying to keep her hands from grabbing him and pulling him towards her. 'No, it's never been Billy.' She put her hands under her knees to stop them from shaking. 'Wait… What? You've been wanting to kiss me for how long?'

'Since the moment I met you. Well, after I'd got over the shock of you telling me via the art of storytelling that you witnessed my brother going down on my girlfriend. It's really not Billy?'

'Why would you think it was?'

'The way you talk to him. Look at him. Every time I see you, you're dancing with him or sharing some joke. You think he makes the sun shine for you. You told your friend he was lush. You let him stay with you in your room. You're always touching him. He teaches you filthy words. When he was hurt, you practically fainted. You kissed him in front of everyone. Dad says you pine when he's away and ask questions about him.'

Pip didn't know whether to laugh or cry. 'You really thought, all this time, that I was in love with your brother?'

'He's easy to love.' Leo looked miserable.

'Whoever said it should be easy? You should know this about me: I never seem to be able to choose the easy way. And I don't pine when Billy's away, I pine when *you're* away. And I talk to him and joke and flirt to get your attention, but you're so bloody Leo-ish, you give the impression you don't know I'm alive. You paid me to watch DVDs with him in my room. Remember? *He* touches me. *He* kissed me. And you never come near me.'

'Because if I did I knew I wouldn't be able to handle it.'

She stared at him. 'So what's changed now?'

'I think about you all the time, when I shouldn't be thinking about you. I'm hungry but I can't eat. I'm tired but I'm not sleeping. It's like… I'm unravelling. I had to do something, say something because otherwise I thought I might go mad.'

'Sorry.'

'Me too. The timing sucks.'

'What do we do? Three months until the Olympics. What do we do to… umm… ravel you up again?'

He smiled slowly. 'I can think of a few things.'

'Yeah?' She couldn't help smiling back at him. 'Like what?'

They kissed again, lowering themselves down until they were lying next to each other. Leo's hand stroked the back of her thigh and tugged her leg over his. She put her hands on his back and crushed herself against him. Waves of heat rushed through her body. She kissed his face, his neck, his shoulders, her breath quickening. He was shifting his weight on top of her and she knew she had to stop, before it was too late.

'No. No.' It wasn't in the least convincing, but she had to try to stop him. 'We can't do this. Not here.'

'Shall we go somewhere?'

'No. We can't.' She sat up. She tried to be firm. 'This is not going to happen. I think it's a really, really big mistake.'

'Why?'

She didn't answer.

'Why, Pip? You can't just stop there, in the middle of the best kiss of my entire life, and not give me a reason.'

'Because. I'm… not… I'm.' *The best kiss of his life.* How was she going to say this? 'I have things… I need to sort out. I… we haven't had that talk. We're doing everything the wrong way round, can't you see? We said we'd talk after Sydney. If we start this now, and then I tell you stuff later, and… it's a huge mess.'

'Do you mean your Australian boyfriend?'

'Ex. Yes. I need to talk to him and tell him it's over.'

'And is it?'

'You think I can kiss you like that and still be in love with someone else?'

Leo balked. 'You were in love with him?'

'No. I don't know. I thought I was. Let's not talk about him.' She was starting to panic. She had to try to avoid telling Leo any outright lies about Troy. 'I'll sort it out, I promise. Your dad's given me time off while you're in Sydney, I'll see him then and after that we can carry on where we left off. Is that enough? Will that help you focus?'

'I don't know. Either I'm going to have to stay away from you completely or you're going to have to be with me constantly. Every minute of the day. In that underwear.' He was fiddling with the strap of her bra.

'As long as it's not the stuff I threw away.' She tried to laugh, but her heart sank. 'You're busy, I have to work. Your mother has her eye on me. She already thinks I...' *Probably not wise to say anything more about fancying Billy.* 'She doesn't like me much.'

'She doesn't like any of our girlfriends.'

Pip felt a thrill. *Does this mean I'm his girlfriend?* 'Not even Roxy?'

Leo smiled at her. 'Especially not Roxy. Although the two of them are frighteningly similar. High-maintenance, spoilt, attention-seeking.'

'What did you see in Roxy, then?'

'I liked discussing Greek philosophy and quantum physics with her.'

Pip raised her eyebrows at him.

He laughed. 'OK, busted, I'm shallow. Do you forgive me?'

'Yes. I'm feeling quite shallow myself at the moment.' She trailed her fingers along the muscles on his arms. How could she have ever thought that he wasn't good-looking? 'But' – she stopped him kissing her again – 'we really can't. What if I tell you something about me, when we talk, and you hate me?'

'I could never hate you.' He moved towards her again and put his hands on her arms.

'I thought you had more self-control than this.' He was kissing her neck. She groaned.

'Come home with me,' he said. 'Back to the Sixth Floor.' His hands were all over her.

'They'll be setting up for your party.'

One of his fingers slipped under her knickers at the side, separating the wet material from her skin.

'A hotel, then?'

She felt her resolve melting away. 'Yes. No. Not today.'

'It's my birthday.' His other hand was on the clasp of her bra.

'I already gave you your present.'

'But I want another one.'

'Bet you anything you can't even remember what the book was called.'

She felt his lips smile on her neck. '*Power of One*. Your favourite book. Sports. Inspirational. Now pay up. You said anything.' He licked her ear, and at the same time, his fingers moved around inside her knickers to the front. She felt a powerful, tightening kick inside her and rose up on her knees, juddering against him, her legs squeezing against his fingers, a noise escaping from her throat, her embarrassment making it end as soon as it had begun.

Oh God.

She sank down again and looked at his bare chest.

He had stopped moving.

She couldn't look at his eyes. *What just happened? He barely touched me.* They were on a riverbank, in broad daylight, in plain view of anyone who might walk past, and she'd come? It wasn't even physically possible, was it? With Troy it had never happened; with Sven it had seemed to take ages. How could it have been so quick? She felt ashamed, exposed. Young.

'You beautiful girl,' he said, and she looked at him underneath her heavy eyelids.

She was confused. She hadn't wanted to have sex with him until after she'd told him about Holly, and if necessary, about Troy. He said he wouldn't hate her but he would, if he knew. She wanted to curl up, disappear, remove herself from him, but he wrapped his arms around her and held her tight.

'Hey. Don't cry,' he said. 'Sorry. I know you said stop, but I couldn't resist. You're so sexy. Did I hurt you? I'm so sorry, Pip. I didn't want to make you do anything you didn't want to do. Pip. Please. Talk to me. I'm so sorry. Say something.'

'I'm scared shitless,' she said.

They made plans to not make plans. They had to try and stay away from each other. Three months. Ninety-five days until the Olympics started. Then sixteen more days after that, it finished. They separated at the river, Leo running up to the house to collect his car and go back to the Sixth Floor.

After waiting for an hour, she pushed the bike back up the hill, not riding it because the saddle rubbed against her in a very disturbing way. She thought, *Did that really happen?* It seemed like a dream. When she got home, still wet between her legs, she went straight to her room. He was gone, but so was *The Power of One*, which he'd left earlier on her bed, and in its place was a slip of paper, on which he'd written, *Best mistake I ever made. 112 days to go.*

14

Pip tried not to think about what had happened at the river with Leo. It wasn't that she still felt embarrassed about it: she, and apparently he as well, had waited so long for it to happen, so wasn't it completely natural and normal? It was more that the memory of it was so delicious and thrilling, she didn't want to wear it out by replaying it too much in her head. She didn't email Nadine about it – how to describe something so out-of-body, so unheard of in her limited experience, something so intimate? She had been fine to share every last detail of her encounter with Sven with her best friend because it had meant so little, but the things that Leo had done to her body were hers and his to keep, only for them.

That evening, while she sat with Max and Ferdi half-watching *Toy Story* and *Toy Story 2*, thoughts of him filled her head. What was he doing now, at his party? Was he thinking of her? Was he batting away Roxy's advances? Was he sitting at the table on the balcony, talking about sport? She wanted to text him but didn't want to seem needy, and anyway it would be too risky – Billy was always borrowing Leo's mobile when he lost his or it ran out of battery.

She was in the kitchen early the following morning when Leo arrived alone. He froze at the kitchen door and, rushing towards her, took her face in his hands and kissed her.

'What are you doing to me? I can't think straight.'

'Same here.'

It was an unbearable feeling, to have this man right here in front of her, miraculously wanting her as much as she wanted him, and to have to pull away from him. *He doesn't know*, thought Pip. *He thinks I'm going to tell him I failed my A Levels or my dad's secretly gay or something trivial like that. He only wants me because he doesn't know.* She pushed him away.

'Work it off in the pool. Get out of here.'

He turned reluctantly and she sat down at the table before her legs gave way. Shortly afterwards, Billy arrived and Dominic came downstairs. The three of them swam together while Pip made breakfast for Max and Ferdi, who changed the Sydney countdown number. She smiled to herself – she had a different countdown number now.

'Hello? Pipster? Did you hear us? Will you take us to the club today? Please?'

'Your mum might want to take you – ask her first. If she's busy, I'll go with you.'

They went outside to water Max and Ferdi's sunflowers, and when Leo had finished his lengths, he came over to them and stood behind Pip with only a towel wrapped around his waist. She could feel his warm breath on her neck and the heat radiating off his skin. She knelt down and, with shaking fingers, helped Max adjust the ties on the stake. She looked up at Leo, squinting into the sun, and shook her head. He gave her a look of mock exasperation and walked away.

Later, when they had left for the club and Pip had finished some jobs that Elisabeth had given her, making it clear she didn't need to come with them, Pip found a new bookmark in her book: *111 days to go.*

Every day a new note: 110 under her pillow; 109 on her computer keyboard; 108 in her trainers; 107 folded into her towel. They had snatched kisses, whispered conversations, hurried touches when no one was in the room with them. Once, Leo rubbed his leg against hers under the table and she lost the feeling in her body, dropping her spoon with a clatter onto the table and knocking her coffee cup so that a drop of hot liquid splashed onto her hand. She sat and stared at the spill, unable to move, her lungs emptied of air.

'Did you burn yourself?' said Billy. 'Are you all right?'

Pip couldn't speak, she was so turned on.

Billy fetched a cloth and she locked eyes with Leo, who mouthed, 'Sorry', and for a moment he looked it, before his face cracked into a smile.

'Why are you so chirpy?' Billy asked him, giving the cloth to Pip, who dabbed at the table half-heartedly.

'No reason.'

'No reason, my arse. What's going on with you these last few days? Did you pull at your party?'

'Might have.'

'I didn't see you with anyone. Come to think of it, I didn't see much of you all night. Who the hell... it wasn't Rox, was it?'

'I'm not even going to dignify that with an answer.'

'Caro?'

'Nope.'

'Was it that au pair... Whatshername?'

'Tara,' said Pip. 'The au pair's name is Tara.'

Leo stood up, grinning. 'You're getting closer, but no. It wasn't Tara. We should go, Bill. Team meeting at the club in ten minutes.'

'What about?'

'The double-header at the weekend.'

'Sounds vaguely pornographic.'

'To you everything sounds vaguely pornographic. Come on. Let's run there.' Leo was jumping on the spot, pulling his brother's sleeve, buzzing with excess energy.

Billy looked at him. 'Whoever this girl is, she's made you into even more of an eager beaver than before.' He stood up and shook his head. 'I think I liked it better when you weren't getting any.'

The following weekend, Leo was away in Berlin on Saturday and Stuttgart on Sunday. On Monday morning, Pip's phone beeped.

08.23: Come to the club if you can.

She deleted the text and ran full pelt through the woods. She didn't have much time – Elisabeth had asked her to clean every ground-floor window today as they were smudged.

The club was deserted. She'd expected to see Leo on the AstroTurf, but it was empty. She opened the door to the clubhouse, calling out, 'Hello?' and heard a noise from the basement. In the gym downstairs, she found him on the seated leg-press machine. She said under her breath, 'Quads, hamstrings, glutes, calves.' And to him, 'Hey.'

He turned and smiled at her, swivelling to sit sideways. He wasn't wearing a T-shirt and his face and body were slick with sweat. 'Come here.'

'You come here,' she said.

'Can't move right now.'

She laughed and walked over to him. It was the first time they'd been truly alone since the river. She bent her head and kissed him, tasting the salt on his lips. She wanted to lick it off his face.

When they came up for air, he said, 'New plan.' He stood

up, stretching and wrapping his arms around her. 'I've been thinking. We should tell people. I know you have all your stuff to deal with, and I know why you won't sleep with me and that's fine. But if we told people we would at least be able to talk—'

'It's not going to work. Your mum will fire me.'

'So? Come and live with me at the Sixth Floor. At least until you find another job. Or you could study. You don't need that job anyway.'

'I don't have any money, so I do need that job.' Leo wasn't going to say it, she knew he wouldn't. But she also knew he was thinking it. 'Anyway, have you thought about how that would affect your family if there was no au pair? Your mum's not exactly in a good place at the moment. Your dad's at work all day and Rosa's busy in the shop. Billy keeps your mum company but she's unreliable and the boys need routine. They need me.'

'I need you.' His hands were exploring her. He kissed her collarbone, her shoulder, moving her T-shirt aside, his hands all over her, until she was gasping, panting like a dog. She had to stop, but she couldn't; he had to, but he wouldn't; and she could feel him, he was hard against her, it was her fault, she'd come to him and not pushed him away and they were both out of control. There was only one way this was going to end.

'No. No.' She pushed his shoulders but they didn't budge. 'Leo. Stop. For fuck's sake. Stop.' She was still out of breath and he was panting too, his eyes wild and glittering, his hair messed up from where she'd scraped her fingers through it. She punched him as hard as she could on his left arm. His face was bewildered, like she'd woken him up from a deep sleep. She closed her eyes. *Give me strength.* She moved away from him and sat on a mat.

He sat down beside her. They were both miserable, both longing to touch each other, neither able to speak.

'Is this right? It doesn't feel right.' His shoulders slumped and he put his head on his knees.

'The only question is, how's your hockey?'

'Good,' he said, his voice muffled. 'Better than ever.'

'Then this is right.' She paused. 'Are you sorry I came to Munich, that I appeared in your life?'

'No. Never. I'm just sorry I'm behaving like a randy teenager.' He turned his head towards her and gave her a lopsided smile.

'I'm sorry I hurt you.' She touched his arm where she'd punched him.

'That? That didn't hurt. It was like a fly hitting me. You're going to have to try harder than that if you want to cause some damage to this perfectly honed machine.'

'It hurt, didn't it?'

'Yeah, it hurt.' He rubbed it. 'I deserved it, though. I don't suppose there's a chance you'll kiss it better?' He leant towards her, but she ducked away.

'You need to concentrate on your hockey. Seriously, Leo, or I'll stay away from you altogether. All of this – everything we're trying to do here – it's for Sydney. Ninety-five days to go until the end. Have some willpower, please. I thought you were supposed to be the strong one?'

He searched her eyes. 'Is it because of what happened? At the river? When you... when I made you...?'

'No. I'm fine with that, I told you.'

'But you cried.'

She looked at the floor. 'It was a bit of a surprise. And quite intense. It had never happened... like that... so quickly before.'

He touched her elbow. 'I think about it all the time.'

'Me too. But I promise you, it's not because of that. It's because I'm going to mess with your head after the Games. If we've kissed, nothing more, then there's a chance it will be less messy than if we've slept together. You have to trust me. I'm trying not to screw everything up for you. I just don't want you to make promises you can't keep.'

'Seems like you're the strong one here, then.'

'Don't sulk.' She kissed him again, and he groaned.

'This is nearly killing me.'

'What doesn't kill you makes you stronger. I have to go and clean some windows. Get back on that machine, Stein.' She scrambled away from him and ran out of the door.

94 days: in the coffee cup she always liked to use, the one with the chipped handle. *93 days*: in the pocket of her shorts. He left for a week, and every day a letter or a postcard arrived with a number on it. He came back, and it was Max and Ferdi's birthday party – they turned eleven and nine within days of each other. He stood at the barbecue with the dads, drinking an alcohol-free beer, and she felt him watching her as she organised games and gave out prizes. She ached for him. The afternoon turned into evening and the house was full of guests. Elisabeth, hand on a bottle of white wine, snapped at her that she wasn't needed and could go to her room.

Leo appeared through the back door, quickly kissing her before he pulled away. 'It feels weird, not telling Bill about us.'

'Are you going to?'

'Not if you don't want me to.'

Pip thought about it. 'Maybe, but not yet. It… it's simpler like this.' He nodded and kissed her again. 'You should go. With Billy, just think of it as us playing a massive practical joke on him.'

Leo smiled. 'OK. Sleep tight. Dream of me.'

The days ticked away; the notes kept appearing. Pip had no free time because Elisabeth was becoming more and more demanding. She seemed to take pleasure in finding ridiculous, fiddly tasks for Pip. *80 days*: Pip found a note attached to the sunflowers, now as tall as she was, and spent all day polishing the silver. *75 days*: she found a note on the bench outside her door and she cleaned Elisabeth's car, inside and out, and the oven, and weeded the flower beds.

There was no more time for trips into Munich. She missed her aimless wanderings and regretted all the things she hadn't seen yet: the park with the river running through it, where people gathered at the weekends like it was the seaside; the beer gardens shaded by horse chestnut trees; the museums that looked like castles; the street markets and the cafés and the libraries and art galleries she hadn't yet visited.

When the boys were at home, they whined because no one would play with them, and fought with each other, bickering over toys that, before Elisabeth arrived, they'd been happy to share.

Max and Ferdi's school broke up for the holidays and still Elisabeth insisted that she would take care of the children while Pip shopped and cleaned and ran errands for her. Only when Elisabeth had a lunch date, or an appointment at the hairdresser's or beauty salon, or when she had Pilates or an AA meeting, or a party or coffee morning or was meeting friends to go shopping, was Pip allowed to take over.

'This summer sucks,' said Max. 'We don't do anything. It's so boring.' He was floating on his back in the swimming pool. He and Ferdi had argued earlier that morning and they were still sulking with each other. A game of Twister had gone wrong when Ferdi had accidentally-on-purpose bitten Max on his arm. Max asked if he could swim, so Pip sat by the side of the pool watching him, as Ferdi went to the end of the garden to climb his favourite tree.

'It's only two days into the holidays,' said Pip. 'You're going up to Hamburg next week to see your cousins and watch Leo and Billy play. After that it's only a few weeks until Sydney.'

'Is Mum coming?'

'To Hamburg or to Sydney? Both, I think.'

'Why can't you come instead? You're much more fun.'

'I'm going on holiday myself. Get away from you terrors for a week or so.'

Pip looked up as she heard a scream from Ferdi's tree. There was no crash or thump – could he have fallen off a branch without her noticing? The tree was a good twenty metres away, but she thought she would have heard it if he'd fallen. He appeared at the base of the tree, covered from head to toe in mud. His mouth wide open, screaming. He was standing, so he hadn't broken his leg. Was it his arm? Pip jumped up. Max swam to the side of the pool and peered over it.

'What's up with him?' said Max.

'He's fallen in a puddle.'

'Huh? There's no puddle under that tree.'

'But he's covered in… oh no. Shitting shit. Max, get out of the pool and go into the house. Quickly, just do what I say. Listen. Find the phone and call an ambulance. You know how to do that?' Pip was walking towards Ferdi. She looked back over her shoulder. 'Max, did you hear me? Go and do it now, please.'

'But what do I say? What's wrong with him?'

'He's covered in wasps. There must be a nest. Go inside, close the door behind you. Call an ambulance. Then… go round to Rosa's, OK? If she's not there, call your dad's mobile. But first the ambulance.'

She turned back to Ferdi. Behind her, she heard Max splash out of the pool and the French window slam. She breathed in, breathed out again, her heart hammering in her chest. She was a few steps away from Ferdi and she could see that his left arm, his T-shirt and shorts, and both his legs were crawling with dark bodies. She could hear it now, the dense buzz filling the air as if the hundreds of wasps were one growling animal. Ferdi was still whimpering, and seemed to spasm and shiver every few seconds. *Are they stinging him?* She'd been stung by wasps a few times and hated that searing, sharp pain. What else did she know about wasps? Was it wasps or bees that died once they stung you? Which one, wasps or bees, could sting again and again? And were these wasps? *How do you tell the difference?*

'Ferdi. Hey. How're you doing? Just look at me, OK? You're going to be all right. Max's inside, he's safe, the ambulance will be here soon. What we need to do is stay calm. Are they stinging you? Don't move. OK, I can see that they are. You're being incredibly brave.'

She could feel the sweat under her arms. She had to stay calm, otherwise Ferdi was going to freak out. She reached forward and took his right hand, the one with no wasps on it. She gave it a squeeze.

'Here's what we'll do while we wait for the ambulance: you stand there and I'm going to try to take the wasps off you, very carefully. Close your eyes, all right? Close your mouth and breath gently, little in, little out, through your nose. I'm going to start with your face because I want you to be able to open your eyes and your mouth soon. OK, here we go. Squeeze my hand if they sting. Hard as you like. Break-my-bones hard.'

Pip knelt in front of Ferdi, whose eyes were closed and who was breathing too fast through his nose. She started there, in case a wasp was sucked up. She put her fingertip next to the wasp nearest his nostrils and laid her fingernail in its way. It climbed onto her nail and she slowly moved her finger away, gave it a gentle shake and the wasp flew off. She hoped to God this was the right thing to do. She thought about hosing him down, or throwing him in the pool, but if that was wrong and all the wasps stung him at once, it would be unbearably painful for the little man.

'One down, three million to go,' she whispered. 'You're doing amazingly well.' The next wasp stung her knuckle as she lifted it off; she gasped with the pain of it. She did three more and was stung again. Ferdi squeezed her hand hard. She looked down at his legs. Good thing – some of the wasps were flying away from him as he stood as still as he could. Bad thing – his legs were covered in angry red marks. Pip cleared his face and checked his hair and neck. 'OK, you can open your eyes now, and your mouth. Good boy. You're amazing, you know that?'

Pip gulped as she saw tears roll down his face.

'I'm scared. It hurts.'

'I know, sweetheart. I know. Just squeeze me really hard if they sting again. I'm going to start on your legs now, so after that you can sit down.'

From the house, Pip heard a knocking sound. Max was at the window, a terrified look on his face. But he was holding the cordless phone in his hand and doing a thumbs-up. He'd called the ambulance. Pip motioned for him to run over to Rosa's and he disappeared from the window. The front door banged and there was a flash as he ran through the gate in the hedge. She turned back to Ferdi. She was covered in sweat, crawling behind him and lifting off the wasps on the back of his shorts and legs. By now she'd lost count how many she'd done and how many stings she had on her hands and forearms. She knelt on one and was stung on her knee for her troubles.

Ferdi started to shake.

'It's OK, I've nearly done your legs. Then you can sit down. Did you know' – lift, shake – 'that there's a planet where the insects rule? They're worshipped and have special powers.' Lift, shake. 'It's called Entomanius, and it's in a galaxy far, far away.' Lift, shake, sting. 'Each type of insect has its own magical power. Bees have intelligence. Ants have teamwork. Dragonflies have speed. And beetles have strength. I've heard that the greatest and most important of all the insects on Entomanius are the wasps. Because wasps have courage. So if you're stung by wasps, they pass on their courage.' She flinched as Ferdi gripped her hand. 'There. Did you feel yourself becoming braver?' She looked at him. There were still tears in his eyes. 'Every time you're stung, you'll feel yourself getting braver.' Lift, shake. Lift, shake. She was going to start crying herself soon. The task seemed endless and she was panicking that Ferdi might be allergic, or that the quantity of stings would make him go into shock. She thought if she could clear his legs and check that none had crawled under his shorts, he could sit or lie down. She had to keep checking his face, in case any of the wasps crawled up or flew back.

When would the ambulance arrive? It seemed like it had been hours since Max called. What if he hadn't explained it properly? Shit, she should have called herself. But how could she have left Ferdi standing alone in the garden, covered in wasps, screaming with pain? Lift, shake, lift, shake. Her mouth was dry and the sun was blinding her; she felt it beating down on the top of head. But she kept going, because whatever pain or fear she felt, Ferdi would be feeling it ten times over.

'I reckon by now, the amount of times you've been stung, you're way braver than Max. I think you're about as brave as your dad by now.' She looked at his face – it was still clear, and he was holding his mouth closed but he was calming down a bit, she thought. Another sting for him. 'With that sting, I'm pretty sure you're as brave as Billy.'

'Am I?' he whispered.

'For sure. Right, that's the last one on your legs. Do you want to try sitting down?'

He whimpered and bent his knees to kneel.

'No, not that way. You still have some on the front of your legs. Hang on, I'm going to come behind you and lower you down backwards. Slowly, just relax into me.' She held him under his arms and shuffled back as he sunk to the floor. 'OK. Good. You want to close your eyes again?'

Ferdi gave a tiny shake of his head, his chin trembling.

Pip started working on his arm and the front of his T-shirt. The ones on his skin were easier to remove; she was getting better at it, quicker, and the wasps were stinging her and Ferdi less and less. She even managed to sweep off a few at a time without any stings to him or her. She heard sounds at the front gate – could be Rosa or Max or the ambulance. She ignored it. She desperately wanted the ambulance to come so the paramedics could take over, but it would be better if the wasps had gone by then. Lift, shake. Lift, shake.

Another sting for Ferdi; he crushed her hand. 'That's right, do your worst. I've got another hand anyway,' she said, and he smiled weakly. 'You're probably as brave as Leo now.' Lift, shake. Her arms and shoulders were aching. She felt like rolling over onto the grass and going to sleep. Lift. Shake. How many wasps had she done? Her head was throbbing. She felt dizzy and wanted to stop, but she couldn't. Lift, shake. She was on autopilot. Lift, shake. She needed water. She wanted shade. Her head was itching, as if there were wasps crawling around in her hair.

Footsteps behind her. Voices and instructions to move out of the way. A man and a woman were talking to her in German, she was nodding and trying to answer their questions. The garden was spinning, she felt someone help her up and she stumbled.

'Are you OK? What's her name?' Someone was right up in her face. 'Pip? How are you doing?'

She said fine. Tired. Water.

'OK, we'd better take her too, let's go, quick as you can. Are you all right to help her into the ambulance? Just the father. No – you'll have to follow.'

On the stretcher in the ambulance, she started to focus again. Dominic was there, holding Ferdi's hand and murmuring into his ear.

'Pip. How are you feeling?'

She was given water by the female paramedic. She said OK.

'Any nausea? Dizziness? Do you know if you're allergic?'

'I don't think so. I've been stung by wasps before. Not like this, though. I felt a bit dizzy, but not any more. No nausea.'

'Headache? Breathing OK?'

'No. Yes.'

The paramedic nodded. 'Good. You were brilliant back there.' Tears filled Pip's eyes. 'You don't have to worry any more. We'll take it from here. This little chap – he was lucky that you were there.'

'Thank you, Pip,' said Dominic, and she couldn't speak because if she did she thought she might start howling.

They took her to a room and Dominic went with Ferdi. Torch in her eyes, blood pressure, pulse, everything checked, everything fine. Free to go. She slid off the bed and saw Leo in the waiting room. Behind him, Billy and Elisabeth.

'Here's the hero,' said Billy, and gave her a bear hug.

'Ow. Stings still hurt.'

Over Billy's shoulder, she caught Leo's eye. He was distraught. She gave him a quick smile to say, *I'm OK*.

Elisabeth snapped, 'Where's Ferdinand? How did this happen?'

'It doesn't matter, Mum,' said Billy.

'It does matter. Where were you, exactly, when my son was attacked by wasps?'

Pip said, 'Max was in the pool. I was watching both of them.'

'Not good enough. He could have been killed.'

'And he would have been, if Pip hadn't cleared those wasps off him,' said Leo. 'He only has twenty stings; it could have been hundreds if she'd panicked or left him. She did exactly the right thing.' He turned to Pip. 'Rosa was watching you from the window with Max and the girls. She's allergic, so she couldn't come out and help. She said you were amazing.'

'It was her fault in the first place that he was in the wasps' nest.'

'Not so loud, Mum,' said Billy, putting his arm around her shoulders.

Elisabeth shook it off. 'You're not fit to look after children. You'll have to leave.'

'You're firing me?' Pip whispered.

Elisabeth said 'Yes' at the same time as Leo said, 'No.'

Elisabeth said to Leo, 'This has nothing to do with you. She's been negligent. I could sue her.'

'Mum—' said Billy, trying to soothe her.

'I've been watching you and all you do is slouch about, making eyes at Billy and Leopold. You never have your mind on the job. You're not capable of protecting my children and you will leave immediately. Maximilian and Ferdinand need their mother. Not you.'

A nurse approached them and asked if they were the von Feldstein family. 'And which of you is Pip?'

'I am.'

'Please come with me. Ferdi's been asking for you.'

Pip hesitated. She looked at Elisabeth, who was speechless, fuming at the slight. Billy was making a theatrical wincing face. Leo took Pip's arm and made her follow the nurse. He said, 'We can sort that out later. Dad will sort it. Let's go and see him for now.'

Ferdi was lying in bed in a ward, Dominic sitting in a chair beside him. He smiled at Pip and she said, 'Would it be all right if I gave you a hug now? I wanted to in the garden but you had those creepy-crawly things all over you.'

Ferdi smiled again and held up his arms. She hugged him gently, his little hands resting softly on her back.

'Your stings OK?' she asked.

'Yeah. Yours? Bet I've got more than you.'

'Oh yeah – let's count and see.'

She heard Dominic and Leo talking quietly at the door. They both disappeared into the corridor.

'Pip?'

'Yes my small friend.'

'Can you tell me again about the planet with the wasps and bees and stuff?'

That evening, Leo drove Pip home. Dominic was staying with Ferdi in the hospital overnight so he could be monitored. In the car, Leo smiled at her.

'Rosa told us what you did.'

'It wasn't much.'

'It was brave.'

'Anyone would have done the same.'

'You're amazing, Pip.'

She was silent. 'Could you sneak into my room tonight and just hold me? I need someone to hold me.'

'I'm the man for that job. I'm going to need a pillow, though.'

'I have a pillow.'

'Then we're on.'

Pip breathed out. 'Say if I'm asking too much. I know how much sleep you need.'

'Do you?'

'Yes.'

'How come?'

Sleep is critical for athletes, especially in the weeks before a big event. It stimulates muscle growth and repair, and improves reaction times, mood and alertness. 'Read it in a book.'

Back at the house, Billy and Elisabeth were sitting at the kitchen table, Billy trying to smile.

'Where's Max?' said Leo.

'He's staying with Rosa tonight.'

'Don't you think he'd be better here? In case he needs Pip?'

'Why on earth would he need *her*?' said Elisabeth coldly.

'There's a chance he might have problems processing what happened. He might blame himself. He might have a nightmare. The person he'll need in that situation is most likely the one he watched save his brother today.'

'Nonsense. Anyway, Philippa has her bags to pack. You'll need to leave first thing in the morning. Ferdinand will be back tomorrow and it would be easier if you left without saying goodbye.'

'Easier for whom?' asked Pip, before she could stop herself.

'For the boys, of course. Who else would I be thinking of?'

'Yourself, for example.' Pip saw Billy and Leo exchange a worried glance. 'It has nothing to do with Ferdi or Max's safety that you want me to leave. It's because they ask for me instead of you. Because I spend time with them and play with them and talk to them. Almost as if they're human beings, and not some nuisances that have to be out of the way at all costs because you're tired or bored or in a bad mood.'

'How dare you?'

'I dare because it's true. Isn't that why you've got me running around from dawn till dusk doing menial and meaningless tasks for you, so that I don't have time to do the job I was brought here to do, which is look after your children because, even if you are here, you can't be bothered to?'

Elisabeth's hand came out of nowhere and landed on the back of her head, smacking her forwards with a surprising strength, so that her chin thudded on the table. She felt a dull pain spread through her. Leo roared with anger and jumped towards her, sheltering her from more blows, while Billy held his mother's arm. They froze, suspended in that moment, blinking at each other, Elisabeth's face dawning with the realisation of what Leo had shown her.

He whispered in Pip's ear, 'We should get out of here', and she stood up shakily, her head pounding, her knees buckling. They left through the front door and Leo drove to Schwabing in silence. He lay her down on his bed and stayed with her, holding her until she drifted off to sleep.

When she woke in the morning with a splitting headache, she was fully clothed and Leo was nowhere to be seen. A Germany kitbag, a suitcase and a stick bag were packed by the door. She heard footsteps in the corridor. She waited until they had faded, nudged open the door and tiptoed through to the living room. She found Leo there alone. He was looking smart, compared with his usual attire of tracksuits and shorts – he had on a pair of light chinos and a checked shirt.

'Morning, beautiful. How're you feeling?'

'Headache.'

'Let me have a look at you.' He stared into her eyes. 'Pupils equal and reactive.' He took her wrist and traced circles on the inside of it. 'Pulse steady.' He kissed her on the mouth. 'Respiration rate normal.' He kissed her neck.

'I thought you'd checked my pulse already.'

'Just being thorough.'

They heard a door, jumped apart, and Martin wandered through in his pyjamas. 'Oh hey, Pip, what are you doing here? Billy's at the house in Solln this week.'

'Oh, is he? Damn, I must have missed him this morning. OK, so now I'm here, how about a coffee?'

'Not for me, thanks, I have a lecture in' – he checked his watch – 'three minutes ago.'

When Martin had left, she breathed again. 'What am I going to do now? You're leaving for Hamburg today, aren't you?'

Leo made them both a coffee and sat next to her on the sofa. 'Stay here, in my room. We'll tell Theo and Martin that you've quit and that you're kipping here for a few nights. I've spoken to Billy already. He's on the way with a bag for you. Then we're heading to the airport. Don't go back to the house tonight. Go and fetch the rest of your stuff tomorrow. By the time we get back, Dad will have sorted this out. You can stay here and we'll tell everyone about us. Either way, don't go back to the house if she's there. It's not safe for you two to be in the same room.'

'I'm not afraid of her.'

'Well, you should be. Don't go near her, Pip, please.'

'Is this to do with what you wanted to tell me, after the Olympics? About you and your mum?'

Leo said, 'Yes. Look, I may as well tell you now.'

'Sure?'

'If it means you take this seriously.' He put his arm around her and pulled her in close. He looked straight ahead of him, towards the other side of the room, and sighed. 'The whole time I was growing up, I knew she preferred Billy and that was OK. It was something I learned to deal with. Dad loved me, and Billy and Rosa. I just got on with it and tried to stay out of her way. Things were good for a while, and Billy and I were away at school in England. I knew how to handle it – if she and I were together, we wound each other up, so I made sure we weren't.'

Pip sighed and curled closer to him.

'I was fifteen when Max was born. That was when it started getting bad again. Billy and I were back for the summer holidays. She was depressed, she was mean and drunk. Dad took some time off work. Max was a difficult baby, cried a lot, and he looked like me, worse luck for him. She spent most of the time in Lindau. Dad hired an au pair for Max and would go down there at the weekends. We were relieved to go back to school in the autumn. But every holiday after that, it was the same – she got worse and worse. Some holidays I didn't go home; I stayed in England with friends, or with our cousins in Hamburg.

'And then she got pregnant again. God knows why. After Ferdi was born, I had to be back here more and more because I was playing for Germany. I saw how she was with the babies – she couldn't be alone with them. The au pairs – there were different ones all the time – they couldn't handle it. Dad was trying to keep it together, but it was a strain. Only Billy being there helped. But you know Bill – often he's just not around.

'One day, I made the mistake of being alone with her and the babies. Ferdi was in his cot, supposed to be asleep, but he woke up and was crying. She went crazy and we argued; I was trying to calm Ferdi down but I didn't know how to do it. She'd been drinking and she ended up throwing a bottle at him. I stepped in front of it and acquired these scars for my trouble.' Leo pointed at his hand and forehead.

'I thought those were from hockey,' said Pip, touching them.

'That's what we told everyone, including Billy. But that was the first time she left, really left, not telling us where she was going and not coming back. And when Dad found her, she went to the clinic.'

'Where was she?'

'That time, Los Angeles. My grandparents hired a private detective. But she has friends all over the world. God knows what stories she feeds them. They always let her stay for as long as she likes, giving her booze and not telling Dad when she pitches up. Fucking idiots – it always blows up in their faces in the end. That's why she crawls back, back to Lindau, back to the clinic. And eventually she comes home and the whole thing starts again.'

'God, Leo. I'm so sorry.'

'Don't be. Not your fault.' He turned his head towards her and buried his lips in her hair. 'So now do you understand? This is the bit, I've seen it so often before, when she starts lashing out. And it'll either be with me, or you. I'm not going to see her again until after Sydney because it'll do my head in. You need to promise me you'll stay away.'

'OK. I promise.' She rubbed her head. 'I'm sorry this blew up now. I wanted to be there – for Max and Ferdi, and your dad, and you and Billy. I thought I could keep my temper, but she's been winding me up for ages and I hate the way she uses Max and Ferdi to blame me for her inadequate parenting. Sorry, I don't want to be cruel about your mother.'

'Be as cruel as you like. She's out of order. Billy has this attitude that she's a free spirit, she's faultless, because she's above mundane things like families and jobs and responsibility. And Dad is loyal to her. I know everyone thinks it's because of the family money, but that's not true. Financially, he's secure because I own the house.'

'Which house?'

'Number Three, Emil-von-Feldstein-Weg. So if he ever wanted to divorce Mum, he and Max and Ferdi would be fine because they'd carry on living there. Dad could find another job, no problem.'

'I didn't know you owned that house.'

'I inherited it on my twenty-first birthday. They've shared out the family property. Mum has Lindau, Rosa has her house, Billy has this flat. The little ones will inherit something – the chalet in Verbier, the hockey club – when they turn twenty-one. It's some sort of tax dodge. Bet you anything they regret giving it to me.'

'Will they really disinherit you if you don't work for the family company?' She blushed. 'I overheard them in Lindau.'

'Ah. Thought you might have done. Maybe, I don't know. Depends on what Billy does, I suppose. If he's a good boy and settles down, it might take some of the heat off me. I honestly couldn't care less. I have enough to live on for now and could stretch it until the next Olympics – and then I'll graduate and start work. Fuck them. Mum, Grandpa, Grandma, they're as bad as each other. I'll be glad to get shot of them, especially Mum. She thinks she can live this separate life from us – with the drinking, the affairs, the lying, whatever – and expect us to welcome her back with open arms. She's the worst kind of person.'

'I think… I'm not sure, but she gave me a look as if to say she knew about us.'

'Yeah, I caught that too. She'll probably have told Bill and Dad by now. I'll smooth it over. Don't worry.' He looked at his watch. 'Are you going to be OK here with these two reprobates?'

'I'll call Tiny and ask her to come over.'

'Good idea. Come here,' he said, folding his arms around Pip. 'You have a whacking great bruise on your chin. You actually look like a hockey player. I need to kiss it better.'

They spent the time until Billy arrived kissing on the sofa, so when they heard his key in the lock, Pip's pulse was no longer steady and she was feeling more dazed than ever. And Leo's shirt was more unbuttoned at the top than it had been.

'I think she might be a bit concussed,' said Leo to his brother, with a serious look on his face. Pip rubbed the back of her head and pretended to wince.

Billy looked from one to the other and burst out laughing. 'You sly foxes, how long has this been going on for?' He banged his head with the palm of his hand. 'I know – your birthday. Since then you've been walking around grinning like a simpleton. But… Pip wasn't even at that party, was she?'

'Think, Bill, think…'

'I can't. It hurts too much. Oh! Got it. You disappeared off earlier in the day for a run. I was injured. Fuck me sideways. This is a bit much for the old brain to process. No wonder you've been so spaced out recently, Pipette.'

'Have I?'

'Christ, yes. You're so jumpy. And clumsy. Flapping around all over the place. I must admit, I am absolutely flabbergasted.'

'In a good way?' said Pip.

'Of course, you muppet. Leo's happier than a pig in shit. Just look at him, the simpering idiot. Also, he's on the form of his life. Whatever sexual favours you are bestowing on him, my friend, keep up the good work and that Olympic gold medal is ours for the taking.'

Pip blushed as Leo said, 'Fuck off.'

'I know you told me I'm like a brother to you, Pipster, but this is taking it a bit far, no?' He grinned at her and checked his watch. 'Taxi'll be here in five. Here's your bag. Message from Dad: he'll try and call you in the next few days about the job. I'll leave you two adorable peeps to say goodbye to each other. Ah, love's young dream.'

Tiny came round and they spent the evening with Theo and Martin, watching TV and eating a Chinese takeaway. Tiny stayed in Billy's bedroom that night, and the following afternoon they went back to the empty house on the way to Tiny's training to pick up the rest of Pip's stuff.

She spent the next week at the Sixth Floor, reading Leo's sports psychology books and watching DVDs. She went for runs in the Englischer Garten and to the cinema with Tiny, who stayed most nights because she couldn't be bothered to go back to her house and the flat was closer to the university.

'What happened, I mean, why were you fired?' asked Tiny. Martin and Theo pricked up their ears.

'It was a misunderstanding between me and Elisabeth,' said Pip.

'A misunderstanding that landed on your chin?' said Theo.

'Typical Pip Mitchell answer,' said Tiny.

Pip said, 'I want to sort it out when they're back from Hamburg, so it's not going to help if stories are swirling around the club.'

'We're very discreet, Pip. If you tell us, it goes no further than these four walls.'

Pip laughed. 'Yeah, right. You are the worst gossip-heads I've ever had the misfortune to meet. Anything I tell you will be round the club three times, each a gorier and more scandalous version than the last. Nope. I'm going to sort it out, then there is no story.'

Leo called every day, at different times, and they spoke for as long as he could between matches. They'd beaten GB and lost to Korea, and were playing Holland on the last day. No injuries.

'And your mum? Have you seen her?'

'Nope, and I don't intend to. I haven't seen Dad or the boys yet either. Billy's been over to their hotel. If she does suspect about us, she hasn't said anything to Dad. Has he called you yet?'

'No, but maybe he's busy. Good luck tomorrow.'

Pip didn't hear from Leo again until he and Billy arrived back from Hamburg on the Monday. Pip was in the flat, alone – Tiny and Martin at uni, Theo at work – when she heard the key in the lock. She jumped up, hesitated and thought, *What the hell, Billy knows anyway*, and ran into the hallway, throwing herself into Leo's arms. He laughed and kissed her and she said, 'I've missed you. I don't want to leave you now, but your dad didn't call and so I don't know if I can go back to the house and if I still have my job and does he know about us?'

'I'd hazard a guess that he knows about you now, all right,' said Billy, who stepped aside. Behind him stood Dominic, mouth open, and Max and Ferdi, glaring angrily at Leo, who still hadn't let go of Pip. 'Oh, and Mum's disappeared. She left last night – packed her bags and got in a taxi to the airport. So I'd say there's a good chance you still have your job, even if you are shagging the boss' son. Am I right, Dad?'

Dominic nodded wordlessly.

Billy cleared his throat and did a loud stage whisper. 'I think, Mary Poppins, now might be a good time to take your hand off my brother's arse.'

15

August 2000

From: pipmitchell80@hotmail.com
To: whatwouldanyado@aol.com

Nadine,
Love the new email address. Sorry I haven't emailed for weeks and weeks, I've been really busy. I know. Pathetic excuse. But wait till you hear about what's been going on in my boring old life.
So, I told you that Dominic's wife came back – was released from the funny farm, I should say. Well, as soon as she moved back in, things here took a turn for the worst. She worked me like a slave, and that's putting it mildly. She was here for two months and I thought about leaving many, many times, but she's totally cuckoo so I thought I'd better stick around; try my best to keep things on an even keel for the little and big men of the family.
Well... finally she left and I'm telling you, the huge dark cloud that was hanging over the house has departed with her. Dominic's been

trying to find her, but all of their friends that he's called claim not to have seen her. Mystery.

But I say good riddance! If I never see the woman again it'll be too soon. You might be getting the impression that we didn't get along, and you might be right.

The main upshot of her leaving is that Dominic's asked me to go to the Olympics with the family. He has a few meetings at the Sydney office that he can't get out of, so he needs me to take Max and Ferdi to some of the events while he's working. First-class tickets, flying out a day before the Games start, back the day after they finish. Tickets to hockey – of course – and a load of other great events – tennis, athletics, beach volleyball to name but a few. Of course, I said yes. I'm not out of my mind.

Which brings me to why I'm writing to you. I had this previous plan to go to Sydney myself, and I already had the plane tickets booked and Troy said I could stay in his room – he'll be in the Olympic Village. I hadn't told the von Feldsteins – all connected to not telling them I'm related to Holly and Troy – so as far as they were concerned, I was going back to England for two weeks' holiday while they were in Sydney.

So, the big question is, do I know anyone who'd like to go to the Sydney Olympic Games and hang out with me while I'm not working? I asked my really close friends and they were all busy, so now I'm asking you.

But seriously – how about it? The travel agent can change the name on the tickets for a small fee. You can stay with me at Troy's pad if you like (there are no rooms left at the hotel where Dominic's staying with the boys, but he's told the hotel we need the first cancellation, so we might end up in five-star luxury). There'll be plenty of spare event tickets if you know who to ask.

Pleeeease come, Nadine. There'll be Pip, and sport, and beaches, and Australian sunshine, and beers, and barbies, and surfing, and fit men and inspirational women, and sluts and Billy.

'Hi, Pip. Where are the boys?' said Dominic. 'Sorry, I guess I need to be more specific these days. Where are Max and Ferdi?'

Pip was washing up and she kept her eyes on the sink. After two weeks, she still wasn't comfortable with living here, working for Dominic and everyone knowing she and Leo were together. Dominic had been – after his initial shock – very kind about it. He admitted he'd thought that Pip might have been keener on Billy – apparently everyone thought that – but he was pleased that she and Leo were so happy. It didn't make it any easier for Pip, though. She blushed.

'They're upstairs.'

'What are they up to?'

'They're having a farting competition. I made myself scarce.'

'Don't blame you.' Dominic laughed. 'Billy will be sorry to have missed that.'

'Oh, he's upstairs too. It was his idea.'

Dominic sat at the table and started reading the paper. He put it down. 'I'm nervous.'

'About tomorrow?'

'What if they don't select him? He's not as reliable as Leo.'

'He'll be selected. He's worked really hard.'

'And if he isn't?'

'Well, only one day before we find out.' Pip looked at Dominic. 'Of course, he must have my ticket if he wants to go out to Sydney to watch. And... I wanted to ask you anyway...

what if Elisabeth comes back? What if she wants to come too?'

'Then we'll buy another ticket. Don't worry about that, Pip. You're coming to Sydney, whether or not Billy is picked and whether or not Elisabeth comes back. Did you sort out somewhere to stay, if the hotel can't fit you in? The advice from the IOC is that there'll be hotel vacancies all over Sydney in the second week, when athletes don't make it through to their finals and their families go home early.'

'I'm staying with friends in Paddington. It's not far from the city centre, so I can work whatever hours you want me to. Nadine's staying there too, with me.'

'It's great that she decided to go at the last minute.'

'Yeah, she's fun. And don't worry about her distracting Billy or trying to lead him into mischief – I've told her, she's not going within ten metres of him until after they've finished playing.'

'A bit like a restraining order?' He chuckled. 'It's nearly time for Billy to go. I'd better fetch him. If I don't appear down here again in the next fifteen minutes, call an ambulance.'

Leo had already said goodbye and was packing his bag at the Sixth Floor. Dominic was taking them to the airport – they were flying up to Berlin with the other two German squad players for the Olympic team selection meeting. Of course, there was no doubt that Leo had made the team; he was one of about six players who were givens. But Billy hadn't played a full game for Germany this year. Pip told herself it was more normal for the forwards like Billy to be brought on and off, and the defenders like Leo to be on the pitch the whole time. Billy had scored plenty of goals this year. He'd knuckled down, just as Beck had asked him to do. And, although it might be unfair to Billy, since he clearly possessed a huge amount of talent himself, he was partly there because he and Leo played so brilliantly together. Leo had told her that tomorrow, the squad players who weren't being selected would be spoken to privately before the team meeting when the final squad of sixteen was announced. Although Dominic was on edge about the selection, and Billy was 'absolutely shitting himself', Leo was calm and confident for him, so Pip took her lead from him.

Dominic put his head round the door. 'Made it in and out without suffocating. You all right to watch the boys while I do the airport run?'

'Sure. Wish him luck from me.'

'Which one?'

'Both.'

When they'd left, Pip walked upstairs to see if Max and Ferdi wanted to do anything. They still hadn't quite forgiven her for the whole Leo thing, even if most of their ire was directed at Leo. She'd tried to talk to them, ask them what exactly they didn't like about it, but they hadn't made much sense.

'Will you leave us?'

'No – not because of Leo, anyway. Some day I'll leave you, but it'll be when you don't need me any more.'

'Do you like him more than you like us?'

'I like you in different ways.'

'When you get married, does that mean you're our mum?'

'Well, we're not getting married, but if we did, I'd be your sister.'

'Cool. Have you Done Sex with him?'

'That's private.'

'Will he hurt you?'

'No. Leo would never do that. You know him even better than me. Why would he ever hurt anyone?'

'If he hurts you, you tell us. We'll make him regret it.'

'I'll be sure to do that.'

Max sighed and shook his head. 'I'll level with you, Pipsqueak: I don't ever want to grow up. The whole thing just seems baffling to me.'

There had been only silence from Troy. Pip was relieved – he'd forgotten about her; met someone else, probably. She would only need to have a quick coffee with him and tell him she wasn't interested and he'd be relieved too, relieved to put their mistakes behind them and act like they never happened. Which meant that Pip could tell Leo after the Olympics about Holly, and that she knew Troy as her brother-in-law, but not about the sex or the plans they'd had until recently to get back together again. She didn't think it was lying. She didn't know – was she supposed to tell him everything about her life before she met him? What exactly was a lie, in this situation? Was it – as well as not answering a question with the truth – not answering the question at all? And if there was no question in the first place? When she told him, everything would be OK. She'd replayed it in her head hundreds of times.

EXT. BEACH IN AUSTRALIA – SUNSET

LEO STEIN, a gold medal around his neck, and PIP MITCHELL sit together, sipping cold beers, facing the ocean. The sun is setting on the horizon, and the evening air is still warm, because that's how it is when there's a big romantic scene at the end of a long story of heartbreak and redemption.

CUE MUSIC: EINAUDI'S *LE ONDE*

> LEO
> So, here we are. What was it you wanted to tell me?

> PIP
> I had a sister. She died, three years ago.

LEO
(puts his arm around her)
I'm sorry. I didn't know. You always looked
so unhappy and I couldn't do anything
about it.

PIP
(in a shaky voice)
Yes. She was a hockey player and you've
met her. Her name was Holly Costa.

LEO
Who? Holly? What...? Are you being
serious?

He stares at her, shocked.

LEO
(continues)
You mean...? Holly... No. It's... Are you
seriously telling me that you're Holly
Costa's little sister?

She nods.

LEO
(continues)
Shit. Oh, shit. No wonder. You poor thing.
How have you managed to stay sane this
year?

PIP
I haven't, really. I hated it at first. It hurt,
every day, so much. Every time I saw a

hockey stick. Every time anyone talked about the Olympics. Some days it was unbearable. But you've been so lovely, and now I can't imagine leaving. I thought, at first, that it would never get better. And then it did. And it's mostly been to do with you lot.

                    LEO
I'm still trying to get my head around this... hang on... what... of course. You know Troy Costa. He's your brother-in-law. Right?

                    PIP
Right. Are you angry with me?

                    LEO
God, no. I feel terrible. Billy and I have been slagging him off all year, in front of you. I'm so sorry.

                    PIP
What? You're... sorry? Why?

                    LEO
It was insensitive of us – he was your sister's husband. It must have been so painful for you, when we spoke about him and her. I would never have been so cruel if I'd known.

He kisses her.

LEO

(continues)

I hate that this happened to you. But now
I get it – what you wanted to tell me but
couldn't, so that you wouldn't mess with
my head before the Games. Thank you.

He kisses her again. He's exceedingly good at kissing.

LEO

(continues)

You're amazing. You hid all this shit from
me so I could concentrate on winning this
medal. You did that for me. I love you.

PIP

I love you too.

They kiss passionately and, as the sun sets, walk hand
in hand along the deserted beach – because beaches are
always deserted when they need to be due to romantic
reasons – to their hotel where they have deeply satisfying
sex all night long.

Who was she trying to kid? Leo was going to be raging; he'd
never forgive her, and she deserved it. She didn't deserve to be
with him, and he was going to realise that in forty-seven days.

Both Billy and Leo were selected to play for Germany at the
Sydney Olympics. When they arrived back from the selection
meeting, with boxes and bags full of kit – training and match
kit, tracksuits, socks and stick bags – Billy was also the proud
new owner of a tattoo of the Olympic rings on his left deltoid.
They'd all be travelling out to Sydney a week before the Games

started and Billy and Leo were allocated to share a room in the Olympic Village.

And Pip thought, *I should be on Cloud Nine – I'm going to Sydney to watch the Olympics, to watch my boyfriend play, to spend time with my best friend in the most exciting city in the world.* But as the days ticked down, she felt a slow, cold dread spread through her; a knowledge that everything she had now would, on the 2nd of October, be destroyed. Her job, her boyfriend and the von Feldsteins would be taken away from her when she told them the truth. She'd be finished with Troy, and would probably never see him again. And Holly – the thought of being in Sydney without her was unbearable.

Pip and Leo spent their nights apart, because neither believed they'd be able to stick to the plan if they were horizontal with each other. On Leo's final evening in Munich before the team flew to Australia, he sat on her bed. He and Billy had been to the local barber's for a haircut – a trim for Billy, but Leo had a buzz cut. There was a line of pale skin around his hair. Pip traced it with her finger.

Leo smiled and said, 'I reckon it'll be best if we stay away from each other in Sydney.'

'Yes. I was thinking the same thing.'

'It'll help me focus.'

'I agree.' She gave him a glum smile. She had so little time left with him. This was the last night she would spend with him before he knew about Holly and the lies she'd told all year. This might be the last time they would have together as a couple, if he broke up with her when she told him.

She put her hands on his cheeks and kissed him, hot tears gathering in her eyes. She kissed him harder, kneeling and shuffling closer to him. He put his hands on her back and pulled her closer. Her breath was coming quicker; she hadn't kissed him like this since the gym, they'd been so careful. But if this was the last time she was going to be with him, she had to make the most of it.

He looked at her face. 'Hey. Why are you crying?' He dried her tears with his fingers. 'What's going on?'

She closed her eyes and tried to stop the tears. 'I know you're going to be so angry at me when I tell you, after the Games, and you're going to break up with me and I want you so badly, and if this is the last time we're together—'

'Hey. I'm not going to break up with you. I told you, I could never hate you.' He was shaking his head. 'You have to stop thinking like that. Firstly, it doesn't exactly reflect well on me, does it? Come here.' He put his arms around her and pulled her down to the bed, spooning her. He shifted his legs a bit away from her. 'And secondly, I want you too, and I'll want you in twenty-seven days, and nothing will get in the way of that. This is how much.' He pressed himself against her and she felt how hard he was. She pushed herself back into him and felt her stomach swoop. She heard him catch his breath.

Should they do it? They both wanted to. She could feel his hot breath on her neck. If she turned and kissed him, and wrapped her legs around him, it would be amazing, the best sex ever, better than she could even dream of. They could do it all night. Her eyelids dipped as she felt his hands move over her, under her T-shirt, down, moving down her stomach, his fingers finding the button on her shorts. He stopped.

She knew he was asking permission, and that she had the power to make this happen or not. Her whole body was shaking; she took a jagged breath and, with the last of her strength, rolled away from him to the edge of the bed. She sat up, pulled her knees towards her and put her head on them, looking at him. His eyes were huge and a bit glazed over, he was breathing hard, in and out, and one of his hands was balled up in a fist, his shoulders tensed.

I love him so much and I can't even tell him. I want to fuck him, but I can't do anything with him, not even kiss him.

She took a deep breath, swallowed her tears and grabbed a pillow, slamming it down in front of him. She did her best to smile at him, and watched as he dragged up the corners of his mouth. They settled down again, his arm resting lightly on her, and lay in silence together – Leo, Pip and the hottest pillow in the universe.

16

As soon as they landed, Pip's phone beeped. A text from Troy to call him. The car that Dominic had ordered from the airport dropped off the von Feldsteins at the hotel and carried on to Troy's house in Paddington.

Dominic said, 'I'll get it to pick you up again tomorrow. I have the address. Call me when you're up. No hurry – opening ceremony's not until the evening.'

In the taxi, she called Troy's mobile. He didn't pick up, so she left a message to say she was on her way to his house. She wished she could stay at the hotel with Dominic and the boys. Dominic had said that he'd asked again at the hotel but they had nothing yet.

The car pulled into Underwood Street and left her on the pavement outside a terraced house with a paved-over front garden. No one answered the doorbell and she started to panic that Troy hadn't told his flatmates she was coming. But she heard footsteps and an unshaven man in his thirties opened the door. He was wearing a crumpled suit and his tie was loose at the top.

'Hi. I'm Pip.'

'Pip who?'

Oh crap. He'd forgotten to tell them.

'Pip Mitchell. I'm staying in Troy's room.'

The light dawned in his face. 'Ah – Pip. Come in, come in, great to meet you. Dump your bag there.' He ushered her into the house. The front door opened straight into a room with a small dining table and four chairs. In a corner of the room was a stack of hockey sticks. The stairs divided the room from an area with a large TV and sofas, and a coffee table in the middle covered in ashtrays, tabloid newspapers and hockey magazines. Through the back she could see a kitchenette, only just big enough for the oven and fridge. There was a smell of feet and cigarettes and burnt food.

Another man in a faded T-shirt and surfer shorts didn't stand up from the sofa. He stared at her, like she was an animal in the zoo.

'Are you... Glen? Or Dean?'

Crumpled suit was Australian – he introduced himself as Glen. Surfer shorts was Dean. He had a northern English accent.

'Cold one, Pip?'

'Umm. Yes. Thanks.' She sat down and felt tiredness curl through her. 'Have you heard from Troy? I keep missing him on the phone.'

'Ah, he'll be at training. Don't worry, we'll take care of you. He's left special instructions.'

They both laughed, but didn't share the joke with Pip. She tried to smile.

'You hungry? We were about to order takeaway.'

'Oh, no – I mean yes, I am hungry but I'm exhausted.'

'Right, well, get that beer down you. We'll sort the grub and then you can kip. You'll be right as rain tomorrow.'

The phone rang and Dean picked it up.

'Costa... yep, she's here... right... righto... yep.' He looked at Pip and offered her the handset. 'For you.'

'Pip? Hi, kiddo. Are you OK? How was your flight?'

'Good. Thanks. Just getting some takeaway; then I'm going to turn in.'

'They taking care of you?'

'Yes. Thank you.' She sounded like she was talking to her parents. 'How's training?'

'Great. Fantastic. We're ready, we're on for the gold. Everything's come together. So how come you arrived earlier than you said? And what's all this about working?'

'Umm. I'll explain it when I see you. Are you free on Sunday? I have a day off.'

'Well, that's what I wanted to tell you. I've... we've got a surprise lined up on Sunday. Meet me at the hockey centre, outside the athletes' gate at ten. Sound good?'

'OK. What kind of a surprise?'

'Can't tell you. Otherwise it wouldn't be a surprise, would it?'

'OK.' She was too tired to be any more curious. 'See you Sunday. Good luck at the opening ceremony.' She didn't tell him she'd be there too. 'And good luck in your first game.'

'Won't need it. We're only playing the Poms.'

'That's a bit rude.'

'Well, you know me. Night-night.'

She ended the call and passed the phone back to Dean so he could order the food. When it arrived, she picked at it, although she'd been starving a few minutes ago. She said goodnight and went up the stairs to the first room on the left.

The room was tiny: a double bed, a squat, heavy-looking chair and a wardrobe filled it with barely any space around the furniture. It looked like Troy had cleaned for her, and there were no smelly sports shirts or shorts hanging around. She looked in the wardrobe. It smelt clean and everything was folded neatly.

Hanging up was a dress of Holly's, a summer one she'd bought for a party. She fingered the material as tears pricked her eyes. A window looked out onto the street, and on the windowsill were photos of Holly, including a black-and-white one of Troy and Holly on their wedding day, coming out of the church under an arch of hockey sticks held high. She could see herself in the corner of the picture, thirteen years old, in the most revolting dress, beaming and on tiptoes, holding her stick up with the others. The hockey-stick salute – Holly's friends had done that at her memorial service too, as David Bowie sung through the fog of Pip's stunned grief.

There were other photos too, of Holly and Troy in hockey gear. Of Holly on a beach, laughing – that was from their family holiday in Ireland, just before the wedding. Troy hadn't been with them, which meant Pip's dad had probably taken that picture. Photos from that life they'd had, a distant memory, when they were happy and oblivious.

Pip sank down into the bed. Fresh sheets, but she wouldn't have cared if they'd been a year old. She was here. It was happening. Not how she'd wanted it to happen. But she was here.

Day One: Friday 15th September

Pip left early in the morning, taking a key that either Glen or Dean had left on the table near the door. It must have been Troy's key because it had a Canterbury Hockey Club keyring on it. She took that off and left it on the table, scribbling a note to say she'd be working all day and back late at night.

She spent the day with the von Feldsteins, exploring the streets and parks around their hotel, taking pictures of the Harbour Bridge and the Opera House. They had lunch at the hotel. In the evening, at the opening ceremony in Stadium Australia in Homebush Bay, she watched the show and tried not to feel blue at the prospect of her first Olympics without Holly. When the German athletes came out, she joined Max and Ferdi in people-spotting. They pointed out the athletes they knew – Heike Drechsler, Nils Schumann, Jan Ullrich.

'Which one is Franzi van Almsick?' said Pip.

Dominic smiled at her reassuringly. 'You know that was just gossip, don't you?'

'Yes, yes, course.' *Phew.* Tiny was right about one thing, though – Franzi was drop-dead gorgeous.

They saw Leo and Billy, and Pip's whole body welled up with happiness. Max and Ferdi were going mad, screaming at them and jumping up and down, until Billy caught sight of them and waved his German flag, tugging at Leo's sleeve, who also smiled and waved. Max and Ferdi reeled off the name of every hockey player, male and female, as well as the almighty rowers and cyclists and the equestrian team.

After Germany came Ghana and Great Britain. Pip braced herself. A few new faces, but there were her sister's friends too. She wondered how the new players felt, if any one of them was aware that they'd replaced Holly Costa after she'd died. Were they thinking about Holly now?

And right at the end of the parade, a spine-tingling roar filled the stadium and Team Australia walked in. She saw Troy – he looked fit, tanned and excited, waving at the crowd and chatting to his hockey teammates. As he passed by the GB team, he looked over at them and waved, and the women's hockey team returned his wave. He put his fist on his chest and walked on. Pip's eyes filled with tears.

Day Two: Saturday 16th September

Pip went with the von Feldsteins to Homebush to spend the afternoon watching a young swimmer called Ian Thorpe win some gold in the pool. While they were at the aquatic centre, in a gap between races, results from other events were announced. The Australian men had beaten Great Britain four-one in their opening hockey match. *Huh*, thought Pip, *Troy was right.*

Afterwards they walked next door to the hockey centre and watched Germany beat Malaysia. They bought T-shirts and caps and draped themselves in German flags. In the cold wind of the huge open-roofed stadium, bigger than any hockey stadium Pip had ever seen, they huddled together for warmth. Dominic explained that it seated fifteen thousand fans, which was more even than in those Dutch stadia. They watched Leo playing brilliantly, solid and impassable at the back. Billy came on for the last twenty minutes and won a short corner, which Germany scored and which turned out to be the winning goal.

In front of them sat other German families. One woman, the wife or girlfriend of one of the players, was explaining the rules of hockey to her friend, and Dominic whispered that Pip should listen, so she could learn them too and might enjoy watching more.

Pip was quiet for most of the game, content to let Max, Ferdi and Dominic think she was only there to watch Leo. She felt that familiar pressure in her chest; she remembered it from when Holly had played. The nervousness of watching her sister play had been multiplied when she was in a crowd or a stadium. The bigger the match, the more she felt it – and these were the biggest matches of all. The stadium, the crowds, the pitchside cameras and microphones, and the photographers with their zoom lenses added to the feeling of twitchy dread she hadn't felt for so long.

After the game, the teams warmed down with a couple of laps around the pitch. Max and Ferdi ran down to the fence that separated the stands from the pitch, and the team stopped to say hello to the boys and sign their autograph books. Pip stayed in her seat. She saw Max and Ferdi point up at her after Leo said something to them. He looked at her and smiled, and she smiled back.

Day Three: Sunday 17th September

Pip took the train out to Homebush with Glen and Dean, who were heading to the hockey stadium to watch the early matches in the other group. She found out they also played hockey for Troy's club. They knew Holly from the time she'd spent in Sydney before she died, and muttered their condolences to Pip. She was pretty sure they just thought she was Holly's kid sister. Troy would never have told them he'd slept with her. He wouldn't have told anyone.

They had some cans in their rucksacks, and opened them on the train.

'Start as you mean to go on. Want one, Pip?'

She thanked them and shook her head.

She left them at Homebush station and walked around for a while, drinking coffee and people-watching. Shortly before ten, she waited at the athletes' entrance, having double-checked that neither the German men nor the British women were playing that morning. Buses were pulling in and out. She saw a German tracksuit and tensed – but it was the women's team and none of them knew who she was. She saw Indians and Argentinians and New Zealanders arrive, but no sign of Troy. She felt a pair of arms pick her up from behind and squeeze her hard.

'Pip. Man, is it good to see you.'

'You too,' she said shyly. He had wet, clean hair and he was in his Australia tracksuit. He looked good, much better than when she'd last seen him, which wasn't difficult. But she felt about him like she'd felt when Holly had been alive – daunted, in awe of him, but nothing else. He kissed her on the lips and she had to stop herself from pulling back.

He didn't seem to notice. 'You got time for a coffee?'

'Always.' She realised after she'd said it that he would probably interpret her passion for coffee as passion for spending time with him.

They walked up the Olympic Boulevard, away from the hockey stadium, past the aquatic centre and stopped at a street vendor where Pip bought a coffee and Troy a bottle of water. They sat near the fountains next to the Olympic Stadium and watched the children play. One of them spotted Troy and ran to his friends. They came over cautiously, stretching out their arms with autograph books at the ends of them, as if they were too scared to stand closer. He signed the books and handed out miniature 'Troy Costa' hockey sticks from his Team Australia rucksack.

When they'd gone, Pip took one of the sticks in her hand and looked at it closely. It was gold, with green and white stars on it and his name in massive letters. It was brash and ostentatious, a bit like Troy himself. But she had to admit, it was pretty impressive that he had his own stick design.

She waved her hand around at the wide boulevard, the stadium looming up behind them, the flags fluttering in the warm breeze, the clear blue skies, the people smiling around them. 'This is amazing. I love the Olympics. But here, in Sydney – it must be so awesome for you.'

He smiled at her. 'Only one person missing.'

She nodded, and they were silent for a while.

'Good result yesterday.'

Troy shook his head dismissively. 'Malaysia tomorrow – they won't be so easy to beat. D'you have time to come to my games?'

'No. I'm working. I'm here with the family – the dad has meetings in their Sydney office and I have to go with the kids to the events. Otherwise I'm supposed to hang out with them at their hotel or take them to the beach. It's a hard life. I'll see your matches if they're in the same session as Germany's, and when you play against them next week. And if you're in the final rounds against them.'

'We're going for gold, kiddo. You'd better believe we'll be in the final rounds. You've got tickets to hockey? They hockey fans, this family you work for?'

'Sort of.'

'But you have the rest of the day off today?'

Pip nodded.

'I have to go back to the Village now, but can I meet you here again at three?'

'What for?' Pip knew the GB women were playing at 3.30.

'Pauline and Jane got in touch with me. They want to retire Holly's shirt. The number nine.'

'What does that mean – retire her shirt?'

'It's like a ceremony: they want to play without it – an eight, then a ten, but no number nine. They'll do a little speech at the beginning of the match against the Hockeyroos this afternoon and they want to give me the shirt. But you should be there too. Jane said she'd tried to call you at home but there was no answer. So when I told her you're here—'

'You told them I'm here?'

'Yeah. Is that not right?' Troy looked confused.

'No. Fine. It's just… I didn't tell the family I'm working for who I am… who Holly was… I mean, they don't know I'm her sister.'

'What? What d'ya do that for?'

'I was upset. I didn't want anyone feeling sorry for me or talking to me endlessly about her. Sort of a new start. Never mind. It doesn't matter.'

Troy was fiddling with his tracksuit zip. 'So you'll come? To the shirt thing?'

'No. I can't – someone might see me. If they're playing Australia, it'll be on TV.'

'They won't televise that bit – just the match.'

'Of course they will, Troy. Because of you. Because she was your wife.'

267

'You could watch from the sideline?'

'I'll think about it.' She didn't want to do it, but Troy was clearly upset and confused about the way she was acting. Could she do it? Could she get away with it, without anyone from Munich seeing? It seemed doubtful. This was exactly the kind of thing she needed to avoid. In the end, she said she'd come and meet him at three and see how she felt. Troy kissed her again, on the cheek this time, and left.

She spent the rest of the morning at Homebush, soaking up the atmosphere and reading *The Subtle Knife*, the second book in a trilogy by Philip Pullman that Rosa had given her to read while she was in Sydney. The place was buzzing. After lunch, she lifted her head and saw loads of people wearing GB T-shirts and hats and flags walking towards the hockey stadium. From where she sat, back from the street and behind a tree, she recognised at least three families of the British team. Parents, sisters, brothers, boyfriends, girlfriends – people she'd known for years, with whom she and her parents had watched hundreds of hours of hockey.

She had to resist the urge to run over to them and say hello. How many times had she spectated with these people, shivering and passing round flasks of tea? There was the mum who always brought far too much food and shared it with Pip and her parents; there were the parents who always got tipsy in the bar after the matches and argued about who was going to drive home; there was the girlfriend of one of the players who videoed every game; and there was the dad of another who always cornered the umpire afterwards, furiously disagreeing with every decision. She missed them. Could she risk a quick hello?

She stood up, and saw Leo.

He wasn't wearing his Germany tracksuit, just jeans and a white T-shirt. He walked from where Pip supposed the Olympic Village was, over a bridge, towards the stadium. He saw someone and waved. A man in a GB tracksuit. They shook hands, stood together talking and walked towards the hockey stadium. Was Leo there for the shirt-retiring ceremony too? He had said that he'd met Holly. That sealed it for Pip. She hurried to the station and caught a train back to Paddington.

There was no one at Underwood Street, which was a relief. She turned on the TV; she couldn't help it, needed to see if she'd been right about them televising the ceremony. She flicked through the channels; sport on all of them, or people talking about sport. Finally, she found the hockey.

We're here at the hockey centre in Homebush Park to see the Hockeyroos play in their opening match against Great Britain. The Hockeyroos are of course favourites to win this competition. They're the reigning Olympic champions, world champions – is there anything they haven't won in the last few years? Ha ha, yes, that's right, and there's the great man, head coach Ric Charlesworth, bringing the girls onto the pitch.

But we're here today for a special reason. I don't know if you were aware, but our Kookaburra star Troy Costa lost his wife Holly in a tragic accident three years ago. Holly was part of the GB women's team, but also played and coached right here in Sydney for many years. Here, we see the teams lining up... Now what are they doing here exactly, can you explain it to me? Well, yes, of course. Holly Costa, wife of Kookaburra hero Troy Costa, played in the number nine shirt for GB. Her teammates are retiring her shirt today. That means they'll play for this whole Olympic tournament without the number nine... Well, that's a touching tribute to a well-loved and much-missed member of their team.

And here's the legendary Troy Costa now, proudly sporting his Australia tracksuit, coming onto the pitch to receive the shirt. My goodness, what a truly memorable moment... brings a tear to the eye, doesn't it? We'll come back to the match, but first, news from the aquatic centre, where the Thorpedo has won another gold...

So. Troy had been wrong: it had been televised. Good decision to have stayed away, especially since Leo had arrived to watch it. Pip hoped that he wouldn't approach Troy – no, he definitely wouldn't; he'd tried to do that three years ago and Troy had told him where to go. Disaster averted – for now. She was tired again, still jet-lagged, and went upstairs to nap. Nadine was arriving tomorrow. After that she'd have someone to play with when she wasn't with the von Feldsteins. All she wanted to do now was sleep.

She woke to someone shaking her shoulder gently. Opening her eyes, she saw Troy sitting on the bed beside her.

'Hey,' he said softly. He had Holly's shirt in his hands. Pip reached out to touch it and felt tears in her eyes. 'Come here,' he said. She sat up and he put his arms around her.

After a while, they both shifted and sat opposite each other with the shirt between them.

'When does this start to get easier, do you think?'

'Don't know.' Troy hung his head.

'Sometimes I think, *How can she be dead?* It still doesn't seem real, even after three years.'

'I know. And all this carries on, hockey and the Olympics and our lives, even though you feel like it should all stop, too.'

'Exactly.'

'And sometimes, I feel OK – you know, I have a happy moment – and then I remember her again and it all comes crashing down. Do you think that's always how it's going to be? Forever?'

'Maybe. Probably.'

Pip took comfort in Troy's wretchedness – whatever his faults, he had loved her sister as much as she had.

'D'you think after the Games it'll get better? This might help.' She laid her hand on the shirt. 'It's just so hard that she's not here.'

Troy brushed away tears from his face.

'I watched it on TV. I couldn't come. I wasn't ready. I haven't seen any of those girls since… the funeral.'

'They said.' He sniffed. 'They want to see you, Pip. I gave them your mobile number. I couldn't not – they were asking me for it.'

Pip nodded. She'd have to do it. See them. Just not yet. And not so publicly.

'This shirt's for you. And,' Troy seemed to brighten, 'I can stay for a bit.' He looked into her eyes, and she dropped her gaze to the bed. His hand reached up to her face. She stiffened. 'Pip?'

'I… don't think… I don't want… to.'

His smile was stiff and uncertain. 'Oh?' He moved his hand, stroked it down her arm and held her hand. 'You got the curse, then? Only joking. What's… umm… OK.' The disappointment in his voice nearly made her give in.

'Can we just talk?'

'Yeah. Sure. Let's talk. Actually, I've been thinking and I want to ask you something. It's just that I've missed you so much, more than you can imagine. I've been working hard but I think about you every day. You're the best, Pip, the best thing that's happened to me since… since Holly. And I was thinking. What if we got married?'

Pip couldn't say anything. She opened her mouth and closed it. *What?*

He smiled at her. 'I know – that's come out of nowhere. What am I like? But I feel so great when you're around. You know, all this – my hockey, the Games – you just get it. And you get how I feel about Holly, and we're good together. So I… will you marry me?'

No no no. Pip couldn't keep track of what was happening in her brain and her body. She felt sick. She felt her vision blur and sweat prickle on her back. She heard his voice and it sounded like it was in the next room.

'And I want to make some babies with you. I think we should start as soon as you're ready. You like kids, don't you – you're

271

good with them, yeah? Pip, don't you think this is a great idea? You and me, together. We can have as many as you like. What do you say, kiddo?'

Pip finally found her voice. 'I… need… to think about it.' He seemed so optimistic. 'Is this really what you want?' She tried to calm down and make her voice steady.

'It is.' He leaned forward and kissed her, his mouth pressed on hers. She felt cold and shaky, but she opened her mouth and went through the motions. He became more insistent, leaning into her, his hand on the back of her neck, his tongue ramming into her mouth. His hand moved down her back, and he pushed himself on top of her, crushing her under him as she dropped back. His hand was on her shorts zip. She heard familiar noises from inside him, a short groan, and she knew she had to stop this.

'No. No. Sorry, Troy, I can't. I don't want to.' She pushed against him but he didn't move, looking at her, panting, stunned, his hand still resting on her.

'Oh.' He rolled off her and looked at the ceiling. 'Oh. Only… I thought… what?'

'It's just… so sudden. I'm in shock. I need to think about it. I… I'm sorry.'

Troy's face was baffled. Pip thought she was going to cry again.

'Can we… can you just hold me again?' The tears began, and she bit her lip. He put his arm over her and pulled her to him, their faces so close she couldn't see his features clearly. His thumb wiped away her tears but they kept coming, and he used the corner of the duvet. She turned her face into his chest and lay there until she slept, and when she woke up, he was gone.

Day Four: Monday 18th September

'I think I was on the same flight as Natalie Imbruglia. This is so cool.' Nadine was wearing huge sunglasses and a tiny sundress, her dark hair in two plaits. She'd arrived on the early flight and Pip had gone to the airport to meet her. 'But where's the Australian sunshine?'

She delved into her suitcase and put on a pair of jeans and a cardigan. They took the train to Paddington to dump the case at Underwood Street and decided to walk into town to meet the von Feldsteins for lunch. On the way it started drizzling, and Pip covered them both with an umbrella.

'It's spring here.'

'How disappointing. I'm going to have to go shopping.' Nadine showed Pip what was inside her case and it was all tiny – bikinis, shorts, flip-flops, flimsy tops, strappy dresses. There was a sheaf of typewritten papers in there, which Nadine covered with a hot pink T-shirt. 'Did you see Troy yet?' she said.

'What? No.' It took Pip momentarily by surprise that Nadine would ask about Troy. But she remembered: *Troy's my brother-in-law. Nadine knows this.* And they were staying at his house. 'Yes. I mean, briefly.'

'Was it traumatic? I mean, how's he doing?'

'OK, I think.'

'Does he… is he seeing anyone else? Is that what's upsetting you?'

'No. Yes. Nadine…'

Nadine looked at her, waiting.

'I've… I'm… sorry. I've screwed up everything. I'm sorry I didn't tell you about this. But…' Pip brushed away tears. So many tears. She was so tired of crying.

Nadine slung her arm around her. 'Hey. It's OK.'

'It's not. It's not at all OK. Nothing is OK. I've done something really terrible.'

Nadine searched her face. 'You don't mean… do you mean what I think you mean?'

Pip nodded miserably.

'How far? All the way?'

Pip carried on nodding.

'Oh. Shitting hell.' She thought for a moment. 'How was it?'

Pip stopped on the pavement and stepped away from her. 'Nadine! For Christ's sake. I tell you I've slept with my dead sister's husband and you want to know if he was good in bed? Seriously?'

'Just trying to lighten the situation.'

'Some situations shouldn't be lightened.'

'I'm not sure I agree with you. But OK. I will try to take this seriously.' She took Pip's hand and they carried on walking. 'It's not as terrible as you think. Look, I know you adored Holly. But it's been three years, and God knows you've suffered and suffered, and so has he, and it's gone on and on. If you like each other, in a way that's only natural.'

'But… no. It wasn't yesterday. Yesterday we just talked. We were… we did it… when he lived in England. In 1997.'

'What? What the fuck?' Nadine dropped her hand. 'Jesus Christ almighty, please tell me that's not true.'

Pip stared at her. 'I thought you said it wasn't terrible and it was natural?'

'That was if it happened last night.' Nadine shook her head. 'You were sixteen? Seventeen? Holly had only just died. That's wrong. Pip, can't you see that? Did he… did he… force you? Did he make you?'

Pip shook her head.

'Are you sure? Because you were so young. You were a virgin. Weren't you?'

Pip nodded.

'Ugh. God. I feel sick. What an utter, fucking, cocksucking twat.'

'Me?'

'No, not you, you massive goon. Him. Troy. How could he? I'm going to kill him when I see him.'

Pip was crying, great waves of guilt and agony rolling upwards through her body. They sat down on a bench in Hyde Park and Nadine put her arm around her again.

'Oh, honey, don't. Please don't. It's not your fault.'

'But I started it. Well, he started it' – sob – 'but then he stopped' – sob – 'and I insisted. I was the one – it was my fault it went so far.'

'Don't you ever say that or think that. It's not true. He took advantage of you. You were barely legal. And you were grieving.'

'So was he.'

'Don't stick up for him,' Nadine snarled. 'No way, Pip. You are absolutely not allowed to stick up for him. He's a fucking creep. Don't interrupt me. If he was feeling horny, he should have shagged someone who hadn't just lost their big sister. If he wanted to comfort you, he should have talked to you, not opened your legs and stuck his dick into you. You think he was being nice to you? Of all the fucking depraved, selfish—'

'He wants to have a baby.' Pip said it without looking at Nadine. She had her face in her hands.

'He what?'

'He wants to get married and have babies. With me.'

'And you think that means he loves you?'

'Yes. It does. Doesn't it?'

'No, you retard. Oh my God, where does this guy get off? He's not content with screwing up your teens, he wants to take the rest of your life away from you too. He's emotionally blackmailing you.'

'He wants me.'

'He doesn't even know you.'

'He does.'

'Bet he doesn't even know your middle name.'

'Nad. You know I don't have a middle name.'

'Of course *I* do – but I bet *he* doesn't. He wants Holly, darling.' Nadine's voice softened. 'He doesn't want you – he wants the closest thing to Holly. And he wants a baby because that's what they wanted, too. Your baby with him might look like Holly.'

'But that's OK. It's what I want too. I want Holly back. If I can do that, it's like having her back.'

'This is so wrong, Pip, can't you see? He doesn't love you. He only wants to mate with you. He wants your genes. He wants to pollinate you. Please don't even consider this. You've just started to get over Holly. He has to as well. He has to let go of her, and of you and of this awful idea. You won't be happy together because he wants Holly and you're not her.'

'You don't have to tell me that.'

'You're better than her.'

'Yeah, right.'

'It's true.'

Pip raised her head. She could feel her face, heavy and puffy, her eyes tired with crying. 'You try – you just try and find even one thing that I can do that's better than Holly.' She laughed harshly. 'You never will.'

'You're clever. You're kind. You're unselfish.'

'She was all those things.'

'Not as much as you. And you're prettier than her.'

'Now I know you're making this up.'

'I forgot how useless you are at taking compliments. Look at yourself. You're gorgeous. I'd do you, if I were that way inclined. You don't even know it, but Billy told me that he and Leo have been fighting off the whole of the hockey club in Munich all year, who've been trying to get into your knickers. To defend your honour.'

'You're just being kind.'

'When have I ever been kind to you?'

'Good point.' Pip sniffed.

'And here's another one – why would you even consider Troy's suggestion, when you're deeply and madly in love with Leo Stein?'

Pip stared at Nadine in disbelief. 'I… but… what…?'

Nadine laughed. 'You are so transparent. I know what you're like with boys. Remember that party, straight after GCSEs, when you spent the whole night mooning over Jason Merrick? You couldn't even talk to him, you were so love-struck. You're exactly the same with Leo. And he's just as bad as you. On New Year's Eve, he wouldn't dance with anyone. Not even poxy Roxy. But he couldn't take his eyes off you. It was so obvious. So I went up to him and said, "Would you like to dance with me, and then I'll say, 'Switch' after the next song so you can dance with Pip?" and he said, "Yes please." Just like that.'

Pip couldn't help smiling. 'OK, I admit, I really like him.'

'Like?'

'OK. That other thing too.'

'Say it.'

'You are very annoying. I… umm… I love him. Satisfied?'

'Not even close.' Nadine grinned. 'Did you tell him yet? You did, didn't you? That's why you're looking so smug.'

'It's… complicated. It was bad timing, I didn't want to distract him and he's totally committed to the team. And he doesn't even know the half of it.'

'You haven't told him about Holly?'

'No. I couldn't. Because he'll know that I know Troy, and he has this sort of rivalry with Troy on the pitch and it makes it difficult for him. So we said we'd talk after the Games. I'll tell him about Holly then.'

'And the sex? Is it mind-blowing?'

'We haven't... really... not, you know. Because it doesn't seem right to be that involved, not having told him who I am. We're waiting until—'

'After the Games. Wow. He must have seriously impressive self-control. And you, too. You see him every day, don't you? How can you stop yourself grabbing him and shagging his brains out, right there, in front of everyone?'

'You are so gross. How did we become friends?'

'You had an older sister who bought us alcohol.'

'When we were six?'

'Oh, then. Holly paid me to be your friend.'

'Ha ha.' Pip rubbed her eyes. 'I'm terrified that when I tell him, he's going to hate me for lying to him.'

'Has he actually asked you if you're Holly's sister, and have you lied about it?'

'No.'

'Well then. He'll understand. You were upset, you were grieving. You wanted to make a new start. It's not the sort of lie that's going to make him fall out of love with you. If anything, it'll make him love you more, because you've been shielding him from the crap that's been rotating around your head all year.'

'And you think he'll be so understanding about Troy?'

'No, because you're not going to tell him.'

'But—'

'No buts. Pip, you don't have to tell him. He doesn't need to know about that. It happened way before you knew him and it's not your fault. *Do not* tell him.'

'If I don't tell him, he'll find out later and it'll ruin everything.'

'No. No. Don't you dare. Don't you go and do some stupid *Tess of the D'Urbervilles* letter under the door on the eve of your wedding. And don't look so surprised – you're not the only one who reads, you know.'

Pip flushed.

'You have got to put this behind you. You can't have this hanging round your neck all your life. Here's what you do: tell Troy ASAP you're never going to see him again. Fess up to Leo about Holly, he forgives you, you get it together and live happily ever after.'

Pip started crying again. 'I can't see how it's going to work. They play against each other all the time. I can't avoid Troy if I want to be with Leo.' It was hopeless. 'If I tell him, he'll hate me. If I don't tell him and he finds out later, he'll hate me even more. Either way, I lose him.'

'It's not like that in the real world, Pip. You know your problem – you read too much.'

'You sound like Billy.'

'You watch too many films. In the real world, you don't have to spew out every single bad thing you've done in your life to the man you love. Sure, if Leo asks you straight out if you've slept with Troy – which he will never do – you can't lie. But unless he does that – which he won't – you don't have to tell him. It's not lying, it's just not spewing. You gonna tell him about that time we tickled Penny Finnigan on purpose until she wet her pants?'

'No.'

'Or when we stole those flowers from Mr and Mrs Cleary's garden and gave them to our mothers on Mother's Day because we'd spent all our money on sweets?'

'No.'

'Or when we—'

'OK, I get the idea. Are you going to list all our childhood misdemeanours?'

'I can if you want. Or you can promise me never to tell Leo about Troy.'

Pip paused. 'OK.'

'Say it.'

'Annoying as crap. I promise.'

'And you need to promise that you're going to dump Troy and tell him to find another surrogate mother.'

'I promise. Anything else?'

'You have to tell me the bedroom details, when you and Leo finally get it on.'

'Nadine. Not helping.'

'Well, it was worth a shot. Come here. Give me some Pip loving.' She opened her arms and Pip leant forward to hug her. While they were still holding each other, Nadine said into her hair, 'I think I need a drink now. Did you see that? Was that Venus Williams?'

They met with the von Feldsteins for lunch and Dominic offered to take Max and Ferdi to the hockey match alone, if Pip wanted to spend time with Nadine. But Nadine wasn't having any of it.

'I want to see Germany play. I've heard they have a couple of decent players. Come on, Pip, we're going, right?' She insisted on the full Germany regalia – including the black, red and yellow stripes of the flag painted on her face. 'We're hockey groupies,' she laughed.

'Do you play hockey, Nadine?'

'I used to at school. I was awful. But I had this friend, when I was younger. She was an amazing player.'

Pip glared at Nadine – *Please don't do this* – but was ignored.

'All the time we were growing up, I used to go and watch her play. She was way better than anyone else our age. She played for our school, the county, and she was selected to play under-sixteens for England. I loved watching her.' Nadine sighed. 'Then I moved away. I lost touch with her. You know, I must look her up one of these days. She was my best friend.'

They wore see-through rain ponchos, and Dominic bought them both a beer to drink while they were watching. Despite the teasing, Pip was grateful that Nadine was there. Everything was more cheerful with her around. She must have been whacked, but showed no signs of flagging all the way through the afternoon, cheering and screaming whenever Billy or Leo had the ball, egging on the boys when they started shouting at the umpire, so that Pip could sit quietly and watch the match, hiding under the hood of her misted-up poncho, the emotions swirling around inside her.

Of course it was wrong to have even considered Troy's proposal. When she'd been with him, she'd felt so weak and could have easily said yes just to please him, to make him happy again. She had a connection with him that no one – not even Nadine – would understand. And even if it was true that Troy didn't love her, they both loved Holly and neither of them was ever going to find anyone who had that in common.

Nadine was the first – and the last – person she had told about her and Troy. Her reaction was exactly as Pip had expected: disgust, anger, worry about whether Pip had been abused or taken advantage of. It hadn't been like that, but that would be how anyone would see it.

Germany beat Canada two-one, all three goals in the last ten minutes of the match, and when the team jogged round the pitch for their warm-down, Max and Ferdi scrambled down to the fence. Leo stopped and Billy did too, and the rest of the team. A few of the other German team families went down. Billy looked up to where Nadine was sitting and blew her a kiss. He was slick with sweat and rain, his white shirt sticking to his body, his face flushed and glowing.

'Oh, my,' purred Nadine.

Day Five: Tuesday 19th September

Pip texted Troy and asked when they could meet, if he had another day off or a few hours one evening. She had to do this before she weakened. If she waited, she'd forget why she was saying no. Troy said he could meet her at the Novotel hotel opposite the Olympic Stadium at six the following evening.

She hated the idea of hurting him again, after what he'd been through losing Holly. And confrontation had never been Pip's strongest point. She rubbed her head to try and clear it of a dull headache she'd had since she woke up. Her only consolation was the small hope she had that, when all this was over, she and Leo could have a normal relationship – no more lies, no baggage, no secrets.

'I feel bad about telling him, right at the start of the Games,' she said to Nadine.

'If he was so worried about it, he shouldn't have asked you now. Own fault. The thought wouldn't have crossed his mind that you'd say no. Arrogant prick.'

The day was sunny and warmer, so they spent it on the beach at Manly, bodysurfing in the low waves. Dominic had to leave before lunch, and after a trip to the zoo, Nadine, Pip, Max and Ferdi took the ferry back to Circular Quay and hung out at the hotel, swimming in the rooftop pool with a view of the bridge and the Opera House.

'This is the life. I could get used to this,' said Nadine. Pip looked at her, in a tiny bikini, her skin already dark, and wondered if she was thinking about Billy; if the idea of marriage crossed her mind. She could have this all the time, if she was in the von Feldstein family. Pip blushed at the thought of Leo. *Stop it*, she thought. *Don't jinx it. You have a long way to go, and many lies to confess, before you can think like that.*

Day Six: Wednesday 20th September

Dominic had to work, so reluctantly gave his tennis ticket to Nadine. They watched Lleyton Hewitt and Billy arrived with a friend to watch Tommy Haas' match.

'Nadine, Pip – this is Tom, a school friend.'

Nadine looked at Tom's GB tracksuit and said to Billy, 'Are you consorting with the enemy?'

'Yes, but don't tell Leo. He'll have a shit-fit. Mr Team-Man.'

'Do I know you, Pip?' said Tom.

'No.'

'Sure? Your face is awfully familiar.'

'Nice try, but she's taken. By my brother.'

Tom raised his eyebrows. 'Is that right? Well, Leo's a lucky guy. Still, I'm sure I've seen you somewhere before—'

'She gets this a lot,' said Nadine. 'She must have a common face or something. Loads of people think they know her or have met her before.'

Tom wouldn't give up. 'Do you play hockey?'

'No,' said Billy. 'She's a civilian. Hands off, I tell you, or you'll have Leo to deal with.'

Tom didn't ask her again, but Pip, who was concentrating very hard on the match, could feel him looking at her a few more times. She had never met this man in her whole life. He wasn't a Canterbury player. If he was Billy's age he'd have been too old to have played under-sixteens at the same time as her. He might have a younger sister who was her age. Or he could have been thinking of Holly, but Pip was fairly sure that they looked so dissimilar, he wouldn't have made the connection, even if he did know Holly. She sat with her back partly turned to Tom and tried to relax her aching shoulders and clenched-up stomach.

After the match, Tom left with Billy, who had a training session and team meal, so they took the boys to the fountains and Nadine said she'd watch them.

'Good luck,' she said as she squeezed Pip's hand. 'How he reacts will tell you everything you need to know about whether he's the right man for you.'

'You mean to say, if I reject him and he behaves like a gentleman, I was wrong to reject him?'

'No, but if he behaves like an arsehole, you'll know you were right. I'm here if you need me.'

Pip asked a cheery volunteer where the Novotel hotel was. The volunteer laughed and pointed upwards to a curved tower rising behind them.

Troy was already waiting for her in front of the entrance. He was in his Australian team tracksuit and was signing an autograph for a young boy, who ran off shouting, 'I've got it, I've got it, I've got Troy Costa.'

'Hi.' He didn't kiss her or touch her. He pointed to the hotel lobby and for one awful moment Pip thought he might have booked a room. But of course that was ludicrous – every hotel in Sydney had been booked up months ago. Instead they went to a restaurant on a terrace that looked out onto the stadium and down the Olympic Boulevard. Pip could actually see Nadine and the boys. She was in the fountains with them, splashing them, soaking wet. She could hear them screaming and laughing.

They sat for a while in silence. But Pip knew he wouldn't have much time, and so she had to say it.

'Troy. I'm sorry. I can't do it.'

'Do what?' His face fell. 'Oh. That.'

Silence.

'I don't want to hurt you, especially not now. At the moment. You know, while you're playing. But I can't do it. I thought it was best to tell you straight away.'

Troy shifted in his seat. 'You wanna think about it a bit more?

How about we still go away after the Games and talk then? Just so you're sure.'

'I'm already sure.' Her voice wobbled.

'Are you? You don't look it.'

'I'm nervous because I don't want to muck things up for you. I'm sure. I just… I don't… love you. I don't want to marry you. Sorry.' She hung her head.

'Hey. It's OK, kiddo.'

Pip wished he wouldn't call her that.

'I knew it was a long shot. I mean, why would you want some old bloke like me?'

Was he fishing? He knew how good-looking he was. He was a national hero. Everywhere he went at the moment, he was surrounded by adoring fans. And if they won the gold it would all be multiplied by a hundred. Pip couldn't think what to say.

'It's not that. I… what we did… when… after Holly died. It was wrong. You said so at the time.'

'But now. Now it wouldn't be.'

'Yes. I think it still would.' She took a deep breath and rushed it out. 'I don't want to be a stand-in for Holly all my life.'

'You aren't, kiddo—'

'Stop calling me kiddo.' She said it louder than she meant to. Troy's eyes widened, and a few people looked round from their tables. 'Sorry. It was her name for me. And it just makes it weirder. This. This is weird. Don't you think?'

'No. Maybe it was. But I think now we'd be good together.'

'You don't even know me.'

'Sure I do.'

'OK, then what's my middle name?'

His eyes hardened. 'What's that got to do with knowing you?'

'What is it?'

'I don't know.'

'I don't have one.'

He looked annoyed. 'What are you trying to prove?' But he checked himself. 'OK, so I don't know every little thing about you. But I want to. And we have the chance now. Just you and me. I've booked a hotel. Nice one too. In Port Douglas, up the coast. We can swim, snorkel, relax on the beach, get to know each other properly, slowly...'

Pip shivered. 'You should cancel that booking. I can't come, Troy and I can't see you again. Not ever.'

'You're just going to ignore me? What if I see your parents? At a hockey match?'

'They don't go to hockey matches any more,' Pip said dully.

'They will if I ask them.'

'Then don't. You've been getting along fine without them since you left Canterbury. What's so important about seeing them now?'

'Because of you. Because I want to see you. Don't break up with me.'

Pip noticed that Troy hadn't said he loved her. 'There's nothing to break up. We didn't have... what we had wasn't real. We were both in a very bad place. I don't even want to think about it. I think it's best if we pretend it didn't happen.'

'What are you saying, kid... Pip? Wait. Are you – do you have another bloke? Is that why you didn't sleep with me the other day? I thought you were just being a prick-tease.' She winced at his words. 'Is that what this is about?' His eyes had narrowed into slits. Pip had to be on her guard. Holly had told her he was the jealous type; that she couldn't talk to any other men when he was around. And Troy had gone nuts when he'd seen her talking to Leo that time.

'No, it's not that.'

He ignored her. 'Is it the guy you're working for? The Kraut?' He raised his voice and more people were looking at them. 'Is that it? Am I right? The dad of those kids you look after? And all this time you've been stringing me along. Jesus, Pip. You sure like older men, don't you?' His face was twisted, his eyes hard and mean.

'You don't get it. I don't want to marry you for the reasons I said. Look, if Holly and I were both standing here, right in front of you, can you honestly say that you'd choose me?

Troy frowned. 'Of course not. She was the love of my life. But—'

'Well, I want to be the love of someone's life. Not just the next best thing. And I think maybe I could be. So, yeah, I met someone else.'

Pip thought some of that might have sunk in, but Troy's face was furious. She stood up to leave. 'I don't think this is helping either of us. I'm sorry I can't give you the answer you want. I hope it doesn't distract you from the Olympics.'

'You're not that important,' he muttered.

And there we have it. Pip paused. 'Then my conscience is clear. I'm going. Have a good Games, Troy, and have a nice life.'

As she walked away, shaking, she heard someone ask Troy for his autograph and he swore loudly. There was a crash. She didn't look back.

Day Seven: Thursday 21st September

At the hotel, Nadine and Pip sat reading the papers while Max and Ferdi played in the pool. Dominic was due to meet them at Homebush for the afternoon hockey session. Pip closed her eyes – the sunshine was making her head ache and she felt lethargic.

'You OK?' whispered Nadine.

'Troy's playing at 1.30. Right before the Germany-Pakistan game.'

'So?'

'So, they might see each other.'

'They won't. The teams aren't exactly going to be socialising, are they? When is Germany playing Australia, though? Don't want to miss that humdinger.'

'A week on Friday.'

'Hey, check this out – a profile of Troy in the *Sydney Morning Herald*.'

'Don't want to read it. It'll be about Holly.'

Nadine scanned the article. 'It's only a bit about her. God, he is so far up his own arse. Listen to this: *The group stages are just a formality. We're not expecting any upsets. India is the only real threat to us. Argentina and Spain are not on form at the moment and we're at the top of our game, so we can use those matches as goal-scoring practice. We have the right training, the right attitude and the right players to make it all the way to the final. We're ready for all of them. The Netherlands are always overrated and Germany have selected a bunch of schoolboys. We're the best in the world and we're going to prove it, right here in Sydney.* God, I hope they lose every match. And what's this glittery gold stick all about?' She showed Pip the full-page colour photo of Troy holding his stick. 'You know where I'd like to ram that ultra-camp sparkly piece of shit?'

'I can imagine.'

Nadine picked up an open file from the table. 'What's this?'

'Press cuttings about the hockey team or Leo and Billy – from German and European newspapers. Dominic has them faxed over every day, so he doesn't miss anything.' Pip stretched out in the sunshine. 'We should go soon, shouldn't we?'

Nadine looked at her watch. 'Why so early? We don't need to be there until 3.30, do we?'

'Oh. Don't you want to watch the Australia-Canada game before it? The tickets are for both games.'

Max and Ferdi climbed out of the pool and were drying themselves with their towels near the sunloungers.

'Not particularly.' She scrutinised Pip's face. 'Do you?'

'Yes, yes, let's watch the Aussies,' said Max. 'Then we can shout Aussie, Aussie, Aussie.'

'Oi, oi, oi,' said Ferdi.

'That seems like an excellent reason *not* to watch Australia lose to Canada,' said Nadine.

But Max and Ferdi were insistent, and even wanted their faces painted with Australian flags. 'How many bloody stars are there supposed to be?' complained Nadine. 'Oh, never mind, I'll just do a bunch. Will you do a Canadian flag for me, Pip?'

'What? You're not supporting Australia?' Max and Ferdi were outraged.

'I think one of their players is a knobhead,' replied Nadine.

'You're such a potty mouth,' said Max admiringly.

Nadine lent Pip her face-covering sunglasses, and she wore her Germany cap. 'The stadium's so big and it'll be full to capacity. No one's going to see you. Everyone ready to go? OK, little dudes, let's make like a maple.'

They looked at her in confusion.

'And leaf? No? I'm wasted here.'

They met Dominic outside the hockey stadium. Their seats were in the middle of a group of noisy Australian fans. At half-time, or 'the intermission' as Nadine called it, the score was one-all and Dominic took the boys to go and buy drinks. There were two women sitting in front of Pip and Nadine, draped in Australian flags.

Girl One said, 'So, are we going after this? To Mac's barbie?'

'Yeah, why not? Will any of this lot come?' Girl Two pointed at the pitch.

Pip looked at Nadine, who cocked her head to one side, listening.

'No chance. You know what they're like. We won't even see them until after the closing ceremony.'

Nadine mouthed, 'Groupies?', wrinkling up her nose disdainfully.

Pip mouthed back, 'What, like us?', and Nadine stuck out her tongue at her.

Girl Two said, 'Well, not always. Remember...?' Both girls giggled. 'Shit, that seems like such a long time ago.'

'Have you seen him since?'

'Here and there.'

Nadine was scribbling on a blank page of Max's autograph book. *WHO???*

Pip shrugged.

Girl Two said, 'He is gorgeous, the best-looking in the whole team, I think.'

Girl One said, 'Undoubtedly. Was he good. In bed?'

Nadine wiggled her eyebrows, grinning.

Pip looked along the rows of seats to check if Dominic was coming back.

'No, he was awful to tell you the truth. Very disappointing, size-wise.'

Nadine wrote, *HARSH.*

'And he wasn't exactly sensitive to my needs, if you know what I mean.'

Nadine nodded and grinned.

'It was just wham, bam, thank you, ma'am. And he started crying halfway through.'

Pip stiffened. Surely not…

'Oh God, I heard he used to do that a lot. But it was always about his wife. You had to feel sorry for him, didn't you?'

Pip felt Nadine's hand close over hers. She bit her lower lip.

'Did you see him the other day, with the shirt thing? I watched it on telly. He was in floods when they gave him her shirt. Poor guy.'

Pip was trying to breathe her way through it.

Girl One said, 'Ever since she died, he always cries when he sleeps with someone. It's kind of his thing. That's what I heard, anyway.'

Girl Two lowered her voice, but not enough. 'Oh no, you see, it was before she died. He and I… we went with each other when she was still alive.'

'No.'

'Yes.'

Pip steeled herself to look at Nadine, whose face was clouded with anger. She was shaking her head. She wrote on the pad, *NOT POSSIBLE.*

Girl One: 'Are you sure?'

Girl Two: 'Yes. Look, normally I wouldn't remember, it was ages ago and who cares, right? But I remember. Definitely. It was when he was playing in the World Cup, beginning of the summer. It was here, in Sydney…'

It would've been 1994. A few months after Holly and Troy were married. He left England in November and Holly joined him in Australia after Christmas.

'We talked about it, you know, afterwards. He said it was funny because that day he'd played England, where his wife was from, and she was going to be mad at him because the Aussies beat the Poms two-nil, and I said I reckoned she would have more than that to be mad at him about.'

Nadine's arm slipped round Pip's shoulder. She brushed away the tears. Why did she have the feeling she was always on the brink of tears these days?

When Dominic arrived back with coffees for them, Nadine stood up and said, 'We're going to need something a bit stronger than that.' She tugged Pip's arm, and Pip followed her.

At the bar, Nadine ordered drinks and Pip stood in a daze. Nadine sat her down on a plastic chair and slammed the four beakers onto the table, some of the liquid splashing out. There was no one else around – the second half had just started.

'Fucker,' Nadine said. 'Stupid, arrogant, cheating motherfucking fucker.'

Pip stared at the table.

'I'm speechless. No, I'm not, actually. I knew he was a dick-brained twathead, but I at least thought he loved Holly. And now... God damn it, I'm so angry with him.'

'Maybe he was missing her,' Pip said quietly.

'You have got to be kidding me. Sorry, Pip, but can you hear yourself? Can you hear how ludicrous some of the things you say are? No.' She banged her hand onto the table and the drinks spilled again. 'No. No excuses. He's a fucking slag. I'm actually, definitely going to kill him when I see him.'

They heard a huge roar and the announcer said, 'Elmer scores for Australia. Australia two, Canada one.'

'Typical,' grumbled Nadine loudly. The people serving behind the bar looked over at her.

'I wouldn't have thought you'd be that bothered about it. You said that it's OK to sleep around, and that being a slut just means you're having lots of brilliant sex.' Pip didn't know why she was arguing with Nadine. She didn't even care. It was so complicated – love and marriage and sex and life. She'd never get the hang of it.

'Yeah, and you know who taught me that? Your amazing sister. She talked to us both, d'you remember, when we were fifteen? I'll never forget that eye-opening conversation. Up until then, I'd thought that girls should stay virgins for as long as possible and boys should get laid as often as possible. The other way round – no way. But she said, "What's the difference between men and women? Why shouldn't we have as much sex as men? What is the reason that girls are labelled bad if they enjoy sex and boys aren't? It defies logic."' Nadine took a large gulp of her beer, burped and wiped her mouth on the back of her hand. Pip couldn't help laughing. Nadine wagged her finger at Pip. 'But that, my friend, is if you're single. Not if you're married. When I get married I'm going to commit to being madly and truly in love with one person. And until then I'm going to shag my way through as many boys as I like.'

Nadine, as always, was right. Troy – who had freaked out if Holly even spoke to another man – had cheated on her, God knows how many times. Why was it OK for him to sleep around and still be possessive over his wife? What a sexist hypocrite. Pip picked up her small plastic beaker and drank the water. 'What was that?' she gasped.

'Gin and tonic,' said Nadine, and necked hers too. She held up a beer and said, 'You know, thank God we heard those two. Just think – if I wasn't here, and if we hadn't heard them, you might have said yes to Troy and this time next year you'd be married to *Troy Costa, the biggest wanker in the world—*'

'Shhh, don't,' said Pip, but she couldn't stop laughing.

The bar staff were staring at Nadine as she shouted at the top of her lungs.

'*Troy Costa, who has the smallest knob in the world—*'

'Don't, Nad, stop. We'll be arrested.'

'*Troy Costa, who's rubbish in bed.*'

Pip was doubled up with laughter. She caught sight of the bar staff, one of whom held a walkie-talkie to her mouth. 'Come on, we have to go. They'll chuck us out of here.' She pulled Nadine's arm and they took their beers back to their seats.

As they sat down, two Australian players scored in the space of a few minutes, making it four-one, and the crowd erupted, the chants of 'Aussie, Aussie, Aussie, oi, oi, oi!' echoing around the stadium. When play started again, Nadine cheered loudly for Canada every time they touched the ball, earning dirty looks from the fans around them. At the end of the match the score was five-two, and the Australian team warmed down with a lap around the pitch, Pip sinking into her seat as Nadine glared at Troy and the two Australian girls in front waved at the team as they jogged past.

There was a break between the matches. The Germans came on to warm up, music pounding out of the speakers as the stadium emptied and filled again. Pip helped Max and Ferdi wipe off their Australian flags and painted on the black, red and yellow stripes.

'Who are we playing?' Pip said.

'"We"?' said Nadine. 'Are we German now?'

'Of course.'

Dominic said, 'Pakistan. These guys are seriously good. That player – Sohail Abbas – he has a killer drag flick that'll take your head off. They beat GB eight-one a few days ago; he scored three times.'

Pip remembered reading about Abbas in Leo's notebook, when she'd found it in his bedroom last October. She breathed in and out to try and calm herself. She had to try not to panic too much, but Dominic's choice of words wasn't helping. She could barely watch the match and had to look away any time Abbas went near Leo.

'You're missing the best bits,' said Max, noticing that her eyes were closed.

'You tell me what's happening,' said Pip. 'I can't watch. It's too frightening.'

So she listened as Max and Ferdi commentated on the match, and Nadine added her own version.

'That one with the tidy bum is racing down the white line on the other side from us... he must be tired now – he's just having a little rest on the floor. No one seems to want the ball; as soon as they catch it they boing it back to the other one again. That bald guy seems to be very angry about something... Now they're having a chat and doing some stretches... look, here comes Billy – *go Billy* – *pass the goddamn ball to von Feldstein* – sorry, is that not what you say?'

'Will you put a sock in it?' yelled an Australian from above them in the stands.

'You wanna come down here and say that?' said Nadine, standing up.

'Sit down, love. You carry on. It's the best commentary I've heard for years,' said someone else who was sitting right behind them.

'Hear, hear,' said another voice.

Nadine turned back to face the pitch, sitting down just in time to see the ball passed to Billy, who bounced it up once and smacked it into the back of the goal, scoring his first Olympic goal. Their section of the crowd, full of German supporters, went mad. Pip and Nadine screamed and hugged each other. Max and Ferdi were jumping on their seats, chanting their brother's name, and Dominic was taking pictures of Billy and the rest of the team celebrating. One-nil to Germany. Play began again, and Pip closed her eyes.

'Looks like they're having a game of tennis now... blimey, didn't know you were allowed to do that... ow. That'll smart a bit.'

'Who is it?' Pip said.

'Mayerhöfer – it's all right, just an elbow in his mouth.'

Pip groaned.

'He's up again, laughing. You can look again, Pip. Billy's going off – *don't take him off* – *he's your best player, you morons...*

what's that yellow bit of plastic they're waving at him? Those guys must secretly fancy each other – they keep rolling around on the floor together… oh – what's this called?'

'A penalty corner.'

'And that?'

'A goal for Pakistan.'

The match ended one-all and Pip's heartbeat slowly returned to normal as she sat in her seat and watched Max, Ferdi and Dominic go down to the fence to tell Billy how awesome he was. Remembering her promise to Dominic, she made Nadine stay with her. She felt drained and fragile. Why was she putting herself through this? Dominic had said she didn't need to watch the hockey. Leo wouldn't notice if she wasn't here. And she was in serious danger of having a panic attack at the thought of a ball from Abbas' stick taking the head off Leo or Billy.

Day Eight: Friday 22nd September

Nadine and Pip took the boys to Bondi to watch beach volleyball, and when they arrived back at the hotel, Dominic told them he'd managed to procure a room for them. He had the taxi ready and waiting to take them back to Paddington to pack their stuff and bring them back to the hotel. Dean and Glen weren't at home, so they packed quickly, hoping to avoid them. Pip left a note to say thank you and bye on the table by the door.

Nadine said, 'I'm so glad we're not staying there any more. I hate to think of you alone in that house with those weirdos, before I arrived.'

'Were they so bad?'

'Yes. The whole house was filthy. Glen was OK, I suppose – but that other guy gave me the creeps. I didn't like the way he was looking at you. Shifty.'

'You're imagining things.'

'Well, you'll never see them again anyway. I hope it's OK for me to stay with you in the hotel.'

'Dominic said it's fine. You're helping out so much with Max and Ferdi, so it evens out.'

'A couple of school friends from London called me yesterday. They've rented an apartment in Manly and said I can kip on their sofa.'

Pip said, 'You don't have to, honestly. Dominic's really generous. He'll be insulted if you don't stay.'

'Well, I might go and see them tomorrow or Sunday anyway. You'd like them – you should come too, if you're not working.'

After they'd had dinner, they sat and watched TV in Max and Ferdi's room while Dominic worked in his. The phone rang and they heard him say Billy's name. Nadine made a curious face at Pip and they both tried to listen.

'It's a bit strange… no… I don't think so… I'll ask her. No? You sure? Well, let me know. It's probably nothing. OK, I won't. Good luck tomorrow. Ha ha. Yes. She has quite a few fans of her own. OK, I'll tell her. Bye.'

Dominic's head appeared in the doorway. 'Billy says he appreciates your support, Nadine.'

'Oh yeah? What other news from the Village?'

'Nothing much. Just some… nothing.' He waved vaguely and disappeared again.

Nadine's face was puzzled. '"I'll ask her" – what? What do you think that's about?'

Pip shrugged and gently squeezed the sides of her thumping forehead. She had a bad feeling about – well, about everything.

Day Nine: Saturday 23rd September

'Hey, Pip, d'you want to go over to Manly today? I'm meeting my friends at the beach. There's a party later. You in?'

'Nah, it's OK, I think I'll skip it this time,' said Pip, who was feeling exhausted.

'Are you going to the match this evening?' Germany were up against Great Britain – Leo and Billy would be playing against their old school friend.

'Nope. I hate watching it. I mean, I love watching Leo, but I'm terrified. I keep imagining he's going to get hurt. It's better if you're there, but I think I'll sit this one out.'

'Won't Leo want you to watch?'

'I don't think he'll mind either way.'

Nadine smiled. 'You're doing really well, Pip, you know that, right? It's incredibly brave of you to even be here. Take it easy on yourself, will you?'

'How d'you mean?'

'I mean, you look knackered. You're carrying around a lot of grief still, and it's bound to make you feel overwhelmed. Everything – your first Olympics without Holly, all this marriage-and-babies bullshit from Troy, the pressure you're under, protecting Leo – it's a lot to cope with all at once. That's bound to take its toll. Go to bed early, don't watch the match; watch a film, or do something by yourself. Just be away from this shit for a while.'

'OK.' Pip smiled. 'When did you get so wise?'

'I think it was when my best friend lost her big sister and needed help but was too spaced out to ask for it. I know you didn't read my letters or answer my calls, Pip. But I thought about you every day and I tried to imagine how awful it must have been for you. I think you're incredibly brave and I'll always be around if you slip a bit and need someone to talk to.'

'Thanks, Nad. You're the best.'

'I know.'

Pip changed into her pyjamas and ordered room service. She watched a bit of the Germany game, which they were losing, before she switched over and found, with some difficulty, a channel that wasn't showing sport. She watched *Tootsie* for a while, checking the time every now and again, and at ten o'clock, switched back to see that Germany had drawn two-all with GB. *Good, better than losing.* She carried on watching the film and was thinking about going to bed when her room phone rang.

'Hello?'

'Pipster, hi, it's Billy.'

Oh God. Oh no. Her brain scrambled. There was only one reason why Billy would call her, and she started to shake at the thought of Leo in hospital or lying on the ground.

Billy said, 'Funny thing—'

'What's happened? Is he OK? What is it?'

'What? Who? Leo? No, he's OK. What, did you think something had happened to him? Did you not watch the match?'

Pip closed her eyes and breathed out. He was OK.

'Never mind. What I'm calling about is this – a funny thing. Well, maybe not so funny, actually. This guy from the Australian team comes up to me yesterday, in the Village. He's a complete wanker so I don't know whether he's just trying to wind me up or what, but he asked me how I know you.'

'Oh?' was all Pip could manage to say.

'Yeah. Weird, huh? I told him you work for my family and tried to leave it at that. But this morning, there he was again. Said something about how you'd been spotted by a couple of his mates at the game on Thursday. Apparently you gave the impression, from your reaction to my goal, that you and I are an item. "So what?" I said. "What's it to you?" Then he told me that he's known you for years and that you and he had a thing. So I'm a bit confused. Because you said you had an Australian boyfriend. But you didn't say it was Troy Costa.'

Pip couldn't speak. How could Troy have told Billy that? She thought he'd be discreet about it. The bastard.

'Babe? What's going on? Is this guy for real? Because he's way older than you, and you might not know this but he was married for a while, to a hockey player, but she died.'

Pip covered her mouth with her hand.

'Pip? You still there? You wanna tell me what's going on?'

'Does Leo know?' There was silence at the other end of the phone. 'Billy? Does Leo know? Did you tell Troy that I'm going out with Leo, not you?'

'No. I was too surprised to tell him he had the wrong brother. And I didn't say anything to Leo. I wanted to talk to you first. I don't understand. You're saying it *is* true, then? How did you even meet him?' Billy's voice was full of worry.

'I can't tell you. Yet. Please. I… sorry. I… have to talk to Leo first. But not until after the Games. What… what can I do?'

'What do you want to do?'

'I have to tell Leo myself, not have him hear it from someone else. Can you talk to Troy, so he carries on thinking it's you, not Leo?'

'Dunno. Can't promise that he won't blab to someone else. I might not even see him again, except on the pitch. And all sorts of stuff is said on the pitch. There's nothing I can do about it.'

'But will you try? I'm sorry to ask you to do this. I… wanted so desperately for Leo not to know until the end of the Games.'

'How did you think you were going to manage that?'

'I don't know.' Pip was crying. 'I… it's just, everything happened at the wrong time. I didn't want to get together with Leo until after the Games but it happened, and then I said I would end it with… with Troy and I warned Leo to stay away from me until I'd finished it but he wouldn't listen and now it's fucking blowing up in my face and… shit. This is all shit.'

'Don't panic. Try to calm down. Listen, I'll do my best. God knows, I don't want Leo to hear about this either. I'll try and find Costa and make up some story about you and me. You are a dark horse, Pip. I thought you were all sweet innocence when you arrived last year, and you've been screwing the biggest dick-brained macho he-man in international hockey.' He started laughing.

'Don't tease, Billy. It's not a joke.'

'Oho, I beg to differ. Does Nadine know?'

'Yes. She's the only one.' Pip sniffed and wiped away her tears. 'You didn't… did you say something to your dad yesterday?'

'Don't cry, little Pip. I only told him about Troy asking how I know you. I'm gonna sort this out, OK?

'Please don't say anything else to your dad. I have to talk to Leo first. You really don't mind?'

'Well, I'm bored out of my tiny little brain here at the Olympic Village. There's so much time between the matches. All we do is talk about bloody hockey. Blah, blah, blah. I'm seriously tempted to do something I might regret involving alcohol or a cute Swedish volleyball player. So a bit of intrigue and plotting will be just the thing to keep me on the straight and narrow. I know – shall I start a rumour about him – match-fixing or something? They'll be burning his effigy this time tomorrow.'

She rolled her eyes. 'No. Don't get into trouble. He can be… quite aggressive… sometimes.'

'Don't I know it. How on earth did *you* end up shagging *him*? Never mind, tell me another time. Listen, got to go. Stay calm. I'll be in touch. What are you doing over the next few days?'

'Tomorrow we're going to the rowing. On Monday to watch Cathy Freeman.'

'Lucky sod. Wish I could come too. Might be able to meet you during the day, though. I'll arrange it with Dad. Laters.'

Day Ten: Sunday 24th September

After a terrible night's sleep, during which Pip had a nightmare about Troy beating the shit out of Billy with his glittery hockey stick, she was woken early by Max and Ferdi who were overexcited about going to Penrith for the rowing. Of all the events at the Olympics, this had been the one she'd been looking forward to the most – Steve Redgrave was racing that day and everyone was on tenterhooks to see if he'd win that fifth gold medal. But now she was too wound up about Troy and Billy and Leo to care. Should she call Troy? What was he up to, telling Billy like that? She broke out in a sweat at the thought of what might have happened if Troy hadn't believed, like everyone always seemed to, that it was Billy she was in love with.

They were sitting near other British fans, including some of the hockey families. Luckily, she'd worn Nadine's face-covering sunglasses. She barely saw the race and had to paste a smile on her numb face for the benefit of Max and Ferdi when the British team won the gold.

Afterwards, Pip took Max and Ferdi back to the hotel while Dominic went to the office for a meeting. When he returned, he joined them on the roof by the pool, where Ferdi and Max were having a Connect Four marathon. His face was serious and his voice concerned.

'Pip, I need to talk to you. I'm sorry about this, I wouldn't normally pry, but…' He was holding the file with Billy and Leo's press clippings in it. He pulled out a fax. 'Only – I was sent this and I thought it was an article about the boys, and I'd read too far along before I realised it was about you.'

Pip looked at the document. It took her a few seconds to focus, but it had her name on the top. 'What is this?' She grabbed it and started skim-reading.

Philippa Mitchell, born 28.11.80 in Canterbury, England. Parents: Justin and Anne Mitchell, retired police constables. One older sister, deceased 9.9.97, Holly Costa, née Mitchell. Cause of death: brain haemorrhage after impact with ball during a hockey match in Sydney, Australia.

More stuff about Holly, about Pip and her parents. 'What is this?' she repeated in a whisper.

'It's my parents-in-law. Well, also my wife. Apparently, before she left, she told Maximilian and Maria about you and Leo. Let's just say, she expressed her severe reservations about you. She's a terrible snob, I'm afraid. They all are. It's rather embarrassing, and it's not the first time they've tried to dig up dirt about girlfriends of Leo or Billy. They have the private detective who we usually use to track down Elisabeth when she's run off, and he was tasked with finding out more about you. If it's any consolation, they did the same to me when I first met Elisabeth.'

'Oh.'

'Pip, don't worry about this. It doesn't matter to me. Not one bit. I wouldn't have even read it if I'd been concentrating. But I glanced down and saw something about hockey and the Olympics and then I read your name and... I really am sorry.'

'I'm the one who should be apologising.'

'I don't agree. I understand, Pip. This – what happened to your sister – I remember it. It was terrible. I'm sure you must have been devastated. Is that why you didn't tell us?'

Pip nodded.

'Is that why you've been so nervous around the hockey club? And when Billy was hurt? And why you wouldn't play for our team? And why you were terrified of Sohail Abbas?'

She nodded again.

'Oh, you poor girl. This must have been a terribly difficult time for you. I can't even begin to imagine. Of all the families in the world, you couldn't have chosen a worse one.' He thought for a moment. 'You know, accidents like Holly's are so rare. I mean, players are often hurt, it's a physical sport, but to be killed… it's all the more cruel and devastating for you. But what I'm trying to say is, the likelihood of what happened to Holly happening to Leo is one in a million.'

She smiled weakly at him.

'Nadine – she knows, of course? You've been friends for a while?'

'All our lives. Yes, she knows. She knew Holly.'

'She… she was talking about you, wasn't she? When she said she had a friend who played? You played? England under-sixteens?'

'Yes.'

'But you haven't told Leo or Billy?'

She shook her head.

Dominic thought for a moment. 'So what Billy said – now it makes sense. This Australian player – Troy Costa. He's your brother-in-law. That's how he knows you?'

'Yes.'

'Ah.'

'I warned Leo ages ago, even before we got together, that I had something to tell him, something he wouldn't like. I didn't want him involved in it before the Olympics, because, you know, it's complicated and I didn't want him to lose his focus. He accepted that, but I don't think he realised how bad it was. I think he thought it was some stupid thing, like I'm adopted or I was caught shoplifting or something. When we got together, it was worse – I felt like I was sending him into the Colosseum to be eaten by lions, because he didn't know about me and Holly and Troy. But I thought the one saving grace was that Troy didn't know about my connection to you and Billy and Leo.'

'How do you think he found out?'

'I think it was his housemates. That's where I've been staying. They must've seen me with you and Max and Ferdi, and if they saw Max and Ferdi talking to Billy... I don't know. I guess there are no secrets in the hockey world. Don't need a private detective to know that.'

'You might be right about that. Listen to me – don't worry about this. It's fine.'

'Really? You don't care that I've lied to you about who I am? About the hockey?'

'No, of course not. I can understand that it must have been a very difficult thing for you to stay with us. Why did you?'

'Because you're all so kind.' She swallowed a sob. 'And because I love my job. And because of... well, you know. Leo.' She blushed. 'Do you think he'll be OK with it?'

She had expected Dominic to say, 'Yes, he'll be fine. Don't worry about it.' But he frowned.

'I honestly don't know, Pip. He's sometimes... well, I don't know. It's not my call. But whatever happens between you, if you want to stay with us next year, and for however long, we'd like you to stay. Leo will have to deal with it.'

'So you mean that he won't want me to stay?'

'I think he'll need more time than Billy and me to get used to the idea.'

'I can't stay if he doesn't want me to.'

'You can – for me, and for Max and Ferdi. Leo doesn't even live with us any more. He'll be busy with his degree. We need you, and he'll have to put up with it.'

Pip felt herself sink under the weight of his words. 'You know he'll never forgive me. Don't you? That's what you're saying, isn't it?' *If he says he doesn't know, he's just being kind. He knows his son. Better than anyone.*

Dominic loosened his tie and rubbed his eyes. 'I don't know, Pip.'

Day Eleven: Monday 25th September

'Hello, troublemakers.' Billy kissed Pip and Nadine on the cheeks and sat down between them at the bar. He was wearing his hockey kit and a baseball cap on backwards. 'What are you drinking?' He looked longingly at their glasses of wine.

'It's a smooth, chilled glass of heaven from the Barossa Valley. What's new?' said Nadine.

Pip was too afraid to ask. She'd updated Nadine about the fact that Billy knew she'd slept with Troy, and that Dominic knew she was Holly's sister, and that Leo still knew nothing but could find out at any time. Nadine had said, with a grin, that there was never a dull moment when Pip was around.

They were at the bar in the Deutsche Haus, the meeting place for the German Olympic team and their families. Dominic had been given passes for them for the whole week, so they could come and go as they pleased. There was a restaurant and a bar, meeting rooms and video analysis rooms, a gym and physiotherapists for the athletes. The boys could eat and drink as much as they liked and watch the sports on the big screens.

'Nothing new,' said Billy. 'Only, we're playing them tomorrow and it could all kick off then.'

'Do you think I should come to the game or not?'

'Not. Sorry, I know you'd probably love to see your paramours fight it out on the pitch – a bit like pistols at dawn, except on a hockey pitch and with sticks – but it might be best to watch on telly in the hotel again.'

Pip nodded.

Nadine said, 'I'll stay with you. We can watch the game together, get drunk and slag off Troy without fear of arrest.'

Billy said goodbye; he had to go to a team meeting. Pip was so on edge – Dominic was just over the other side of the room.

Leo was next door, going through the tactics for tomorrow with the coaches. Billy, as well as being totally indiscreet, was about two connections away from knowing about her and Holly. She should tell him, she should have done it straight away, but she hadn't and now she didn't want to complicate things further. She never, ever wanted Dominic to know that she'd slept with Troy. He'd been really kind so far, but probably wouldn't feel so understanding towards her if he knew what she and Troy had done.

She felt like everything was closing in on her. There were too many complications, too many bits of jigsaw puzzle that anyone could join up to make the full picture. And that wasn't even counting the fact that she'd had a couple of missed calls from a British number on her mobile, which probably meant the GB women were trying to reach her. She wondered if she should call Troy, to persuade him to leave Billy – and more importantly, Leo – alone. But if she did that, he might be so angry with her that he'd take it out on them instead. On the pitch. With his stick.

Nadine told her to leave it and, for good measure, deleted his number from her phone. 'No offence to you, but I think he'll have forgotten all about this by now. So, you hurt his pride, but he has more important things to think about than a completely un-heartfelt marriage proposal to a woman he doesn't even love.'

'You really have a way with words, Nad.'

'Oh, talking about a way with words. I brought something with me.' She fished a sheath of typewritten pages out of her rucksack and placed it carefully on Pip's lap. 'This is for you.'

Pip looked down at it. There was no title or heading. She started reading and recognised the words she'd written to Nadine over the past few months. She frowned. 'What is this?'

'It's all your emails to me. I love getting them. I read them over and over and I started putting them into order and editing them a bit. There's a bunch of fab material in there. It's like *Bridget Jones's Diary*, but with sport.'

'I'm still not with you.'

'You should get some of this published. There are women's magazines, creative writing competitions, stuff like that. One day, you could pull it together into a novel. It's great. It's funny and sweet and exciting. Read through it – you'll see.'

'Nadine, you're crazy. I can't write a book.'

'You almost have.' She lifted up the pile of paper. 'This is thirty thousand words, Pip. I did a word count. And you've written this in, what, nine months? You keep on writing like that and you'll have a full-length novel this time next year.'

'I couldn't. I can't. I don't know how to.'

Nadine tapped the paper. 'Clearly, you do. Look, just read it, OK, and think about it. You never know, it might help you along the way – they say writing is great therapy. And take the compliment, you big twerp.'

That evening they watched Cathy Freeman win her four hundred metres in a packed Stadium Australia, every one of its 110,000 seats full, cameras flashing, the roar from the crowd deafening. It was the most exquisite race Pip had ever seen. Freeman running in her hooded bodysuit, oblivious to the screams of her adoring fans; she was the eye of the storm, elegant, serene, looking for all the world as if she was alone in an empty stadium.

Day Twelve: Tuesday 26th September

Dominic gave Pip the day off and took the boys to the beach, and afterwards to the Deutsche Haus. Nadine and Pip spent the day shopping and ate lunch in a pub by the harbour, but Pip felt like she was sleepwalking. She had to keep reminding herself to relax – her shoulders were so tense, she had backache and her head was thumping.

At six o'clock, they settled in front of the TV in their hotel room to watch the warm-up and the match. There were pre-match interviews with Troy and the Australian captain, and the captain of the German team and both coaches. Neither Billy nor Leo was interviewed, although Leo was mentioned as a key player and 'one to watch'.

'Oh, we'll be watching him, all right,' said Nadine, sipping a revolting-looking cocktail.

In the first half, there were three penalty corners, two for Germany, one for Australia, no goals. Troy was shown a yellow card, which the commentators said was completely unjustified.

'Shall we turn off the sound? These guys are so biased,' said Nadine.

'And we're not?'

At half-time it was nil-all. Pip and Nadine ordered food from room service but when it arrived, Pip hardly touched it. So far, Leo and Troy hadn't been close to each other on the pitch, or not that she'd seen anyway. Billy hadn't come on yet. Had he said something, done something to get himself into trouble?

In the second half, two goals were scored in the first five minutes, making the score one-all. Billy came on and the game changed. What had been low-level unpleasantness in the first half – stick-tackles, body contact, a few hard stares – became nasty fouls, bodies thumping, and players shouting at each other and the umpire. A player from each team went off injured – one with a broken finger, one with a stick to the head that required stitches.

'What's going on, Pip? It's so fast – can you even follow this? And why is everyone suddenly so angry?'

Pip did a few calculations. 'This is the last match of the first round. Up to now, Australia and Germany both have eight points. Whoever wins this match wins the group. The other one comes second. If they draw, Australia wins with a better goal difference.'

'So only one team goes through?'

'No. Two. But if you win the group, you play the second-placed team in the other group, theoretically an easier team to beat.'

'Which is…'

'South Korea. I think. Anyway, there's a lot at stake. Ouch. Shit.' Billy was on the floor and Germany had been awarded a penalty corner. They missed. Two more players were given green cards.

'What's that for? Are they sent off?'

'No, it's just a warning. Yellow is when you're sent off for five minutes, and red is for the rest of the match.'

Troy was marking Billy, but the cameras weren't ever on them long enough to see what they were doing – or saying – to each other. There were four more German penalty corners. Two were saved, one missed the goal and the other was stopped before Germany had the chance to shoot at all. Pip watched, her shoulders tight, and it seemed like the whole match was crackling with an electricity that was about a second away from exploding. One more push, one more tackle, one word would set the spark alight and the whole thing would go up with a bang.

The Aussies were pressing harder and harder. Leo was as solid as ever, but on close-ups, Pip could see the sweat on his face and hair, his grim expression of concentration, his laboured breathing and the way he moved, his body clearly battling exhaustion. She thought the game would never end. If the umpire could just blow the whistle, a point each, and no more chances of Troy blasting Billy's head off or Leo being body-slammed for the twelve-millionth time. Oh God, it was torture.

But in the last five minutes of the match, disaster. Leo, standing on the goal line, stopped a shot with his arm and Troy stepped up to take a penalty flick.

'What? How's that allowed? Surely Leo should get the ball – that guy hurt him.'

Troy put the ball in the back of the net. Two-one to the Aussies.

'Not how it works,' mumbled Pip, watching with dread as the minutes and seconds ticked down.

The final whistle blew and Australia had won.

Day Thirteen: Wednesday 27th September

After a morning at Bondi beach, where a massive kids' beach cricket tournament had been organised, Pip and Nadine took the boys, exhausted, sweaty and sandy, to the Deutsche Haus to meet Dominic for lunch. With only three days of the Games left, many of the German athletes had completed their events and were busy making up for months or years of abstinence at the bar or in the restaurant. Rowers, swimmers, fencers and archers were finished, as well as the triathletes and most of the cyclists. The men's hockey team, grim-faced, filed into one of the meeting rooms to pick apart last night's match and prepare for the semi-final on Friday.

They emerged after an hour for a break and Billy came over to them.

'Hey, Pip, can I have a quick word? Maybe outside – breath of fresh air? I've got twenty minutes.'

While Nadine played table football with Max and Ferdi, they walked around the park and Billy updated her on what had happened last night.

'Costa was giving it some on the pitch – he didn't say anything but he was simmering the whole time. They all were. Jesus, I can't believe we lost to them.'

'Is Leo OK? His arm?'

'Yeah, he's fine. The dude's made of stone, Pip, you really don't have to worry about him. Anyway, at full time I see Costa in Leo's face, so sprint over there, in case I need to step in.'

'What did he say?'

'Costa's all, "Take that, you Nazi", and Leo says, cool as, "That's an original insult", which only riles Costa more. Then he gets going about you – but this is the best bit. He says to Leo, "That chick your brother's shagging is a whore."'

Pip winced. *Charming.*

'Two things I'd like to point out – one, what a hypocrite, like *he's* not a total whore. Also, please note that he doesn't let on that he's shagged you himself. What a knob.

'Anyway, of course, Leo thinks it's Nadine he's talking about. That's the brilliant bit. So he just shrugs. And I'm laughing so hard, I can't even see Costa, he's coming towards me, fists flying, and then a couple of his buddies hold him back, and he's shouting rude and frankly ungentlemanly things about you-slash-Nadine, even stuff about how you shouldn't be looking after kids, which is perfect because Leo knows Nadine's been helping out so much with Max and Ferdi, so doesn't suspect a thing.'

'But you didn't fight, did you? I mean, no one got into trouble?'

'No, relax.' He put his arm round Pip. 'I told you, no one's going to get into trouble – well, not me and Leo anyway. Costa's such a psycho, I bet his teammates have pulled him off many a man before.'

'I'm sorry about all this, Billy.'

'Christ, no, don't apologise. This is the most fun I've had for ages. You certainly know how to spice things up, my friend.'

'You don't think… you don't think I'm a cliché? A groupie? For sleeping with one hockey player after another?'

Billy laughed. 'Why on earth would I have a problem with pretty girls who like to sleep with hockey players? They're my favourite type of girls.'

Pip rolled her eyes, but he cheered her up a bit.

'And by the way, you once told me that your life was anodyne – see, I remembered that big word. That's a load of horseshit, isn't it?'

'It really is true.'

Billy counted off on his fingers. 'First time I meet you, you catch me and Roxy in the sack. Then you tell everyone about it, by mistake. You somehow manage to not know who Leo and I are, even though you're working for our dad. Then you become the first girl ever to resist my advances. You learn skiing in about twenty seconds. You can figure out when I'm playing a trick on Leo in ten seconds. You dance. You drink. A lot. You do dares for the love of your new best friend. Your other best friend is a sex goddess. You nurse a house full of people back to health. You save my brother's life from a swarm of wasps. You make up stories and write plays. And you've shagged—'

'Enough, OK, Billy, enough. All of those things were either stupid mistakes or just mucking about with children. Or I was drunk. Really, I'm very ordinary and boring.'

'You keep telling yourself that, Pipsqueak. It won't wash with me any more.'

Back at the Deutsche Haus, the big screen was showing Germany against GB in the women's hockey. Pip knew, because she'd followed the scores, that they were playing off for seventh and eighth place, which would be a huge disappointment for Holly's old team. She should call them back this evening and arrange to meet them. She locked eyes with Dominic, who smiled at her reassuringly, understanding that watching the British women play without Holly would be unbearably poignant for her. There were cheers as Germany won two-nil, but Pip didn't feel like celebrating either way.

Day Fourteen: Thursday 28th September

Semi-finals day for the men at the hockey centre. Pip was torn – should she go, could she bear it? With the misunderstanding about which girl Troy was shouting about, she felt like she'd dodged a bullet. Maybe she and Nadine should both stay away. But there was a gap of four hours between the Germany-South Korea semi and Troy's semi against Holland, so there would be no contact between the two men today. In the end, they decided to go. Nadine was so proud that she'd become the diversion in the complicated mess of insults and intrigue.

At Homebush, Nadine received a text from her friends – they had a spare ticket for the women's doubles tennis finals that evening, and would she like it?

'Would I?' said Nadine, squealing with excitement. She hero-worshipped the Williams sisters. 'Is it OK?' she said quietly to Pip. 'Will you be OK without me?'

'It's fine. Go. It'll be great. Have fun.'

'I'll probably crash at theirs afterwards. So don't wait up for me.'

'Got your Anya Amasova overnight emergency bag? Good. See you tomorrow.'

Pip watched the hockey match with Dominic and the boys. The crowd was mixed – around them, Germans and neutrals, including the German women's hockey team; but a large Korean group was at either end, making lots of noise and lending the place a party atmosphere. Only Pip felt down. The time was close when this would be over – the Olympics, her relationship with Leo, her life in Munich. In a matter of days, everything that she'd kept from Leo would have to be spoken out loud, by her, and she felt her courage failing because she wanted to be with him for a while longer. Just a few weeks. Or days. Maybe one single day. But she'd promised him, and she knew she had to go through with it.

Germany lost one-nil and the von Feldsteins trooped back to the Deutsche Haus afterwards, knowing that in two days their team would be playing either Holland or Australia again, but only for the bronze medal. There, amongst the families and friends of the hockey team, the atmosphere was muted.

Pip was silent and thoughtful. She watched TV with the boys while Dominic chatted to his friends. They had some dinner and Dominic suggested she go and meet up with Nadine.

'It's OK, I'm not really in the mood,' said Pip.

'You look exhausted. Why don't you go back to the hotel and get an early night? I'm all right with the boys this evening. This can't be much fun for you, Pip. You don't look well and I'm worried about you.'

'I'm fine, but thanks, yes, I'll go. See you later.'

Back at the hotel, Pip put her hand in her pocket for her room card, and with it pulled out the key to the Underwood Street house. She'd forgotten to give it back. And she realised that, in her hurry to pack, she'd left Holly's number nine shirt at Troy's house. It was *her* shirt – Troy had given it to her – and it would be lying there, on the bed, waiting for her. She felt like a jog. It would only be an hour there and back, so she changed into running clothes, tucking the key and her mobile phone into her pocket. Her shorts were an old pair, indecently tight and short, but she wouldn't be seeing anyone she knew, so it didn't matter. She left a note on Dominic's door to say what she was doing and set off away from the harbour towards Paddington.

As she turned the corner into Underwood Street twenty minutes later, sweating in the still-warm early evening, she heard music and voices. There were people in the small front garden and a barbie was smoking. Tubs of beer were set out along the length of the fence, and people were coming in and out of the house.

'Pip! Hey. How're you?' Glen saw her and opened the gate. 'Thought we'd never see you again.'

'I forgot to give you back my key,' she said quietly. 'Also, I forgot my T-shirt. I left it—'

'Never mind that,' said Glen, taking the key from her. 'Have a beer. Have lots of beer. We're watching Troy in the semi later. Stay for a bit.'

Pip smiled and looked down at her sweaty running gear, plucking at her shorts to pull them down a bit. 'I'm not dressed for a party.'

'You look smashing,' said Dean from behind her, putting his arm around her shoulder. Pip cringed. He was swaying and his breath smelled beery and meaty. 'Really, you do. Doesn't she, Glenno?' He leered at her, pinched her bum and staggered away. Glen gave her a quick smile as if to say sorry.

'You can go upstairs and shower, if you want. But no one's bothered. Look around you – it's hardly formalwear.'

'Thanks, OK, I will have a beer.' She stood by the barbecue with Dean and his girlfriend Tracey, who played hockey at the same club as Glen, Dean and Troy. She had met Holly, she said, and told Pip how sad she was when she'd died. Thirsty from her run, Pip drank her beer quickly, meaning to leave, not wanting to have this conversation, but the match was about to start, so she went inside with another drink and sat down.

She barely watched the match, but listened to the chatter around her and accepted drinks whenever they were offered. She sat next to Tracey, who was really friendly – a big, solid girl, with short, no-nonsense hair and a pretty, freckly face. She reminded Pip of a larger version of Tiny.

'So, Glen tells me you're an au pair, is that right?'

Pip looked at Tracey, to see if it was a loaded question. But her face only showed friendly curiosity. Still, she didn't want to talk about this now.

'Yeah. What do you do?'

'I'm a police officer,' said Tracey, and Pip felt comforted and, at the same time, thrown off balance. 'This is my first night off since the Games began. We're all working back-to-back shifts. I'm at the central station near Darling Harbour.'

Pip said, 'My parents are retired police.'

'I know. Holly told me. How are they?'

'Not great. Don't know. I'm not in touch with them much.'

At half-time she sat on the stairs, in a queue for the one loo, and thought to herself, *Must remember to pick up Holly's shirt before I leave.*

The match went on and on. At full time it was a nil-nil draw, so there was extra time. Still neither team scored. Pip drank and yawned and was about to leave, but extra time ended and there was a penalty shoot-out.

'You can't leave yet,' said Glen or Dean or Tracey as she stood up.

Whoa. Pip's legs nearly gave way. She climbed up the stairs, hanging on to the banister, and sat on the loo with the window open to breathe some fresh air. How come she was so drunk? She'd only had a few beers. Sure, she'd not had much to eat from the barbecue, but she was light-headed and could hardly keep her eyes open.

She could hear cheers from downstairs. Was Troy one of the five players who'd take a flick? If so, she hoped he'd miss it. But on the other hand, if Australia beat the Netherlands, they'd be in the final against South Korea and not the bronze medal match against Germany. Out loud, she said, 'That would be referable... reperable... preferle.' *Shit. I'm hammered.*

Instead of going downstairs, she crossed the tiny landing with one step, narrowly avoiding falling down the steep, narrow stairs, and went into Troy's room. It was exactly as she'd left it, and Holly's shirt was hung on the bedpost. She put her hand on it.

319

'I'm sorry Troy is such a wanker,' she whispered to the shirt. 'I'm sorry you ever met him. I'm sorry I fucked him. I've ruined everything. It's all my fault.'

She buried her wet face in the shirt and felt waves of despair and loneliness roll over her. 'What am I supposed to do, Holly? I've landed myself in deep shit and I don't know how I'm supposed to dig myself out of it. I'm a complete fuck-up. I hate myself. No wonder Troy doesn't love me. No wonder Leo's going to run a mile when I tell him.'

She lay down on the bed, hugging the shirt to her, curling her body around it. 'If you were here, you'd hate me too. But if you were here, none of this shit would have happened. Why did you die, Holly? Why did you have to be killed by something so insignificant as a hard, round bit of plastic? You were my hero. You were so strong, but you died in a pointless, crap way. And you left me alone to deal with this stuff by myself. I hate it. All this shit. The shitness of my life. I hate that you're not here. Where are you? Why won't you come and talk to me?'

There was no answer, and Pip ran out of steam. She cried some more, not wiping away the tears. She felt her eyes close and relax... she sank into the wet pillow... she heard cheers and the sounds of feet and voices downstairs, on the street... fading out... then black.

A hand on her arm, stroking from her shoulder to her wrist. A voice whispering her name. Her mouth was dry. Her head thudded. She cranked open her eyes – it was dark outside the window.

'Troy?' she said.

'No, it's me.'

She turned her head and saw Dean's big face hovering over her. She tried to sit up but crashed down again onto her back. She felt dizzy and sick.

'Relax,' he said, and began stroking her arm again. She shivered. 'You like that?'

She gagged, but nothing came out.

Through the fuzziness of her brain, she felt the springs on the bed beneath her move, and she turned her head towards him. 'Stop it,' she said, but her tongue was furry and thick and it sounded wrong.

His hand gripped her wrist and she started to panic. Why couldn't she move? A small, sharp thought was forming in her head. In the beer she'd drunk... what if... she'd heard stories of drinks being spiked. She raised her other hand to try to loosen his grip, but he grabbed it and pushed it down on the bed beside her.

No. No, no, no. One of his legs pinned her down. No. He was kissing her, his sloppy mouth, stale and rank, on hers. No.

'No,' she shouted. 'No.'

'Whaddya mean, no? You want this, Pip. I know you do. With Costa, with me, what does it matter?'

'No.' She gagged again. 'What did you put in my drink?'

'Little something to help you relax. You're much too wound up. I can see it. Just relax. This'll be fun.'

He put his mouth on hers and pressed down on her closed lips. She couldn't get enough air, he was blocking her nose and she opened her mouth to breathe.

'That's better. Good girl.'

'No.' She kicked under him, tried to wriggle out, but he was fully on top of her. He was so heavy, she felt her strength drain away. 'Help me,' she shouted as loudly as she could.

'There's no one here. Everyone's left. Gone home.'

'Glen,' she shouted.

'He's gone too, to his bird's house. Just you and me.'

'Glen. Tracey. Help,' she screamed.

'They're not here. Shout all you like. Actually,' he laughed, 'she's a bit of a screamer too; the neighbours will think it's them doing it. Go for it,' he said. 'The louder the better.'

He lowered his mouth again and she bit down, feeling something rip and a liquid trickle into her mouth as he yelled.

'What the...?' He sprang off her, his hand clamped to his mouth. She struggled up onto her elbows and rolled off the bed, slamming onto the floor, shoulder then head then knees then feet. 'You fucking bitch.'

It was all shadows in the room, the only light cast from a street lamp outside. She heard the bedsprings move and put her hands in front of her, pressing down on the floor. Her head felt so heavy. Under the bed she saw a long, thin shape, many shapes, gleaming in plastic covers in the dim light. She reached out her hand and it closed around a hockey stick as she felt Dean's hand grip her ankle. She wriggled the other way, under the bed, but he pulled her out and she felt the carpet burn her elbows. Writhing around, she turned to face him as he landed on top of her, the weight of him knocking the wind out of her and making her let go of the stick.

He took hold of her T-shirt at the neck and, his body pinning hers down, yanked it. It sliced into her neck at the back and the fabric ripped. He sat up on her, his knees gripping her thighs, holding her wrists above her head with one hand, the other fumbling with the zip on his jeans.

'You hurt me. I'm going to hurt you too,' he said. He had a dark smear of blood on his chin. He lowered his face and wiped it off with the remains of her T-shirt. She kicked again, but he was too heavy. She felt weary. Was this going to happen? Was this what happened to brainless fuck-ups like her? Was this simply another way that life was going to shit all over her? His hand was on the top of her running shorts, trying to tug them down, one side, then the other.

Her body went limp and her head flopped to the side. If she let him, it would be over soon. It wouldn't hurt, if she let him. Would it be so bad? It might only hurt a bit. She felt her chest rise and fall, her heart thump, the hard floor beneath the back of her head, his hands on her shorts, the bruises on her neck and wrists and thighs and knees, the carpet burn on her elbows, the scratch of his fingers.

He swore under his breath, struggling with the tight shorts, and let go of her hands. Her arm moved of its own accord, sliding across the carpet under the bed, reaching out until she felt the plastic and the hard stick. She had one chance. He was looking down, and she opened her mouth, letting out a roar as she swung the stick up from under the bed. It caught on the underside of the bed, taking most of the momentum out of the swing, and glanced off his shoulder, only skimming the side of his head. But it was enough for him to stop what he was doing.

'You bitch—'

She screamed again, holding the stick with both hands and ramming it up against his throat. He fell backwards off her, and she scrambled up and stood above him, pulling up her shorts with one hand. He was sitting on the floor in the corner of the room. She put her face right up to his, his ragged lip, coughing and clutching his throat.

'Don't. Call. Me. A. Bitch.'

Now she didn't know what to do. Should she hit him again or just get out of there? She raised the stick and lowered it. Time to leave. She took Holly's shirt and tugged it on over her ripped T-shirt, one arm and the next, swapping the stick from hand to hand, not letting it go. Then one foot in front of the other. She stumbled towards the door and heard a shuffling behind her. As he reached her, she looked back and yanked open the door, meaning to hit him, but she did it too soon and felt it thunk against her head as he made a lunge for her, missed and fell through the open doorway.

The room swam, and she reeled back and sat down on the floor, managing to kick the door closed as she heard a series of thumps. *He's falling down the stairs. Did he knock himself out?* She heard him swear loudly. No such luck. She looked around the room, crawled to the heavy chair in the corner and dragged it across, wedging it between the door and the bed as a body crashed against the door from the other side. The chair held. There was no space for anything to move. She was safe, for now. But trapped in the room.

Dean banged against the door and it shook in its frame, but didn't open. She sat on the bed, her head pounding, trying to think. Mobile phone. Yes. It was still in her pocket. With trembling hands, she pulled it out and jabbed at it. *Calm down. Breathe.* Slowly, she pressed 999 and held it to her ear. There was a dead tone. What was the dialling code for Australia? She tried 0061-999, but again, a dead tone. What was the emergency number in Australia? Why didn't she know this? She tried 911 and 999 again.

There were more thumps and curses from outside the door. Dean said, 'I'll wait here all night. You've got nowhere to go. I'm not going anywhere.'

There was another thud, and silence. Had he passed out? Fallen down the stairs again? With the stick still in her hand, she crept to the window and opened it. The street was deserted. She could hear loud music from the main road. She put her hand to her head and felt the lump on it. No blood, though.

She only had the numbers of three people who were in Sydney in her phone – Dominic, Leo and Nadine. She tried Nadine. It rang and rang, but no one answered. She tried again. She tried Dominic. It went straight to voicemail. Her thumb hovered above Leo's number. No. It was the middle of the night. He had the bronze medal game the day after tomorrow. He'd be asleep in the Olympic Village; she'd wake him and Billy. No. She tried Nadine again. Her left hand was shaking, and she had to hold the phone with her right hand to press the buttons. Her head throbbed, her limbs felt heavy. Nadine would be in a bar or club. She would have to hear sometime, if she even had her phone with her. Pip kept pressing, kept calling, sent a text to Nadine: *Come in a taxi to Underwood Street right now.* Tears burned her eyes, she had a metallic taste in her mouth, there was dried blood on her chin, and she felt nausea and exhaustion pour over her, through her. She couldn't pass out, she had to stay awake. She had to call Nadine. She texted her again, fumbling with the phone, dropping it. She jabbed at the buttons, her vision blurred by tears. Back at the window, she shouted, but there was no one on the street.

She slumped onto the floor underneath the window. The cool night air washed over her and she felt only tiredness. *What will be, will be. He's asleep on the landing. Just a quick nap. Just close my eyes. Then I'll be safe. Or not. Doesn't matter.*

Outside, the screech of tyres. Did someone call her name? A hammering, far away. A crash, splintering of wood. She was awake. Noises on the stairs. She heard her name.

A thump, and a groan.

'Get out of my way. Who are you? Where is she? Pip?'

'Leo?' Her voice snagged in her dry throat. What was he doing here? 'Leo?' she said, louder. 'Leo. In here.' She pushed herself up and staggered towards the door, heaving the chair aside. He was standing in the hallway above the prone form of Dean. She collapsed against him, sobbing.

'What are you doing here? Who's that? Are you hurt?' He pushed her gently away from him and looked at her. 'What's happened?'

'He... he tried to... he... I hit him.' She showed him the stick in her hand. 'I hit... my head. I... Leo...'

He was looking at her, taking in the state of her, and around her into the dark room, at the bed with its covers tangled, at the windowsill, the street lamp outside lighting up the row of photos. 'Whose room is this? His?' He pointed at the slumped Dean.

'No. He... I think he spiked my drink. Leo, can we please leave?' She was shaking against him, and he nodded and took the first few stairs, holding on to her arm to steady her. They walked out of the broken front door onto the street and into the taxi.

She rested her head against his shoulder, feeling the warmth of him, shivering as the taxi sped through the dark streets. Neither of them spoke. His face was set in a hard mask. She was trying to stop her teeth chattering. Her tongue felt heavy and large in her mouth. She was so thirsty.

The lights of the hotel were bright in her eyes as they walked together through the lobby. She looked at Leo's face – he had a fading black eye and a red graze on his jaw. Her gaze dropped to his arm and to the perfectly round, purple-black bruise. Up in the lift, along the corridor, she gave him her key card because her hand was shaking too much to fit it into the slot. But he had his own. He opened the door for her. She stepped inside, but it wasn't her room. The bed was in the wrong place. The door to the en-suite bathroom was on the other side.

'Where are we?'

'My room.'

'Huh?' She felt bleary and weak.

He sat her down on a chair near the window and fetched her a glass of water, kneeling down in front of her. On the table next to her was his copy of *The Power of One*, spine up – he was about halfway through.

'Dad reserved it for me. I come here for some peace and quiet. The Village is crazy; the athletes who've finished are up all night partying. I can't sleep, so I come here, kip for a few hours and go back before everyone else is up.' While he was talking, he examined her, his fingers brushing the bruises on her head and neck, his callused hands turning over her wrists and arms, looking into her eyes.

'Leo, I'm so sorry, I didn't mean to call you. I don't remember...'

'You sent me a text. *The* text.' He showed her his phone with the *HILFE* message on it.

'I didn't mean to. I would never have—'

'You said you hit your head?'

She nodded. 'On the door. It's fine.'

'Dizzy?'

'A bit.'

'Nauseous?'

'Not any more.'

'How many fingers am I holding up?'

She looked at his hand. 'Three.'

'Now?'

'One.'

'He gave you something? In your drink?'

She sipped the water. 'I think so. Before – I was tired. Just really, really tired. I fell asleep. I think.'

'And how much did you drink?'

Something in his voice made her look up into his eyes. They were blank and hard. She blinked. How much had she drunk? 'I don't know. Five. Beers. Or more. I don't know.' She rubbed her head. She needed more water.

'When we were there, you said he tried… you don't mean that he tried to…? Did he…?'

'No. I hit him. He fell down the stairs.'

He released a breath, but froze as he followed her eyes to her hand. She was still holding Troy's stick. She dropped it. He looked at her again, then at her shirt, which was Holly's.

'Leo—'

He stumbled away from her. 'What? Pip? What is going on? Where was that? I got your text and didn't know where you were. Then I found the note on Dad's door. Who lives at Underwood Street?' His voice was quiet and angry.

'No one. No one you know. Friends.'

'No one I know?'

'Just… people.'

There was silence in the room. Pip looked down at her lap. She was having trouble keeping her eyes open. She had to focus.

'You're lying. You know who lives there. I know too.' His voice was ice-cold. 'Start talking, Pip. Quickly. And no more lies.'

'I don't know where to start,' she mumbled.

'How about you start by telling me why the fuck I just found you in Troy Costa's bedroom, wearing Holly Costa's shirt?'

Silence.

'Now! Talk. And don't stop until you've told me everything.'

Pip said, 'She's my sister. Was. Holly was my sister.'

'Holly? Holly Costa?'

Pip let it sink in. She glanced up at him.

'This… but… of course. Her maiden name. Holly Mitchell.' The anger drained out of him. He stood in front of her, his arms hanging down by his sides, wide-eyed. 'Oh, Pip. All this time… why didn't you tell me?'

'I don't know. I… it was selfish, I suppose. When I came to Munich, I was still so upset about her death. I couldn't even bear to think about her. I just wanted to forget. Not be dead Holly Costa's little sister any more. Fresh start. That was the idea, anyway.'

'You didn't know that we played hockey. You didn't know who we were. Did you?'

She shook her head.

'Wait – you used to play. You played hockey, didn't you? Of course – it makes sense now. You're so fit, so coordinated. Holly – she told me, too. I met her once, in Atlanta; we watched one of Costa's games and chatted. Oh, man. Oh. She told me all about you, couldn't stop going on about you. She said you played, that you were a great little player. That's what she said. Those words.' He sighed. 'She thought there was a good chance you'd both be going to Sydney, the way you were improving.' He shook his head. 'I never spoke to her again. That stupid bastard thought I was chatting her up; he went mad, threatened to "dismantle" me.' He did air quotes.

'Were you?'

'What?'

'Chatting her up?'

'No, course not. She was great, your sister. I liked her, but not like that. I can't believe you're her sister. Does Dad know?'

'Your grandparents faxed him a report about me from a private detective. He read it by mistake. So yeah, since yesterday, he knows.'

'Oh Christ, not that again. I'm so sorry.'

'He already apologised.'

'And Billy – does he know?'

'Not about that.'

'What do you mean – there's more?'

Pip closed her eyes briefly and opened them. Leo was looking at her with love and pity and kindness. He understood about Holly and why she'd not told him. Now she had to tell him about Troy. She'd always known, deep down, that she couldn't hide it from him. It was the way it had to be. Being with Leo wasn't meant to be easy. It had to be all or nothing. All, then nothing. This was going to be the last time ever that he looked at her like that.

'Leo, are you absolutely sure you want to hear this now? If I tell you... that me being Holly's sister... is the good bit?'

The smile ebbed away and he frowned, trying to figure it out.

'I'll tell you if you want me to. But I don't want to, I never have, not before you've finished playing.'

'Is it to do with Costa?' His voice was hard.

'Yes.'

'Then you have to tell me. I can't go out there on Saturday—'

'You're playing them again? They lost against Holland?'

'On penalty strokes. So we play them again, for the bronze medal, and I can't win against him if I don't know what it is. You have to tell me everything.'

Even now, he couldn't guess. He couldn't imagine the awfulness of what she was about to tell him. She covered her face with her hands. *Don't cry, don't. Just don't.*

'Pip,' he said sharply. 'Tell me.'

Still hiding behind her hands, she took a deep breath. She couldn't look at him or she'd lose her nerve. She felt like she was standing on the edge of a cliff, about to take that step off solid ground. Soon there would be nothing but air beneath her feet.

'I... Troy and I... we... we slept together.' There was no response from Leo, so she continued. 'It was in England. Three years ago. After Holly died. We didn't know what we were doing. It was... I was too young. We were both... It was a massive mistake. I didn't know it then, but since I met you, I knew I had to end it with him.'

'Wait. Let me get this straight. Your Australian boyfriend is Costa?'

Pip looked at him. His face was crumpled up in pain or disgust or incomprehension. Or all three of those things.

'Is he?' Leo spluttered. 'Answer the fucking question.'

All she had to do was say it. Then it was over.

'Yes.'

She took the step off the cliff. She was falling, spiralling towards the ground, nothing to stop her, the ground rushing up towards her. But now she'd said it, she felt relief. It was done. The anticipation she'd felt, the dread that had been building every day since she'd met Leo, the tight knot that she'd had in her stomach since she'd arrived in Sydney – all over now.

He sat on the bed and put his head in his hands. He was muttering to himself. Pip couldn't hear what he was saying. She felt calm. She knew she deserved whatever he was going to say to her. She was light, she was free, floating towards the ground.

He stood up. His face was furious.

'Do you have any idea how much you've fucked up?'

'Yes.'

'You can't possibly. You think this is OK? You think you can mess around with stuff like this? I've worked so hard, my whole life, and it comes to this? A fight over a fucking girl? You have no idea.'

'I do. I have every idea. I know this inside out. From Holly. From Troy. From you.'

'Don't you fucking dare say his name. Jesus. Why did I think this would even work? I must have been mad.'

'Because it did work. It still could.'

'You're joking, right? You must be. Otherwise you're a complete moron. I never want to see you again.'

'Don't give up on this, please, Leo.'

'There's nothing to give up on. You said, before, that it would be easier for both of us if we weren't too involved with each other. Well, you were right.'

'This is easy for you?'

He was silent.

'I did the only thing I could think of, to try to stop this happening.'

'You lied,' he spat.

'No. I just didn't tell the truth.'

'Same thing.'

'No, it's not. You didn't tell me that your grandparents would hire a private detective to find out about me.'

'I didn't know they would.'

'Of course you did. They did it before. They did it to your dad. To Roxy, even.'

'How do you—?'

'The Swiss grandmother? You knew what they were going to do and you didn't tell me.'

Leo said nothing.

'You let them. And you told me you didn't want to know about me until after the Olympics. That was as much a lie as anything else here.' She sighed. 'I know I've screwed up. I started screwing up three years ago when my sister died and I basically haven't stopped screwing up, every minute of every day since then. The only thing that I did right was meeting you and falling in love with you.'

'You couldn't love me and do this to me. You of all people should know that.'

'It was too late. It was in the wrong order. I'd already started not being Holly's sister by the time I fell for you. You said to me, on the Night of Saying Yes, that we didn't have to tell each other everything. That not everyone has a perfect life that they want to shout about. I thought of telling you loads of times. Then when we got together, it was too close to the Games. I was trying to protect you.'

'Bullshit. You were trying to protect yourself. Oh Jesus, that was you, wasn't it – Costa was talking about you, not Nadine, on Tuesday? He thinks you're with Billy. Join the club. He's giving Billy all sorts of shit about you, trying to wind us up… Wait. So he knows about us, but you didn't think to tell us about him?'

'I didn't tell him.'

'How does he know?'

'I don't know. He must have… his housemates might have seen me with Max and Ferdi and… I guess they told Troy.'

'You must have known he'd find out. For fuck's sake, Pip, how naive are you? We were together, you and me, and you took his side over mine? Shit. This is so fucked up.'

'I didn't take his side. I tried to keep it from you and Billy told me Troy thought it was me and him, so he said he'd carry on pretending so you wouldn't find out and mess up your concentration—'

'Oh right, but it's OK to mess up Billy's concentration?'

'He said he wanted to help. He said it was OK,' she mumbled, studying the floor.

'What the fuck does he know? What kind of a thoughtless, selfish, spineless person are you? You mess up your life and expect him to sort it out for you, in the middle of his first Olympics?'

She had no answer for that.

332

'And by the way, you said you were going to finish it with Costa, face-to-face. So that means you've seen him? Since you were here, in Sydney?'

'Yes.'

'When?'

'Last week. I was staying at his house.'

'In his bedroom? That was his bedroom, wasn't it?'

'Yes.'

'And what... you broke up with him, just like that? No final sympathy lay? For old times' sake?'

'No.'

'Nothing?'

Pip swallowed. 'He kissed me.'

He looked at her scornfully. 'Oh for Christ's sake, you have to stop this innocent little virgin act.'

'It's true. He kissed me and I stopped it.'

'You do this again and again and you think it's OK, but you're putting yourself in danger every time. You get drunk and you let guys like Bredenkamp feel you up and Billy kiss you, and now there's... this with Costa and whoever that person was I found on the stairs.' There was no kindness left in his voice – it was steel. 'You were drunk, asleep, alone, in his house. You have quite a habit of falling asleep uninvited in people's beds, don't you?'

Pip stood up, her guilt and grief turning to rage. 'You fucking bastard. You think I asked for it? How dare you? After what just happened? You came to his house, you saved me from that... man. He drugged and attacked me. He was going to... he would have... have *raped* me. You think I want that? You think I want men like him and Troy Costa crawling over me? *You* don't get to say stuff like that. *You* have no idea what it's like to be someone who's smaller and weaker than half of the population. To be so afraid when they come towards you, when they grab you, that you can't even move.' She glared at him, speaking slowly so he'd understand. 'And if you say "stop" to them, and they don't stop, and they know you don't want them to come near you, there's fuck all you can do about it.'

Leo's face was white. 'Are you talking about me? About us? At the river?' He looked like Pip had punched him.

'I told you to stop and you didn't. I said no, I told you it was a mistake. But you went ahead anyway. You don't know how that feels, do you? How could you? Well, I'll enlighten you: it's terrifying. You, as a man, are not allowed to not believe me. Do you hear me? You don't get to call bullshit on it. Not ever.'

'Seriously? You're bundling me in with Costa and that piece of shit at his house? That's what you think of me – that I raped you at the river?'

She stepped towards him, but he stepped back from her. 'Forget about the river. Listen to me. I'm trying to tell you that it's because I'm female, and not because I'm pretending to be some "innocent little virgin" as you so charmingly put it, that I get scared. And I don't know what to do when men who're twice my size and strength want something from me. You think I drank too much tonight. And I saw you looking at my shorts. If you think that I led him on, you're wrong.'

'I didn't mean that, I only meant—'

'Shut up. I've made a lot of mistakes, but this wasn't one of them. And sleeping with Troy is something I absolutely regret, but I did it when I was sixteen. I was too young and I was out of my mind because I'd just lost the one person in the world who loved me, and who I loved.'

'What about your parents?'

Pip waved her hand dismissively. 'My parents couldn't give a stuff about me. I had no one – I was lonely and confused and I didn't know what the fuck to do. I know you think I've been acting like a sixteen-year-old, and that's because, to all intents and purposes, I am. Everything after Holly died was a blank for me. Nothing mattered. I wished over and over that it was me who'd died and not her. But then I met you and I tried to do the right thing and failed, but it doesn't mean that I don't love you because I do.' She wiped the tears off her face with her sleeve. 'I thought we had a story together.'

'Oh, you and your stories.' He raised his hands in exasperation.

'Not my story, *our* story. And it was a good one. I thought it would have a happy ending. But I'm starting to realise that there's no such thing as a happy ending. Otherwise it wouldn't be an ending. I mean, let's face it, nothing in my life so far has ended well. Holly and me. Troy and me. You and me.'

'That might be the only thing you've said tonight that makes any sense.' His voice was full of contempt.

She said fiercely, 'But what you don't know, because you've never lost anyone that you love, is that I'm going to get over you. I lost Holly and nothing – not even you, not you at all, not in any way – is as painful as that. So if I can get over her death, breaking up with you is Mickey Mouse. I'm tough as shit.'

'Right. I need some sleep. You can leave now.'

Pip didn't move.

'What do you want? You want me to thank you for lying to me, or for finally owning up to the shitstorm you've unleashed on Billy and me? We could lose our places in the side, if Costa provokes us and we slip up, just once. I could lose my captaincy. All because you can't keep your legs closed.'

'Fuck you, Leo.'

'No, fuck you. You're weak and selfish and naive.'

'You can try, but you won't be able to make me feel any smaller than I already do. You can't break my heart because Holly's death already did that. And you can't hate me as much as I do myself.'

'Oh, believe me, I think I can. You've jeopardised everything I've ever worked for.' He pointed out of the window at the view of the harbour. 'This – all this – matters to me, more than anything. This is my whole life.'

'Then why did you come to Underwood Street?'

'I don't know. Get out. And don't even think about coming to the game on Saturday.'

She stood up and walked unsteadily to the door. As she closed it, she looked at him and he turned his back on her.

Day Fifteen: Friday 29th September

'Pip, Pip, wake up. Are you all right? What happened?' Nadine was shaking her.

'What time is it?'

'Nearly eleven. I just saw your texts. What's happened? Oh my God.' She caught sight of Pip's face and arms as she sat up in bed. 'What the hell happened to you?'

'Where were you last night?'

'I didn't have my phone with me – it was running out of battery so I left it at the apartment. We only got in a few hours ago, I crashed and then saw your texts and caught the next ferry over. I nearly went to Underwood Street but you sent that message so long ago, I thought I'd check here first.'

Pip told Nadine the whole story, about the barbecue and Dean and Leo. She held Pip's hand and they dried each other's tears.

'You hit him before he did anything?'

'Yes.'

'Let me see you. Shit. Oh my God. He's really done a great job.' Nadine turned over her wrists, as Leo had done last night. She smoothed her hands over Pip's shoulder, which was black and blue, her red-raw elbows, her knees and thighs with their scratches and bruises. 'You're not just saying it to mollify me, are you? He didn't rape you?'

'I hit him in the throat with a hockey stick. Troy's stick.'

'At least it's useful for something.' Nadine smiled wryly. 'It's over, then, with you and Leo?'

'He was seriously angry. So was I. We both said some pretty unforgivable things.'

'But in the heat of the moment. He'll come round.'

'No, I don't think so.'

'Well… one thing at a time. What do you say you have a quick shower, I'll find some coffee and breakfast and we'll go together to the police station?'

'No. What? Why?'

'Because that creep tried to rape you.'

'But I can't.'

'Oh yes you can. And you will. Come on, up.'

'It's not important.'

'It bloody well is and you know it. I'm not going to let you start blaming yourself for this.'

'I don't.' But she wasn't sure if she did or not.

'You're going to get up and shower – actually no, don't shower. And then we're going. No buts. Get your arse in gear, Mitchell.'

'You'll stay with me?' What was the use in arguing with Nadine?

'Of course.'

Pip slowly dressed, her body aching and stiff. She looked in the mirror – she had dark circles under her eyes and the bruises on her arms and legs looked like paint splatters. At the desk in the hotel lobby, Nadine asked where the nearest police station was and the receptionist said, 'Darling Harbour' at the same time as Pip did.

'How d'you know that?'

'Tracey. Glen – the other housemate – his girlfriend. She's a copper. I met her last night. Before. She's lovely.'

'Perfect. Then it is Tracey we shall ask for.'

Within two minutes of them walking into the police station, Tracey had taken charge. The T-shirt with Dean's blood on it was taken away in an evidence bag. Pip gave urine and blood samples. Her bruises were photographed. She wrote a statement and gave her address in England, not the one in Munich, since she didn't think she'd be there for much longer. Another police officer asked her questions, but Tracey and Nadine never left her side.

The male officer asked her, 'How much alcohol did you consume?'

That question again. 'I don't know. I thought he spiked my drink, but I honestly don't know. Probably too much. I lost count. I suppose that ruins everything, doesn't it?'

But Tracey interrupted her. 'No. Listen. I saw you arrive, and you went upstairs before I left. You didn't drink any more after that, did you?'

Pip shook her head, confused.

'I know exactly how many beers you had – four. Because I was drinking at the same pace as you and I had four. I remember thinking how it was funny that we got along so well and our bottles were finished at the same time.'

'Tracey, you absolute star.' That was Nadine.

'You want to make a formal report? That means we take this further – arrest him, prosecute him.'

Pip shook her head as Nadine said, 'Yes. She does.' She turned to Pip. 'What if he does this again to someone else? What if that girl's not as strong as you? He has to pay for this, the skanky fuck-face. Excuse my language,' she said to Tracey, who flashed them a sympathetic smile as if to say, *I think your language is perfectly acceptable in the circumstances.*

Tracey said, 'Listen, if you go ahead with this, we'll need to take a statement from your friend too.'

'Who?'

'You said your friend came to pick you up. You said you spoke to him immediately after the incident. We need a statement from him. Whatever he says will corroborate your version of events, make it stronger if this goes to court.'

Leo. Oh no, not Leo. 'No. You can't do that. He's not... he can't... he's not available to give a statement.'

'Why? Has he left the country?'

'No. Yes. I don't… he can't, OK? Not until Sunday.' Pip felt the sweat forming on her palms.

'Whatever he's doing, this is more important, Pip.'

'No. It's not going to happen. I won't sign a formal report if you want a statement from him.' She pointed to the documents lying on the desk. 'I'll take back all of this.'

'We may prosecute anyway. Then both of you will have to be called as witnesses.'

'No, please don't do that. Leave him alone.'

'It's not as simple as that.'

'Yes it is.' Pip felt anger and panic rise inside her. No way were they going near Leo until after he'd played. And then it came to her. 'Nothing happens until Sunday, and I'll tell you why. This went down at Troy Costa's house. He has an important match tomorrow – the bronze medal is up for grabs, at his home Olympics, and he's a Sydneysider and a national hero. If you hit him with this, and the Kookaburras lose, the press is going to crucify you. You really think anyone will understand that you couldn't wait twenty-four hours?'

'It would be a PR disaster,' added Nadine, shaking her head ominously.

The other policeman looked nervously at Tracey, who made the call. 'We'll wait until Sunday. The ideal situation is that statements are taken as quickly as possible after the attempted sexual assault occurs. But we'll wait. We'll just have to hope that Dean doesn't do a runner. You'll give us your friend's name?'

'On Sunday.'

Outside the station, Tracey gave Pip her email address and private phone number. 'If you want to talk. I doubt I'll be on the investigation, because I know the parties involved. But I'll make sure you're assigned some good people. And I'll request to be your liaison.'

'And you'll talk to Troy?' said Nadine.

'On Sunday afternoon.' Tracey hugged Pip and turned to Nadine. 'I don't need to tell you to take care of her.'

Nadine hugged Tracey. 'Nope. You don't. Thanks, Tracey.'

They walked back along the side streets near the wharf, a warm wind whipping up the flags and bunting above them. They stopped at a restaurant called the Slip Inn for a late lunch, sitting in the sheltered courtyard at the last free table. Nadine ordered them both a glass of wine while Pip looked around her at the other customers. Groups and couples, laughing carelessly, enjoying a lunch break or a day off, chatting excitedly about the last few events they were going to see before the end of the Games. Just like she would have been in her parallel existence.

'I'm in awe of you, you know,' Nadine said as she took Pip's hand in hers. 'I don't know how you managed to fight him off. He drugged you and he's twice your size. You're so brave.'

'I'm not.' Pip felt dirty and uncomfortable in her skin, still with the memory of Dean's mouth and hands on her, and the camera and needles and specimen pots from the police station.

'Holly would be proud of you.'

Pip's face crumpled. 'I've made such a mess of everything. What a huge fuck-up.'

'Don't you ever say that. You've been given some kind of shit to deal with, Pip, and you've dealt with it all. God, you even managed to guilt-trip Tracey into laying off Leo until after his match. Genius. You're amazing.'

'When Holly was alive, I felt amazing. She always made sure I knew how much she loved me. It made me feel like I was the most special person in the world. We talked about everything. Now, I don't feel special any more. I'm just another person in a crowd in a world full of people and crowds.' She pointed at the high-rise buildings on the street. 'I feel like one of those windows in those blocks of flats. No one knows which one I am.'

'I do. Leo does. Billy and Dominic and Max and Ferdi do.'

'Not Leo.' *I never want to see you again.*

'He'll come around.'

'He won't. I made sure of that.' *Fuck you, Leo.*

'Just wait and see. He will, if he has any sense. And if he hasn't, well then, he doesn't deserve you anyway.'

'I won't wait for him. I've done enough of that to last a lifetime. I'm going to have to forget about him.' *I'm going to get over you. I'm as tough as shit.*

'Sure? Because I get the impression you and he are the real thing.'

'Whatever it was, it wasn't real. For a start, I'm not even a real person.'

'D'you mean because you didn't tell him about Holly?'

'No, I mean because I stopped being a person when Holly died. I don't actually do anything; I can't tell you who I am or what I like or all the little things you learn about when you're growing up that tell you what kind of a person you are.'

'That's not true.'

'It is, but it doesn't matter. Because from now on, I'm going to start being a real person. I pressed the *Pause* button on my life.' She looked at her watch. 'It's time to press the *Play* button again. Two-fifteen on Friday the 29th of September 2000.'

She heard the clatter of plates against cutlery; the quiet zoom of traffic on the road outside; roars and cheers from a TV set showing an Olympic event. She smelt burgers and beers and sweat and perfume. This was the everyday into which she would sink, immersing herself gladly. She was profoundly relieved that the drama of the last twelve months was over – the drama she'd created and that had been buzzing menacingly at the periphery of the happiness she'd tried and failed to find with Leo.

She said, 'It's not about how Holly died or how my parents ignored me for most of my life; it's not about how I slept with Troy or was attacked by Dean. It's not about how I sat in my room for two years, or how I ran away from England and the whopping great lies I told. None of that matters any more. It's what I do now – after I've fucked up every which way but Sunday – that's what matters. Now I think I will have that drink – in fact, let's buy a bottle. Urgh. Actually, no, just this glass will do. I feel like shit.'

Day Sixteen: Saturday 30th September

They had all day to wait – the bronze medal match was at 5.30. Pip tried to keep busy – she and Nadine climbed the Harbour Bridge, awestruck at the spectacular views. In the water they even could see some sailing events. They walked through the Botanic Gardens and had lunch at a pie shop called Harry's Café de Wheels, which Nadine's friends had told her about. After that, they went to the Deutsche Haus. Pip wore a long-sleeved blouse with a scarf around her neck and jeans to cover her bruises. The one on her forehead was partly covered by her hair and some make-up. She and Nadine were going to watch the match on the big screen. The commentary started with a male and a female presenter in the hockey centre studio.

Now, Brendan, what do we know about this German team? Are they going to break Australian hearts this evening and rob the Kookaburras of their bronze medal?

Well, Shannon, that's an interesting question. On paper, the Kookaburras are the favourites. Last year they won the Oceania Cup, the Champions Trophy, and in Atlanta four years ago, the Aussies beat the Germans in an exact same repeat of this match, to win the bronze medal. However, in the year leading up to the Olympics, the two teams have met eight times and the score is tied at four-all.

So it's anyone's game.

As well as the home crowd, another big psychological factor will be our – I mean the Australian – victory against them in the group round.

Yes, tell me about that, Brendan.

Sure, sure. The Kookaburra star Troy Costa—

Nadine booed.

...scored a heroic last-minute penalty stroke to win the match two-one. This will certainly be on the Germans' minds as they go into this all-important bronze medal match. Can they beat the Australians? There must be doubts in their minds.

'Rubbish,' yelled Nadine.

Now, tell us, in case there's someone out there who's been living on the moon these past few months, about the one and only Troy Costa.

Yes, I certainly will, Shannon. He's had an astonishing tournament, he's top scorer for the Kookaburras and is an inspirational figure in the team.

'Bullshit, they all hate him.' Everyone watching the game laughed with Nadine.

Pip sank down in her seat but she didn't mind. It was just Nadine's way of showing Pip that she was on her side.

Yes, he's certainly looking sensational, hockey-wise. Here's an interview with the brilliant man himself.

Troy's face flashed up on the screen.

Troy, we're all very excited about your bronze medal match. How're you feeling going into it?

We're very confident of winning. The German team has its weaknesses and we aim to exploit them. We're going to be gunning for them and that medal is ours.

And what are those weaknesses?

They're a very young team, and that means they can't handle the pressure of the big stage. We've got the crowd behind us, we're at home here. They have a few players who are mentally quite brittle. We'll certainly be taking advantage of that.

Do you mean anyone in particular? Or would that be naming names?

That'd be naming names. But I will say they're brothers.

Ha ha, righto, Troy, say no more.

'What a fucking cheek. Is he allowed to say that? I hope they chew him up and spit him out,' Nadine said.

But on a serious note. We were all very saddened to hear about the passing of your wonderful, talented, beautiful wife three years ago. How has this affected your Olympics?

It's made me stronger. Holly and I played in the same clubs for years. We were at two Olympics together – we met in Barcelona. I feel the loss of her here, when I'm not playing, but when I'm on the pitch, she's with me and she inspires me. Everything I do, I do it for her. Love ya, Holl.

'Oh God, I think I'm gonna puke,' said Nadine.

'Shhh,' said Pip, smiling. 'You're so cynical.'

Thank you, Troy, and we wish you all the luck in the world today. Don't need it, but thanks.

And now, back in the studio, let's talk more about the German team. The captain, Christian Mayerhöfer, says his players are ready for the match and confident of a good result. There's a lot of young talent in this team – the average age of their squad is a mere twenty-four, and none of them are over twenty-nine years old. They certainly seem to be the underdogs.

And let's focus on a couple of players who are a key part of this young, inexperienced squad.

Pictures of Leo and Billy appeared on the screen. Nadine wolf-whistled and there was more laughter from around them.

Here we have Leo Stein and Billy von Feldstein – they are brothers, but Leo prefers the shorter version of their family name. Just what do we know about these players?

It's Leo's second Olympics and he's a force to be reckoned with. He's a defender and is one of the best players in this position in the world. Twenty-six years old, he's been exemplary in this competition and is well known for his cool temperament. Here are a few clips of him in action. Watch his control, his poise with the ball, his immense presence on the field – it's going to be very difficult for our Aussie boys to get around him.

And here's Billy von Feldstein in action. It's Billy's first Olympics and he's been impressing everyone with his explosive pace and raw aggression. Check out this goal against Pakistan. He certainly has flair, you've got to give him that.

And what do you think these references to their mental weakness might mean?

Well, there is a rumour that these three players – the two Germans and Troy Costa – have some history.

Pip frowned and looked at Nadine, who grimaced.

We were talking to our boy Troy earlier about his lovely wife, Holly. And a little bird tells me that not only was Leo Stein involved with her – before she married Troy, of course – but that Billy von Feldstein is currently dating her much younger sister. Troy feels very protective about his wife's sister, and Billy is a notorious... well... shall we say, heartbreaker?

'Where do they get this absolute shit from?' someone said.

All in all, the von Feldstein family is not in Troy's good books. We heard it on good authority that heated words were exchanged after Germany's defeat on Tuesday at the hands of the magnificent Troy Costa. He believes – quite rightly – that the brothers should try and keep their personal issues away from the hockey pitch.

Rightly so. Now, the teams are running out so we'll watch their warm-ups and here's our pitchside commentator...

The match started and Pip forced herself to watch. Australia scored an unstoppable field goal from a volley after twenty-two minutes, to which Germany responded with a goal from a penalty corner five minutes later. The German goalkeeper saved three more Australian shots and Leo was kept busy. He never lost his cool.

At half-time it was one-all and Pip's hand shook as she accepted the Coke Nadine had brought back from the bar. Pip thought her heart was going to pound right out of her chest as the whistle blew for the second half. Within minutes, Australia scored again, a scrappy goal, and Germany had a goal disallowed.

'When are we going to bring Billy on?' Nadine's voice betrayed her anxiety.

Pip smiled faintly. '"We"?' she said, and Nadine rolled her eyes.

With twenty-five minutes to go, there was nothing between the teams except the score: two-one to Australia. There was plenty of aggression – a green card for Troy after a stick tackle, and a yellow for the German captain, who gave his armband to Leo. Nadine nudged Pip and beamed at her.

Someone said, 'Look! He's on. Billy's coming on.'

'Finally. Now we're talking,' said Nadine.

Sixteen minutes left on the clock, Billy scored. The crowd in the Deutsche Haus was on its feet. Two-all.

Five minutes later, he scored again, this time from a penalty flick. Nadine was jumping up and down, someone bumped into Pip, jolting her sore shoulder, but she didn't care. Three-two to Germany.

Seven minutes to go, Billy dived in front of the goal, Pip's heart hammering, he slid along the AstroTurf, Pip's eyes glued to the screen, he stretched out his stick, Pip's mouth opening in a scream, he gave the ball the lightest of touches to send it into the back of the goal. There were yells around them, Nadine's face up close to Pip's, mirroring her euphoria. Four-two to Germany.

After that, the countdown – all Germany had to do was hold on, keep possession, and close down the increasingly desperate Australian attacks. Leo tackled Troy, taking the ball off him, but Troy turned, slipping his stick under Leo's feet, who crashed to the ground. The whistle blew, Leo stood up and, as the umpire walked towards them, his hands reaching for a card, Troy squared up to Leo, shouting and gesticulating.

This is it, thought Pip. She sat as still as she could, tensed and waiting. The camera was side-on to the two men. Troy's face in profile, his neck craning forwards, veins protruding, wild eyes bulging, his mouth opening and closing, roaring God knows what at Leo, who stood calmly, his face a mask. Leo didn't even flinch as Troy lunged at him like an enraged animal. As the umpire reached them, Troy planted his hands on Leo's chest to shove him backwards, but Leo didn't budge. The umpire showed Troy a red card, and this time the pitchside microphone picked up the sound. Pip clearly heard Troy say, 'Fuck you, I've had them both.'

'Whoa. Did I just hear that right?' said Nadine.

Someone in the Deutsche Haus leaned over to Pip and Nadine. 'What does zis crazy kangaroo man mean – had zem both?'

Nadine shrugged.

Thank God he made me tell him, thought Pip.

Leo didn't react. He stood motionless as Troy left the pitch, in his fury kicking out at his team's bottle holder, which sent water spraying into the dugout.

The cameras turned back to the game until the final whistle blew. Germany won the bronze medal.

Nadine hugged her, everyone hugged each other, there were champagne corks popping and glasses were passed around.

Pip said, 'That was the best hockey match I've ever seen.'

She sat, with her knees pulled up to her chin, tears pouring down her face. They'd done it – Billy and Leo and the whole team. It wasn't the gold, but they had a medal and they'd beaten Australia, in Sydney, against Troy, who'd ended up looking like a tantrumy child. He'd tried every trick in the book but it hadn't worked, because neither Billy nor Leo was stupid enough to let him get to them, Billy with his I-don't-give-a-shit attitude, and Leo, who was as cold as ice.

The stamping and roaring in the room quietened as Leo and Billy's faces, dripping with sweat, filled the screen.

I have here with me the stars of the German team, brothers Leo Stein and Billy von Feldstein. Leo, how're you feeling after that amazing performance?

Fine. Great.

Leo's face was unsmiling. The female interviewer paused, waiting for more before trying again.

You're happy with the bronze medal?

Yes.

Pause.

What was it that gave you the upper hand over the Aussies today? How did you formulate a plan to beat them? When they've got the home crowd and they beat you only a few days ago, and have a vastly more experienced squad than yours?

We scored more goals than them.

Leo's face was deadpan, but Billy cracked up and put his arm round his brother's shoulders.

The interviewer gave up and turned to Billy.

Now, Billy, this is your first Olympics. How are you feeling right now?

I'm on top of the world, Shannon. The whole team's worked so hard and it all came together today. We couldn't be happier. I mean, just look at my brother. He's never been so excited.

The Deutsche Haus erupted in laughter as the camera zoomed in on Leo's impassive face.

You scored three goals, Billy; you must be very proud of your achievement.

It was a team effort – that's what's so great about it. It's an amazing feeling to be part of a team like this, Shannon.

What's your take on comments made before the match about you and your brother's personal lives?

Billy laughed.

We don't actually have personal lives, Shannon, didn't you know that? We eat, sleep and drink hockey, all day, every day. I haven't got a clue what the fella's talking about. Maybe it's because I'm just a schoolboy.

The crowd behind the interviewer cheered off-camera, and Billy waved at them, making a call-me sign with his fingers.

Ah, OK, thank you, Billy. And now that your first Olympics are over, what are you doing to celebrate tonight?

Well, that's a bit forward of you, Shannon. I hardly know you.

Billy winked at her and was dragged away by Leo, who ruffled his hair. The camera followed them as Billy jumped on Leo's back. They were stopped by a German interviewer and camera crew, microphones stuck in their faces, Billy still piggybacking Leo. The camera turned back to Shannon, who was blushing, clearly flustered, and through the roars of laughter in the Deutsche Haus, Pip could just about hear what she was saying.

The charismatic Billy von Feldstein there, setting the record straight. He's certainly got bucketloads of talent, and even more charm. He's been described as a heartbreaker, and I can see why. Fathers of Sydney, lock up your daughters tonight.

'We have to go. No, actually, *I* have to go,' said Pip. 'You stay here – there'll be a massive party here tonight.'

'I'm not staying if you're not,' said Nadine. 'We stick together, remember?'

'What about Billy? You can't tell me you want to spend the whole night with me, when you could be with him.'

'Pip, I couldn't give a stuff about Billy. He's going to be getting smashed with his team, and I'm going to be with mine. That's you, by the way, if that wasn't clear.'

'I got it. But I'm going back to the hotel. You can't miss this party. I'll never speak to you again if you come with me.'

'And I'll never speak to me again if I do. Which I won't. That's a bit confusing. Look, let's just stay here, OK, and if it's awkward with Leo—'

'Which it will be—'

'Then we'll disappear. It's going to be fine, anyway, isn't it? They won. It's over. Honestly, what has he got to complain about?'

'I don't want to hang around here if I'm not wanted. And last time I checked, I'm not wanted.' *Don't even think about coming to the game.*

Nadine looked at her watch, betraying the fact that she gave a very large stuff about seeing Billy. 'How long will it be, anyway? Before they're here?'

'Oh, ages. Relax, they'll be hours yet. There's still the final, and afterwards the medal presentation. Let's go for a walk, shall we?'

They set off back to Homebush and wandered around, taking photos and soaking up the atmosphere. Pip pointed out the GB hockey girls to Nadine. They were sitting at tables outside a wine tent, drinking from plastic glasses.

'You want to go and say hello?'

Pip nodded.

When they saw her, Pip was sorry that she hadn't contacted them earlier. They were so relieved she was OK, after all this time. Pip and Nadine had a few drinks with them and, as the time of the medal ceremony neared, which they wanted to watch in the Deutsche Haus, they stood up to say their goodbyes.

'So, tomorrow we need to see you again. Just before two o'clock, at Circular Quay. You have to come, Pip. Where are you staying? We'll send someone to your hotel to drag you kicking and screaming if you aren't there.'

'She'll be there. I'll make sure of it,' said Nadine. Her flight was leaving in the evening, during the closing ceremony.

Pip said, 'What's it for?'

'A surprise. A good one. You'll like it.'

'OK, sure, yeah, I'll see you then.'

They made it back to the Deutsche Haus in time to see the Germans being given their medals. When Billy was given his, a roar went up in the crowd and there were wolf whistles, and Pip was sure she could hear girls screaming. Leo earned a huge roar too, and even cracked a smile when he waved at the crowd. People knew that Pip and Nadine were friends of the von Feldsteins, and they were congratulated by the other athletes and their families, which they found hilarious.

Someone shouted, 'They're here,' and since there were no other German medal-winners that evening, it had to be the hockey men. As they walked in, wearing their medals, the entire house erupted in clapping and cheering, a standing ovation that they acknowledged with waves and handshakes and hugs. Max was on Leo's shoulders and Ferdi on Billy's. Billy put Ferdi down, vaulted over the bar and grabbed a bottle of champagne, spraying it over his teammates. Dominic, Max and Ferdi spotted Pip and Nadine sitting at a table in the corner and came over to them.

'That was an awesome game, Pipster. You should have seen it. Why weren't you there?'

'Why are you wearing all those clothes, Pip? Aren't you hot?'

'I saw it on TV. Weren't they brilliant? Here, I saved you a table – come and tell me all about it.'

She listened and nodded, sitting in a corner seat tucked out of the way, not wanting Leo to see her there, and if he did, to make it easy for him to avoid her. She didn't want to ruin his big night. But she did need to say one thing to him, and so she watched him and when he stood up to leave his teammates, she followed him to the men's loos and waited for him when he came out.

'Congratulations.'

'Thanks.'

She stared at him, stared him down, until he dropped his eyes to the floor. He had that blank, dispassionate look on his face. Was he still angry with her? Or was he just impatient to be back with his team?

Pip felt suffocated by his indifference. He couldn't even ask her how she was doing? She was an idiot, a stupid girl, childish to think he cared. But she had to be hard and say it. 'They need you to go to the police station. Tomorrow, first thing. Ask for this officer.' She gave him Tracey's card. 'You have to write a statement.'

He took it without looking at her or touching her.

'They want to arrest him and prosecute. It will help, they said, if the person who saw me first after the attack gives a statement.' Her voice sounded strange – she was trying to keep it even but it came out sounding formal and over-polite. 'I made them wait until after the match.'

He was silent. He wasn't going to say thank you. Of course he wasn't going to let her off the hook.

She looked at him, his mask-like face, his dark eyes that gave nothing away. She'd been shut out. Well, fuck him then. Nothing more to say. She turned away from him without another word and went back to the table. Max's eyes were half-closed and Ferdi was asleep on his dad's shoulder.

'Shall I take them back to the hotel?'

'I've already ordered the car. But I can take them back – you girls stay here and enjoy the party.'

'I'm not staying, Dominic. Leo doesn't want me here. You stay, I'll go.'

'He told you to leave? You've spoken to him about your sister?'

'You were right – he's not taken it well. So you can come back to the hotel if you want, but I'm definitely going, so why don't you stay here with the other families?'

Dominic smiled regretfully and thanked her.

'It's OK, really it is. Nadine said she'd come with me. Where is she, have you seen her?'

Nadine appeared, straightening her dress and smoothing down her hair, with glittering eyes and a huge grin on her face. She whispered in Pip's ear, 'Quickie in the ladies' loos. I'm all class, me.'

Pip tried to keep a straight face. 'Taxi's on its way. Last chance to stay here and have fun rather than spending the evening with me crying on your shoulder.'

'I consider it an honour to offer you my shoulder. I'm all yours.'

They each took a child by the hand and went to wait outside for the car, just as it pulled up. Nadine sat in the front seat, humming along to the tunes on the radio and chatting to the driver. She seemed cheerful, but Pip knew it must be killing her to leave Billy there. Pip sat with the boys either side of her, their hot heads lolling onto her shoulders. She had to cherish these last few moments with Max and Ferdi. She would miss them when she was gone. They both looked so angelic when they were asleep.

At the hotel, they tucked the boys into bed and sat on the sofa with the sound on the TV down low. Nadine sighed.

Pip said, 'Still time to go back to the party, if you want. I'm safe and sound here, no one's going to hurt me.'

'You don't get it, do you?'

'Get what?'

'I want to spend my last evening in Sydney with you. Even if you're not as joyful as Billy is, nor as pretty as him at the moment, and I'm thinking there's no chance of hot, dirty sex with you – this is still where I want to be.'

'Mates before sexy bronze-medal-winning Teutonic Olympians?'

'That's right, and don't you forget it.'

Pip smiled at Nadine and said, 'The feeling's mutual.' She was glowing again – Nadine did that to her. *Who needs men when you can have a friendship this strong?*

'Besides, Billy was off his tits already. He was wittering on about having a haircut tonight. He thought that was hilarious. And something about a Swedish girl he wanted me to meet in the Olympic Village. Said he had a plan to sneak me in. Sounded a bit dodgy. I think, to be honest, I got the best out of him in the loos at the Deutsche Haus. Sex-wise, it's going to be downhill for him all the way to the closing ceremony.'

Day Seventeen: Sunday 1st October

At two o'clock the next day, with fair-to-medium-sized hangovers, Pip and Nadine were waiting by the docks at Circular Quay. There were the hockey girls, standing by a boat, and they waved to Pip, calling her over.

'What's going on?'

'Wait and see.'

Pip stepped onto the boat and sat down on a seat near the front, turning to see who was there and who was arriving. It was the whole women's hockey squad and about half the men's. There were other GB athletes too, including some she recognised from Holly's funeral or from the TV. She thought some of the Australian hockey players were there too, and she saw Troy and froze. He came straight over to her and sat down near her, leaving a few seats between them.

'What are you doing here?'

He shrugged, not looking her in the eye. 'I was summoned. What's happening?'

'Your guess is as good as mine.'

'This guy bothering you?' said Nadine, sitting down between them.

'No. Troy, do you remember my friend Nadine?'

Troy nodded non-committally and stuck out his hand, but Nadine ignored him. Over by the entrance to the boat, Pip watched as more and more people climbed up the ramp. She braced herself, because if this was something to do with Holly and her team, then... yes, there he was. Leo. He was with Billy, and Dominic, Max and Ferdi too – they'd kept that quiet. She stood up to go over to them, but caught Billy's eye, who shook his head quickly. She sat down again. Troy was fiddling with a rip in his jeans and staring into space. Clearly he found it awkward to be there with her. Well, she wasn't going to help him out with that.

The boat set off and the captain of Holly's team stepped forward. Everyone fell silent as the boat chugged out of the harbour.

'We're here today in this special place, in our own special way, to say goodbye to a very special person. Since Holly's death, three years ago, we've missed her like hell and we think about her all the time. Today, believe it or not, was the first opportunity we had to get together all her hockey friends in one place – which tells you a lot about Holly, because she had so many friends from all over the world. We've got the Brits and the Aussies and the Dutch and the Germans. And, of course, we've got Troy. And finally – because she's a hard person to track down – last but not least, Pip.

'More than anyone else here, we know that Holly's death must have hit you the hardest. Whatever she was to us as a teammate and friend, she must have been a thousand times over to you. And you were so young. We feel for you, Pip, and we don't want you to disappear again. We want you to know that you have sixteen older sisters now. And some of them are younger than you.'

There was a smattering of laughter from the crowd.

'Holly was a great player, and she had an amazing career behind her when it was cut short. She would have been here with us, wearing her number nine shirt, and I'm sure we would have done a lot better than eighth if she'd been here. No offence, Hels.'

'None taken,' said Holly's replacement in the team. More laughter.

'The way that Holly died shook us up, but I want to say this about it: she died doing what she loved, and she was totally that kind of player – she was never afraid of hurting herself; she would never have hesitated to put her body in the way of that ball. It's just the way she was.

'We miss her on the pitch, but she was also a great friend to us. She kept us together. She was the person everybody loved. She was like a sister to us all. She always made time for us – to listen to our problems, sort out our arguments, give us advice on our love lives. Nothing was too much trouble for her. I can even hear her now, whispering in my ear – *Wrap it up, dude, people are thirsty.*'

More laughter.

'So, OK, I will wrap this up. We didn't know how to be at an Olympics without Holly, so we brought her with us.' The captain held up an urn. 'Her parents kindly agreed that this was what she might have wanted – so, Troy, Pip, will you do the honours?'

Troy stood up and looked at Pip. Avoiding his gaze, she stood up too, and took a handful of the ashes, letting them run through her fingers, fly up in the breeze and disappear into the water. She heard the first bars of *Beautiful Girl* by INXS – the guitar and the piano – and closed her eyes to stop herself crying. She didn't want to cry any more. It felt like she'd cried enough in the last three years – enough to fill the whole of Sydney Harbour.

She felt an arm around her, and didn't shake him off because she couldn't be that cruel. Even with the rays of disapproval from Nadine and with Leo watching, even then. They had to understand that Troy was her brother, a bad brother, who'd done bad things to her and Holly, but a brother nonetheless. And when he stepped off the boat, Tracey would be waiting for him and he'd have to deal with all of that, too.

She stood and watched the ashes that she and Troy tipped into the water float and sink away to nothing, thinking about Holly and how strong she was, and how she would have hated to see Pip blundering and crashing through her life, making mistake piled on mistake, and how she would have helped her. But Pip didn't need Holly's help any more.

Leo – and Billy and Tiny and everyone she'd met in Munich, but especially Leo – had unravelled her, too. She'd been dismantled by them, by their large hearts and their persistence and unswerving belief that she was someone worth their love. Now she knew she had to gather up the pieces and build herself again, from whatever she could find.

She knew something else: that there was no proper time to stop grieving Holly's death. Her sister, who had been her friend and her mother and her hero. Who had died at exactly the time when Pip was no-more-a-child and not-yet-an-adult and hadn't known how to understand her love and pain and lust and fear – had mixed up where one ended and the next began. So she'd just given up and hidden away, for want of any better ideas. Holly was a part of Pip, and her death was also a part of Pip. It ran in her veins and in her beating heart, and she could feel it when she dreamt or woke, when she ran, when she read books and listened to music, when she danced, when she smiled or when someone smiled at her. Holly was inside her and always would be. Pip thought, *But now I'll grow older; and Holly will not.*

She would do something with her life that would make Holly proud, and she would do it on her own, making more mistakes, no doubt, but making them with no Holly – with no number nine.

17

Munich, October 2000

Pip could feel the autumn chill in the air on her way to work. Friday afternoons and Saturdays, since she'd been back from Australia, she'd been helping Rosa in the shop. It meant she only had Sundays off, but she preferred to keep busy and the extra money was going to come in handy next year. She'd been thinking about applying to the university in Munich, and had been looking at courses. There was one called *Literaturwissenschaft* she liked the look of – Literature Studies. Or *Sprache, Literatur, Kultur* – Language, Literature and Culture. There were loads of choices.

She wanted to stay in Munich, but she was desperate to leave the house at Emil-von-Feldstein-Weg. Rosa had offered to take her on as their au pair, but it was too close. Leo had been avoiding the house since he'd returned. He was staying away from his own family because of her and she couldn't bear it any more.

On the flight on the way back to Munich, once Max and Ferdi had fallen asleep, she'd spoken to Dominic.

'I've been thinking – I'm going to resign.'

'That's not necessary. Don't hurry into anything. He just needs time.'

'He can have all the time he likes if I'm not hanging around, getting in his way.'

'Max and Ferdi would never forgive you. They'd never forgive Leo, either. Where would you go? Back home?'

It took a moment to understand that Dominic meant England. But Pip hadn't thought of England as her home for a long time. If she could, she wanted to stay in Munich.

'I thought I might speak to Tara. She's unhappy with her job and – if you're OK with it – she'd probably be up for swapping. Tara will be great with you lot. She plays hockey, she gets on well with the boys. Will you be OK with that?'

'I suppose so, but it won't be the same without you. Are you sure this is what you want, Pip? Why don't we play it by ear – work out your notice and let's decide then.'

Three weeks later, nothing had changed. In the summer Leo had avoided his own house while Elisabeth had been there, and now he was doing it again – because of Pip. She'd done more damage to him than she could ever have imagined.

She knew that Leo had been cruel to her in Sydney – he should have taken her to hospital or to the police station straight away – and his judgements about her had been hurtful and inaccurate. But in her anger at him, she'd also stepped over a line, making him believe that when he'd touched her at the river, it had been the same as what Dean had done to her. How could she have said that, or even implied it? She'd ruined the memory of that day at the river, which had been so precious to her, forever. It was unforgivable. She'd written a letter to Leo to explain and apologise, but she hadn't sent it because she didn't want him to think she wanted anything from him. She had to behave properly. Better late than never.

Also, the longer Leo ignored her, the more doubts she had that his feelings for her had been as strong as hers for him. He had always been difficult to read, showing little or no emotion about anything, but what if that was real – what if he actually didn't *feel* any emotions? When he'd been with her, he'd made it clear he wanted to sleep with her, but what if that was it for him, and now, after their argument in Sydney, he was over it? It might have just been a thrill-of-the-chase-type thing for him. She'd been so available, so easy, such a sure thing – had he lost interest? He'd admitted he was behaving like a randy teenager, and he'd said he was shallow. Or maybe he wanted to nick a girl off Billy for once; get his revenge for what Billy had done with Roxy. There was also a very real possibility that, on the evening of the party in the Deutsche Haus, he'd got together with someone else. Another German athlete, one of the hockey girls, or Franzi herself, who'd also won a bronze in Sydney.

Either way, he'd probably had second thoughts – after all, who was she? An au pair from the opposite end of the social spectrum, too young, too poor, a nobody.

Why had he blown so hot and cold all the time? She had never known where she was with him. One minute treating her with such solicitude that she'd been sure he'd loved her; the next ignoring her as if she didn't exist. Then the way he held her and kissed her – showing his need for her physically. But what did any of it really mean? How well did they really know each other? She'd thought that what they had, limited as it was, had been special, unique to them. That they could see inside each other, without the need for small talk or getting-to-know-you conversations. But she knew now that it had all been a crock of shit. She was so naive.

It all came back to the same thing anyway, no matter how much she turned everything around in her brain and tried to work out what he'd meant when he'd said certain things. No matter how much misunderstanding there'd been between them, or how little they really knew each other, there was the stark, staring fact that he knew where she was and he wanted nothing to do with her.

She didn't blame Leo for avoiding her. She didn't hate him. Not nearly as much as she hated herself, anyway. But she did hear Nadine's words in her head; words that she had repeated in emails and on the phone. The way that Leo had reacted told her everything she needed to know about whether he was the right man for her.

He was the wrong man for her.

Or rather, she was the wrong woman for him.

INT. BACK ROOM, ROSA'S BOOKSHOP – DAY

Pip is sorting through a box of books. She hears the bell on the shop door ring.

PIP
(shouts)
I'll be right there.

There is silence in the shop. Pip frowns – why didn't the customer answer? She walks through.

INT. ROSA'S BOOKSHOP – DAY

PIP
Sorry, I was just...

Leo is standing in the doorway of the shop. He looks terrible. All the health that glowed from him in Sydney has vanished. He's pale, has bags under his eyes and a thick beard on his chin. He looks like he hasn't slept for weeks.

Pip stops. She walks behind the desk, as if it will protect her. She looks at him and then down at the desk. She breathes deeply to calm the hammering of her heart.

She bites her lower lip and looks sideways at one of the bookshelves. Anywhere but at Leo.

> LEO
>
> I'd like... I wondered... Do you have the sequel to this?

He holds up his copy of *The Power of One* and takes a step forward, just one. He's trying to be brave.

> LEO
>
> I loved it. It really was inspirational. There is a sequel, isn't there? I didn't want the story to end.

> PIP
> > (barely audible)
>
> Yes. There is.
> > (a little louder)
>
> Yes. It's called *Tandia*. I think we have it. English or German?

> LEO
>
> Pardon?

> PIP
>
> Do you want it in English or German?

Leo looks at the book in his hand, as if he's forgotten it was there.

> LEO
>
> I'll stick with English.

Pip walks around the desk slowly, towards one of the shelves. There's still distance between them. Her mouth is closed in a tight line, and she's breathing hard through her nose, trying to keep it together. Why is he here? Why this bookshop?

Her hand reaches up and plucks a book from the shelf. Again, she needs a moment to collect herself before she turns her back on him, stepping behind the desk – easier now there's a barrier between them. She rings it up on the till.

Leo steps closer to the desk. Pip flinches. He's too close. He unfolds a scrap of paper.

> LEO
> I... I need some more books too. I've got a
> list.

Pip sits down at the computer, her fingers poised above the keyboard.

> PIP
> (manages to keep her voice steady)
> Which ones?

> LEO
> (clears his throat)
> The first one is *I'm a Huge Idiot.*

Pip starts typing, and then stops. She stays very still.

                         LEO
          The second one is *I'm Really, Really Sorry
          I Hurt You.*

Pip stares straight ahead of her, the words on the screen
blurring.

                         LEO
          There's also *I Should Have Taken You To the
          Hospital.* Then there's *Will You Forgive Me,
          Because I Can't Believe How Badly I Fucked
          Up and I Swear I'll Never Do It Again?*

                         PIP
                      (whispers)
          Snappy title.

                         LEO
          Pardon?

                         PIP
                       (louder)
          I said it's a snappy title.

She turns her head and looks at him, speaking more
resolutely.

                         PIP
          We don't sell those kinds of books. There's
          a self-help bookshop in town. You should
          try there.

                         LEO
          Pip...

(Beat)

                    LEO
                (continuing)
Dad told me you're leaving. Don't go.
Please.

                    PIP
Why not?

                    LEO
Because I love you.

(Beat)

                    LEO
                (continuing)
I did everything wrong in Sydney. I don't
give a shit about Costa. I shouldn't have
got angry. I should have taken care of you.
I was so obsessed with that last game, I
forgot that you were more important than
anything. I asked you the wrong questions.
I should have gone back to that house and
finished off that filthy bastard. I was upset
about completely the wrong things. I
didn't listen to you. I was an idiot. A stupid,
unkind, selfish fuckwit.

Pip stands up. She's angry. She's not going to let him off
the hook so easily.

                    PIP
It wasn't just in the hotel room. You saw
me after the last game. I was there. You

couldn't forgive me then. And on the boat –
you wouldn't even look at me.

LEO

I know. I was scared.
(there are tears in his eyes)
You were all muffled up in those clothes
and that scarf to hide your bruises. I
wanted to hold you and never let you go,
but I was terrified you didn't want me to.
I tried, but I couldn't say what I wanted to
say. I'm so sorry.

PIP

This – whatever this is you're trying to say
now – it's not good enough. It's too late. For
fuck's sake, Leo. In that hotel room I told
you everything about Holly. Someone had
just tried to rape me, and I was hurt and
you ignored me, doubted me. You said you
hated me.

LEO

I tried to hate you. That went well – for
about half an hour. Then I sat down and
wrote on the hotel stationery.
(his voice is unsteady)
I wrote everything down – from when your
text came to when you left the hotel room.
I thought you might need it – if you went
to the police. And as I wrote it, I realised
that I'd been completely wrong. I basically
accused you of leading on a rapist.
(his face is twisted with shame)

And I realised that my behaviour at the river, and every time I saw you since then, hadn't exactly been perfect. I'd been pressuring you to do something you weren't comfortable with.

Pip tries to interrupt, but Leo holds his hand up. He can't stop now – he has lots more he needs to say.

> LEO
>
> I thought – I knew – I was so sure I'd fucked it up between us irrevocably. At the Deutsche Haus, you were so angry and I was ashamed of myself for even thinking that winning a stupid medal for you could get you back. And on the boat, you were with him. With Troy. So I knew it was too late.
>
> (his voice cracks)

He brushes his hand over his eyes.

> PIP
>
> What did you say?

> LEO
>
> When?

> PIP
>
> You did... won a.... what?

> LEO
>
> (hesitates)
>
> I did it for you.

This is absolutely the last thing she expected him to say. She doesn't understand.

                    PIP
        I don't...

                    LEO
        The medal. I won it for you. After I'd finished
        writing and I'd sat up half the night, there
        was only one thing I could think of to do. I
        went out there and played the best game of
        my life. I wanted it so badly – not for me or
        Billy or for the team or the captaincy, but
        for you.

Pip can't speak. She knows it's not just some line – she knows he's telling the truth, and for him, the ultimate team player, this is a very big deal. She is struggling with the idea of it.

She thought Leo hated her because she got in the way of the one thing that mattered to him. She thought she hated him because he was cold and unforgiving. Turns out she was wrong on both counts.

                    PIP
        I thought you didn't believe in grand
        romantic gestures.

                    LEO
                  (quickly)
        Well, it is only a bronze.

(tries to smile)

Since I've been back, I've been thinking about us non-stop and I can't talk to anyone about it. No one understands; everyone either makes a joke of it or tells me I'm being an idiot. The only person I want to talk to about it is you.

PIP
(still not sure)

Leo—

LEO
(interrupts – he's desperate; this is his
only chance to get through to her)

I want to make you happy. You've had a shit time of it, and quite a large proportion of that is because of me. And now I'm miserable too, even more miserable than I was before, and that's really saying something. I know we can make each other happy.

PIP
(now it's her who sounds miserable – she
hangs her head, her shoulders slump)

We don't have anything in common. Half your family hates me. I can't stand hockey. I'm too young for you. I don't know what to do with the rest of my life.

Leo hears something in her voice that gives him hope. He takes another step closer.

LEO

Bullshit and you know it. We've got plenty
in common. That half of my family hates
everyone, and the other half, the important
half, adores you. And you don't hate hockey,
I know you don't. Who cares that you're
younger than me?

Another step closer. He's within reach of the desk, which
is still between them.

LEO
(continuing)
And I have a few ideas about what you can
do with the rest of your life.

Pip looks at Leo properly. He's smiling at her wonkily.
They both think this is going to happen. But Pip also
knows she has to make the first move. She climbs up onto
the desk, on top of books and papers and flyers, grabs
Leo by the shoulders and pulls him to her. She kisses
him hard, and his eyes widen in surprise – he came here
today not believing that anything he might say could
make it up to her. He responds enthusiastically. His arms
slide around her back, he shuffles his hips closer to her.

It's the kiss to end all kisses – the one they've been
dreaming of. There are fireworks exploding in the sky.
There's music swelling and soaring, possibly a choir.
There's a dizzying ARC SHOT and an EXTREME CLOSE-
UP. There are lips locking and hands fumbling and it's
a big old-school Hollywood, swoon-worthy, glorious,
romantic, sexy, dramatic kiss.

LEO
(coming up for air)

Whoa.
(he's out of breath, his eyes glazed over)
I'm going to have to... is there somewhere
we can... Pip?

She understands what he wants – she wants it too.

PIP
There's a room upstairs. I'll have to shut
the shop.

LEO
Will Rosa be OK with that? Actually, I don't
give a shit.

He lets go of her and she lurches, steadying herself. He
walks to the door and flips the sign over, locking the door.
She's still perched on the desk and he slams his lips back
onto hers, dropping the book on the desk with a thud, his
hands on the backs of her thighs, lifting her up to him.
She wraps her legs around him.

LEO
Not sure we're going to make it upstairs if
we carry on like this. Come on.

They untangle themselves from each other. He grabs
her hand and they run around the desk, Pip turning off
the shop light and groping in the darkness for the light
to the stairs.

INT. STAIRCASE – DAY

She leads the way up the stairs. He watches her every step, and she knows he's watching; they can't move quickly enough for what they're feeling. At the top of the stairs, she opens a door, which leads into:

INT. LARGE STORAGE ROOM – DAY

Shelves line every wall. They gaze around the room, and everywhere there are hard edges and dark corners. There is nowhere to do it, except for up against a wall or on a dusty floor.

They hesitate. They're both thinking the same thing: it's a let-down. They look at each other.

> PIP
>
> It's not quite...

> LEO
>
> It's a bit...

> PIP
>
> Why don't we...

> LEO
> (starts laughing)
>
> No. This won't do. Not at all. I mean, I'm not a fussy man when it comes to having sex with the woman I love. But not here. Not the first time.

PIP

(laughs too)

Thank God you said that. I'll meet you at the Sixth Floor later.

LEO

No, everyone's there tonight. I'll pick you up when you finish here. I'll book something. A nice hotel. The last time we were in a hotel room, things didn't go so well. I need to make it up to you.

PIP

I said some things that night... I'm so sorry. Everything I said about the river – it wasn't true. That was the biggest turn-on in my life. And I trashed it.

LEO

(laughs again)

We'll go there again, in the summer. Recreate it. And the summer after that. And every summer, forever.

PIP

Every summer? Even when we're eighty years old?

LEO

Especially when we're eighty. That's when we'll fit in the most.

                              PIP
              I can't decide if that's really romantic or
              really pathetic.

He smiles at her.

(Beat)
                              PIP
              I've never felt safer with anyone than I feel
              with you.

He kisses her softly. There is no urgency any more – they
know that it's going to happen later and that it's going to
be amazing. They kiss for a few seconds, enjoying it, then
break away and stand looking at each other shyly.

                              PIP
              Cup of coffee?

                              LEO
              Sounds like a plan.

INT. STAIRWAY – DAY

They clomp down the stairs, holding hands, into:

INT. ROSA'S BOOKSHOP – DAY

There is a face peering through the shop door. Pip drops
Leo's hand and he stays in the back room, making the
coffee, until Pip has dealt with the customer.

Pip and Leo sit together and drink. Leo pats the sofa
they're sitting on.

                        LEO
    Could've done with this upstairs.

                        PIP
    Yes, what an oversight for Rosa not to have
    installed it up there for us to have sex on.

He laughs and kisses her. As he does so, she sees the
slip of paper sticking out of his shirt pocket and takes
it out. He tries to grab it back, but she holds it out of his
reach.

                        PIP
    Just let me see. I won't laugh, honestly. It
    was sweet – it's how you won me back.

She looks at the paper, starts laughing and puts her hand
over her mouth.

                        PIP
    Sorry. *I'll Make It Up to You, Every Day for
    the Rest of My Life.* I like the sound of that.

Leo groans; hides his face in his hands with
embarrassment.

                        PIP
                      (reads)
    *I Can't Stop Thinking About You. You're the
    Best Thing That Ever Happened to Me.*
              (looks at him and smiles)
    Adorable.
                 (giggles and reads on)
    I'll Give Up...

(she stops, her face shocked)
Seriously? *I'll Give Up Playing Hockey for You?*
(she frowns, suddenly serious)
Leo? You didn't mean this, did you?

LEO

Well, I was hoping I wouldn't have to use that one.

PIP

I would never ask you to give up hockey for me.

LEO
(cheeky grin)
Yeah, I knew that.

She thumps him on the arm and he pretends it hurts. They kiss.

LEO

You know, I've been thinking about what you said – that you didn't know what to do with the rest of your life. Why don't you write?

PIP
Write what?

LEO
(gestures at bookshelves)
One of these things.

PIP

Oh. Well. I don't think I could.

LEO

Course you could. Nadine told me you've
written most of it already.

PIP

Those emails? That's all just nonsense.
What kind of a book would that make?
It's just about me and my grief-stricken,
coffee-fuelled, lovesick misadventures.
Who wants to read about that?

LEO

Great title. *Grief-Stricken, Coffee-Fuelled,
Lovesick Misadventures in Munich*, by Pip
Mitchell. Everyone wants to read about
that. It's a love story. There's nothing
better than a love story.

PIP

OK, that's quite enough with all the shite
titles. Don't give up the day job, Dr Stein. Your
mum; your grandparents – they'd go apeshit
if I wrote about you lot. They'd sue me.

LEO

So? Write under a pseudonym. Change
our names. Change the city, the country.
Change the sport we play.

She thinks about it. Maybe, just maybe it's something
she could do. It might just work.

                              PIP
            Should I write it in English or German?

                              LEO
            Both. Start with English, then write the
            whole thing again in German. I'll help
            you. Then write a screenplay for it. They'll
            make it into a film, and all our friends can
            be extras.

                              PIP
            It's a love story with a happy ending – how
            corny is that?

Leo takes her hand and looks into her eyes.

                              LEO
            It's not a happy ending. No such thing,
            remember? What happens at the end of
            your book is a happy beginning.

FADE OUT

THE END

Glossary

Bratkartoffeln: fried potatoes.

Deutsche Haus: meeting place for German athletes and their families.

Englischer Garten: a park in the middle of Munich.

Freikörperkultur (FKK): nudist area.

Hilfe: help.

Isar: the river that runs through Munich.

Liebling: darling.

Ostbahnhof: east train station.

S-Bahn: suburban railway.

Schatzi: see *liebling*.

Süddeutsche Zeitung: a newspaper printed in Munich.

Weg – way (as in a street name, so Emil-von-Feldstein-Weg is Emil von Feldstein Way).

In 1999–2000, Germany still had Deutschmarks (Marks) and Pfennigs. When the country adopted the Euro in early 2002, the exchange rate was about two Marks to one Euro.

More books by FJ Campbell

The Islanders:
A young adult novel inspired by Thomas Hardy's *Far from the Madding Crowd.*

***

One girl, three boys. Which one will Beth choose?
The safe choice: Milo
The interesting choice: Edward
The thrilling choice: Zack

Far from the Madding Crowd, teenager style.
With sex and drugs.
With parties, holidays, pranks, school plays and rugby matches.
With lust and friendship.
With love.
But with whom?

***

"It has the potential to be a classic."

Matt Rudd, journalist and author
"*The Islanders* is a fantastic read – a sexy, intelligent, romantic story about the lives and loves of a group of teenagers at a boarding school. It is sure to appeal to fans of E. Lockhart."

Sam Mills, author

***

The Islanders by FJ Campbell will be published in late 2018. To find out more, go to www.fjcampbell.net and sign up for the mailing list – you'll be contacted when *The Islanders* is on sale.

Author's Note

I have taken liberties with the results of the men's hockey competition at the Sydney 2000 Olympics. For this I apologise, and here set the record straight – the Kookaburras won the bronze medal and the Germans came fifth. They weren't even playing in the same group, but I needed them to be for the sake of the story so I changed it all around. Sorry to each and every Aussie, their children, their grandchildren, et cetera, et cetera until the end of time.

The fact is, Sydney 2000 was the best Olympics I've ever attended – the city was beautiful, the people were friendly and welcoming, the venues were stunning. The atmosphere was amazing. Best ever.

So please don't be offended, just enjoy the story and ignore my fiddling with the facts. It was all about Leo and Troy, you see.

Acknowledgements

I'd like to thank Faye Booth, Joe Shillito and everyone at Troubador – you've made the whole process of editing and publishing this book feel like fun and not at all scary.

Also, thanks to friends, and friends of friends, and sisters-in-law-once-removed who helped with hockey details – Tissi, Stefan Tewes, Philipp Crone, Simon Triggs, and Helen Richardson-Walsh. Any inaccuracies are my fault, not theirs.

Thanks to all of my friends and family, for always showing interest in something that was, for a long time, just a pipe dream. When I'm in the middle of writing a book, I am annoyingly uncommunicative because in my head I'm elsewhere, and you've been brilliant at putting up with that for the last few years.

Sarah and Andy: you weren't sarcastic about my writing and that means a lot to me. Vikki: thanks for your perfect combination of kindness and honesty. Rachel McIntyre: you've been unbelievably kind to help me improve my writing and I am forever grateful. Gesa: thanks for starting up the FJ Campbell Official Fan Club. Florence: thank you for your help with everything, but especially the rude French. Lara: thank you for your sharp eyes, in particular for spotting the names of sexual partners; and for loving my characters as much as I do. James: thanks for your Verbier expertise. Les and Loz: you're amazing and your enthusiasm has kept me going. The Neons: thanks for your unending support and praise. How lucky am I to have found you? The Perlen: thanks for your Bavarian name suggestions and for being the inspiration for all the lovely hockey players in this book.

And most of all, thanks to Rick for telling me not to worry and that nothing's a big deal (because it turns out, it really isn't).